THE LAKE ON FIRE

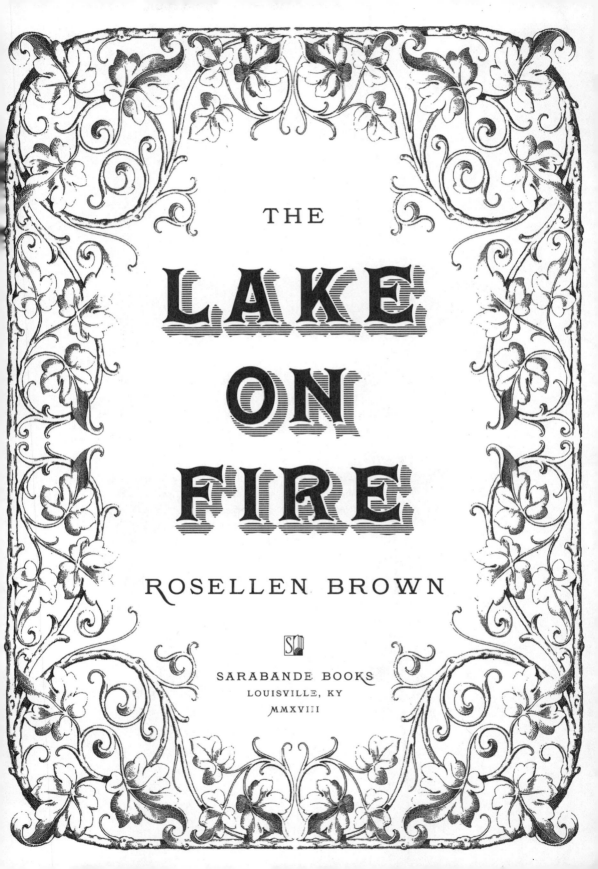

THE

LAKE
ON
FIRE

ROSELLEN BROWN

SARABANDE BOOKS
LOUISVILLE, KY
MMXVIII

Library of Congress Cataloging-in-Publication Data
Names: Brown, Rosellen, author.
Title: The lake on fire : a novel / by Rosellen Brown.
Description: First edition. | Louisville, KY : Sarabande Books, 2018
Identifiers: LCCN 2017058702 (print) | LCCN 2018000390 (ebook)
ISBN 9781946448248 (ebook) | ISBN 9781946448231 (pbk. : alk. paper)
Classification: LCC PS3552.R7 (ebook) | LCC PS3552.R7 L35 2018 (print)
DDC 813/.6—DC23
LC record available at https://lccn.loc.gov/2017058702

Cover and interior design by Alban Fischer.
Manufactured in Canada.
This book is printed on acid-free paper.
Sarabande Books is a nonprofit literary organization.

This project is supported in part by an award from the National Endowment for the Arts.
The Kentucky Arts Council, the state arts agency, supports Sarabande Books with state
tax dollars and federal funding from the National Endowment for the Arts.

FOR MY GIRLS-NOW-WOMEN,

ADINA AND ELANA,

AND FOR DALIA, SPARK OF OUR FUTURE

I carry a brick on my shoulder in order that the world
may know what my house was like.
—BERTOLT BRECHT

We must admit there will be music despite everything.
—JACK GILBERT

THE LAKE ON FIRE

1

FOR ALL the years of her life, this was the story Chaya-Libbe told.

The missing parts stayed missing.

THERE WERE many brothers and sisters Shaderowsky but Chaya-Libbe loved Asher best, a thousand times best. He was her only vanity. She was the oldest sister; between them there were six—Yakov, Beryle, Binyomin, Yitzhak, Dvorele, and Masha—and, in two different graveyards, the large one there, in Zhitomir, and the fresh one here, in Christa, Wisconsin, a few more, souls shaken out of them like seeds from a burst pod, early or late.

The only one lost in the new land was Sorele who, as a baby just learning to walk, caught a fever that almost killed the rest of them: She was one of the helpless pioneers of the stone-hard graveyard, out in the fenced place as far from the barn and the house as they could take her. (The first act a community of Jews must perform, even before they build a place to pray, is to make a burial ground, and fence it away from unhallowed soil. They understand the priorities of the universe too well to be frivolous.)

The children's mother was brusque to them all, so busy they remembered her mainly as motion—sewing, darning, cooking, planting, sweeping—all the -ing words, her hands flashing faster than barn swallows. There wasn't much left of her for loving, although they knew that the motion was somehow meant for them. Chaya was the one who, back in the grim city where they were born, caught Asher's first word—two words, actually,

3

spoken clearly at six months, while their mother dozed over his nursing: "It's curdled." Or so her mother heard it.

"Curdled?" she gasped back at him, rudely awakened. Her nipple, abandoned, quivered like a lip before tears. "*Shoyn!*" Finished.

Chaya tried to console her mother. She had been a smoother, a reassurer, a peace-bringer from the first day she discovered discord. It was a treasure and a fault, this desperation she felt to rush ahead of anyone headed for a painful confrontation, to cushion the blow about to land, whether out of kindness or, out of her own need to be loved, in gratitude.

"Mother," she whispered, looking regretfully at the basket into which her baby brother had been thrust to quell his thirst alone. "Mother, sweet." Which she was not. "Little Mama." But she saw the way the affront misted her mother's eyes. Who was this Asher, stranger than any of her other children?

He was the most curious child who ever lived, Chaya understood, and he became, early, early, a little mill for grinding words into questions, a memorizer, a challenger, a declarer; it was not her mother's imagination that he seemed to have been born talking. He was never still and never silent. "*Gay avek!*" she would shout at him—"Go away!"—and swat at him as if he were a horsefly. Silent herself, Chaya was glad to give him her ear. She loved them both.

So, in a single gesture, Asher had been weaned, and, in spite of Chaya's placating murmur, his mother never forgave him. He seemed to have slipped between this year's pages of who-shall-live and who-shall-die as a special case, larger than mere life, exempt from all that burdened the rest of them into ordinariness.

Asher was not relatively astonishing; he was an absolute. Still, condemned to crawl on a cold Russian floor in the lee of the drafts that came in under their door, his genius was not—except to his sister—cause for celebration.

And now they lived in a place called Christa in the state of Wisconsin. A joke, such a name for a pack of disheveled Jews, some of whom swayed and prayed, others of whom blasphemed. The pathetic piece of land they lived on, seventeen of them before the addition of any new life or the subtraction of old, had been assigned by the powers of the Hebrew Emigrant Assistance Society. With the best of intentions and a dangerous optimism, the association's clerks moved pins randomly on their map as the hordes poured by the thousands out of the Pale, ahead of (or behind) the pogroms, the empty stomachs, the laws and the threats and the curses. Undoubtedly, they looked at their maps with satisfaction: they were not making exiles, they were making Americans.

CHAYA-LIBBE was fourteen, newly arrived at the age of self-consciousness, when they left Zhitomir. She would forever remember their arrival with feelings of exhilaration turned to shame: how Asher came leaping down the narrow stairs of the SS *Stettin* into the crypt called steerage, slipping on the damp floor, clinging to the walls, shouting, "We're here! We're coming in! Everybody on deck, *schnell, schnell!*" Her brother was now eight: small, lithe, with slanted gray eyes that looked for action wherever he could find it, movement, sparking energy, and danger if there was any to be found. One of those boys fueled by risk. He had a map of ringworm on his scalp that had eaten his spiky hair away in a spiral. His eyes, when he yelled at his family to hurry, were as round as the portholes no one in steerage had so much as glimpsed. He blinked them rapidly, signals of his earnestness, and was gone.

And so they hurried. They washed themselves off as best they could without much water, mothers showing the way to children, and straightened their stringy hair that they had sweated in for weeks, adjusted their clothes—Chaya's thick dress smelled vaguely of vomit and, worse, not even hers—and as if it were *shabbos* and they were rising into its light and sweetness, trusting, they rushed up the many narrow sets of stairs single file to crowd against the rail. The air was so thick with fog it beaded up on the steel sides of the ship, making the rivets shine.

Their mother had one fist over her heart the way she did on Yom Kippur when she beat her breast for her sins. "Oh Lord, let it not be London!" she muttered (to herself; she could never alarm her children on purpose). But she had heard of cases where a family bought a ticket to New York and found itself dumped with frightening finality on the dock in Liverpool or London, duped by the agent and out of luck.

In America, Father had said and said again, in public and alone, they encourage Jews to be people of substance, not only the people of the Book, which doesn't feed their children. Here we will take care of ourselves, eating from our own crops, owing nothing, working with our animals— though no one had animals in Zhitomir, no one had crops, it was not even a shtetl with a concave cow and yards full of geese—ruling ourselves without fear of pogrom or famine. We will support ourselves cleanly and healthily, not in the city and not in the village which everyone knows is a foul sty, a blight of dependent paupers. "Faivel," she had heard him say. "Every town has a Faivel like ours, or a Velvel or a Yossel, who sits on a box at the corner of our street. The most decrepit of beggars, a walking swarm of flies, an animated rag pile. Is that what we want the world to see when they see a Jew?"

Chaya-Libbe would listen, a little moonily, respecting and slightly fearing the avid swell in his voice. "Now imagine Faivel sitting on a bench beneath an apple tree, watching his sheep graze." She knew Faivel: He was lazy, he was inept, he might even be a little bit mad. But that was not the point here; it was the saving balm of the barnyard her father wanted them to think about, when the mysteries of the farm still seemed simple to unmystify and master.

He himself was a bookbinder, adept at intricate finger movements, which, though the work kept his hands busy, left his mind (and his mouth) free for endless political debate. In another world, he could have been a senator, possibly a journalist. In his world he was only a dreamer, which meant that his wife worked harder than he did to keep his family in herring and stale heels of bread.

"And when we arrive, the Americans will meet us with a band," the dreamer assured them. "This I have heard." Ah, he could be persuasive. She ought to have asked where he had heard it, but even had she doubted, she would not have dared. "Trumpets and a drum?" one of them asked, smiling, and he said yes, really. "And with flowers. They will give us tools and the animals we will need to start our new life, and bring us in a wagon and show us to our own spot of clean dirt." His father, their grandfather, had farmed a piece of a peasant's land illegally and had been stripped of his goods, beaten in the farmyard by the Czar's inspectors and laughed down the road and out of sight, long before their father was born. To be a farmer, legally . . .

But the children had to wonder what he meant by "clean dirt," the planting dirt he promised. Their mother and Chaya and the other girls had enough trouble keeping the house straight, swept, swabbed. There was no such thing as dirt that was not an affliction. But their father tended to be right most of the time. A wise family did not separate its hopes from its father's.

Up on the deck Zanvel-the-hatter had the flag; he had kept it standing up out of the muck. He wore a smile so wide his stubbled cheeks crushed up under his eyes while he struggled to pull the flag loose from its carefully tied binding of rags. Then, with a flourish, he shook it out and it sent a sharp report like the crack of a gun. It was a moment they had dreamed of. There it was, still crisp and clean, never yet used in the real world that preceded this dream: AM OLAM carefully embroidered in gold upon a red field, below that all ten commandments (the sewn letters tiny as ants) and a plough standing by itself waiting to be seized, its two handles wide as the horns of a barnyard bull. Across the bottom the words, proud and square, in a Yiddish with grand serifs: ARISE FROM THE DUST, THROW OFF THE CONTEMPT OF THE NATIONS, FOR THE TIME HAS COME!

Zanvel, having protected the flag from Zhitomir to Hamburg to their ship, was the one they chose to hold it up. They raised their fists and cheered and shouted and made a happy racket, this unspeakable journey almost done. The children jumped so that they could come down hard and noisily on the damp deck. Zanvel was wagging the banner in the fumy air, gold on red, a rag of color against a cloud, and all of them were cheering, when a man in a dark blue uniform and a hat—he looked rather like a trolleyman but did not carry himself like one—poked through the rows with a face like a hard fist made for bruising. What, he demanded none too nicely, were they doing. No—what did they *think* they were doing, as if they just might be misinformed. Between them, as it happened, there was no more than a thimbleful of English, but because Zanvel had already been in America before, "in *Bal-de-more*," (and returned in a fury, full of himself, when his wife threatened to divorce him if he stayed away a minute longer, so they heard when their mother spoke in her gossip voice) he was able to say something about celebration and (perhaps badly put) the land, the land, he said, something about taking over the land: Am Olam means People of the Earth. It must have seemed that he dragged his words under the man's nose like cat scent to a dog. He meant ten acres, a fence, a barn. The official repeated Zanvel's last words with astonishment: *Take over the land?!* By the descending movement of his hands they could see that he was ordering Zanvel to lower the flag, couldn't they? Couldn't they?

"No," Zanvel said. He was a squat man, amiable, hairy as a hound. Now, though, he looked like a small guard dog ineptly preventing passage.

"Or else," the man threatened.

"This is a free country, that is why we are here," Zanvel flung at him, something like that, though not comprehensibly. The crowd tried to make taunting noises in their own language, or halfway in it, in something they took for the sound of democracy, in which they knew they were free to say anything they pleased.

The trolleyman's face deepened a few shades and a cord beat in his forehead as if it were counting off time. Under a wide mustache he bit his lip, considering. Then, like a schoolchild, with an awful sound he lunged at Zanvel, whose cap flew off over the rail as if it were a shot bird, and floated for a while till it picked up the weight of the water. Then it sank.

They tussled for a moment or two—the rest of the men cried out in anguish and leaned in to try to help but they were afraid to be too bold. The women simply shrieked and the trolleyman managed to seize the broomstick that was the pole of the flag, bang it angrily against the shiny rail to try to break it in half, then in frustration raise it over his head whole and fling it as hard as he could into the white wake of the ship. It came down slowly and spread itself out for just an instant like a tablecloth, a fancy *shabbos* cloth, against the dirty greenish spume—ARISE FROM THE and one horn of the plough—and then, whipped into a frenzy of bubbles and shreds, it was dragged under the body of the ship and down.

He smoothed his mustache with both his forefingers, restoring his dignity, as if he were soothing it. *There, there.* Then he nodded curtly at the rest of them and disappeared behind a curtain of fog.

So much for the flowers and the ploughs. Chaya was afraid to look at her father. Blame, and its suppression, would come later. Now she wanted so devoutly to go home that she'd have been grateful, would have borne another two weeks of stink and turmoil gladly, if the ship were to turn and make for Hamburg, to return them to Europe, all of them, safe.

The vibration that had thrummed under her feet as steadily as a heartbeat had broken off for good and she was overcome with panic laced with disappointment and, another layer beneath that, a roiling anger for which she had no words.

2

WAS THERE a Biblical curse that promised five years of squalor, spoilage and rot? They called themselves the Fields of Zion and, for all their hope, they came naked to their future. Native-born farmers from Massachusetts, from New York and Vermont, flowing westward on a river of restlessness and ambition, faced every cruelty of nature but, not innocents, at least they were familiar with the soil, with animals; they knew how to build.

But the Fields of Zion farmers were gray-faced and weak-fingered from too many years in a murderous city. Their lungs were coated with factory smoke, their minds fixed either on a book full of holy exhortations ("O Lord our God, be gracious unto Thy people Israel and accept their prayer. . . . Remember us this day for our good, and be mindful of us for a life of blessing. O may our eyes witness Thy return to Zion") or on the Socialist mission to undermine all that and blame Forces equally abstract for every evil. None had ever stood behind a plough, or seen hail flatten a greening field.

Their first bewildering night, fresh from Castle Garden and an endless train ride, they had slept in a field in one large circle, feet toward the center like the spokes of a wheel. They managed to find a sawmill, and with no English, bought wood—more costly than they'd expected—and built the fewest buildings possible. Given the cost of pine, the Commons, one large building, was going to have to suffice for a very long time. Each family had a single porous-walled room.

The wood that had been loosely assembled was so green it still bled sap; in time, great rivulets ran down its surface like those marvelous paintings of the Madonna that weep miraculous tears. It rejected nails, actually gobbled them into ragged holes that meant that no one could hang any ornament or picture without quickly discovering it in a tangle on the tilting floor. Then—not counting two outbuildings, one for men and one for women so that modesty could remain at least technically unbreached—came a barn, leaky and canted, and finally a chicken coop that the chickens avoided when they could, never confiding the source of their dissatisfaction.

CHAYA WAS repelled by the spectacle of her respected elders reduced to gawking children, inept and unprepared. She could not forget the trolleyman cursing at the little crowd as they huddled on the fogbound deck. What must he have been saying in that language she knew not more than three words of, *hello* and *thank you,* assiduously practiced in her bunk. *Go home? We don't need your kind here?* Whatever it was he shouted when he ruined the flag, at that moment were they cursed? How else could the end have been written at the very beginning?

She was a girl from a gray and stony city. When she studied the Field of Zion's buildings thrown up quickly, crookedly, by the light of their faith that such approximate carpentry would hold, and then the chicken coop when their birds spent too much time hiding—still she was glad they had not been turned back to Hamburg. Unpainted, gray as the sky, the buildings seemed to be riding an ocean of green. When the wind blew, and it did, viciously, without barrier, the long grasses danced like surf, swaying, bowing, miraculously recovering just to be leveled again. She was bewitched by a beauty she had never seen: the fat spread of rain drops on the doorstep, the sweet smell, better than warming dough, that rose from the damp ground. There was such a promise of peace here, and safety. Empty space without a shadow on it. She had never really seen the horizon before. Perhaps she could be happy here.

But there was work to be done and bills to pay from the little they'd been given, a small packet alongside their train tickets. The buildings sometimes swayed in the wind; when the cold poked through the walls, over the sills, it whistled, a thin sound like an unattended kettle.

Slowly, slowly, the ship began to list and take on water.

Chaya began to feel it one worry at a time. The hens were either very dumb or very smart—they left their eggs, some but not all, in the low bushes outside their coop. Either the coop was all wrong—built badly, somehow, its sills already splintering—and they preferred to nest in the dead leaves on the ground, or they were being clever and having a good morning laugh. But when she came with her basket looking for the eggs, it wasn't funny. Hollering at them didn't help—not only do they not tend to be clever but one did not reason with chickens.

The cows were bad milkers. There were two, called Eyn and Tsvey, One and Two, because in a muddle of tradition someone had insisted that giving them human names would insult the memory of a departed soul who happened to share that name. "Do you say Kaddish for a cow?" Zanvel, it was. Zanvel-the-hatter.

The cow pond. Coated with scum like fat on soup, only this soup could not be skimmed. There was no clean water for a *mikve*, which tormented those who cared, the women monthly, the men before holidays and holy events. You were supposed to immerse yourself completely, over your head, your hair slicked, but if you did that in the cow pond you came up cob-webbed with green silt and mucous weed, reeking like foul breath. No honor to God or self in that.

The dry rows of growing greens, stunted, crooked, choked. Nothing burgeoned, nothing spread, little flowered. Tomatoes hung riddled with worm holes, hard and pale pink; lettuce bolted before it could thrive. Onions went dead in the ground, their green flags browning from heat and lack of rain.

Rusted tools (bought used: cheap, but a bad bargain). The wheels of the blue wagon did not match; every trip, sitting in the remnants of hay, clots of manure on her boots, she rattled so badly she came unstrung and quivered like an old woman the rest of the day. The horse, poor ratchedy horse, reorganized the flies with a frayed tail and watched her smooth her dress and try for dignity after a ride like that.

And then there were the Others: *Yenem*. Some Chaya loved (Toibe with her kind, kind face, Uri the jokester); others were either too pious (Pesye and Zanvel, Mordechai who had no wife, Lazer and Itzhak who fasted Mondays and sometimes Thursdays and, famished, could not work) or simply *meshuge*, too crazy for this world. (Muttel spoke to no one, Bunya was a secret drinker, but not so secret that he didn't tip over tables, fall asleep in the snow to be found by the bony old dog; weep, loom, cower.)

Why did nothing thrive in this place? Whom could she ask? She could not ask her mother and father because they had chosen this, or at least chosen the idea of it. She seethed at the casual way in which the men from HEAS, upstairs at Castle Garden—pink-skinned, clean-scrubbed Germans, who handled them with their fingertips like dirty laundry— had sent them forth no questions asked, with no support but that small wallet of cash and no instruction. She was not quite a child, not quite an adult when she'd heard someone say, *Beginnings are more than beginnings, they make the next things happen the way they do.* She was older now and she did not like the way those next things were happening.

AS FOR her affinity with Asher: He was a born provocateur. Communal life created the flimsiest of separations, boundaries, borders. And it seemed that if anyone spoke so much as a word, Asher could hear it and, made irritable by discretion, retail it to anyone who would listen. He did not hesitate to invade a privacy: Pesye, round as a wheel of cheese, stock-still in her undergarments. ("Do you know the fat hangs down off her arms, it's like candle drippings.") Muttel at prayer alone, hiding out when the *minyan* needed a tenth man. Itzhak pinching the cows and secretly tormenting Shlepper, their pathetic horse.

It was Asher's curiosity that pulled him along; he wanted to know everything. One night he saw Rivke and Munya huddled in the shadows of the barn, very close together, face to face. Attached, in fact. They were mouth to mouth and he could hear them breathing. "Why are you doing that?" His small voice. They fell away from each other, and stared at him and ran behind the barn. He saw Batya beating her child with a mixing spoon, holding her by her hair and swinging her high and wide while the little girl shrieked. Again his voice, undaunted: "Stop! Stop! You are making her bleed!"

When he saw these things, these and more—the secret hoard of extra food that Mordechai hid under his bedclothes, the way Reuven slept behind a hay bale instead of swinging his scythe—petty, they were, but he told them all to Chaya. "Ssshh," she soothed. "Those are not things you ought to be seeing."

"But they're true." He could look quite petulant. He stared her down. "I saw them."

"They may be true but people do not want to hear them, Asher. Adults," she amended. "Adults do not appreciate being talked to that way by a child."

"Do you want to hear the kind of hens we have?" He didn't wait for an invitation. Listing the things he knew, miscellaneous, was as natural to him as running and wrestling were to the others. "Leghorns, Rhode Island Reds, Araucanas, barred rocks, two langshans and one Australorp." There were no words for these in Yiddish; they made an indecipherable sentence.

"How do you know those?" She didn't ask why he wanted to know them, which he probably couldn't answer.

"I listen. I like to listen." He clapped his hands. Modesty was a far reach for Asher, as impossible as silence. For a boy his age, he still had the kind of little ears, far forward, that make babies irresistible. His skin was tender, and though his features were sweet and regular and promised a later lifetime of dangerously good looks, now his eyes were almost perfectly round and his hair stood up stiff as a whisk broom, the hair newborns lose in their first weeks. In his intensity, he did look the far side of peculiar.

His mother still looked wary around him; she gave him a wide berth. Chaya watched him kick at the pebbles under his feet, watched him try to resolve to cease his judgments on everything he saw. But his conscience was his curse: She knew he would fail. "Oh, Asher. *Ketzele*." Kitten. Or no, not kitten; rather, little cat, which is something different: the animal mature but miniature. She could not imagine what kind of adult he would make but she suspected he would not have it easy.

3

SMALL FIRES flared between the opposed houses: The Socialists, who observed no ritual, constrained themselves from jeering and contributed their bodies to be counted in the *minyan*. In return, the zealous religionists, not cheerfully, refrained from carrying on like prophets in the town square of Sodom. For the most part, they left each other's souls alone.

But very early, Zanvel-the-hatter and Mordechai disappeared for a week, gone to Milwaukee to purchase a Torah, which they had laboriously located via a series of letters to names they had gleaned who-knows-how. They returned triumphant, the heavy, hand-lettered scroll swaddled in blankets so that it looked like a child protected from a snowstorm. Once back, they confronted the fury of the half of the Fields of Zion that had never been consulted about such a waste of the colony's slim resources.

The battle lines were drawn: How dare the "godless" work on the Days of Awe? *Shabbos* was bad enough, but the most profound of ceremonial days? "Do the cows stop giving milk?" Father demanded. "Do the hens refrain from laying in honor of the day?" The children stood at the door when their screaming parents confronted one another, fully expecting them to fall upon each other like dogs.

BUT, TOO, there were joyous days. The Commons had seen one marriage—the couple Asher had discovered behind the barn, Rivke the very young daughter and Munya the son of cousins, had arrived indifferent to each other but had discovered an affinity during the blank days and nights of their first Wisconsin winter. Almost at once Rivke was blooming with a bellyful of child.

And there was a good bit of dancing in the Commons, single sex and not, Mordechai wielding a tolerable violin. High spirits drove the dancers, women flattered by the temporary attention of their husbands, even if they could not touch; children lifted and swung, shrieking. Melodies swelled with longing and loss, sweet songs floated into the chill *goyishe* Wisconsin air, crying out to those left behind across the ocean.

4

THE FATHERS of some of the children chose to teach them Torah and Talmud and leave the learning of English to chance. Somewhere along the way, between There and Here, they had lost heart and were not so eager now to transform their children into *Amerikaners*. Might they not, if they mixed with the local stock at the schoolhouse, be taught forbidden subjects like Christmas and hymn-singing? Might they be offered a bite off the haunch of a pig at lunchtime? A guzzle of milk after the poisonous meat? So the children stayed moored out there on that dusty road with starving animals and scrappy harvests, bored when they were not working, bored when they were, taught in whatever stray idle moment occurred, neither There nor Here.

The adults needed someone, though, who could be a courier to the world, someone to interpret, to speak for them, and in spite of her sober silence—or perhaps because it made her seem scholarly, a girl of moderating temperament, double-sighted—they consulted and considered and finally chose Chaya. She was so often the conciliator between antagonists, they were convinced she would be the best one to walk with a foot in each language, each life.

For as long as it took her to drink down her new language and, nourished, make new bone with it—English her stepmother tongue—she walked the very long way into town and into the whitewashed schoolhouse. There she sat at a desk too small for her, her knees pushed tight up against rough boards, so that she could learn what the littlest ones were learning, those shapes and sounds, those capitals of the world, those numbers. "*Kah-ya?* What kind of name is that?" asked a girl smaller than she, who stood with one shoulder cocked like a dare. They had said hello to her the day she first appeared but when she told them her name they laughed.

"It's *Chy-a*," she said, exaggerating the throat scratch. "*Ch*," that gargle, "not *Kuh*." She tried looking straight at the girl who was half her size, to protect her pride.

"Uch, you sound like you're going to spit!" Her own *ch* passable, still the girl made a disgusted face.

Chaya stood eyes wide, lips parted. *Yes, like that, like uch,* she wanted to say but could not. Boys fought with their fists; girls mocked. She swallowed her defense.

Impatient, they turned their backs and left her standing in her pool of silence. Something stubborn—dignity, for which she had no word—kept her from approaching them again. There was a German boy in the school as well, but he and the other boys didn't worry *his chs.* They shared wordless pleasures without difficulty, threw rocks at birds, squashed frogs and grasshoppers, chased the girls around the lilac bush that stood in the middle of the scuffed-up yard.

She had not expected it to be easy. Could someone be born lonely, Chaya wondered. The possibility did not leave her feeling bereft; she looked at it, rather, with a consoling dispassion. Like so much else, it was simply a question she had no one to ask.

Like her brother, she had been an infant early full of words; she could still make herself remember what it felt like to learn them—those hummed *mm*'s behind a closed mouth, the ticklish glottals and fricatives, *ssh* like a wind brushing forward from the back of her throat. Endless experiment, a sensual feast for herself alone. It was an ecstasy to blow and click and suck in, then try the sounds in dozens of shapes and then, after a while, know they formed words she could use to make herself understood.

But that was the old language. Now she had to move her mouth in a dozen new directions, suppress the sounds she had lived in. Pick out of the welter of noise vowels she had never heard before, a musical scale with intervals she could barely discern. Walking home from the schoolhouse she said them over and over again, sang them like a song no one could hear. Or no, they were a prayer and she was a convert who had to learn them, but her tongue would not cooperate. *This* not *zis* was the hardest. *This, there, theirs.* Not *oy* but *O. O O,* and *O* again. If only someone at home could listen and know when she got things wrong. Asher, pulling at her sleeve, begged, "Talk to me in that English, Chai, I want to talk it too," and—she was not surprised—he learned it faster than she could bring him words.

Her teacher, impressed with the speed of her learning, slipped books to Chaya on her way out the door: *Jane Eyre*, which was not easy to parse; *Wuthering Heights*, which inflamed her like a forbidden dream; romantic novels, ladies' books in which strong-willed women broke themselves on the rack of society's demands but justified their capitulation, all, all for love. They were always beautiful or, with love, became so; they were always good. She wished she could speak with someone about their fates, these heroines of Mrs. Humphry Ward, of Francis Marion Crawford, of Chester Bailey Fernald, whose major challenge was which man, among two opposing types, to marry.

Her teacher, for all the generosity of the loan of her library, frightened her. Though many school mistresses were barely older than their charges, Miss Singlet was a very thin, straight-spined older lady—she seemed to have been compressed, as if in a vise, and the striped skirts she favored made her look even longer, like a candy cane. Unmarried, monocled, she did not appear to be the woman to interpret these passions for Chaya. Nor did her own mother, so work-worn, so respectful of her husband but voiceless.

Then one day, Chaya made the mistake of reciting for her parents a poem she had learned in school. She thought that the English that now poured easily off her tongue would make them proud. "Announced by all the trumpets of the sky, / Arrives the snow, and, driving o'er the fields, / Seems nowhere to alight..." It was what they had wanted of her. Obliging them had been bliss, though it hadn't been easy. It had simply strained her capacity for empathy to be isolated from both sets of companions, at home and in the little schoolhouse. She had won the oratorical competition with the poem and had been given a whole book of verse called *Pillows to Dream On* for a prize; she allowed herself to be dramatic as it hurried to its close, because it made her feel like someone other than herself: "Stone by stone, / Built in an age, the mad wind's night-work, / The frolic architecture of the snow." Beaming, her mother applauded, her father banged his mug on the pine table, and she felt, perhaps for the first time, that her voice had carried forth into the world her true feelings.

"That is a fine way," Father said, looking hard at her, his frank face above his mustache red with pleasure, "to end your time at school. We were right to send you, of all the children."

She was confused.

"Now that you have learned so much, you can help us when we need to speak in town. And you can come back to work here at home. Where we need you."

She argued, she wept. She was not competent at this work, she did not care about this work. It made no sense. Chaya loved her parents and felt for their difficulties—her mother breathed for them, she was their pulsing machine. She admired her father for the dignity of his commitments. He was a man who bled for others, who ought to have been given a chance to work for the well-being of strangers. But they were living someone else's life, she was certain of that. Driven to improve their chances, they had chosen wrong, and were covered with the dust of failing farmers. They seemed to attract catastrophe—the rain that soaked the hay before they got it in, the calf that strangled in the womb and could not be pulled out until its poor mother expired, the wind—so harsh it could not be measured—that took down the chimney pipe and let the rain flood in and soak the quilts and bother the babies. Each, if you traced it back a few steps, was the result of their incompetence. And luck—luck was nothing but their enemy.

By now, too, she had heard of other ventures all too much like this one, sent by HEAS to Dakota where they froze, to Louisiana where they flooded and died of yellow fever, only a few in New Jersey less than laughable. Even those had to hire themselves to the factories of New York. They tilled and planted and harvested after hours and how could they not have broken under the burden of their double work lives? So much optimism undone. So much energy wasted.

"You are ready for the Academy," her father told her, "but the Academy costs money we can't spare." He sipped weak tea, no sugar cube between his teeth because white sugar also cost money. "Do you think we enjoy the loads we lift? The bending, the carrying, the calluses on our hands? Why do you think you can exempt yourself?" He looked at her gravely. "We are doing this for each other."

She breathed in deeply and then dared to say to him, "We should never have come." It was the first time she had not run to apply a salve of absolution before she struck. The worst of it was that he knew she was right.

He looked back at her with a harshness she could see he was trying to contain and joined his hands together as if they could squeeze back words he did not want to say. Just as well: She would not have liked any response he could give her. Asher was the only one who saw her disappointment. The others would hate her for thinking herself superior.

In Zhitomir, everything lay ahead, in another country. She had had enough of the horizon. In Christa, she dreamed of the city. Why could she own not a single fine dress, so that she was condemned to wear her poor faded school dress to the Oratorical Competition? In spite of its difficulty, she had loved going to her school because each new thing she learned promised to be useful for her next step: reading those books to be diverted from boredom but also to lay down a road that she might travel.

She had bent her head over the times tables, each combination a different shape in her mind—for some reason, eleven times eleven amused her, twelve times twelve felt solid and round and reassuring. But chiefly, numbers would be necessary to calculate her way, some day, to independence. Pared to the bone by skimpy diet and endless labor, she could feel fury bubbling like a caustic, burning everything away but hope. She was going to correct the mistake that was her life as soon as the moment came clear. She had never before deliberately hurt someone. She was prepared for regret.

In the meantime, she woke up one morning with a plan: Passivity. Refusal, like a stone, many sharp little stones, in her palm, clutched but not thrown. She would grow calluses to blunt her pain. Against every instinct, she was going to render herself useless. If they would not give her what she needed, she would not give them anything at all. And if she became a burden, wouldn't they expel her? Instead of pulling the peas off their spiraling vines and then shelling them into the pail, where the first layer made a pinging sound like rain against tin, she hid beneath the farthest tree in the orchard, reading *Mrs. Dancy's Fortune* (another story of a girl who, finally, for all her early spirit, does as she must, as others demand, and smiles prettily in her arbor. Miss Singlet had wanted to lend her a very big volume called *Moby-Dick*, but wondered if she could manage it. She would make herself manage it).

She did not come when called. When her mother handed her a basket of laundry to take to the pond, she turned her back and walked away, hoping her desperation would finally convince them to set her free. She ate sullenly beside them meals she had not helped cook, and when the dishes were ready to be cleared and washed, she vanished without a word of apology, walked off across the low rows of green shoots she had not planted. She was appalled at her insolence, and thrilled by her daring.

Her mother called down a *cholerya* on her—cholera, an all-too-familiar curse—and prayed that her disobedient feet would wither. Chaya, clenched tight so as not to be too badly hurt, smiled to hear it. Her poison was working its way. She closed her eyes and let the stunning curses fall on her head.

They looked at her with contempt—no one understood what she was doing. Only Asher could console her. Sometimes their bond was uncanny. Chaya would think something and Asher, as sensitive as a leaf in a slight breeze, would respond. There were too many things that she wanted and knew she could never have, down in town, at the mercantile. In fact, the more she was denied, the more she desired; she suspected she was not alone in this. But whenever they went into town together, some one or two of these precious objects would appear in the burlap bag that Asher carried with him everywhere. When they were safely at home and out of sight, he would carefully unknot the shoelace that cinched it closed and, smiling, hand her his booty. Hair ribbons, a set of ornamental pins stuck through a little square of velveteen—one the sun, the other the moon—made out of mock silver. A belt that seemed to be a long chain of flower petals in many colors of leather she had never seen before, green and red and a bronzy gold. A *Farmers' Almanac* that told her the dates of great events—the Battle of Hastings, 1066; the frequent eruptions of Mount Etna, with the probability that there would be another within the year—and predicted weather catastrophic and benign and warned, this year, that winter would be more harsh than usual, damp and windy. The little yellow book seemed full of threat because it made no comment, only promised, in the very same print that recorded events already past.

She had never mentioned these covetous yearnings to Asher. When they came to town, did he watch her eyes to see where they lighted? Did he monitor her breathing as it changed intensity in the presence of all that she coveted? Sometimes he couldn't even wait until they were at home to give her his gifts. At Doreen's Mercantile, he would stand close to her, press himself to her side, and, below the height of the counter she would feel his warm hand slip something into hers. The tiny cameo, bone-white against umber. The packet of ice-white buttons. Palm-sized surprises. One time she lingered over a length of water-blue ribbon, rubbing it beneath her fingers to enjoy its silky gloss, and in what seemed an instant he thrust a length of it at her, unsmiling, as if he were fulfilling a duty. Innocent-faced, silent, he was her little criminal and she was complicit, and no one in the family paid them sufficient attention to wonder how these fancy accessories had materialized or to ask to search Asher's bag, no matter how lumpy.

If only she could know all that he knew without studying, she would not need school. Asher was blessed, his tongue sweet without costly sugar, and she was cursed. Sometimes she thought he did not really exist. In the dead, dark of the country night, lying beside him, listening to his sticky small-boy breath, she feared that out of her own need she had invented him.

5

AND THEN it all closed in on her.

Her mother, who should have known her better, abandoned her to an idea, and, already far from her best self, she had to fight to keep herself recognizable. Mother and her good friend Fraydl became conspirators to marry her off.

The boy was a recent arrival, Fraydl's nephew, who showed up unannounced one hot August, having begged a ride with a neighbor who was heading past their turn-off in his wagon. With his eyes he raked the girls where they sat in the too-warm Commons in relative undress idly gossiping. Not that there was such a thing as undress, only the chance to suspend a few layers of bombazine and country cotton to roll up their sleeves and unbutton their collars.

Chaya had pulled her reddish hair back and tied it with a rag, uncaring. Though it was thick and usually rumpled, below it her face surprised with its delicacy. Her gray eyes seemed to be influenced by the colors she happened to be wearing; today they echoed the blue-green of her wash-worn shirtfront, tomorrow they might tend toward brown. Had she ever noticed that, she might have thought it an expression of her own irresolutions. High cheekbones and those forthright eyes, wide apart and deeply set, gave her face a gravity that matched her darkest moods, like the one she was entertaining on this airless night. Some wild man from across the Caucasus, she always imagined, had ambushed her great-great-grandmother—she liked to envision him lifting her onto his horse and fleeing across the icy fields—and left her unsanctioned descendants with a vaguely eastern cast. She did not think herself beautiful or even pretty; in fact, she suspected she might strike some people as odd and hard to place. Though saying that to herself did not entirely protect her from vanity, she knew it best not to think about it at all.

The nephew's move to America had actually been trumpeted in a letter from Fraydl's sister more than a year ago, and now that he had finally arrived, exhausted, from too many adventures, Chaya could see a dangerous look erupt like a sudden rash across Fraydl's face. Reuven's Fraydl was a milkmaid of a woman, rounded everywhere, pink and wire-haired, a sort of dray horse, sweet-natured but thick, and her sudden interest, which made her pinker than ever, was not subtle. How efficient it would be to fold this boy right into the batter, whatever he might or might not contribute to its flavor.

He was a tall, pale, ghostly looking young man, Shimmie—Chaya had the feeling that she could run the palm of her hand right through him the way you could through a candle flame. His eyes were colorless, his skin the gray of fish just slightly too long out of water, his shoulders narrow and sloping: apologetic. Something about his frailty made her want to pinch him. How could he have done the things he reported? Possibly, she thought, as generously as she could, he had been starving and would, like a flower in dry soil, revive with a rain of attention. He looked famished for warmth and moisture, and for the sun, and there they sat, girls in their summer dresses, loose-haired, returning his gaze because they were so tired of each other's. Their lives had slowed to a dull drip, nothing to look forward to, no temptations to regret taking or refusing. Bleak, bleak, Chaya was thinking, she who had loved the swaying grasses and the starry nights. Now the only excitement was the chance that, if you kept your head cocked back, you might see a dead star falling.

Shimmie had been five months in New York City. He had had every experience—had found good work unloading wagons, been robbed and beaten, had shaken the hand of the mayor, had even seen Sarah Bernhardt just returned from Paris. To the Fields of Zion, these feats were equally miraculous, all of them, they who had been whisked past the city without a minute to see it or even smell it. Had they not spent a day in the tumult of Castle Garden and a night on a parched lot on the corner outside the building, a city of tents and shanties, while they awaited their orders and train tickets, she would never have seen the awesome variety of people the world contained: women "from the East" with coins dangling above their eyes, and those eyes blackened and sooty, white-haired children, girls wearing vests wildly embroidered with flowers and birds in violent color. Their fathers would not allow them to wander into the city, though they cried and begged; they were not allowed curiosity, which was dangerous, which was tempting. (The mothers wanted to go up to Fifth Avenue, but they too were constrained.) The women and girls were stupefied with envy. Their husbands and fathers had been bent on delivering them to green fields and open air, and forbade them even a day to walk in this wonderland that might have made the crossing worthwhile. It hardly seemed plausible, now, that Shimmie, this long drink of water, had so much life in him, such memories of dazzle and tumult—maybe all he had was an imagination and the brazenness to lie.

He told his stories around the table late into the evening of his arrival, his jacket off and his sleeves rolled up on hairless arms and flaccid wrists that hardly looked capable of lifting a cup to his lips. (Unloading barrels off wagons? This was a puff of smoke, not a teamster!) "Sarah Bernhardt!" Gittl breathed and leaned her buxom chest closer. "What was she like?"

He answered in a quiet voice, as if all of it were too ordinary for comment, and shrugged. "Oh, she was nice enough." His eyes lingered on her bosom. "She was more delicate than I expected of a woman of her reputation." Either he was such a pirate of a man that nothing seemed exceptional or, just the opposite, he had no capacity for wonder. Both were repulsive.

But here was the worrisome thing: Chaya's mother caught her eye across the room. Widened *her* eye a thousandth of an inch—less—a little glint of collusion, a twitch of possibility so miniscule she was not sure her mother would have acknowledged it to herself. But her daughter was seventeen, a bud about to open; she was fatally without prospects here in the middle of the alien Wisconsin corn, and she had become impossible to keep, her refusal to work an affront and a mockery, from which no amount of opprobrium would budge her. And at their rickety table sat a *landsman*, who seemed brave and honest, worldly but modest about his exploits and—this was what made all things happen for a reason, wasn't it *bashert?*—destined?—that he had happened to arrive among them just now, and none too early, now and not too late? Her mother and Fraydl glowed at each other across the assembled heads.

Betrayal fouled the air, sharp as manure. The way things worked on the farm, if her mother suggested to her father that Chaya's future had just arrived on a passing cart, dusty but intact—not even a stranger but vouched for by Fraydl!—and if he agreed that the boy had promise, she would not be consulted. There was no other girl, quite, of marriageable age just then—Gittl, for all that she was more *zaftig* than bird-thin Chaya would ever be, was younger, so was Rochl—no one to graciously pass him on to. She envisioned this frail, leafless twig tight against her, the two of them in their own little room off the Common, bundled under a quilt lovingly made for them by *di veyber*, required to lie close. Required to breed like the chickens in the hutch. Chaya did not dare to think she deserved a prince, but she saw her body pass through his like that hand through candle flame, and she believed she would sooner throw herself in their stagnant pond than let him near her. She did not know much but she knew enough—and if she shuddered, it was not because a sudden breeze had found her where she sat. There were no breezes there that night in the whole hellish state of Wisconsin.

And then he winked at her. One of those pale reptilian eyes creased in a coy flicker of greeting, as if she had agreed to something, and she could feel her hands becoming fists in her lap. Suddenly, then—it made so much sense that she gasped out loud—finally, finally, she understood that she had been waiting for this: She was going to leave the Fields of Zion.

Shimmie could stay to inherit the stricken fields of hope gone dead, good labor after bad, God versus Marx. If they had so little respect for her that first she was starved of the education she wanted, and then was considered communal property like Eyn and Tsvey, obedient cows, and their poor decrepit horse, an asset to be made the most of, she would inscribe herself in the debit column. Before she appeared as black ink in the ledger, she would quietly subtract herself. Let them write her name in red. And when she returned triumphant, a queen who could rescue them, let them try royal purple!

When they had all gone to bed, she sat on the doorstep imagining a life. She stacked all she could not wait to leave behind—the caught-ness like a dress snagged on a hook that bound her tighter every time she tried to move forward. She was too bitter these days, she could see it, to be kind to the children, she was harsh with the animals, short with her friends, and, ever since she'd been bereft of school, she had been a parasite on the community and a shrew to her mother. Everything disgusted her: They still lived in the Commons, waiting for—who? The messiah?—to build their own house for them. There was nothing here that was not chipped or cracked, soiled or deformed. Gouges in wood. Fetid flowers in a jar, in green and stinking water. Egg stuck to the wooden table waiting to be picked at with a fingernail. Dust bolls, sour cleaning cloths. Mordechai's violin dead silent. Cow dung on her soles, yellow-brown in the cracks. Maggots in the outhouse. Coughing at night in the next room, Yankel and his endless catarrh. The taste of milk gone slightly rancid, the distant taint of onion on every dish. She had read—half, at least—of that *Moby-Dick* that her teacher let her keep for the long time it took to make her way through its forests of new words and elaborate sentences. She understood perfectly why that man called Ishmael said when he found himself following funerals, it was time to go to sea.

But, as if something had leaped out from behind a bush to frighten her, one idea made her chest lurch: How could she leave Asher behind? It would be a cruel abandonment, for her perhaps more than for him. For one thing, she was the one who had taught him to read and figure and she loved it that he seemed to swallow books in one great bite. Now she feared he too would be conscripted as a pair of hands, a back, a shoulder, his access to books curtailed, his mind turned to practical matters and none of that frivol and fuss they both so loved. She told herself (though she did not quite believe) that, being the boy he was, the lovesome, worrisome boy, he would object to leaving his mama and papa and the brothers who had ridden him around on the sweet saggy horse, or pelted him (as they did each other; it was never hostile) with fallen apples. Now she had to trust his ingenuity, his refusal to heel, and believe he would manage somehow without her help, though she was not so certain of herself.

She did not dare take one last look at him while he slept sprawled like a puppy in a litter beside his brother Beryle for fear she would waver. Instead, she lay in the dark, clenched listening to the breathing around her, some even, some disordered, of far too many of her unbeloved neighbors.

THE NEXT morning, so early the sun's red fire was just beginning to lick the dark side of the barn, Chaya stood in the way of Henry—the girls called him Horny Henry—when he came to pick up the milk cans' to deliver to the railroad siding. Every morning he propped them there to go to market on the 8:10. She had to seize all her courage to whisper her request to him because he had always half frightened, half disgusted her. Henry was cruel-faced because of a brutal scarring he'd received when he was just a boy working at the tannery. In fact, the edges of his scars looked terribly like leather themselves, thick and brown and impervious as hide, and he looked as though he'd given up washing around the same time. But he was as regular as the sun that revealed the barn each day, and she suspected he was hungry. She surely was.

So when he made clear the price for his assistance, she didn't hesitate to pay it: one fast swipe of his shovel-sized hands across her breasts, and one pretended thrust against her where she stood with her back to his shaking wagon. Poor Henry. She thought of the dogs in their barnyard hurling themselves at the yelping bitches. But he didn't steal anything from her, she reasoned, that cost her anything. She was still the same—a girl full of books and bitterness—when he was finished pressing against her, the first man ever to fit himself to her, mussing her dress. Her rough burlap apron must not have been quite the texture he had in mind. *Cheap at the price*, she thought, even though she knew she would have to yield this same favor again tomorrow, on the actual day when, her few belongings in a seed sack, she would hunker down invisibly between the cold silvery cans that chattered against each other in the rank body of his wagon.

HENRY PICKED up the milk cans in a number of towns and she asked him to let her off in Columbia City, which was the next town over, so that, if anyone came asking questions of the stationmaster in Christa, he wouldn't have seen a girl carrying a sack stuffed full—she had looked in vain for the Gladstone with which they had arrived and had "borrowed," instead, twelve dollars in coin from her father's hiding place behind *The Coming End of the Capitalist Monopoly*, which he did not have sufficient English to make sense of.

SHE STOOD alone on the platform—Columbia City was no metropolis—trying to look casual, as if she made this trip frequently, off on a visit or to shop for things she could not find near to home when, craning to peer down the track, she heard from behind an empty baggage cart, "Chai! You *left* me!" and out sprang her little brother, arms wide in triumph. He nearly knocked her over diving at her. Here, to complicate her escape, was a small short-pantsed boy, dark hair shining, knobbly-kneed, vibrating with energy.

He was not asking absolution for following her. "Where were you *going* without me?" His outrage was not child-sized: When he stamped his dusty boot he looked like a petulant little man. Should she be angry or pleased that he simply would not be abandoned?

However he had tracked her down, here he was as solid as Chaya, casting his shadow beside hers in the fresh morning sun. And so she chose to be pleased—flattered, even, though it might have been the hope for adventure that had brought him and not his need for her or his bone-deep love. From inside the station a tiny high-pitched bell announced the arrival of the train. Asher nearly leaped with pleasure as it crept toward them.

Her own knees were watery. Car after car came worming out of the distance and pulled beside them far, far more colossal than she had somehow remembered—heavier, noisier, obliterating the horizon. Brutal. Thrilling.

When they had been helped up the high steps—the conductor picked her brother up and swung him right past her like a light valise and took her hand with surprising gentleness, giving a little bow as he did so—Asher had found his first teacher. He tapped the man's uniform at the top of his dark-blue thigh and asked about the silver ticket punch that dangled from his belt beside a tangle of keys, "What name is that?"

The man laughed from very high above both of them, and they were off. By the time Chaya had settled herself and her sagging bag of belongings, Asher had the conductor in thrall, and had sat tight against the engineer a while and, careening like a drunk, walked the length of every car. By then, in that peculiar way he had of staring at a thing as if he were a camera and committing it to his voracious memory, he had learned every word in the conductor's vocabulary from *clerestory* to *sandbox* to *standpipe*, to *trailing truck* and *coal tender*.

Asher's profile, beside the dusty window, was sharp as cut glass; his eyelashes, more lush than his sister's, were separate as though they were always wet, his eyes and his nostrils black and comically round. He was— was this blasphemy?—like a boy in the funny papers! And every time he opened his mouth to speak he made a little popping sound like her snap-purse opening. It was the small noise, not quite moist, she would think later when she had met more than a few, of a gourmand anticipating a morsel of something delicious.

Her dual—no, triple—acts of thievery, abandonment, and kidnapping, had exhausted her. She had executed in fastidious Yiddish a simple note that, contrary to every pleading by her consoling side, refused apology, and left it propped against the pillow (stuffed with their own chickens' feathers) on her parents' bed:

> *Dear Mama and Papa,*
>
> *I am not yours to give away. So I am going to hide for a while. Please do not look for me. I promise to keep myself safe. Some day I may even make you proud.*
>
>

Your loving daughter,
Chaya-Libbe

Then, like Jonah who escaped into sleep at the bottom of the ship that bore him from Tarshish, Chaya hid from what she had done and, finally, from the knowledge that she could not imagine where they were going and how they would survive there. She had said, *No. Yes* was not something she could afford to think about. When, reluctantly, she woke to clamor and flashing lights, what she saw was the chaos of engines, freight cars, wagons and cables, thick and daunting, and tracks that scrolled to the left and right in a shining script that she had no trouble reading. They had arrived in Chicago and no one would be there to greet them.

6

ALL THEY had eaten on the train was a piece of unbuttered brown bread
Chaya had ripped off a loaf in the bread box—why she hadn't taken the
entire loaf she couldn't imagine, unless it was some vague gesture of con-
trition for the way she was about to slip so secretly out of their lives—and
a sweet the conductor had offered to Asher, which Asher unwrapped with
great ceremony. Listening to the rumble of her hunger, she concluded
that she was going to have to do for them whatever might be demanded
if they were to survive here. This category was no longer merely abstract:
She was a confirmed sinner laying plans for further mischief and they
had not yet even arrived at the station. This, she understood, was why the
doomed farmers of the Fields of Zion had refused to persist in city life;
they thought their resistance would keep them *good*.

They stopped tantalizingly close to their destination and sat, and sat,
and sat still longer in gathering heat, while Chaya restrained Asher from
rushing to leap off the train. Her legs had begun to feel as inert and heavy
as fence posts. In fact, theirs had subsided right beside another train that
was also stopped and when, without a lurch, it began slowly to inch forward, she had the illusion that they were the ones moving. The faces in the
other cars seemed calm and peaceful, all those lives floating by in silence,
going away from Chicago just as they were arriving, and she was seized by
a fearful curiosity—why were the others retreating just as they advanced?
Was that an omen, a warning that she might fail here, and take her Asher

down with her? But they might, she reasoned—these days there was a debating society toiling in her brain—be going on a day visit or to fulfill a family obligation. Why must she assume that because she was fleeing *they* were fleeing?

Then, with a ferocity that would have knocked her down had she not been seated, pinned in place by perspiration and exhaustion, she wished her mother were there to comfort her, and her father to let her lean against his shoulder. How could she not recall how different were his dusty, time-worn vest and jacket from the spruce outfits of the men and women beside them, and there in those passing windows? The hats! She could just see, above the seat in front of her, a spray of dark purple feathers and the very top of something extravagantly leafy; there must have been a virtual garden below it, combined with a rookery. She hadn't seen it earlier—perhaps the woman had defied propriety by removing it for the trip and had replaced it as they approached the station. What would Pesye or Fraydl have looked like in a concoction like that, or any of the women who never removed, in public, the headscarves that they trusted to keep them safe from a world of lust and provocation? She giggled at the idea.

Mama, possibly—she had, or could have had, in a different life, a certain bone-bred elegance: She was tall and her posture was proud, which sometimes made her seem unbending. But Chaya could see her in a hat like that, though under Father's severe tutelage, she could hardly imagine her daring to want one. That was the kind of constraint that kept them ordinary. A crown, a brim worn up or down, she knew, expressed a woman's most secret self; it was practically an organ of the body, plain if her dreams were plain, abloom with life if she herself was vital! If ever she was rich, she would own a hat for every mood.

They weren't moving. If only to contain her apprehension, she made herself concentrate on everything she saw: the shiny brown valise that sat on its own seat upright, like a child. The pull-down shade rolled up at her window. The gay checkered suit jacket of the portly man across the aisle, complete with a carefully folded handkerchief in the breast pocket, which matched the dark green of the plaid but which, though he was perspiring in the stilled train, he did not use. He was, she was sure, what she had heard called a "drummer," a man who travels with a case of samples and sells things far from home. Did his feet drum on the ground as he walked? Did he drum on the ears and nerves of shopkeepers or housewives until they surrendered and bought of his goods? There were customers' men and, undoubtedly less privileged, the back-door men who wandered down their lane with their cunning cases of needle-and-thread and lengths of dry goods, and the occasional ball or toy soldier to make the children cry and wheedle until their frugal mothers surrendered. They had received one recently who clambered up in a wagon, and on the wagon what did they find but the extravagant addition of a photographer's necessities. The children had convinced Mama that they needed a portrait, and now, Chaya realized with a little inner grimace, that would be their only record of Asher and his evil sister more enduring and objective than memory.

What she had come for was to entertain spectacle. Having lived so long at the end of that washboard road where nothing offered color and movement, she admitted to herself, and proudly, she had come to be provoked. And if that meant that she left goodness behind, well, they would see about that.

IT WAS June of 1891 on the day that same kind conductor handed them down onto a little wooden footstool so that they might meet the ground gently, and there in the late afternoon she was overwhelmed with the certainty that they would be safe here in the province of strangers. (In her inflamed state, it took little to overwhelm her.) And this was illusion too, perhaps, but she felt the very rhythm of her perceptions change. So much passed so quickly that had it been music, it would, all of it, have been staccato. Her nearly weightless little brother pulled her along like a dog at the end of a tether.

And then, what was their initiation into the city's strangeness but a real dog, only a dog not restrained by any tether. As they inched down the platform alongside the great army-green flank of the train, a dog as tall as a horse came running, loose, toward them and then, having nearly knocked them down, right past. He was the color of a bale of hay, but shining, and his tail ended in a long elegant spiral. This was a rich man's dog, and when he got to the end of the platform where it entered the station, he stopped and looked back, over his dog-shoulder, teasingly, with imperious eyes, to see if his rich man was coming. Still no one came rushing forward; he loped, then, casually, arrogantly, into the station and when the two of them saw him next he was sitting, quite demurely, before the information booth, his feet together, waiting to be caught up with. *No rules,* Chaya thought (which, of course, was not true, only the dog had long since eaten the instructions and taken them into his muscles). No prohibitions. *Beauty, free to run everywhere.* Who did she think she was and what did she think she wanted or needed, not to say deserved?

AS TIME passed, she would think about those things long and hard and each time she reached an answer, she watched it change and change again. She only knew that she was not angry any more, she was apprehensive but not at war with her possibilities. Anticipation seized her. So *this*—hopeful expectation unsupported by the most rudimentary detail—was what had gripped the Am Olam pioneers when they disembarked on the New York shoreline! Now—not when the motors of the SS *Stettin* cut off but here in Dearborn Station, Chicago—she was certain her real life had begun.

WHAT SHE had not foreseen was that this first glimpse of Chicago, bursting on all her senses, a riot of color and shape and movement, would nearly drive her baby brother mad with excitement. Given his voracious nature, there were simply too many things to be seen, counted, ordered, remembered.

He studied the departure times posted at the gate of every track: Springfield 2:48, Kankakee 4:15, a long skein of numbers, unwinding. And in the waiting room, when she bent to inspect the guidebooks for travelers, he guzzled down the names of the newspapers on the stand and said them back one by one under his breath. Their existence was so exciting he named each like the discovery it was. "*Tribune! Times! Herald! Daily News! Evening Mail! Hotel Reporter! Inter-Ocean!, Evening Journal! Neue Freie Presse! Staats-Zietung!*" She watched him with the greatest alarm: He thrummed like a little motor, but a motor running too fast for safety.

His bright eyes darted everywhere at once, and he balled his fists and then unballed them—he was ten years old, still in short pants and a cut-down shirt, courtesy of his brother Yakov, with a wide, frayed collar, and a good many ineradicable food stains. His cap had been knocked askew by someone whose carelessness could only be forgiven if he was late for his train.

Yet there were things he did not notice or, if he did, he remained more placid than perhaps he should have. While he was memorizing the names of the newspapers his sister, in rather inelegant fashion, knelt to the ground before the travelers' guides with her skirts bunched before her as tightly as she could arrange them so that she could slip into her bag quite invisibly *Glossop's Street Guide, Strangers' Directory and Hotel Manual of Chicago*, and pull the strings tight with inspiring finality. She was already so devious, she reasoned, that she granted herself license to do whatever needed doing to survive. That was a great relief: She would draw the line at hurting another. *From each according to his ability, to each according to his need* seemed a capacious motto that could suffice for her needs.

Asher saw her tuck away the unsanctioned green pamphlet. Instead of making note of it, he told her, "I looked and seven of the engines are the same." Perhaps actions seemed too illusory for notice; they were not *facts*. They made their way against a strong current of men, women, and even traveling babies done up in their best bonnets. "Three are different, and I also have to find out how they get from the front of the train to the back so they can leave. Do you know how?" He tended to whine when he needed to know something. Asher's hunger. She shook her head, disappointing him. "How can I find out?"

She told him, too impatiently (and, if he had been any other kind of child, alarmingly), that she couldn't think about such things before they had an address to retire to. She didn't like to frighten him, in case he had some hidden part that froze with anxiety beyond her capacity to see it, but (as he should have appreciated) facts are facts. To assuage him, she took him to a counter and with one precious coin, bought him a tumbler of milk and a muffin, of which she begged a bite.

Then she studied her *Glossop's* and was staggered that, far beyond her capacity to have imagined, they had come to a city so bedizened with theaters, music halls, opera houses, restaurants, hotels and public parks—all except the last wildly unaffordable, given the pitiable sum her kleptomania had provided. There were instructions that amused even as they depressed her, for there was no way their warnings and directives could affect two such beggars, and she vowed that if she ever lifted them from penury, she would write a guide for the impoverished. They had come here to be joyous in their freedom, but joy this side of heaven, she reflected, had a steep price attached. "When (as you ride into the city in a 'palace on wheels') the omnibus agent calls for your baggage checks (which he certainly will do before reaching the depot), have no hesitancy in giving them up, designating where you wish baggage taken. You will be agreeably surprised to find your 'luggage' at your hotel within a few minutes of your own arrival. This admirable feature is all owing to the Frank Parmalee Omnibus Service, which is most efficient, accommodating and entirely trustworthy. Place yourself in their charge and you have nothing to fear." What would Mr. Parmalee make of Chaya's bulging burlap bag before he deposited it in the nearest waste can?

So, while Asher continued to whip his attention from one set of memorizables to another—the name over the shoeshine stand, Jasper's, Home of the Slick Shine; the barbershop (which, since it was called Foote's, should have belonged to the shoe man); the bar (While Away), and the restaurant lit by the white of its tablecloths (The Metropolitan)— Chaya's mood wavered like a fever chart from exhilaration to gloom to absolute terror and back again to a slightly hysterical delight. She searched in vain for some desk that might give aid to confused travelers; wished, hopelessly, for an office of HEAS like the one to be found up a flight of stairs at Castle Garden. But, of course, that was a gathering point for immigrants by the thousands (and for all she could appreciate at the time, there were similar offices for other nationalities as well). Dearborn Station, she understood from her purloined Baedeker, was not the largest in the city. Could there be more assistance at another, where the trains arrived from greater distances?

For all her desperation, she could feel herself maturing on the spot, like an adolescent who can feel her limbs lengthening, and that gave her some strength, built upon no foundation except her capacity to get them into interesting trouble that she had no idea how to get them out of. She was a fast-growing plant, and she would simply have to master blooming. How they could have used some real such plants back at the farm, rooted in soil. She was rooted nowhere, but she would be, she had faith—*they* would be, without resort to prayer or begging (though perhaps to petty theft!), and soon. She would be a girl in one of Miss Singlet's cheering novels; though they foundered, they never failed.

She studied her *Glossop's* for more information than it could give her, chiefly: Where in this teeming city did the Jews live? The little book was more inclined to leap from a history of the birth of Chicago, c. 1837, to the fact, recited with pride, that its 4,711 manufactories employed 152,280 men, women, boys, and girls to the not very helpful disclosure that Asher and she had been but two riders on the 463 regular passenger and suburban trains which entered and left the city daily. She detected in the publishers of *Glossop's Strangers' Directory and Hotel Manual* a penchant, familiar to her in her brother, for disconnected facts whose mere existence was their justification. But the listings of retail establishments—sculptors, portrait painters in oil colors, charcoal renderers of landscape and animals; dyers and scourers; purveyors of artificial limbs, birds, goldfish, and popcorn (wholesale, on the ear or shelled); architects and detective agencies—were of little use to her, as was the sudden pronouncement of a lively editorial voice bristling with advice. "Avoid the unsolicited proffers of strangers as you would that of a savage Zulu or a mountaineer Afghan. They are equally to be feared. For any and all desired information not found in the Guide consult the hotel clerk; for what that human storehouse of knowledge don't know is beyond the scope of ingenuity to find out." Mr. Glossop was clearly impressed. Onward he marched, with advice irrelevant to the two of them and their seed sack luggage. Asher clutched his own favorite book, which his sister doubted would prove particularly useful in their new home. It was not the *Red Fairy Book* or the *Blue*; it was surely not the Bible; it was *Hopkinson's Book of Forest and Jungle, Illustrated.* Some children need one blanket to comfort them. Asher needed his "exhaustive compendium of curious animals and daring expeditions" to keep him secure far from the vine-entwined habitats of four-legged predators.

Chaya had been standing beside him at the counter, leaning her elbow in the two inches or so of space allotted each of them, undoubtedly not sufficiently ladylike to qualify her for city living à la *Glossop's*. She was reading her way through its lists and maps and so she neglected to notice that her brother had vanished from her side—or, rather, from the folds of her skirts. When she did cast around for a sign of his presence and failed to see him, she flung herself like a madwoman through the crowd, uncertain whether to call his name or simply to search for the top of his head. It was difficult to penetrate the density of rushing patrons. Asher, who lived at ground level, moved as quickly as a fox, and with a fox's independence.

She was faint with terror at having lost him—half an hour in the city and her competence was already inadequate, fatally so. But when she did nerve herself up to bleat his name her voice was like some rusty hinge squeaking in a high wind. Women in daunting dress stared at her; men hardly noticed but only hurried on. She ran to the heavy doors of the station nearest to where they had consumed milk and muffin and tried to see outside. She raced back again when she saw him running, shouting who knew what, circling the information booth in pursuit of another boy around his size. Flailing their arms, they wove between skirts and pant legs, bringing down curses on their heads.

She wrenched Asher's arm ungently, until she found a quiet pocket where she could scold him for frightening her out of her skin and putting himself, however invisibly, in danger. "You can't simply show off like that here, this is a *city*, and who knows what could happen!" All this in English. They were finished with Yiddish for now, if not forever, though speaking it made her feel suspended in midair, somehow, her feet not touching solid ground.

His small, earnest face pink with exertion, Asher met her eyes levelly— he was never insolent and, though larcenous about solid objects, those many things he slipped into his grasp, he was never really devious. "Then tell me, what is this *city*? That wasn't dangerous except so many people bumped into us and didn't care."

Chaya tried to see him as he must appear to these strangers, a slight child with a clear voice and an accent in him unidentifiable, dressed in his bedraggled small boy's outfit, who had not yet grown into his ears or, for that matter, his dusty, ill-shod feet. He had such a pretty face, and, shining out from under his scuffed cap, such healthy dark hair for someone whose diet was unreliable at best, such a clarity about him—that was the thing about Asher, not his brilliance but his light!—that again, Chaya saw, he was like an illustration of a boy, not a real boy.

Not for the first time she was reminded that his kind of genius without experience could be a dangerous kind of idiocy.

"You have never lived in a place with thousands of people you never saw before and will never see again!" she began. Zhitomir had thoroughly faded for him. Let him be frightened; it would serve him well.

"And so?"

"And so, and so, they are not your friends!"

"That's all right. I don't need thousands of friends."

Frustration washed in upon Chaya like water climbing a shore. "It is *not* all right! They owe you nothing. You are not an adult, Asher. You stay beside me, I don't want you wandering off on your own again."

He made a sour face as if to say, *What do you know about what I need.* This was a new defiance and it frightened her. "I thought we came here so you could be sweeter. You said."

This was not fair. "I mean it. I've lived in a city, you haven't." Men on tall horses, spurring them to thunder down on the Jews of their quarter, who scattered like vermin. She had watched from a window, pretending to be safe, as they plunged bayonets through her neighbors and waved their rifles like flags of victory. It was not only hunger that had made them travel across half the world. "You had better trust me, little boy. I will skin you for your own sake, Asher." She was shaking with anger. But perhaps it was not his fault: What she needed was not what he needed.

That was when Chaya felt a very gentle hand on the arm that ended with her accusing finger. "Pardon me, miss," she heard in a male voice, carefully modulated not to alarm. She had, in fact, to look up, actually had to cant her head as she would soon do to encompass the buildings outside.

"May I be of some assistance? You seem rather agitated over this little man's stunning performance."

Her *Glossop's* had warned against accepting unsolicited proffers of generosity. *The nerve of the man!*—that was her first thought. But first thoughts are not always best thoughts. She looked again and registered his height— extreme; his eyes—not the blue of the sky, an expectable blue, but the darker blue of the birds that liked to eat the seeds from the fields and leave their lovely feathers like calling cards on the ground; his face, in total, that of a man of perhaps thirty or so years, with kindly lines from nose to mouth where frequent smiling tends to carve them. That inviting face seemed to be divided by the contested border between concern and amusement.

But Chaya was still caught in her moment of uncontrollable panic at having lost Asher, for she saw that if she lost control of her boy, this Chicago would casually gobble him up. She had not given so much as an ounce of thought to the risks of the city. All her dangers had been the insidious ones she knew too well at home: death by boredom, by depression, by regret.

She looked into the face of this man from behind the veil of her anxiety. "Thank you but I have no need for—" But then, by now third thought, "I could—we have no—" She was helpless with confusion, and, as brilliant as her brother must have seemed, she appeared to be feebleminded.

"I would be pleased if you were to invite me to help you."

She had never heard a sentence so graceful. And it gave her responsibility for proceeding.

"We have no—" Which, of all their needs, should come first? "I am trying to find a place for us to go to—"

"Do you have the address?" Seeing him standing beside Asher was ludicrous, a giraffe beside a newborn chick. But she too, most probably, looked ill suited to absorb his attention, this thin girl with a weight of unruly hair (lusterless these days beneath a veil of farm dust) and a dusty jacket over a shirtwaist whose hopeful yellow had faded off-white with a hundred washings.

"No, no," she began, and it did feel hopeless. "I mean, we have no particular place. I am just trying to find the—where—" She hesitated, frightened at the disclosure on her lips.

"Where then?" He bent down towards her and seemed to listen with something deeper than patience; he vibrated at a slower pace than most, some slow beat of the blood or the nerves.

"Where the Jewish people live." Chaya was mortified by her bluntness. And might he tell her that in this democratic city, they were dispersed in every direction?

His constant smile did not dim. "Well—I will happily escort you there, if you will allow me. You don't have anyone to whom you could go?"

She shook her head bitterly but—in spite of their father's insistence that they cover their ears to circumvent the opportunistic prayers of the holidays—she knew she would have to believe that something, call it God or call it chance, would provide.

Her new friend lifted his valise and she, awkwardly, raised her absurd tan burlap bag tattooed with lettering concerning the potency and durability of the barley seed therein, whose contents poked out irregularly, as though she were hefting a sackful of unruly animals. Mercifully, he did not offer to carry it for her, since any man with functioning eyes had to understand how humiliated she would be were he to acknowledge that he had so much as *seen* it. He did seem to be offering his arm—at least, she believed he was, but she was pitifully uncertain of every move, and were he not offering it and she were to try to take it, she would melt into a puddle at his feet.

Outside the station, as she clutched Asher's hand, what awaited them were squares of dark, lozenges of light. Brick, cement, macadam, glass. The setting sun seared the far edge of a hewed-stone building with fire. A cable car screeched wildly at the corner, a wild jungle sound, as it lurched to a stop, but everything else moved. *Everything moved.* Of course she knew in theory, but it hardly seemed possible in fact, that they had lived on that prairie—nothing but slender dancing grass and scrabbled earth— while *this* existed. The air was thick, rich, rank, fishy, buttery, harsh with manure. And the hurrying crowds, thousands of skirts in thousands of colors sweeping the street, and more, by far, black-suited men beneath bobbing hats! They pushed forward with an energy that suggested their survival depended on gaining the next crossing. How many ways there were to live! She wished she could follow everyone home.

The man who had made himself their guide turned and watched Chaya at the door, standing so still it seemed she must be looking or listening for something in particular.

She saw him regarding her with a slight smile and was so embarrassed she had to restrain herself from fleeing, turning back in to the station. Then he made it worse. "This city's architecture is probably its greatest gift to the nation," he began, like a lecturer, but the rest of his comment was swamped by the shame with which she furiously quizzed herself: *Architecture? Arches? Texture?* What did that *mean?*

The Samaritan, as yet anonymous, ushered them to a hansom behind two horses who stood with their heads down respectfully, still as stone. He stepped up behind them. "Let me think now, for a moment," he said and then, definitively, to the driver with the whip hand, "We should like to go to the Maxwell Street area, please. I will tell you more precisely when we draw near."

"And what is there?" How could she not inquire, though why should this person know such a thing? Were the Jewish people of Chicago so notorious that a Christian should be familiar with their neighborhood?

"Some preliminaries," he said. "My name is Gregory Stillman. I have had some traffic with your community, so it seems a fortunate circumstance that your need coincides with my experience." He seemed quite satisfied with himself for this.

Self-consciousness had reddened her cheeks and made it difficult for her to look at him. When her lack of etiquette did not stir her to reciprocate with her own name, he quite straightforwardly asked it.

"I am," Chaya told him, still too abashed to meet his eyes, "Chaya-Libbe Shaderowsky. This is my brother Asher." She could hear her accent change—regress—as she spoke. It had been years since she had sounded like this!

"And you have never been in Chicago before." Was he a masher or simply a kind man? She had never, after all, been the subject of any man's attention, unless she counted that weak tea, Shimmie, who had winked his snake-eye at her. (If the boys of Christa had shown any interest in her, their mothers would have knocked it out of them.) She watched Gregory

Stillman watching her, quite openly, really, but she had no way to read the return of her gaze, except to note that it was steady, not guileful, and that the same slow pulse and unhurried sense of well-being seemed to rise off him the way the air sometimes falls upon the skin with perfect temperateness. Those are the days when there is no shock of change between indoors and out and such sublimity tends to make one feel at peace.

"We are—" How to say it? Runaways? Wayfarers? Adventurers? She had none of the necessary language on her tongue, not yet, nor would she for many years. "We hope," she said instead, with every small fragment of pride she could assemble, "to make our fortune here." That phrase came directly out of one of those books she had read; she could hear it as an echo, as if someone else, a Brontë or a Dickens, were speaking from inside her mouth.

Gregory Stillman laughed as if he recognized that, somewhere between sympathy and mockery. "Oh, nothing less than your fortune!"

Irony demanded more of her than she could spare. She could not muster a smile.

"Again, please tell me where are you taking us?"

It was soon enough made clear: They had clattered on blocks of stone and wood through rows of narrow brick and wooden-sided houses, and now the shopfronts and the signs above them were a riot of Yiddish lettering, each clamoring louder than the next to be seen. Not since Zhitomir had she encountered her alphabet in any public place; her heart beat hard with relief. There were tailors; there was a matzo company and a baker of sweet rolls and butter pastries. The butchers promised economical cuts, strictly kosher. She recognized a few men walking in the deliberate way that would deliver them to the door of some synagogue. It was time for *ma'ariv*, evening prayers.

But her guide had already gestured to the cabman to stop before a dark-brick building that had the shape of the solemn business within. "Here," he said to Chaya. "I am certain these people will be eager to help you and this young gentleman." He patted the boy on his bare, scabbed knee.

Chaya began to thank the gentleman, still concerned as to his motives. With the casual ease with which she supposed those well-placed in the world could go about their pleasures, he shook off her gratitude and asked, "Will you be all right? I am certain the good people inside will help you, but beyond today—am I wrong to suppose that you might need—"

"Nothing at all," she replied with a dignity that strained her last resources. "We will be—" She feared he was going to offer them money, which would have undone her.

"Four turns," Asher announced. He had been so silently absorbed Chaya had almost forgotten him. "The way he just turned the carriage doesn't count. Four real turns from the station, two railway crossings, and one bridge."

Mr. Stillman pinched his cheek, which made him buck like a horse refusing the bit. "You are a young genius and nothing less, my friend. I think you will do very well for yourself and your sister."

He helped them down and then, with delicacy, handed Chaya his calling card. She had never seen hands so kempt and clean on any man. "My dear Miss—Shadow?"

"Sha-der-ow-sky!" Asher said impatiently, breaking the name into emphatic syllables. "And the *vuh* is a *w*."

She took the card, cream-colored with a soft, fuzzed edge, between her soiled fingers and wondered what to do with it. Her sack seemed an inadequate receptacle for anything so fine.

She was too flustered to try to thank him again as she should have. She had, in the course of reading to her brother from their sinfully secular books, encountered fairy godmothers, rarely fathers, but she knew that, male or female, this was not the form in which they generally appeared: that is, fairly near one's own age, dressed in tweeds and spotless footwear, clean-shaven, even-featured, with a seductive solicitousness; the ones she remembered were gnarled little hunchbacks and warty old women with hairy chins. She bowed her head in lieu of thanks, seized her brother's equally sullied hand, and fled inside the doors of Ner Kodesh, one of who knows how many synagogues *Glossop's* had not named, and was greeted with the surprise she deserved—none at all.

But after much back-and-forthing, and a considerable number of eyes turned upon her as though to measure her virtue as well as her capacity to pay her way, she was offered the name of the widow of a recently deceased congregant who had just today, by coincidence, announced that she was yielding to the economic catastrophe brought about by his death, and wished to take in a boarder.

She was put in the hands of someone's young son, in knickers and cap, to be shown the way, and together the three of them wound through darkening streets of depressing sordidness, loose refuse stinking against the posts that held up sagging porches, the wooden planks of the sidewalk uneven and, occasionally, punctuated by holes that they barely avoided stepping into. Chaya saw a rat, just its unmistakable ringed tail, disappearing into a yard whose privy she could smell, one among many, but she did not tell Asher.

7

ASHER CAME to consciousness in a single blow.

It was the smokestacks, the scaffolds, the shafts—hard, all of it. Stone and iron. Wooden Wisconsin was soft and yielding, it was a pillow, a pelt. The city commanded sight, imposed hearing, and it stank. Reached up into his nostrils and raked them. Once, he had inhaled smelling salts—tried to leap from an apple tree onto the sagging back of their horse and fell straight as a plummet onto his head when the horse moved nonchalantly off. A shriek went up, the whole farm running, and someone shoved a vial under his nose. The wild acidy insult to his membranes brought him back intact and he loved it now, helplessly. It was like scratching an endless itch, better than bread baking, better than chicken on the fire.

And here, this *Chi-ca-go* was something different in its particulars but just as harsh. Ugly. He breathed it in and held it, held it deeper, his eyes closed.

Off the train and into the crowd he felt he was walking in a swarm of bees, in their noise, in their wind, in their threat. He wanted to run through them fast but his sister held on to him as if he had become a dog on a leash. In fact they saw a grand dog on the platform, a princely hound. No country dog ever looked like that.

He whirled through numbers—got away from Chaya—Chai—snaking through the underbrush of skirts and pant legs and, hanging on to a post, up on a ledge to give him height, called off departure times for the trains that stood out in the light, chuffing. Lovely sounds: Lafayette, Peoria, Madison. *Pee-or-i-ya* felt in the mouth like custard going down. Applause, that strange thing people did, banging hands together like a baby playing patty-cake. Who invented such a thing to show appreciation? A child? Did everyone in the world do that, people who ran naked in jungles and rowed boats made of tree bark? Clap? Here, in and out underfoot, beneath an endless vault bright as sky above, carved, thick with designs and carvings, he expanded. He had been asleep and now he was altogether awake. He would never slow down. In this place he was going to be happy.

But she caught him again. She was going to herd him, her face like someone else's—Pesye's, Zanvel's—with a rare anger. No words were ever worse than "for your own good." Every sip of medicine was for his good, if he survived the taste. He wanted to gag. Then someone with a calm voice spoke so that she let go of his arm, sat them in a carriage and Asher began to count. That was the only way to hold still the streets, contain them in his mind.

The farm was all blank space, the prairie beyond nothing but distant green and hazy horizon; in town those separate little houses and their fences and timid rows of tulips were frail as paper. Here, everything was fierce, even the air was a different color. The shadows were dark, thick, deep—solid. You could almost pick them up. Beside the stony buildings, the tops of the horses' heads looked warm and breakable.

Thousands of everything! He would die of it, fall into exhaustion keeping up. Thirty-four shops with signs even before they turned a single corner. Fourteen full stops. Trees here and there, but spindly and parched. Were there any trees as glad to be here as he? He couldn't wait to tell Chaya he was never leaving. He dangled his arm over the side to feel the rush and the wind pickled his fingers.

"Four turns," he told them when the carriage pulled up to a halt. His sister was blind to him. The man's face had entered her, he could see that. She was not a policeman now. Her face was stricken (he liked that word though it didn't sound like what it was. *Ick* should be funny, *icken* even funnier). Her expression was soft as sheep's wool and between her pretty gray eyes a new line lengthened, something worried, something bewildered. (There was be-whiskered. There was be-jeweled. What was *wildered* that one could *be* it?)

THEN HE saw a rat but he didn't tell Chaya. That tail, raw and unhaired, like a string in sections—disgusting, though he didn't know why. They had rats in the barn sometimes, but they felt cleaner—rats, groundhogs, chipmunks, prairie dogs, raccoons, everything incessantly making its way, finding what it needed, most of it still alive. Sometimes he lay in the grass and listened to them move. The ground was drilled with mole holes.

Chaya had gone into a broad brick building, up the steps and disappeared; he followed her in and saw her being looked at up and down by a dozen men, and then they were rushing along behind a boy whose knickered legs flashed faster than Chaya could go. That was when he saw the rat bent over something it was liking for supper, hunched and busy. Its long nails were pearly in the falling light. So: no more chickens, no cows, what would a city have but horses, people, rats. And birds. There were fat gray ones with rainbows, beautiful rainbows, around their necks and their bulging chests; dozens swarmed around like the crowds in the railway station, this way and that. He would have to find out what they were called, though probably not from Chaya.

Everything on the ground scattered when they went by. Pretend you're a prince—he had met royalty, endlessly, in his books—and those are your people, paying homage, hurrying out of your path. *Make way for the Prince of Chicago!* Why not?

8

THOUGH SHE was honest enough to warn Mrs. Gottlieb that they had only a modest amount of money from which to pay her, the widow seemed desperate to install a living body in her rooms, as if to prove, against great odds, that it could be done. Furthermore, Chaya assured her, she would have work as soon as earthly possible.

Mrs. Gottlieb was not relying on earthly powers: "With God's help," she breathed, and Chaya hoped such piety would not remind her too much of Pesye and Zanvel and the rest of the grim lot she had left behind. "I'll tell you honestly, I hope I'm not offending, that I am not feeling very friendly toward God just now after he took my husband, *olav ha-sholem*, but yet you should remember who holds your good fortune."

Still in widow's crepe, shamed by the very idea of sharing her tiny, dark, unlovely flat, she was nonetheless very kind. Perhaps she took to the two of them because she had no children—when she referred to herself as a barren woman Chaya blushed for her because that word made her seem the victim of a Biblical curse.

Mrs. Gottlieb's bosom was like the wall around old cities, an awesome barricade. But behind it, she was meek and stunned still by having been abandoned—suddenly one morning, just as she turned away to bring him his tea—by her good Nachman, who fell on the floor *right here*. (She gestured beside a chair.) Her husband, she told Chaya, had been in the ground now only three weeks. Her eyes, in the full light of day, had disappeared behind circles of defeated flesh. If Chaya had hoped to find high spirits after her years of woe, this was the wrong apartment. But glee and good cheer, she understood, were not a roof and a floor. Like her attention to the buildings downtown, they would come later.

It was dark outside when she dropped a scant few coins into Mrs. Gottlieb's hand but she could feel her wince, shamed, as they fell into her palm. "Come dear, look at this," Mrs. Gottlieb said, perhaps to cheer herself, and showed Chaya, on the little shelf on which stood her candlesticks and *kiddush* cup, an old country photograph of herself as a very young woman with a mammoth bow in her hair, standing stiffly between brothers and sisters, her stern, bearded father and unsmiling mother safely between them. They sat within a scene, pillared before and grassy behind, out of something more like Rome before its fall than any vista in their own *shtetl.* "When I was young like you," she said with a pale smile. She would have regretted the ripple of fear that sent through Chaya like a shiver of oncoming fever.

Then, "Your brother, your *pitsele*, is very smart," Mrs. Gottlieb murmured from behind her hand, pointing not so secretly at Asher. He had impressed her by counting the steps up to her apartment—forty-eight— and announcing the total, divided evenly by the number of landings. It was on the fourth floor, through a hallway so dark that the single gas lamp at the foot of the stairs illuminated nothing.

"Oh," Chaya answered her, "he is just an eager boy who loves to use his brain, far from home and hungry. He tires me out." She wished she had not said that last thing to a woman who had no child, smart or otherwise, but she was left with her regret.

She would herself, their landlady told them, sleep in the front room, which had no bed that Chaya could see. She would have to be planning to push her three unmatched wooden chairs together so that she and Asher could share the bed in the one lightless bedroom. This seemed preposterous to her; Mrs. Gottlieb was a grown woman, weighted with age and grief, and they were children—even she, by all measurements, was as light as a child. *Her* bosom must have weighed a feather. And so they fought gently, like cats with their claws drawn back, over whose head would lie where.

"But you're paying me," Mrs. Gottlieb insisted, balling her apron in her veiny hands.

"Not very much," Chaya insisted to her. She wanted to say, *That bed is still warm with your husband's heat!* Instead, she told her, "You will hurt yourself trying to sleep on those chairs." She did not add that she would mortally wound the chairs as well.

Chaya pushed together the chairs, which were not quite of the same height. But when she'd spread a quilt over them, they served well enough, since her standards were still more Wisconsin than Chicago. The quilt hung far over the side onto the floor, and here her Asher, like a small faithful dog, made his bed, protected from the harsh punishment of the floor. This was not an arrangement anyone would call comfortable for either, but as Chaya laid herself carefully back she tried to imagine how painful it must be for Mrs. Gottlieb behind the curtain that separated one darkness from another—there was no door—to have to hear the intimate sounds of strangers preparing for sleep. How unreal the world must feel to her, whose husband had awakened beside her of a morning and then, after an instant of time like any other, no longer existed.

"Chaya," Asher whispered out of the silence.

"Yes, dear?"

"What is a widow exactly?"

She never knew whether Asher needed a word in English or a definition. But they were surely tuned to one another. "A widow is a wife who has lost her husband."

He took a minute to digest this. "Lost? He got lost coming home?"

Now she put aside her concern for their landlady (whom she could hear praying quietly, like soft music, and then sobbing, muffling her grief in her pillow), and tried, instead, to see into her darling's mysterious head. The only time she could tell the difference between what he really knew and what he only seemed to know was when he was curious enough to ask a question. Then she was relieved that *he* recognized the difference.

And every time she dared to fear that his astounding head was hollow as a doll's, he knocked her flat and shamed her. "No, Asher, it's just a way to say that he died." She paused, trying to run ahead of him. "Do you know what it means to die?" He had seen a dog die, and chickens eaten by a fox. His baby sister Sorele's death had been dealt with quietly, outside his notice. But she had disappeared—what did he make of that?

His own pause. A little laugh, either of comprehension or of incomprehension. "It's too hot in here. I don't need all this blanket. No. To die?" He was turning over and twisting and thrashing irritably below her on the floor. "To die. No. Do you?"

CHAYA WOKE more sore than she thought she could bear. Sleeping on raw ground, on rocks and tree roots, would have been kinder. Mrs. Gottlieb was still asleep in the bedroom behind her curtain, which she could see in the fresh morning light was a faded Turkey red cloth that had probably been a bed cover, its swirling pattern meant to suggest a tapestry far grander than it had ever been. The more she studied it, and the smeared windows at the front, the worn sprigged cloth on the table—not an ill-kept house, only a house sinking under its place near the bottom of fortune's wheel— the more she saw the motes of dust, smudge of coal, street dirt, peeling paint, smut of kerosene that hung between everyone and every thing in a room like that. There was no getting it clean. This was all too familiar. And for this she had traveled. For this she had slept on a surface meaner than a gravestone. *Still,* she could not help thinking, *better mine than those old bones.*

Having been spared the rack in a living room thick with the daily ghosts of garlic and onion and the weekly yeast of the challah in her oven, Pearl (née Perel) Gottlieb became the first of Chaya's fairy god- parents. Chaya would never know which of Mrs. Gottlieb's gestures of concern won her more reward than the good feeling that must have flooded her with satisfaction. No one knows, really, who (if any) are the souls keeping count.

MRS. GOTTLIEB fed *di kinder* tea and bread on its way to turning stale— this was part of their arrangement but she had not been prepared for them and had in her kitchen only the sad leftovers of someone who was not much concerned just then with what she ate. Asher worked his jaws at the hard bread as if it were gristle. He was used to eating what would best have gone to feed the animals; he did not complain. Then Chaya asked him what she should do with him while she went out in search of work.

Asher was swinging his legs as he subdued his pumpernickel. His feet dangled nowhere near the ground. "I'll come along," he told her cheerfully.

But there was no way he could accompany her. She explained why. "You have to understand that the people who own stores and factories aren't concerned that I have a little brother to care for."

"Why not?" He asked this smiling.

She wondered if he were teasing or trying to disarm her. Or perhaps the absurdity of such indifference seemed to him amusing.

"I promise to stay right outside the door, wherever you go. You can hide me."

"This isn't a game, dear. And you are not a lap dog." She was trying to primp but Mrs. Gottlieb's mirror was cloudy. Just two weeks ago, for the days of *shiva* when vanity of the body was a sin, it had been covered with a cloth. And now, the widow must see a slightly different face when she peered into it.

Asher looked deflated.

"You can take the streetcar," their landlady told her—"It's easy"—and drew an elaborate set of arcs in the air, at the end of which, presumably, Chaya would find herself on a corner from which she could achieve, via cable car, the city center.

And then what? Chaya asked if she had any ideas regarding employment but she had little imagination beyond the obvious: Shopgirl. Garment worker. Do not ask what engaging ideas Chaya was hoping to hear— if Asher was not ready to comprehend the demands of anonymity, she was not quite prepared to admit that she was a farm girl (and that farm uniquely benighted), with no city skills and none but the most rudimentary understanding of how the world worked, of who pushed its buttons and pulled its levers. Her only consolation was to remember that Chicago was swarming with innocents like herself and she trusted they were somehow surviving. Was it not infinite in every way? True, she had heard the stories, discreetly, behind hands, of the ones who ended up selling their one most priceless possession to strangers, but that—surrendering themselves for a drink and a dollar—was too preposterous a fate to imagine, even for someone who had allowed a drayman to imprint his woeful body against hers in broad daylight. They must, she thought, with a primness that would later embarrass her, have wished for—come here for—the pleasures of their profession. They must have lusted themselves and been compelled to sin for its own sake.

Now, at Mrs. Gottlieb's table, she sighed with anxiety. After a while, sufficiently apologetic to cringe but not to be silent, she asked if—assuming she was not too occupied with her own difficulties—her new landlady might watch Asher just for today. How she wished she could have added, *For an extra half dollar.* But she had begun to suspect that she was going to exact favors from many, and, en route to her fortune, she was going to learn humility. "Are there—do you have any books for him to read? You will not hear a word from him all day if you have a good story for him."

"Ah, *kleynele.*" Affectionately, little one. She pondered. "I'm sorry but my Nachman had no time for any books but his *siddur.*" Chaya was sorry too, to have made the widow's whole face quiver like that. Shakespeare would have served but holy books would not do.

When Asher glared at his sister, he knew he could convince her of almost anything; his anger was far more effective than his charm. Now he turned on her with murderous, under-the-brow intensity and refused to blink. Had he held his breath until he turned blue, he could not have provoked her panic more effectively. "I will go back to Mama and Papa." This in a strange, suffocated voice, ghostlike. "I will run off to a part of this *city* where you will never find me. Everyone will help a poor little *pitsl.*"

He could do it, too. Run off and probably do a better job at existing than she was doing. "Where are your shoes?" she said as harshly as she could, and gestured to him to put them on. He still had trouble with the buttons. "*Ganef.*" Thief. "Where did you put your cap?"

OUT THE door, into a new day. Even mean Zhitomir had been nothing like this! There was no escaping it—a king, a god, could have stood with her on that wooden stoop, high above the street, and not been exempt from the dire stink of the stockyards. It fouled more than the nose, she could feel it strafe her windpipe as it traveled toward the lungs, an odor both sour and bitter at the same time, with something more putrid and rotten at its far edges. They were so close to the death-stalls, acres upon acres of them, that she began to imagine she could hear the *shofar* sound of the cattle lowing, pitifully, on their way to slaughter: What they were being forced to inhale was the smell of blood, the hopeless exhalation of captured creatures who, even without comprehension, felt their fate approaching. Futilely, she tried to hold her breath. She could as easily have held back the sun that was just then rising in a riot of flame from behind a heap of a house across the way. That sun flung down on Liberty Street a hard disclosing light.

Movement gone mad, it showed her, up and down the block as far as she could see. Dozens—were there hundreds?—of peddlers were roiling into action, wheeling pushcarts until they found their place, pulling off whatever covered them, flinging back blankets and lids, grating, squeaking, banging. Shopkeepers raised suits and dresses to hang on hooks before the dark corridors of their stores, and the bodiless clothing swayed as it swung on its way upward, sleeves buttoned around empty air, men's jackets collapsed a bit at the chest for want of a solid body inside. On tables, heaps of color lay flung together, sloppily piled, and precarious towers of hats, of caps, flowered scarves and aprons, though she watched one young woman who was probably her age stacking hers as decorously as if she were setting her table for visitors. Tools glinted in that new light. Coops and cages, sagging furniture—the bazaar seemed to have no policy by which anything could be refused the chance to change hands. Way down at the end of the block the food began: She could make out blocks of orange and green, could see the street already littered with rinds and cast-off leaves. And the clamor rose as unstoppably as the stench, mongers crying their wares, calling to each other, arguing. She heard chickens' nattering that would soon be silenced, and, distant, the two-note call of a train. Coming or going? Taking or bringing? She was not sure whether she wanted to be on that train; surely she could put aside her apprehensions if she were going home.

Asher nearly leaped over the railing as if there were a fistfight down below, and he the intrepid rescuer. The coiled, hardy, ample, ready child. Chaya held him still with both her hands.

HOWEVER AFRAID she might have been for him, she could see how the pleasures, for Asher, piled up. They climbed up the wide step of the cable car and it was a wonder, grinding and lurching, all shuddery wood and metal clanging against metal. He watched with huge eyes as a boy only a few years older than he rode hanging precariously over the side, his whole face invisible behind his waving hair, and she could see the calculation with which he tallied how long it would be before he could do the same.

The thronged streets were so thick with moving bodies it seemed they could be borne up, shoulder to shoulder, and never touch the ground. Though he was so excited that his cheeks turned red and stayed that way, the crowds were difficult for Asher because, whatever the age of his radiant mind, he was a smallish boy who wore the crown of his tweedy cap no higher than a grown man's middle. He was buffeted by so many gesturing passersby—male; the women he passed were far less demonstrative—that he finally walked holding it to his side. Around State and Madison Streets, Chaya affronted his pride by clutching at his arm, though she knew she was equally in need of protection.

But could it be survived? Chaya spent a long dispiriting day at the mercy of the shopkeepers of her new city. Some few establishments were called "department stores." She thought them, in conception, really elephantine general stores, with many, many counters on which and under which to display their wares in cool light and, to one who had come fresh from the tumult of pushcarts, the frozen silence of a museum.

These buildings were wrapped in glass, their broad windows vistas into separate little worlds. Dress forms—but with blank-featured faces and stiff, false hair—stood draped in unaffordable fashions, and around them had been placed props, to advance the notion that these dolls were somehow related to the world in which their viewers lived: In one it was a grove of autumn trees dropping their leaves in a carefully disheveled circle, in another stood stacks of books as though the beautiful, eyeless clothes-hanger of a woman, when she was not standing in a humanly impossible position, was a dedicated reader.

The department stores were huge and many-storied and so impressed with their own grandeur that it was not easy to remember that their fortune was made by merchants, not royalty. In their show windows hung signs inviting the most respected customer to enter and be welcome. But when she approached the proper authorities in Marshall Field's, at the Boston Store and, a few blocks north and west, in another called The Fair, she was forced to watch her interrogators run their eyes, with no attempt to hide their insolence, from the rucked-up top of her head in its plain sailor (for this city seemed to be wind and more wind) down her plain white waist with its hopeful placket of yellowing lace to her navy twill skirt and, unsmiling, to her worn shoes, in whose every crease she carried, like a souvenir, the dry dust of the Fields of Zion.

Her hair, which was thick and ungovernable even without those wild gusts to irritate it, bristled out from under the short brim of her hat. Her outfit was beyond redemption and could only, those eyes suggested, be discarded, as if it were contaminated. Her bearing, humble at best, abject at worst, must hardly have seemed capable of the airs necessary to intimidate their respected customers while seeming to indulge them. Her interlocutors had, she was certain, come to their positions from a background not much more exalted than hers; all the more inviting, she began to understand, to put her in the place they had so recently vacated, and keep her there. Many who stood behind the counters were men; they looked out at her blankly, as if she were barely there.

But add, for an extra frisson of unsuitability, this complicating factor: She had an accent, unfashionable, unplaceable, but surely, by their lights, without charm. Had it been French, her stock would have risen. But it decidedly was not French. The first pinprick of disappointment began to burrow under Chaya's skin, not at the inconvenience of being without work so much as a suspicion that she had built elaborate plans upon the imperfections of strangers.

And so she turned to the smaller shops, thinking that their scale would, after all, better suit her temperament. These lined State Street and Wabash, and the old neighborhood along Lake Street, where, apparently, Marshall Field's had begun as a modest haberdashery that led the march south and at the same time led modesty into gigantism. But she was turned away by these as well, as though the selling of shoes or millinery, ladies' undergarments or even candy, loose or by the box, took some extraordinary skill or refinement that such as she could not dare try to imagine. Some very nearly said "No" before she had finished opening the door. In more than one she heard the tinkling of a friendly little bell that turned out not to mean welcome at all, but suspicion. Others led her a long walk through their motives, her motives, the motives of the wretched powers that run Chicago, only to smile sympathetically and, as firmly as any, repeat "No."

A few proprietors informed her, with a patience and consideration that were surprisingly respectful, that she had come at a particularly bad time when sales had slackened: They worried that the city—indeed the entire nation—was declining toward a disastrous "depression." She had never heard that word used to describe anything but the way she was feeling as she dragged herself and her throbbing feet from door to door.

Asher had held her hand, as he'd promised, until she entered these shops, and then had slunk off to lean his small self against the building to wait for her. Once he called forth the wrath of the proprietor of a shoe shop, Ladies and Gentlemen Invited, because he was visible from inside—or rather, the small seat of his pants and his poignantly narrow shoulders could be seen touching the window. The man—a large, pugilistic sort crammed into a jacket narrower than he, which made him look like a boy with a mustache who had outgrown his clothes—ran to his door and, flailing his arms, shooed Asher away. An onlooker would have thought he had caught the child stealing.

"That was unnecessary," Chaya dared to say to him as stiffly as she could before taking the door handle and preparing to follow. "He was not hurting anything."

"Soft hearts, young lady, lead to soft profits." He was eyeing his window for damage. "And soft profits are the death of enterprise."

She looked around at his stock of dusty boxes, of boots lined up like an army ready to march, of chairs unoccupied and his single bored clerk slouching at the rear. "Enterprise?" she echoed. "What a grand name for this"—she knew a very good word for what she saw, though she had no idea how to pronounce it—"this *mous-oh-leum*!"

All he did was, cruelly, laugh at her. She tried hard to flounce out the open door with outrage, but what she had to hear was even crueler. "Take yourself on back to Germany, lady. We don't need foreign scum ruining our city."

Bad enough that she was hardly German, but she did not have a clue what *scum* meant. But neither, she understood, was it a promising thing to be called. Asher was sitting flat on the ground below the visibility of the shopkeeper next door—Antler's Dry Goods and Carpets, Foreign and Domestic—and she dusted off his bottom so vigorously he must have thought she was angry at him.

"It's all right," he reassured her and reached into his pocket. "Here." He held out a folded paper, light blue, containing a set of black bootlaces scored like a rat's tail. "I'm sorry I couldn't get you some nice shoes. Your shoes look like you walked to Chicago in them."

Chaya, not too appalled to laugh out loud, led her little brother around the corner onto a narrower street where they did not have to consider the irritability or suspicion of unlucky shopkeepers, and pulled them toward a peculiarly bright horizon, away from the signs of commerce. In fact, the air was growing more translucent with every step, as if they were walking into a pearl. Then—she never, in all the years to follow, forgot what this was like, the sight that burst upon her like a blow that lanced a blister of hardship and fear—there was the lake! They had been plying the streets of Chicago hand in hand like Hansel and Gretel in the dark wood under the beetling cornices of tall buildings all day, and had never thought to turn to the east.

Now they hurried across Michigan Boulevard, past its private houses, gray granite, built right to the corner. On the far side it was half swampy, half striped with railroad tracks; many impediments prevented their drawing close enough to touch it. But as they came near the azure water, Asher pulled his hand from hers and, whooping, ran as far toward it as he could. She should have scolded him but she was every bit as aghast as he was. Here was a treasure, and they had not even suspected.

Far out, the sky met the lake in a thick unwavering purple line the color of a nasty bruise. But no, that was wrong because it brought to mind ugly things, called up pain and accident, while this was so lovely, the colors so unlikely, she vowed that when "depression" came upon her—when she forgot the glory of all that man has *not* made—she would bring it to the water and be freed of it. Here in this place where air and water, two parts of the same mysterious substance, merged in utter silence, each became the other.

This lake was so serene, so much flatter than the shore, that she felt as if she had come to the end of solid earth, and was gazing, quite unexpectedly, over the edge into another realm. And the color of the horizon, she decided—it was time to search for joy—was the color of lilacs. They had no such bush on the farm, but a large one grew beside the door of her old school in Christa, so laden with those lavender flowers-made-of-flowers that its branches bent humbly toward the ground. She would have to master these jabs of homesickness, the faces of her Mama and Papa that made her wince with guilt. When she felt them, she promised herself, she would come to the lake and throw them in the way, on Rosh Hashanah, you were commanded to empty your pockets and fling what you found there—crumbs become sins—into moving waters.

WHEN THEY were home again—how quickly Mrs. Gottlieb's flat had become home—and when Chaya had answered the widow's earnest, worried questions about where they had inquired and how they had been treated, when she had removed shoes so painful that she wondered if she could put them on again tomorrow, Asher demonstrated that he had learned the plat of downtown streets and could have named for their concerned landlady every single shop into which his sister had tried to insinuate herself and her indispensability.

"That's very fine, but weren't you bored?" Chaya asked him. "Admit it, Asher, wouldn't you rather stay here and find some friends to play with?"

Asher pinned her with that gaze. Since he had never had to go in search of playfellows, she had never thought about the peculiar impression her little brother would make on children his own age. Hadn't he been the odd little sultan of their community, where he was already known? He had had his brothers and sisters, always. Hadn't he, the nervy boy, his nose in everyone's business, inspired amusement, affection and—perhaps it should be called tolerance? In his assorted interferences and curiosity he had been a challenge, an incitement, but a benign one, surely. She lacked the words for any of that, lacked them in two languages, but she could feel it: He was strange and strangely loveable.

But here on Liberty Street, around the corner on Maxwell? Would they eat him up out of jealousy? Out of bewilderment? Would older children, who could read, who went to school—would they allow him into their circle? Chaya saw them roughly playing, careening between the pushcarts, calling down the curses of the housewives they lurched into as they ran. Many were already working, she saw them selling everything from hats to brooms to bridles. Their voices were sharper than their elders', their cries sliced through the air like wind instruments, harsh but clear.

Did he refuse to stay at home because he could guess how hard it would be, or did he simply prefer to be his sister's shadow?

Asher was going to be a lonely boy.

SHE PULLED a chair from the row that composed her bed, dropped into it hard and sank her inflamed feet in a basin. At first they were so sore that even the water hurt. Asher was reading his book of jungle tales with his elbows on the table and Mrs. Gottlieb was fussing over the stove. They cost her effort: She had hauled the water up four flights of stairs for them. But she was relieved, Chaya could see, to have voices and movement in her house, and though they might not have been her Nachman, they came between her and her loneliness. They made her necessary.

Chaya could not exactly have said why she would not look at garment work. Something about its predictability made her recoil, and though she did not like to seem vain, there was something about joining the ranks of the thousands of girls bent over their machines—tied to their ceaseless movement—that repulsed her. Or, since she found that she shivered at the thought of using one, perhaps she was afraid of the machines themselves. Pesye's cousin Fanya, who lived with her family in Cleveland, came once to the farm for a visit when she was unable to work because she had had an accident with her machine that, after infection and other hazards, cost her her right thumb! Chaya was not prepared to sacrifice a limb or a digit, even to pay the rent.

But their downstairs neighbor, Mrs. Seychek, gossiping with Mrs. Gottlieb at the water pump in the yard, told her there were openings in the cigar factory where her brother's daughter worked. No sooner had Chaya heard this than—lacking any idea of what such a manufactory would be like, or the recognition that there may well have been nearly as many women at such work as there were in the garment shops—she found her way to

A. H. WINKLER'S HAVANA CIGARS

which was a broad, nondescript three-story building in a deserted-looking neighborhood a long walk from the trolley. She would discover at the end of the day that the quiet of its streets was only the result of the hundreds of workers' immurement inside those factories: Had they been connected to a dynamo, they could have powered all of Chicago. And when they emerged, the street was transformed, a hive without a queen.

Here she had no reason to regret her dress; she needed no hauteur with which to impress the customers. The less interesting her demeanor, she quickly surmised, the more she must have seemed a promising worker who would not complain or demand or otherwise attract attention. The only thing she would have to do, though she could not yet have imagined it, was to allow herself to be overworked, underpaid, insulted, derided, and, from time to time, afflicted with a response she could not name until someone called it an *allergy* (a lovely word that sounded like a lullaby!) to the tobacco dust that hung in the air. The murk was like the fog that routinely shaded the farm in the spring when it was cool at night and warm in the morning. But this fog did not burn off.

When she climbed the stairs and entered the "floor," she saw dozens of people—men, women, and a few suspiciously young children seated on boxes to elevate them—bent over wooden, desk-like tables, some facing each other, some beneath long windows that were covered with a sickly greenish-brown slime as if they were stagnant water. Chaya watched them bundling their cigars quickly but with great care, lining up tops and bottoms and binding them tightly, to be put in boxes that could be bought for next to nothing. The restaurants, the theaters, the dinner tables of Chicago were clotted with cigar smoke, unapologetically, from the humble to the grandiose. But at this point early in their creation, she wondered who would put such a rank thing in his mouth. One by one they could smell sweet, but together, and far from completed, they stank so badly she almost gagged.

The sour smell, grassy-turned-rancid, lifted Chaya off the sore soles of her feet. Surely the stockyards were worse, but this would take getting accustomed to. She barely existed in the eyes of A. H. Winkler, a jowly man with a shiny face and such heavy eyelids he seemed in danger of falling asleep as he spoke. He assigned her a salary: half the wage for six weeks and then if she proved satisfactory—at this he opened one eye wide as if to challenge her—a "raise." The raise he promised was a small inducement, but she was without alternatives and so she smiled and nodded, though he wasn't so much as looking at her for a response. Then, with a wave, he assigned her a sallow, freckled girl named Sara to instruct her, and ceded to her no rights to lag, complain, refuse, demand, or go anywhere near "that union," or out she would go, "through that door the way you came in."

Sara, who looked as if Mr. Winkler's intimidation had worked perfectly on her, sapping her of whatever vitality she might have arrived with, took her to a little desk, sat herself down and as Chaya craned over her shoulder, and with barely a word, made her stogie, the lower-caste relative of the substantial Havana, lumpier, less well-wrapped and much cheaper—the people's cigar, priced to sell to those who could not even afford it but bought it nevertheless.

"These are easier for you when you're new. Upstairs they make ten-centers and Havanas." She laughed. "We're not in Havana last I noticed but I don't care. I'm going up there soon."

She removed a moist brown leaf from beneath a piece of damp cloth, stripped its spine in two viciously accurate slices, cut it with a cunning, lethal, moon-crescent of a knife, stuffed it with short unruly fragments over which she nonetheless had perfect control—"Not too loose, not too tight"—stood it in a mold that squeezed it hard, wrapped it, folded this side over that and that over this like a baby blanket, making little half-turns, dipped her finger into a cup of paste, applied it invisibly, lovingly smoothed the tip with her index finger as if she were testing a dog's wet snout for its state of health and—there it was, a snub-nosed, slightly dewy, simultaneously soft- and hard-sided projectile fit for nothing but a man at leisure who did not mind its stink and, worse, its after-stink.

"You want me to do that?" Chaya was in awe of her. Though Mr. Winkler had warned her, she was about to issue her first refusal.

Apparently Sara had only been tense before her performance. Now she softened; she even gave Chaya a snaggle-toothed smile that made her look like a small child. "Just do it slow and I'll show you. Don't worry, you can ruin a couple of leaves, your first day nobody's counting." Chaya had not budged. "It don't just come, I can remember I was so scared I nearly"—she giggled—"I nearly peed my pants. But it will."

Chaya sat and was handed a leaf, which turned out to be an implausible combination of dry and damp, strong, fragile, and subject to tearing. It was a mess, her first stogie. It was tumorous and leaked under her quivering fingers, and, like the first piecrusts she had mangled, its end stubbornly refused to seal. Tensile and resilient and silky smooth it was, but with a kind of nap; with an infinitesimal catch, like fur. In time she learned to have her way with this tobacco, to be, in fact, on intimate terms with it, until she saw too much of it, too many hours of the day. But for a while she actually relished it as if it were still, somehow, alive.

9

DESPITE HIS passionate desire to follow her to work, Asher needed his own occupation, and Chaya, accordingly, took him the next morning to the fortress-like school down the block and around the corner. This red-brick structure, three stories tall, windows the height of houses, was so unlike anything they had ever confronted—surely, unlike Chaya's beloved white wooden schoolhouse, it was not built to be inviting to its constituents, small children and the motherly women who taught them—that Asher rolled his eyes when he saw it. Was that fear or curiosity or some other nameless refusal to do as she bid him? He went forward, given no choice by his sister, hand tight in hers, with the reluctance of a collared prisoner.

It was July; there were no classes. But when they finally found an unlocked front door, heavy as a palace gate, and Chaya went in search of some kind of officialdom, Asher gave a colossal tug and broke her grip. She let him go—there was no kind of trouble he could find himself in down these deserted halls with their floors that shone like spilled water, and the smell of disinfectant pricking her nose. Why did they make everything so huge, so heavy, so dark, when the small souls who would reside here were still so tender? It seemed built to intimidate. The glass of the windows was caged with something like barbed wire.

She had yet to turn up anyone in the office when Asher came racing down the hall waving his hands wildly as if to stop her before she embroiled him in anything. "I don't want to stay here. I can do all this already." His voice was querulous. "This is for babies!"

"What can you do?" She knew, of course she knew, that his reading was far beyond the capacity of such a place—probably beyond his teachers'—and so was his figuring, but where could he stay safe while she was at work? "There must be things you can't do that they could teach you," she began in the consoling voice she felt dishonest adopting with him, but Asher was already at the huge door, head down, pushing so hard his frail arms quivered, and was out and down the stony steps before she could think of a single one.

10

WHEN CHAYA came out onto the top step to look for him, wearing her police face, Asher ran full speed down the street and ducked between two houses. And so began his career of alley-running. He looked both ways. Could it be the entire city was connected by these invisible rivers? He could see there was a second city, darker than the first. It stirred him like a secret.

He slowed to a walk, and the walk took him between privies, some open, some closed; many of their doors hung crooked, the whole little shack collapsing in on itself. The morning stank of dead animal, that corrupt sweetness, and the sizzling, sodden garbage piles that lay every few feet. All the neighborhood's digestion happened back here: what went in at the front came out at the rear. No wonder you could stay out of sight in these shadows—he tried to imagine his sister chasing him down this narrow aisle, her skirt hem damp and staining. and failed. He suspected you could meet others who were not welcome on the street.

The first he came upon was a man so dirty he blended with the ground he was sitting on, a camouflaged animal. Asher stood before him, feet planted. The dirt-colored man was eating a handful of something he must have salvaged from a rubbish pile; surely he hadn't cooked it, nor had anyone served him. "Good?" Asher asked. not to taunt but curious. Same food as the rats'. Same foraging place, same hunger.

The man, whose fingers were lost in an unruly gray beard, looked back at him with surprise—Asher, in short pants, could alarm no one larger than a pigeon—his eyes widening, handful of food folded out of sight. Asher, large inside, smiled to reassure him.

"You lost?" the man asked, demonstrating his toothlessness.

Asher considered his freedom. "No, no," he said jovially, "I never get lost." This felt rich, smell and all. He did not need classroom walls adorned with the ABCs, windows decorated with paper ducks in a row, cut-out flowerpots bristling with cardboard daisies. The school he needed was right here, stretching before him in both directions, unknown at either end. "Hiding."

BUT HE came home for supper before darkness demanded it—he did not fancy sleeping in any of the crevices he could have crawled into; too many things could crawl in around him. He had hiked a good long way and back. He passed a whole family chattering in some language made up entirely of shushing sounds, gentle as rain. He passed a legless woman mounted on a platform with wheels, who was singing, though he'd have expected her to howl. He stepped lightly past a sleeping policeman, hat over his eyes, shoulders against a fence, feet out into the alley, splayed this way and that.

No one menaced him. Asher knew they were all invisible. He knew they could only see each other.

The only thing he would need if he spent his days hidden here were some books. His eyes itched for print and the odd consolation of turning the final page, completeness at war with the wish to continue. "The end." He always said that when he closed the covers, like "Amen," quietly to himself. Without books he would be lonely, the way his friend Mordechai, back at the farm, felt when he had no music. He knew he could find some if he walked far enough—there must be stores that sold books the way they sold food or shoes, because people needed them to live.

When he came home (seventy-four streets crossed, two turns when an alley ran out, three schools passed or sighted, six churches, two dogs at his heels, neither vicious, four yards where chickens pecked hopelessly at gravel, a rooster who tried to attack him, a man probably dead but possibly asleep facedown, unmoving even as some unidentifiable animal snouted under his pant leg and nipped at his ankles), Chaya said nothing. That meant she was stifling her words. Mrs. Gottlieb circled them silently, knowing it was not her place to intrude, laying out herring and old tomatoes collapsing toward their stems, preceded by a thin soup the color of the brine in a pickle barrel.

When Asher lay down to sleep, on the floor at the side of his sister's bed of chairs, he called out to her, "Chaya, kiss!"

She bent to him, stared straight into his eyes, waiting, but he had no confession for her, no apology.

"You are not yet eleven years old," she said against his face. She had to know she could not keep him.

"I am almost eleven years old," he agreed, cheerful, and looked expectantly back. *What*, he did not, would not say. "Chai, I love Chicago. Do you love Chicago?"

She sighed. After their trip to that school, she had spent her first day at work. She looked very tired. Saggy and a trifle gray. "I don't know yet, Ash. Why do you love Chicago?"

He closed his eyes to see what it was that invigorated him. "Because it goes on and on forever. Not like the farm. Like the stars at night, the Milky Way. You can't *count* it."

She kissed his nose, his eyes, one ear. "I am glad you are happy, dear. I am very glad someone is happy."

THE ALLEYS, when he headed uptown, led Asher to the streets, inevitable as river to ocean. He had his bad moments with dogs, although a few followed him, sniffing, out on their own travels. Wearing his thin soles thinner, he learned to reach the soul of the city faster every day. Liveries, a staple company, an ink factory, dyers, purveyors of wine and spirits—more than one—many things he could not fathom, endless, endless the count of doorways, some closed, some open, leading to mysteries.

He crossed the threshold of every establishment intended for the public. A few welcomed, or at least did not discourage, his curiosity—what was he but a negligible boy with a dirty mug and scabby knees from his frequent tumbles across branches and protruding stones. Home at night, subject to his sister's scrutiny, he stayed reasonably presentable. But his encounters were not all friendly. Often, shopkeepers assumed he was there to steal— for the first time, did his intentions show, or were they suspicious of all small boys who traveled alone?—and they shouted at him before he put a foot across their thresholds. They watched him carefully to make sure nothing walked out with him. Once a woman in a store that sold clocks and watches made him take his hands out of his pockets and open them to her, palms up. She sniffed and looked into his eyes accusingly. "Those could be cleaner." Lucky she did not try to get him washed. Probably she did not want to touch him.

He chatted with the manager of a shop that sold umbrellas, portmanteaux, wallets, and money clips. "What is that?" he asked abruptly, leading with his shoulder into the open door.

"What, my good fellow?" The proprietor, very short and wide, flattened-looking, asked him amiably. He walked toward Asher, jingling the coins in his pocket.

Asher, at the window, pointed to a silver dollar sign that sat shining on a square of dark blue velvet.

"Why, it's to hold your mazuma!"

"My mazuma." Asher blinked with concern, since he could not account for his. "Does everyone have a mazuma?"

The man, not a head taller, bent down to him nonetheless. He smelled waxy, of a serious kind of soap. "If you work hard and save, you'll have it, and you can come back and spend some of it on that fellow to hold it all together. It's pure genuine silver plate." The man seized his shoulders and held them as tight as a punishment. "Are you a good little man? Do you do as you're told?"

Asher tried to wriggle free but couldn't. "Nobody tells me anything."

"Oh, my. Orphaned, then?"

He was about to pitied, which made him feel mean. He set his mouth to look stubborn. "I never had parents. I just sprouted." He thought that was the word, though he wasn't entirely sure; right or wrong, it came out *shprouted*. "One day I wasn't there and the next I was. Like a mushroom."

"Or a toadstool!" The manager laughed and unhanded him. Toad?

Stool? "Well, come again when you've made your million. The rate business is going these days, the clip might just still be there waiting for you."

He would report this to Chaya—hadn't she told that man with the carriage, that Still-man, that they had come to make their fortune?

One morning when the weather had begun to turn, he found his first bookstore.

The window of the shop was what Paradise might look like: Each book lay behind a cover he must have dreamed once. Their covers were plain but they were opened to show a mountain of ice above a cold-looking sea. A herd of buffalo as solid as the side of a barn. A dragon whose face was obliterated by his own fire blowing backwards, his tail the length of a kingdom. Asher devoured the pictures and all they promised; an ache of longing spread like heat in his chest. The door had a bell, a pretty tinkle, like high laughter, that was so amusing he jiggled it a few times so that he could hear it again.

It took a while for anyone to emerge, but when he did—squinting in Asher's direction, a man with soft tufts of white on his head and above his lip, like the cotton that blows from certain trees in June—Asher had not moved. He stood before the ranks of shelves with the perfect silence of an acolyte about to fling incense from his censer, looking up. Could there be this many books in the whole world?! He had never thought about where they came from, the little chunks and slivers of the rock that Chaya borrowed and brought him—like food, like milk or weather or sleep, they simply *were*, and were his due. He woke, he ate and breathed, he read. Languages he sucked out of the air.

Asher was afraid to talk to the storekeeper because he knew what he needed to do, and he would not want to steal from a friend.

The old man, whose eyes appeared defective, came and stood very close to him, to see him. "May I offer you some assistance?" he asked, respectfully, as though Asher were not three and a half feet tall.

A smile, a shrug. He was safe for now from fraternizing with the man from whom he would, with joy and regret, appropriate as many books as he could hide when he came back tomorrow prepared, with stretched-out pockets and a sack; the man against whom he would commit his first

Chicago robbery of something he really wanted. (The shoelaces had been a tax on nastiness.) In Christa, everything he took from the stores downtown had been for Chaya. Negligibles. Here, he was so hungry, the books would be for him alone.

1 1

IT SHOULD not have come as a surprise: The landlord was at the door relentlessly, and Mrs. Gottlieb, though she tried, was no breadwinner. She took in sewing, not the fancy kind that dressmakers did but fine hemming and minor repairs, until, her eyes clouded over with cataracts, and she told Chaya, "It always feels like early morning just before the sun is up. Gray. But then it never gets light." When she couldn't tell her stitches from the print of the fabric, that was the end of that.

Through her new friends at Winkler's, Chaya heard about another job, at a "buckeye," a tiny band of workers who made cigars, not quite legally, in someone's apartment. As if she had unfilled hours to spare, at Winkler's until five thirty, she began to go directly to Yanowitz's place with—if she could save it from her dinner—half an apple to see her through, or perhaps a banana, gone brown as one of her tobacco leaves by then, from sitting in her pocket in the cloakroom.

The room in which they worked was little better than a sty. The shades were drawn, though after the first few hours their view would have been nothing but darkness anyway. The tables were so crowded together it took an athlete's contortions to pass between them, and from the kitchen at the rear, out of sight, arose the odors of the Yanowitz family's supper, to which they were not invited. Not that his own children did not have to work alongside them sometimes, their small fingers already adept at the craft Chaya was still trying to master. She worried about them—there was one girl of perhaps ten, and a boy not much older. Did they have no school to wake up for? Once she asked the girl, timidly, and she simply laughed, with what Chaya took to be bitterness, but—if she did not enjoy learning from books—might have been sour pleasure.

The other workers were three women and four men, but by the time Chaya climbed the dusty stairs and took her place, she had given too much of her energy to the day's work to have more than a word for any of them. She must have seemed unmannerly, but, truly, she did not care. There were, she had heard, Readers—men or women who actually read from novels to the workers in Cuban factories, and to the cigar-makers in Tampa, Florida, in a place called Ybor City, but whether such delights would have kept her keen or lullabied her toward sleep at ten o'clock when her eyes were crossed with exhaustion she could only wonder.

Her fingers were nicked and a urinous yellow, her back was in spasm when, the trolley clanging into the distance, she walked toward Liberty Street just before midnight. Her wages for the week, both combined, would have made a very stingy tip for the real dinner she dreamed of when, rarely, she passed Richelieu's or Kinsley's or—she had never seen it but had heard it described—the gloriously enticing Palmer House. She had begun to hold her skirt up with a length of ribbon Mrs. Gottlieb stripped off a dress she found beyond repair, but at least her shoes no longer pinched because her feet, like the rest of her, had dwindled.

She saw so little of Asher those days she was worse than wrung out, she was beyond anger. Losing her brother to the alleys was not what she had come here to do. Then again, though he might have gone feral as a cat, he was free. She exhausted herself, sometimes to the point of near unconsciousness, her fingers thickened to calluses that could respond to nothing but the slippery thickness of leaf skin. Now, while Mrs. Gottlieb and Asher slept in silence, she was the one who lay, aching, subject to fits of weeping that filled what little was left of the night when she returned from Yanowitz's shop. When she closed her eyes, her mother's face loomed up, unforgiving.

When she did sleep, she dreamed to the rhythm of her work. Not that she made cigars in her sleep, but whatever phantasms she pursued seemed to rush forward jerkily, and the little dramas that happened in her dreams took place in stages, throbbingly regular—like the splitting, the pressing, the wrapping—so that she woke unrested. One night she felt herself walking a crooked path through a field. From time to time she fell and the tall grass, urgently rustling, hid her till she found her footing, and when she came to the edge of a pond—their terrible stagnant cow pond, so familiar, so foul—she peered down into its still, dark water. But no face came up to her, not hers, not her brother's. She woke to the desolate feeling that they had disappeared. Where were they in the world? She looked around the crowded room, sad furniture hulking in shadow, and heard the sounds of the street pressing their way through the window. She had thought herself heroic, making her way to this place, but she had not come to something, she had only run away from something else. *Chicago? Chicago, so full, so empty.* What had she done to their lives?

After a brief autumn, an early winter had fallen like a doom upon the city. That *Farmers' Almanac* had been correct: Snow piled higher than the refuse on Maxwell Street; the carts and wagons thrust up through it like hulks, the way she remembered the stubbornest survivors of their summer fields, the corn turned straw, the browned cabbage leaves, the sunflower stalks. Horses kicked up dirty slush as they tramped along and the bottoms of her skirts were ringed with filth; once her feet slipped out from under her and she tumbled into an icy puddle that soaked her through to her drawers. The sky was neither blue nor gray but as white as another swathe of snow. The apartment was so cold that any liquid—Asher's milk, Chaya's tea—left on the table turned to ice. She was appalled to discover that the snowflakes stenciled on their windows, which at first she thought were lovely, lived their little life inside the glass, and a long life it was. It seemed no less a blight, this winter, than it had been in Wisconsin: The pump froze, and in the stove, because Mrs. Gottlieb had compelled herself to ration the coal, the fire quivered weakly in the downdraft and threatened to die. Night fell outside Winkler's undersea windows at four o'clock.

Asher, at the least, was still coming home at night. He told her nothing of where he had spent his days, how he had not—in short pants which ought to have been long, with a jacket nearly transparent, and a cap that did not cover his ears—succumbed to the weather. But he appeared to be healthy, he neither coughed nor shivered. For this, she relied on Mrs. Gottlieb's judgment; she only saw him asleep.

She tried to imagine, as her fingers lived their independent life and her vision blurred behind a scrim of weariness, what her brother was doing running free all day, competently making his way home each night. She had begun to hear about the wiles of the boys who wandered the disorganized streets around theirs, Maxwell, DeKoven, Twelfth. It seemed they stole anything that was not tightly secured: milk, coal, candy (it went without saying), kerosene, wood. They pried back the doors of boxcars and sampled their contents. They pilfered boxes of every kind of merchandise from stands and carts, from stores, and the worst of them—in training, she supposed, not for petty vandalism but for genuine careers in crime—from any house they could enter without much ado. And some were truly without shame. Sara, Chaya's teacher at Winkler's, for example, had a freckly faced younger brother, "sweet-faced as Jesus in a painting," she assured Chaya, who was constantly being hauled off to court for a talking-to that did not seem to redeem him or even notably slow him down. He had amassed collections of miscellany he must have appropriated for the challenge alone, since much of it was useless to him: parts for talking machines, fishing reels without the requisite rod, bifocals, and most recently, she confided, a silver-plated tea set in four pieces which he had hoped to present to his mother but was afraid to produce for fear she would know instantly how it was obtained.

Was Asher among them? Was he going bad, like the fleet-footed, lightning-fingered, uncurfewed, ungrammatical, unrepentant older fellows in their tweed knickers and caps, he, following, rushing to keep up, in short pants, knees chapped, lips blue with cold? Would they deign to take him along? Would they goad him? Did they work the streets together, organized like adult thieves, and thus find themselves in need of a decoy or a lookout or a mite to crawl into tight spaces? Were they bringing home their cargo to their mothers and actually being thanked—perhaps Sara had it wrong—because their families were starving like the rest? Had hunger overwhelmed shame? It might have. It might have.

All Chaya knew was that he did not catch cold, his clothes were not torn by splintery fences, his pockets did not sag, distorted by the drag of booty. Which of them would end up on the wrong side of the law, Asher and his possible friends. his theoretical gang, or she for abandoning a child, genius or not, to his own unreliable discretion.

"ASHER," SHE said to him one time. She had just lumbered up the stairs after her double shift. It was midnight, there was fresh snow on her shoulders when she woke him; it was so cold in that apartment, the crystals would cling to the wool like frost on grass until the wan sun came up. "I want to talk to you now." Wrenched from sleep and not yet in full control he might, she thought, confide in her.

"Sleeping." he muttered and turned his head away.

"Would you like me to take you home again to the farm? To Mama and Papa?" She wondered, even as she asked, if the question was for Asher or for herself.

He shook his head so firmly she imagined that she heard the swivel.

"You like it here."

He nodded earnestly and yawned. The inside of his mouth sparkled in the low light.

"But I can't let you run loose like this, Asher. That is impossible."

He stared at her without expression. She was kneeling on the floor beside him, at his level, the level of a cat.

"You are a brilliant boy," she whispered to him, "but you have to understand, and if you don't want to be concerned for yourself, you have to"—she dared to hope this might break through the terrible neutrality of his gaze—"you have to have some sympathy for *me*. We will starve if I have to give up one of my places to keep you in my sight and guard you from danger. Have you no feeling for the one person who cares about you?" She tried a smile so that he wouldn't feel assaulted.

"Take me with you there."

"I can't, Asher. You are too stubborn by half and you only hear what you want to hear. You could never be found near me, so where would you stay? What would you do? You cannot even imagine what it is like in those places."

"I would hide. Read. Get me a book."

"I think the police who protect the factory will discover you if you skulk around like that in the shadows. Do you want to be picked up and taken away? Is that what you are hoping for? Do you want to be separated from me?"

He slumped back against the chair legs. "Oh, Chaya, I only want to sleep!"

"First tell me where you are going every day, and then I'll leave you."

Asher sighed, finally, resigned. "I don't do bad things. I don't, I don't go with the boys, they would never have me. I just—walk around seeing everything. I look. I am visiting Chicago everywhere. I have to be looking at new things all the time or it—you know how it is. I don't feel good."

She heard in his voice that querulous hunger that she knew so well. He was a strange threshing machine that needed to be fed new fodder or it would rust. But she breathed out the breath she had not realized she was holding. "Does anyone bother you?"

He shook his head. "I only like to walk around and look in shop windows, and when it's too cold, I go inside and get warm. Sometimes I have to talk to them to get them to let me stay—I have to make them like me." He shrugged. Apparently that was not difficult to do.

"Now, will you promise me that you won't ever—" Out of the corner of her eye, then, she saw a book she had never seen before, and she reached out to pick it up. *Old Sailors' Tales* it was, and on its frontispiece a furious Ahab of a man stood shaking his fist at the heavens while his meager lifeboat was being upended by furious whitecaps. So much water surrounded him that he seemed to be standing inside a cave. "And you got this *where?*"

He didn't answer. Tears, so rare for Asher, spilled down his cheeks and fell as quick as rain on his hands.

Chaya pulled him to her and she held him fast—she who had secreted *Glossop's Guide* in her bag long before desperation had set in—and wept with him.

1 2

WHEN HER eyesight made her work at home too difficult, Mrs. Gottlieb found herself an opening in a sweat just a few doors down Liberty Street, third floor, front, inspecting coats and jackets. She did not sew, herself, but, quite miraculously, she was able to feel where a seam had deviated and left a tiny rent, to feel where the placement of a button was off by a shade or a hem was not secure. She sat before a window where the light, in spite of ineradicable grime, was good enough that she could hold up close to her failing eyes the garment to be scrutinized, and, better yet, use her experienced touch to discover the flaws with her fingertips.

Sweat, breath, and sour steam that rose off half-singed cloth—the room was foul, and except for her perch, it stayed too dark for exacting work. All day, with an insolent hiss, the mangle expelled gusts of moist fog, gray as smoke. She suspected a frail, sallow-faced woman named Mollie of hiding consumption, and though no bloodied handkerchiefs surfaced, Mrs. Gottlieb was certain her hideous cough hung beads of contagion all around her. A mysterious residue that came off the fabrics sometimes closed her throat and teared her eyes. She and Chaya compared miasmas, laughing (for what else could they do?) about the competition between cigar-murk and wool-fog.

In two small rooms, nine people, most of them related to the owner— wife, daughters, cousins (one male, the presser), nieces—worked with hardly a minute free, to produce overcoats too heavy for some of the machines, too burdensome, when she was very tired, for Mrs. Gottlieb to heft without unbearable exertion. The effort it took to keep the machines moving, by foot or by knee, had hobbled a woman named Bella, who looked strong enough to be a lumberjack but whose legs hurt so badly that she limped like a cripple, and a very young girl (about Chaya's age when she'd made the crossing and so it was painful to hear Mrs. Gottlieb speak about her), who cried piteously for the last hour of every day because her muscles were so strained. But she could not be let go and most likely she did not want to be, for the sake of her paycheck: She was the niece of the owner, which bound her in servitude alongside his own unlucky daughters.

Chaya visited Mrs. Gottlieb there only once, and seeing their awful circumstances, reluctantly she congratulated herself for having had the instinct to choose as she had, grateful that she needed only her eyes and hands to earn her keep. But she was tired of being harangued about speed, speed, and more speed, and threatened for every torn leaf or imperfect seal. Sometimes the leaves she was given were so dry they ripped when she so much as looked at them; sometimes her paste cup crusted over because its cover had mysteriously disappeared. Still, her limbs were her own and that freedom was apparently not to be taken for granted.

She easily picked out of the small group of workers the girl whom her landlady so pitied. She was a thin, pretty thing in a faded pink smock, her pale, hair tugged back in a ragged bow, one strand of which escaped to tickle her brow and cause her to swat at it regularly, without noticing, as if it were a pesky fly. She watched the girl laboring to drag a navy-blue cloak of immense weight, to pull it up under her needle. Her whole body had to move, below the waist, to work the treadle, though this was far from a dance. Then the needle must have broken. She raised the silvery foot and the vast garment slipped to the floor. The foreman shouted; the girl allowed herself but half a minute to close her eyes—in prayer or exhaustion—and then she opened them, wet with tears of pain and frustration and, hand over hand, hauled up the many pounds of winter wool yet again as if it were a net bursting with fish. She was attempting to attach the collar to the coat, and so the whole body of the garment hung down, an enormous weight pulling hard; she readjusted her lap to catch some of its drag, and the thing, a recalcitrant beast with a will of its own, slithered yet again into a dark heap on the floor, littered with scraps and pins and threads, and they adhered to it like iron shavings to a magnet. Chaya could not watch. But when the owner called her a terrible name which Chaya tried not to listen to, her weeping began, and, between hissed interruptions from the presser's corner, there was no choice but to hear.

Still, Mrs. Gottlieb was relatively content with her employment, which allowed her to walk to her work in a minute and a half, and once there, to sit in the light. Even her age, she said, seemed to be respected rather than derided. Perhaps that was because the owner and foreman, Mr. Kraswitz (who, Mrs. Gottlieb speculated, might have taken his lessons in gruffness and whip-cracking from a previous employer but executed with forced conviction, alternating kindness with brutality), had a mother far more ancient than she, who sat at the other window. All Mr. Kraswitz's patience puddled up where, sentient as a barnacle, she clung to consciousness, vacantly staring through the glass where her reflection overlaid the horizon of tenements across the street. He was tender to this husk of a woman, speaking to her in a voice far more gentle than he used with his employees, bringing her tea, Russian style, in a glass supported by a chased silver holder, which she sipped through a sugar cube. Mrs. Gottlieb would look up sometimes to see old Mrs. Kraswitz dribbling her tea or asleep with the tipping glass about to fall from her hands, and would put down the cape or coat she was scrutinizing and pat the chin or remove the glass or straighten the sagging babushka in her chair.

One afternoon, just after Mrs. Gottlieb had returned from the bowl of soup she ate hurriedly in her own rooms, a clamor arose on the stairs and the door burst open without so much as a knock of warning. Mr. Kraswitz, who always wore a vest and a tie so that he looked entrepreneurial even when he was rolling out the rubbish cans, rushed to confront two men with unforgiving faces who stood in the doorway. He huddled with them, gesturing, Mrs. Gottlieb could see, with growing anxiety and cast an arm wildly in the direction of his operators, who had boldly stopped their machines to stare.

The buzz of speculation began, passing with the speed of a needle in cloth from chair to chair: Thieves? Criminals, there to rob the sweatshop of its goods, its payroll? The Law, ready to rescue the youngest workers from their indentured labor now that new rules were astir that threatened to protect the young and force them to school? They did have the menacing neutrality of Government about them, something not so much individual as bureaucratic, dressed exactly alike as they were, with no particularity to their faces except the desire to intimidate. Ready to accuse, the operators turned to the girl whose weeping distressed them daily, as though she might somehow be guilty of attracting these intruders.

But it was worse. One of the men, clearly under orders to appear as inhumanely grim as possible, moved to the bin where the finished overcoats were piled once they had passed through Mrs. Gottlieb's hands, nudged it with a foot as if it might be dangerous, then bent and, his head turned away— "*Gotenyu!*" Mrs. Gottlieb said—he held to his nose a massive handkerchief or perhaps a scarf, something white and voluminous, and with a gloved hand pulled two coats from the pile, one from the bottom, the other from the top. These he wrapped in a sort of carpet, or some such heavy material, and dropped into a cask the size of a steamer trunk that the other brought to him. Then, having closed and locked the receptacle, he began to stalk the little room, peering into the faces of the operators, who sat stunned and wordless. As they passed her, Mollie, the presumed consumptive, began to cough—fear will do that to the fragile—and the man leaped back, bathing her in a glance both contemptuous and fearful. The old Mrs. Kraswitz let out a chilling wail, as if she could feel disaster in the air.

Then the man came and stood beside a seat unoccupied that afternoon and vacant for a few preceding days. "And where is this operator?" he asked, and Mr. Kraswitz, in a voice hardly recognizable, replied that she was at home attending her sick child. And this was the moment that struck alarm into Mrs. Gottlieb. Something about the long unwavering look Mr. Kraswitz received as a result of his reply, and worse—her clear memory that Esther, the woman whose place was so portentously empty, had no child. "I know she lives way over west," she told Chaya, who was hearing the story with numb terror, "with her bachelor brother. Or did, except he died last week."

The man stepped toward Mr. Kraswitz. "And would you happen to know what illness her child might be suffering?"

"Oh," their boss shrugged, " I wouldn't know a thing like—"

"Croup, I think," said the girl who wept. "She told me her little girl has terrible croup."

The man, who had a single caterpillar of an eyebrow that Mrs. Gottlieb knew symbolized stubbornness and immovability and promised exceedingly bad luck, retired to the door at this point. Mr. Kraswitz, who seemed to have lost both height and weight during this encounter, skittered over to speak with them still more, gesturing like a man bargaining for his life. Then, one of them lugging the chest and its overcoats across the threshold, they were gone.

"What?" the younger Mrs. Kraswitz demanded in her most threatening voice. "What was that?" She was a woman one did not ignore.

But her husband threw a hand at her, dismissing her. Instead he turned to command his operators back to work. "They are interested in placing a very large order," he told them with a shrug, "and so we must bear with their intrusion. They have the right to inquire into our operation, after all." He wiped his brow with his sleeve. "Please do not give it a thought. Let's just return to our work and"—here he smiled, most unconvincingly—"if this order works out, there will be bonuses, I promise you, in every pay envelope. Chanukah *gelt!*"

At that, Mrs. Gottlieb was convinced that some doom had befallen the shop, because Harold Kraswitz, attempting to be unapproachable, had never before spoken with such regard for the concerns of his workers, had never promised them a penny beyond the few that he owed them (though he was strictly honest and never cheated them), and surely never dared ignore the demands of his wife. And because, she added, on the word *promise* his voice had broken like a boy's chanting his bar mitzvah portion.

So it was no great surprise—though it was no less grievous—that Mrs. Gottlieb, when Chaya returned from her buckeye the next night, told her that she had gone to her work that morning a trifle cautiously, still wondering what might be afoot, and found the rooms empty. Totally

abandoned. All that remained to identify the sweatshop were the smell
of effort and vagrant threads and remnants and the little glinting pins
that littered the floor. The sewing machines were gone, and the steam
mangle, though each table had left a modest footprint on the linoleum.
The bins were absent, the shelves bare, dust around the places where piles
and boxes had been removed, and—could it really be?—the furniture of
the family was missing as well, give or take a few items too paltry to be
moved: two cracked dishes and a mug, a collapsing wooden chair with
someone's family crest on its back. And all she confronted on the dark
staircase were the two workers, not counting the missing Esther, who were
not Kraswitz relatives.

"It's the typhoid," said Bella, her hand futilely clamped over her nose.
"That's what I heard from my brother-in-law, he works for the alderman.
Those coats we were sending out—he said they must have been contami-
nated." She sounded remarkably matter-of-fact about it. Her gossip usually
turned out to be true. "Somebody must have reported, I don't know how.
Pearl. That means people caught sick!"

Mrs. Gottlieb, who knew she ought to flee, had instead sat herself
down on the step in a kind of surrender. The single eyebrow had promised the worst and here it was. "And Esther? Does anybody know how
she—if she—?"

Bella, still trying to stanch contagion with her bare hand, said, "You
know, her brother died, I don't know about him neither, and Esther—ai,
I don't want to think!" She moved her hand to her heart. "You know
what else I don't want to think?" She didn't wait for a reply. "What that
Kraswitz knew. That snake, did he care who he killed? I hope it catches
him and puts him in the ground."

The other operator, a young woman named Nitze, who spoke only a
few words of English, entreated them with her eyes to explain what was
happening, but there was no way to do anything but pull her into a fierce
embrace and then turn her toward the street and gesture her away. "He
owe money!" she wailed, turning back to them. He did, and they would
never see it, but that was the least of their worries.

"Sickness!" Bella warned her. She did a little pantomime that would have made them laugh if it were only a game, a twitching and a long shivering stroke of her hands along her opposite arms, with a crazy face to go along with it. She did look like a woman jumping out of her skin.

Nitze looked as though she thought them both insane. Finally she backed away and kicked up snow as she moved down the street. You could tell from the way she walked that she was in a fury and used to it.

Bella, whispering, asked, "Is everyone healthy in your house?"

Mrs. Gottlieb pulled herself up very slowly to take herself home. "So far, *baruch ha shem*, everyone is healthy. But I don't feel so good right now myself."

Bella did not make a move to embrace her. "You're just imagining, Pearl. It's only natural."

She sighed. "Maybe I'm sick because he ran away with four days' pay."

"Better that than the other, dear. Go home and say a prayer. I'm putting some garlic around my neck, if it's not too late. This whole city is a cesspool."

As she had turned to walk the fifty feet that separated the houses, Mrs. Gottlieb had seen the doctor's wagon pull up before her very steps, and, hurrying down Liberty Street toward Maxwell, a hearse, black with fancy gold lettering, and two plumed horses, black as a bad-luck cat. Chicago hearses made the death-journey almost beautiful, the way their horses knew how to raise their feet and put them down again in perfect unison.

But just when she thought her landlady was calm about all this, "Chaya-Libbe," Mrs. Gottlieb murmured, keening from side to side like someone already in mourning. "If I brought this disease home with me to you and your brother! Oh!" she moaned. "I don't care for myself, my life isn't nothing with Nachman gone, my eyes are deserting me, I got no more work anyway—but you! You beautiful ones! My *yingele*!"

Her *yingele* didn't stir at the sound of her moaning. Chaya reached to comfort her but Mrs. Gottlieb held her away. "Imagine, those coats! Those coats must have carried the sickness up north to the stores where they sell them. Strangers at the racks at Marshall Field's trying them on, paying good money for them! Those coats, they cost like solid gold. Bringing them home and—" It was too much for her and she wept and wept, but still would not let Chaya touch her. "Imagine—I looked at them so hard, every one of them, I ran them through my hands and I couldn't see nothing. Couldn't see no death in the cloth, Chaya! A plague right there and I was the *inspector* and I couldn't see a single thing."

Chaya led her to her bed—Mrs. Gottlieb was hot with what she prayed was excitement and not fever, and laid her down fully dressed, and from the icy water in the pail brought a compress for her head that startled her with its chill. "And that family, what happens now, that whole Kraswitz family, the sister, the cousins? The old lady! To run away in the night like that, so cold, so black, where would they go?"

Poison in the fibers, poison in the air. Chaya-Libbe had not been there to touch it or breathe it in herself, and she did not believe it could leap so far from their origin that it could find the innocents in apartment 4C, houses away. She would not consider it. She went to her bed—those chairs that punished her nightly—and promised she would not be sick, and neither would Asher.

While they slept, the river boiled on, bubbling with the refuse of the city. Lay a match upon it and it would have roared itself into furious fire. It was a wonder they hadn't all died of it a long time ago.

THEY DID not sicken, Asher and she, but Mrs. Gottlieb hovered for weeks in a peculiar state that Chaya attributed to some elixir of fear and sympathy that she had drunk the day her employer decamped and swept his family away as if they had never existed. She lay in a lethargy, not feverish as she would have been had the disease wracked her; she did not seem to be in pain, her gut, her head, her limbs no way afflicted. Only she lay, insisting on darkness, and slept and woke. Occasionally she called Chaya by the name of her mother or perhaps one of her sisters; she turned away the food they brought and said no more than she asked—not a single thing.

Chaya never told her that her dear neighbor, Mrs. Seychek—the one who had suggested the cigar shop to her—had perished along with one of her half-grown children. (Hers was the destination of the doctor Mrs. Gottlieb had seen entering the house. How could she not have known where he was headed.) Everything lay under a pall, like a spell of weather that would not pass.

IN HER own shop, listening hard while her fingers did their repetitive business, Chaya lived the life of hearsay; heard rumors, before winter locked its clamp around them, that Chicago was still the wonderland of pleasure that she had staked their life on. Sundays in a greensward called Lincoln Park where couples strolled and punted about in rowboats on a swatch of pond, weeknights uptown in the opera houses and music halls—the Haverly, McVicker's, Hooley's Theatre, and Shelby's Academy of Music—gorgeous shows on the stage, dancers in feathers and flamboyant bows, orchestras sawing and soaring, and in their seats, audiences made up of every class and kind, the common to the grand, separated only by the distance of the gallery from the boxes. The streets in summer had been aswirl with comers and goers and children rode the shoulders of their fathers to see above their heads. Even into the uncertain weather of October, sailboats plied the lake, and steamers with crowded decks; regattas ruled the horizon, white-winged and thick as gulls. and across the whole of it one could often glimpse the mayor, a much-beloved Kentuckian named Carter Harrison, astride his horse, wearing a great-brimmed hat and waving triumphantly at his constituents, who gratefully waved back. She had never seen the mayor, her life lived so closely in areas of the city to which it did not seem necessary for him to come, but she had heard descriptions of his legendary romps, and imagined him a sort of king measuring out the bounds of his territory.

Who were the women, she wondered, who possessed the time, not to mention the wherewithal, to enjoy the set table of this city? Were they the ones with husbands or, at the least, sweethearts who demanded they take some rest, and contributed a part of their wages to the project? Had she managed to be granted a salesgirl's place, right in the center of so much activity—she recalled that above the tide of strollers waved a giant balloon in the shape of the World's Fattest Lady (a freak show was coming to the Hippodrome) and clowns on stilts stepped between the dray horses—would she have taken part in those delights that amused the more affluent? In response to threats of insurrection, the cable car had just ceased to cost fifteen cents and could now be ridden for a nickel. Still, if she could have walked there, she'd gladly have done so.

She had no suitors and she had less than no cash money; she also had not an hour to spare. Sundays she could perhaps have gone to some kind of diversion, but she was so exhausted that even the idea of relaxing on demand seemed a burden. And there was no threshold she could cross that did not cost money she couldn't spare. If anything, she wondered, now that her landlady had become but another mouth to feed, whether she should try to find a third employer. But it would be no favor to Asher, she reasoned, if she collapsed in the traces like so many of the horses who lay dead or panting in the street—at least winter kept them from turning foul and nurturing nests of flies and their maggoty offspring—and so she kept that day for recuperation.

She had fallen into a depression only slightly less enveloping than Mrs. Gottlieb's. With winter rapping its icy fist against the windows and no one making a particular effort to seek her out, she burned as feebly as a candle guttering out. The farm had been no worse than this. If she was going to freeze, she might as well have been with people who loved her.

One morning she woke to find her lips coated with a rime of frost. When she parted them, they bled. She was in no mood to credit idealism as a stimulant: Liberty Street, a sty from its earliest day, had been named by a joker or a fool.

She missed so much that her only passion was loss and the anger that accompanied it. What an endless list of deprivations she could make: She missed *red*. The streets were black and white; gray was nothing but *schmutz*, that ugly word for dirt. At work her eyes were fixed on the slime of a greeny-brown; their rooms were so bleak during the short hours she was at home that she would not even assign them a color. With an emptiness she never knew she could have felt, she missed music, which hardly existed without cost—carfare, admission, luxuries beyond her. She almost convinced herself to enter a *shul* if it would mean that she could listen to singing, hear melody, harmony, rhythm; could close her eyes and be salved. But, she remembered, there was, in worship, so much more muttering than singing, so much more swaying than free and joyous movement that it was not worth her angering her father in absentia by joining the pious.

But most, she missed her boy. Asher had gone feral, except at nighttime. He was nothing to her but anxious obligation: to keep him under a paid-for roof, to clothe him badly but prevent him from running bare, to pray that luck ran with him. He was not the only child who spent the day without a guardian; they teemed in this coldhearted place, unclaimed, unprotected, uncontrollable. Winter or no winter, packs of boys still ran through the market, knocking against pushcarts, stealing fruit, menacing, whether or not they intended to be. At least he did not sleep out under the sky.

And she was bereft of one last thing: her body. This was a defect in her life that she kept suppressed, buried as deep as she could keep it: simply the need for touch and warmth. Evenings, when she came dragging home from her buckeye, she sat herself beside Mrs. Gottlieb—their sleeping beauty in her hairnet, her skein of creases—and gratefully laved her face and body with water she had first warmed on the stove, a bucketful that she had carried up in the morning lest she have to go to the pump at midnight. Slowly, allowing herself to feel and enjoy the rises and declivities of a living body, though its pulse beat perilously faint, she swirled the soft cloth over Mrs. Gottlieb's shoulders, under her fallen breasts, along the shriveled planes of her thighs and legs, all the way to her cool splayed toes, and gave thanks that she was alive, perhaps to feel touch in some way that might bring her back to life.

Chaya had, in her years at the Fields of Zion, been pressed to help perform the *taharah* on a few—she had only assisted with children—who had died. This was the purification of the body for burial, an affair that utilized a great deal of water, interspersed with prayers and the humble housekeeping tasks of rooting out dirt from under the fingernails, in the whorls of the ears, and anywhere else the soilage of living might have lodged it. Having done those duties, she never again saw her own nails innocently; they had become memento mori. "Master of the Universe," the women would say in unison, "through mercy, hide and disregard the transgressions of this departed. May she tread with righteous feet into the Garden of Eden, for that is the place of the upright, and God protects the pious."

But the departed was a child, one dead of the measles, another of a fall into their pond, having slipped on the slimy shore; she had not had time to transgress! Her sister Sorele had been one of them, gone in an instant, innocent and unprotected. She was not allowed to prepare her and a good thing: She was so grieved, so uncomforted, she knew that if something terrible happened to her, she would not be one of the protected—she believed none of it. Then—she would always silently apologize for what would have been an affront to the living—they would fling enormous gouts of water they'd dragged from the pond, ignoring the motes risen from its silty bottom, pretending God's own power sanctified and made it clear. "Respect the dead," her father had instructed her the first time she took part in the ceremony, "but bite your tongue on all that mumbling."

At least, she assured herself, Mrs. Gottlieb might still wake if she stung her skin with the cloth sufficiently hard to move the blood around. She could not lay tranced forever, could she? Chaya picked up and scrubbed at the callused hands that had touched so many objects and people in her lifetime, had cooked so many dinners and sewn so many seams, and had so recently felt their way around those dark, doomed overcoats. Perhaps she was sick, really sick with the blight she had breathed, or brought home under her fingernails, but it was easier to believe Mrs. Gottlieb had been laid low by an insult to her pride. Her torpor did not seem physical, somehow; it felt like a refusal. Meanwhile, just to pass her fingers across that flesh, which was warm and still quick, to bathe the sores that sometimes bloomed where she lay too long without stirring—having failed at all else, at least Chaya had not yet finished failing her.

USUALLY SHE rushed from Winkler's to Yanowitz's, one master to the next, with hardly a moment between in which to breathe freely. She walked out the factory door into a street on which the moon alone, with little help from the streetlights, made even the dirty snow glisten like crumbled glass. The city all around was thick with dark; this was not a neighborhood where people lived, its only life the life of capital. These hulks of buildings existed in part to fulfill the needs of the populace, but chiefly to put money in the pockets of men like Winkler, whose pouchy, overstuffed physique seemed to Chaya a perfect representation of his greed. Oily-faced and bulging at every seam of his vest and jacket, perspiring through his shirt on the days when they saw him jacketless, his rolls of neck-fat like a baby's thighs, only not so adorable, he was as gross as his selfishness in the face of his minions.

So it was hardly surprising that this night, emerging a little bit later than the others on her shift because she had misplaced a glove in the cloakroom and had spent too many minutes on hands and knees in a futile search for it, Chaya came into the street alone, one hand plunged into her pocket for warmth. Usually she walked a long, bracing way to her buckeye, to Yanowitz's, where her humiliation was subtler but no less galling.

But on this night, who can say why, she could not, could not, do it. Here was that entropy, though she had no name for it; it was only a nameless stoppage. She was a mule who would not budge. Her legs locked and would not propel her, though they did not feel particularly weak. She felt the way she had one noontime on the farm when she had been stooped weeding the overrun rows in a punishing sun: Her vision was spotted with sunbursts of light and her forehead went damp, until she felt the earth tipping and her poor, light body about to slip right off it. Now she knew that she must keep her footing and not collapse on the hard-packed snow and so she made her way to the wall of the factory and leaned against it while her vision slowly cleared. She might have closed her eyes for a minute or two while she swayed there. She would not have been surprised if she even dozed on her feet, like a bird on a perch.

When she opened them, a man was standing a few feet before her, perhaps a worker from Winkler's, perhaps from another of these sties that contained so many. But as her sight cleared, she saw he was not dressed as workers dress. Some of the high-skilled, high-paid men from up in Havana Golds loved to come to work all dandied up, in slick suits and bowlers that they changed before they sat down, but they overdid it; their crude glamour was only a kind of showing off. This one wasn't trying to prove anything. By his derby and overcoat, and the shining silk scarf that caught the light at his throat, he would have been one of the managers who came to work attired as the gentleman he—at least in theory—was.

"Wouldn't you like to come with me, gorgeous?" he whispered into the darkness. "We can have us a nice dinner and a glass or two."

Just before he came close enough to put a hand on her, she managed to find a sliver of a voice and say, "If you please, sir, you have no reason to approach me."

He stopped short and looked closely at her, head to toe, with a sort of patronizing care, as if he had to ascertain what she had said with his own eyes. "Excuse my forwardness, young lady, but I thought you might be in some distress."

This was all that passed between them, though it was on her lips to say, "That was hardly the burden of what you proposed to me." Instead, shamed, though the shame should have been his, she assured him she was in no need of his assistance. With one finger he touched his hat brim to her and turned away. She felt herself shudder with desolation. What would it matter if she allowed him to put his clean, well-manicured hands on her body like Horny Henry, or gone with him to a room above a shop somewhere, or to a hotel, where he might lay her open to the lamplight and enjoy her youth, her quickly wilting, bone-weary youth? She missed her sisters, with whom she had shared a bed for so long that Dvorele and Masha seemed limbs of her own body. Even Asher no longer put his arms around her neck.

But oh, wouldn't a glass of wine have been lovely!

Why not? she asked herself. Why not go with him, and receive some coins for his exertions? Exactly as she would have had she drunk too much wine or downed too many thumbs' worth of brandy, she could not remember *why* one mode of behavior was better than the next. Whom would it hurt if she gave herself into this or some other man's grip and— in a warmer room than the one she was going home to—invited him to strip her many layers of dulling, obliterating fabric and show her lonely breasts and belly to a windowful of moon? Did she not need, as deeply as any man, to be touched, to be held close and kept warm? Why did women lay such strictures on themselves? At that moment, and many a moment to come, she could not remember. All she knew was that she was so tired of *thinking*.

Had the young man turned back to her instead of heading, she suspected, for some place like the Levee or Printer's Row where many a gentleman tickled an unresistant woman into laughter, who knows where she might have gone with him, and what she might have discovered she could become.

THE NEXT morning she spent bent over her work, wielding her curved knife with a nearly irresponsible vigor born of remorse, when she felt a tiny shift in the air, the way one unaccountably feels eyes upon one's neck, though from behind and out of sight. That, like a plucked string, was the infinitesimal atmospheric vibration she perceived. What could she think but that their warden or *his* warden, either Winkler's officious son-in-law or Winkler himself, was striding towards them across the littered floor.

But there came a swell of laughter—a small ripple at first, as if the laughers were uncertain how to react—and then more and more of her neighbors joined in, stopping their work to gaze into the middle distance. Before she could even change her focus from the pile of leaves on her desk, there came the scraping of a bench being moved slowly and laboriously, with an awful squawk of wood against wood, and then she nearly fell off her own bench when finally she saw: Her brother Asher, little imp, daring creature, was climbing, bare knees first, onto the seat. In one hand he clutched a book.

Asher's eleventh birthday had very recently come and gone with no celebration, as they did not much mark those occasions at home with their parents. He had somehow managed, in the face of scant food and trying weather, both inner and outer, to keep his clarity and—what could one call it but his *shine*? Though she had hardly taken notice lately, she saw through the eyes of her fellow-workers, a few of whom had heard of him but had never seen him, that his radiance, his wholeness of being, were intact. He removed his cap, which he placed carefully by his side— the bench was wide and he was narrow. He looked straight into Chaya's stricken face and then, without a word, he pulled his knees up to make something to lean his book against, and began to read.

It was the best of times, it was the worst of times, it was the age of wisdom, it was the age of foolishness, it was the epoch of belief, it was the epoch of incredulity, it was the season of Light, it was the season of Darkness, it was the spring of hope, it was the winter of despair, we had everything before us, we had nothing before us, we were all going direct to Heaven, we were all going direct the other way—in short, the period was so far like the present period, that some of its noisiest authorities insisted on its being received, for good or for evil, in the superlative degree of comparison only.

"Asher!" she called out in the tone she used for correction.

But he ignored her. "There were a king with a large jaw and a queen with a plain face, on the throne of England; there were a king with a large jaw and a queen with a fair face, on the throne of France. In both countries it was clearer than crystal to the lords of the State preserves of loaves and fishes, that things in general were settled for ever." His accent was faint, his emphases imprecise, but his confidence held every sentence together.

Her bench-mates, even the ones who understood no English, delighted, clapped their hands. She was confused. Was confounded. There were appreciative murmurings from the women, a few of whom flattened their palms to their bosoms and deeply inhaled, as women are wont to do when they are overwhelmed by the charm of someone or something (more often than not, as now, an adorable—an ideal—child).

She left her seat and hurried to him. When he closed his book, she claimed him, clutching him to her, not for the credit his performance might bring her but because he had accomplished what she thought he had hoped to: He had cleared her dimming vision and restored himself there, at its center. He reminded her why they had come to this difficult place and why, in spite of all, she could not take him home again. He had always had unusually unblinking eyes—like a cat's—and he turned them full upon her now. Very simply, and too quietly to be overheard, he said, "You don't let me read to you any more."

She opened her mouth to defend herself and closed it again, rebuked by the truth.

"I have new books you never saw and you don't even care."

All Chaya could do was hold him to her, though she was the one in need of comforting, and shake her head. A murmur of approval surrounded them like smoke.

THAT IS how Asher—who had barely heard of Cuba and never of Ybor City, Florida, or of the Yiddish performers in several factories in New York—became a Reader. He did Shakespeare; he did as much Dickens as the day allowed, and if he could find one somewhere on his afternoon jaunts when he was done with them, the day-old newspaper. "Mayor warns of economic woes," he intoned, in as loud a voice as he could summon. Fortunately, cigar-making is a quieter business than shirtwaists-sewing or die-stamping. Where those were all clattering, stuttering machines, the background music at Winkler's was only the inaudible hiss of knife around leaf rib and the small thump to even the packets of finished stogies against their wooden stations. "That's my last Duchess painted on the wall, / Looking as if she were alive," and "Young Goodman Brown came forth at sunset into the street of Salem Village," and where Asher mispronounced *ocular deception* and *Claus of Innsbruck*, few, if any, of his grateful listeners could tell the difference.

To Chaya's surprise, though he did not cheer, neither did Winkler object. He must have decided that Asher, *der kleyner yingl*, pacified his slaves, kept them awake and attentive and—best of all—cost him nothing. To her further surprise, her fellow workers, especially the women who were not at home with their own children as they would have wished, were sufficiently enchanted that, without complaint, they contributed from their own puny wages. Each week they flicked a coin into a cigar box, and Asher, beaming, emptied it into his palm and then into his pocket. He tried not to gloat but his tight little smile gave away his pleasure.

And so, as the year advanced from dark December toward the light of a sweeter season, they began their slow, word-by-word, page-by-page ascent into a life that would have been preposterous to imagine.

13

HAD THERE been a competition at the time Asher embarked upon—or was abducted into—his celebrity, the city of Chicago would have won the laurels for speediest city on earth. It was called, again and again, a go-getters' town. Its cable cars ran faster than New York's; this had been calibrated; it was provable, by those who cared. Its skyscrapers—a lovely word, so graphic, so arrogant—were taller and more original, its politicians more corrupt, its ladies of the night (and dusk and dawn) more numerous and, it was whispered, more innovative. Scandals broke out more frequently than rain showers: the drug-mad son of a famous industrialist, dead by his own hand in rooms above a red-light crib. Bankers in bed with elected men. News reporters bought with a few rounds of mediocre whiskey. There were a few streets on which brothels alternated with saloons, punctuated by thriving pawnshops, all so unapologetically that it was a market zone as public as Maxwell Street.

Though little of this was apparent to her in the work-worn dimness of that year, it was certainly made clear to Chaya in the bright light into which they had begun to hurtle without realizing it. Asher had been the factory's Reader for a few months when, smirking, Winkler's son engaged him to amuse his guests at a party.

In spite of his unprecedented accomplishments, Asher was a young boy, and frightened.

"You do," Chaya advised him, "exactly as you do on the cigar factory floor. Do as you like—that is what they want you for."

From what height did this sudden confidence descend?

She had begun to suspect the two of them were made of different stuff than the Winklers and Yanowitzes, and that, in spite of their penury— every thin cent went toward bread and milk—was not something to regret. The Owners had the wit for making deals and enforcing obedience; they were, at heart, employers, and would always have servants to command, while she and her brother had a somewhat frailer constitution: So driven to words, books, the ineffable objects of the imagination, what they trafficked in was invisible. If the Winklers or their children were born with silver spoons in their mouths, the Shaderowskys were born teething on syllables, which were less solid but cost nothing. Apparently there was a place, however minimal, however subtly maligned, where both types could meet.

In the wild bazaar on Maxwell and Liberty Streets, on Morgan and Taylor, that throbbed with commerce as many hours of the day as light prevailed, there were two kinds of merchants. There were the staid and steady, who hawked their gloves or their fish or their findings—who stood in one place barking out reports of the falling barometer of bargains, half-price as the day advanced, then quarter when dusk closed in and began to envelop what they had failed to sell.

And then, like fireflies, there were the entertainers. Someone with lithe step could always be seen darting through the crowd, entreating, inquiring, planting suggestions of desperate need where none had been before: "You must own this!" "You cannot dare go home without that!" They thrived on surprise and innovation. More than once, a boy on a high-wheeled bicycle careened through the aisles, peddling hats that he balanced on a stick. When a shopper inquired about one of them, rather than soberly lowering his poker, he would alarm his customer instead by thrusting it upward, making a cap or a bonnet tumble saucily down right into his hand. Just so, there were stilt walkers, hawkers of birds who lifted off an index finger and faithfully returned at a whistle, singers with accordions, fiddlers, harmonica players, drummers: This was the adventuring class, unperturbed at looking foolish, subject to unmotivated grinning, liable to own a tambourine, in every way cleverer—dreamier—than the ones who stood still and waited for customers to come to them. Asher was an artist like these. He was made to wander the aisles of the bookshop rather than the market, but he was closer to their spirit of self-delight and irrepressible self-promotion than to the sturdy entrepreneurs who owned the pushcart and oiled its wheels, kept its inventory and worried about its take. He was not the salt of the earth, Asher Shaderowsky. He was unadulterated spice.

14

ASHER WAS now, his sister told him, public property. Whatever that meant. For his first party he was given a dollar and a dinner. Chaya's Mr. Winkler had a son named Chaz who had a wife and on their anniversary he seemed to think Asher would make an enticing "amuse-bouche." Asher heard *a muse bush* and wondered if he was, somehow, to impersonate a hedge. And which muse? Clio? Thalia? *Mel-pe-money*? It made no sense, but a dollar was a dollar.

He and Chaya were greeted at the back door of a house that looked like a miniature bank or what were those pillars for? He watched the maid whisk her eyes up Chaya and down again, lingering over her collar, which, true, was thready, but *clean*, and raise her nose to sniff as if they smelled foul—he heard the sniff. Did she think she was the mistress of the house? He opened his mouth to remind her she was only a maid but his sister widened her eyes with warning and he wilted.

He had brought Ariosto to read, a little *Orlando Furioso* because it was full of jagged sounds, exercise for his tongue. Chaz's son, a pudgy overgrown boy at least, say, twenty, stared without apology as if Asher had come directly from the zoo. Asher sat on a tall chair like a toy Buddha, ankles crossed and knees akimbo—a kimbo! What was a kimbo?—and bore being pelted with questions. "Who was the third president of our great nation?" "Don't you know that?" he asked before he singsonged, "Thomas Jefferson," and "Where would one look for the River Ganges?" which he took a while to parse because he had never heard the name pronounced. Wasn't it *Gan-gess?* Apparently not. It was rude to ask things just to catch him in not-knowing. The questions were cheese in a mousetrap and he had to snatch carefully lest he be caught.

"Well," Mrs. Chaz Winkler murmured to her husband out of the side of her mouth as if Asher couldn't hear her. "Well, the poor shortpants is a little Jew. They know too much by half." *She wanted me to hear her,* Asher thought. When you overheard something, that meant you heard too much.

"But our son, who reads badly, is also a Jew, as are you and I, my dear," her husband replied bleakly, "and I don't notice that our intellects have been much improved by it."

What's worth a dollar? Asher asked himself as, dismissed, he and Chaya fled down the wooden back steps into the yard. If he asked for two next time—if there was a next time—it might be worth it. That was when Chaya told him he was now public property. If he did this kind of thing he would be fingered, she said, like yard goods.

Yard? Like the grass they were crossing? *Goods?* Bads, more like it. How unsensible, this language, whose strangeness only ceased when he was asleep.

15

AT THE other parties that followed, as Asher was handed from one to another delighted friend tired of tableaux vivants and in need of "original" entertainment, Chaya stood beside her boy in a hall as large as half the common room at the Fields of Zion, and watched the guests giving their overcoats to those whose lot it was only to handle things that did not belong to them. Every surface shone with the gleam of their effort—tabletops, doorknobs, floorboards that showed between the lushly flowered carpets. Bowls of flowers, carefully arranged, chartered their thanks to the parlormaids, or so she fancied. The fringes of the table shawls, paisley, velvet, lace, quivered with the breeze of their hasty passing. Electric lights, dim but steady, warmed the rooms through which they hurried, obedient, carrying to, carrying away.

Chaya found that, identifying herself with them, she regarded those workers as the subjects and the owners of the houses as the mere objects, blank, faceless, whited out to the color of ash. The day she found herself fascinated by how easy it would be to raise, unseen, a long declarative scratch in the mahogany hall table of Mrs. Miles Cantwell—why did this not happen more often, it would be so easy to incise a wound with any sharp stick!—she began to worry about herself.

The Winklers and their friends should have put her out. Furious, subversive in her heart, she was a spy for their ill-wishers. Rather than the awed peasant girl she was certain they saw in her, if they bothered to see anything—the keeper of that little genius boy—she had begun saving up grievances to become their nemesis.

And little by little, as the winter began to thaw, Mrs. Gottlieb stirred from her hibernation. On the day Chaya discovered her sitting, though weakly, on the edge of her bed, she was beyond gratitude. Asher leaned into her empty bowl of a lap, one small elbow on each of her hidden thighs, and stared into her eyes gravely, like a doctor come to pronounce her cured.

16

CHAYA'S FELLOW cigar-makers—not the skilled elite who worked upstairs on the Clear and Seed Havanas or the ten-centers who were well paid in dollars and self-respect, but the peons with whom she struggled for penny-wages—had been threatened, after they submitted a brief list of demands: for longer work breaks (often they had none), for the right to use the toilets when they needed to, for a mere penny more per packet of stogies. They had been told that they were easily replaced, and worse, that their names would be made available to other cigar shops and they would never be employed again. An old, crude story, all of it, and all of it well comprehended. Ill-used, they could hardly feel unique, could only roil about and protest to each other. They were captive and they knew it.

That, one indignity piled on another, was why they decided to strike. Chaya was not deceived by the reputation of organized labor simply because it had its own sufferings—stogie-makers, women all, were not allowed in the union. Their product was considered close to shameful, casually assembled in the eyes of the purists and sold for less than a song, and so they were only a sad band of wives and girlfriends who, after weeks of whispering, gathered one morning before work outside the south factory door to plan their campaign of refusal.

It was a travesty, even Chaya could see that, to try to intimidate Winkler and family when they could hardly catch the eye of the union, white men mainly, a few Slavs, a few Spanish-speakers, indifferent to the peasants downstairs with their jangly languages, their sloppy handiwork, their *voices*. Once she saw Mr. Winkler's son cover his ears and mutter, "The noise those pigeons make! If I didn't have a headache after a trace too much brandy last night, I would have one now after a morning down here!" How fortunate for him that Asher shut them up a few hours a day, piping out, "It was the best of times, it was the worst of times." That was so perfect for the moment that Chaya asked him to repeat it.

But her coworkers did their best, and she loved them for it. They managed to spread the word to two other factories nearby that employed women like herself at the bottom of the stack, where their grievances collected like the muck that thickened the air on the factory floor. They would not stop work but would demonstrate first, civilly, knowing that without support they could not really strike. They would carry signs and picket and hope that, at the least, embarrassment—public shame, even— would weigh on their bosses and chip, even modestly, at their greed. Chaya had never carried a sign before, but not only did she march with a splintery stick in her closed fist and feel how it caught the wind like a sail and threatened to fly away, she had lettered the board herself: FAIRNESS FOR ALL!! it said. Sara carried WE DESERVE TO BE HEARD.

There was no response, neither threat nor—how could they be surprised?—acquiescence. Nor did the union deign to acknowledge them with as much as a word or a gesture. They marched during the short time allotted for their midday dinners, careful not to overstay it. They marched before work and after work, and one day someone brought a newspaper that reported their "nonstrike" with a snide laugh: "The women stamped about the periphery of the buildings like frantic chickens in a barnyard denied their feed. As usual, like Carmen, the pretty ones looked prettier for being peeved." Finally, most patronizing of all, the owner of a factory that faced theirs on Cullerton Street, John Senning—an old man as different from Winkler as could be imagined, white-haired, slender and stiff-cravatted—sent down to them a vat of hot cider "to warm your cold-hearted disloyalty," they were told by his lackey as he set it in the middle of the circle of pickets. They only stared at it, too deflated to drink, knowing themselves the object of derision and all the more fury-driven for that. Sara seized the kettle in both bare hands and, heavy though it was, turned it upside down until all the cider had run into the slush and melted it into puddles so pink they looked like blood many times diluted.

But as Chaya turned to go up to her work, gibbering angrily to herself about power and its obverse, a voice behind her called, "Pardon me, miss," and she turned her bitter face back toward the street. She felt vixenish and liked it. There stood a young man, beautifully clothed in soft, heathery wools of a kind not generally seen on the factory steps. "I believe we've met," he called to her, and removed his hat, while she riffled the empty pages of her memory, incapable of imagining such a thing. He was decidedly not the rake who had issued that lewd invitation the night she had slumped, failing, against the factory wall. Who, though, would she have had occasion to know who in any way resembled this man? One of the parties where Asher had played Fauntleroy, perhaps? He came towards her a step. "The evening on which you arrived in Chicago with your little brother, do you remember? Miss—Shadow—I think."

Her face, she could feel, turned as pink as that spilled cider with mortification. When she could find her voice, she was quite compelled to ask, "Whatever has brought you out today, sir?" Was he, she wondered, one of the owners of these sties? Such a comfortable prince, every hair in place, the kind of young man who could afford to change his shirt twice in a day if his business so demanded. He looked as if he could be the grandson of John Senning.

His answer startled her. "I read about your efforts in the *Tribune*." He frowned and she saw that he was running the yielding brim of his hat between his fingers as if he were less than wholly collected. "And I hazarded to think your group might enjoy some moral support. This must be very difficult."

Truly? She checked his face for incipient laughter at their expense. "You are not here to deride us like the rest?"

"I am not." He smiled, that same benign, undemanding benison she now remembered from their first encounter. Had he been the devil masquerading as a man, she'd have trusted him entirely for the way his smile rearranged his features so ungrudgingly. "I support your efforts entirely," he said, "and I only wish I could bring some influence to bear on the men who hold the tillers of these pirate ships."

She hardly had time, just then, to consider what it entailed for a man like Gregory Stillman to indict these men as the pirates they were, but she would have as much time as she needed when the moment cooled. Now all she could do was wonder at how such a gift could be given to someone who had never prayed, not an instant, in her life.

"PLAYING" THE parties with Asher was like drinking poison for Chaya. She could hardly expect a child to have a conscience about such things; he was properly delighted to be a star that burned in the perfect center of every eye, to be stroked and fed like a cherished pet for his repertoire of tricks and—realistic enough—to actually contribute to their pathetic little household fund. He might have been uniquely literate but, too, he was very good with numbers.

At one party he elicited terrific applause simply for reading a bit of Sophocles in his young boy's unbroken voice. "'Tis plain that thou art brooding on some dark tidings!" Clearly it gave great pleasure to the hosts and their friends to take sympathetic notice of Asher's impoverished clothes, his run-over shoes and rather dilapidated cap, even the stains on his shirt collar whose permanence had long since been confirmed in the hottest water Chaya could produce. She believed the discrepancy between the richness of his mind and the poverty of his circumstances sent a collective shiver up the spine of the men and women who sat on the same delicate chairs that were used for chamber music recitals and, in all their absurdity, tableaux vivants. He was better than an organ-grinder's monkey.

They were finally freed from the kitchen: Their hosts heaped their plates as if in obeisance to someone touched by God. Chaya loved the food, how could she not have, but it felt like alms. She tongued a ladyfinger, opened, halved, spread with something the cook called crème fraîche, and closed again. It should have been bitter but its sweetness blazed on her tongue.

———

AND TO complicate her anger, she had begun to be courted by Gregory Stillman, whose motives she mistrusted but whose decency and concern, not to mention his out-and-out beauty—his forthright gaze, the sharp angle of his cheekbones, the way his hair lay on his neck with a kind of vulnerable softness she had only seen in young boys—undermined her antagonism.

On the day of the nonstrike, before she resumed her bench at Winkler's, he had said, with his usual courtesy, "I would be privileged to hear more about your grievances. I cannot promise to be more than a sympathetic ear for your qualms." He smiled at himself as if to make his proposal casual. "Just a shoulder on which to lean, if leaning might relieve you."

Chaya, blushing, eyed that shoulder beneath its tweed and imagined what it would feel like bare beneath her own bare hand. She told him that she was forced to go every evening from Winkler's to her buckeye, where, if it happened to be unfinished, Yanowitz could complete her day's humiliation. Could reject her careful work if his mood was sour. Could deny her the few minutes it took to walk to the wretched toilet until she sat at her bench clenched against shame. Where, in effect, he could practice the drill of a "big" as opposed to a "little" boss, in case the occasion were to present itself whereby he could embitter the lives of two hundred instead of ten of them.

Thus Gregory Stillman heard every injury Chaya could conjure from memory, nor could she have said which was the stronger, embarrassment at her self-pity or the refreshment of speaking, for once, to someone other than a fellow sufferer. She watched him carefully as she ran through her brief of pains and was thrilled to see his lovely dark-blue eyes actually shine with sympathy at her recital. There was power in weakness, she saw, if it was focused, like a mirror that, aimed at the sun, could set paper afire.

He volunteered to travel with her, sometimes by hack, sometimes in his father's carriage drawn by matching bays, from her large factory to her small—that was the best he could do. This eased the travail of getting herself to Yanowitz's and it gave her a chance to sit tight against him, thigh to thigh, though there were layers of winter wool between them, thick as a bundling board. She could not decide whether he was as good a man as he seemed, or was a practiced dissimulator who understood that some women are wooed more effectively by vulnerability than by mastery and menace. Stories were rife, as she sat at her cigar board wielding her little blade and pinching her leaf ends with callused fingertips, concerning young women who could not tell the difference and sinned themselves into captivity, motherhood, or both.

There was, just then, to pique her guilty conscience, a young man named Hirschl, so thin she was certain he was consumptive, who spoke with her whenever they touched shoulders on the whining staircase at Winkler's, or, rather, tried to speak but was—in spite of that conscience—rebuffed. She hated to admit that he repulsed her, his deflated chest over which his shirt belled out empty as a sheet in the wind, his thin curls, his shoulders hunched protectively, everything about him earnest and unhealthy. She had the sickening feeling that he was searching for one last love before he lay himself down for eternity. When he spoke to her, asking a moment, just a moment of her time, she smelled his sad, moldy breath and thought of graveyard dirt. Gregory had about him the delicate, tampered-with scent of whatever it was men doused themselves with after they bathed. It shamed her to think of him bathing, but there it was, ineradicable as it was indecent. "Please," she said to Hirschl, and passed quickly down the stairs, pulling her skirts away, flattening herself to the wall.

ONE SUNDAY afternoon, having heard from Chaya that Asher was to work—odd how the words *work* and *play* were interchangeable when they concerned entertainment—at the home of a Harry Carter, Gregory came striding toward them, broadly smiling. "I didn't tell you that Harry is my cousin," he said with a grin, and stood closer to her than he ought to, given the number of eyes that surrounded them.

That information only made her want to inch away.

Harry Carter's grand granite house—guarded by lions, heads on paws, which made them more amiable than threatening—possessed a library, which Asher very quickly discovered. When the dessert course arrived, though little boys were expected to bend toward it like sunflowers to light—so said Mrs. Harry Carter, looking anxious—he was missing.

Chaya feared he was rifling the bedrooms upstairs but when she learned that one of the downstairs rooms contained thousands of volumes, she was not surprised to discover him lost in a cavernous brown leather chair, book against bent knees. He was immersed in the verses of Pliny the Younger. "Next week," he said, "when I read at one of these. I'll give them this. 'The living voice is that which sways the soul.' Isn't that nice? But—Chai, what does that mean, *sway*? How can the soul sway?" He moved his shoulders as if they were being stirred by the wind.

Chaya imagined the pious ones back at the farm, bobbing as they prayed.

She held him firmly by one undulating shoulder. "Do you have any-thing in your pocket?"

He scoured her face. It was neutral, which he took for approval she would not put into words.

"Thucydides." *Thusi-dides*, he said, but she did not have a better idea. It was a small green gold-tooled volume, ringed with fleurs-de-lis, so soft to the touch that, when he handed it to her, smiling with the avidity of a victor at an auction, she found its covers to have the exact texture of a fresh leaf of tobacco.

"He won't miss it." Asher said triumphantly. "I'll show you." He stood on his toes, reached up to a wide shelf of someone called Wilkie Collins, and pulled down a book. "The whole *room* is like this." He held the book upside down by its covers and Chaya saw what so disgusted him: how, hanging down, the uncut pages buckled and made little tents on which the letters seemed to crawl like ants.

"He ought to give one of his help a sharp knife and a month's leave from kitchen duty," Chaya said, laughing.

"He needs to hire me," Asher answered, and stuffed the Thucydides in his pocket, where it made a suspicious bulge no one would inspect because who knew what small boys carried—rocks, penknives, the skins of snakes they'd killed. "I could slit the whole lot of them open in a week. But what difference would it make?"

"Asher," she began, not certain where she was going. Could she really defend these vain and empty-headed children?

"Chaya, why don't these people make you mad? All you do is work and work so we can eat and they're spending their money on seeing who can load up their tables with more—trifles. That's all they do, trifles. And they pay money for me to come and make them laugh at me because I read books. Doesn't it make you sick?"

She had never heard anything so adult from Asher, so critical, so disillusioned. She thought he had loved his plate piled with ruffles of ladyfingers and whipped cream like any boy. But this was someone else emerging. She only looked at him in astonishment. When had she stopped knowing him?

17

A CRYSTAL saltcellar. A jeweled bird that cast light all about. A diamond clip, shaped like a butterfly, that somehow—he was exceedingly fast, his fingers adept as a set of pincers—he removed from a deaf old woman's hair, untangled and released without a single suspicious tug. Asher called them souvenirs, the small gifts he gave himself and—oh, may she not put on her police face!—gave to Chaya. More, even, than shopkeepers, these people deserved the losses. It was a matter of balancing the forces of the world.

At first he kept them in a corner of Mrs. Gottlieb's parlor, in an empty milk box on which she had placed a hopeful green plant he and Chaya had kept alive, had watered in her name, through the worst of winter. Later they would become his calling card, his candy. But not quite yet.

NOW. IN the morning, before Asher set out, he would line up his catch, beautiful, beautiful, on the kitchen table, meticulously spaced on the worn cloth: Faded-gold pocket watch initialed TBW in a bower incised by a steady hand, delicately removed from the bedside table of a man whose initials were not TBW. Many-hinged bracelet of square-cut sapphires with a defective catch that fell so easily into his hand, late-season apple from a branch. Evening bag beaded with pearls, cool and intricate beneath his stroking finger—pure frivol. Quill-and-bone pen of possible historic interest, though it was doubtful any pawnbroker would be impressed.

If there was ever a profession devoted to the moment and eager to be unimpressed, it was pawn. He had heard about these shops from an older boy who also ran the alleys, who said it was magic how they changed objects into cash—there was a whole row of them on Wabash behind flashy windows full of shine, above them three balls floating like bubbles, but solid.

"You come in here, you can be any kind of pirate you want to be," his first pawn man told Asher, a huge fellow with basset eyes and a terrier's mouth-obliterating mustache who made spark-quick decisions about the value of anything Asher put down before him. Was he guessing or was there a book you could learn that from? The man didn't seem to think it odd that he had to lean over the counter even to see the boy. "You can con people to get their stuff. You can steal your grandmother's silver, or get it nice, in her will. You can bring me a .22 or turn in your wedding ring." Asher laughed. His .22, his wedding ring! "This profession, we can't afford to be curious about it. Don't matter where it comes from, don't matter why you need the cash money." Asher had dropped a small rainbow of pilfered jewelry on the counter. The man fingered it lightly; maybe it was telling him something, the feel of it, its weight speaking out numbers. "You never look in nobody's eyes, follow me? Last thing you need behind this counter is sympathy." He made a mock-sour face and shook off the idea with a twitch of his shoulder. "Sympathy." He made a little sound of disgust and held one of the bracelets to the light. "Fiver for the lot."

Sympathy was the word that did it. Asher listened to the man's contempt. Probably only last-gasp people came in here, like Christians going to a church when they needed something from God. Why should the pawn man make that seem like a sickness? The word opened wide and took Asher in: He had an idea—new, a light breaking, a sunrise, his spark-quick decision—about how to take the sympathy that brimmed over in him unashamed and do something solid with it.

MONDAY MORNING, the day after a performance, stomach full of pheasant and praline—served in the kitchen, but served, at least—he shoveled the weekend's take off the table and into his lumpy bag.

Up Liberty Street, around the corner to Maxwell, six blocks east, seven north. The bright-white clock tower of the Dearborn Street depot had four faces. He passed, too often, a frozen dray horse collapsed into a pile like a boulder, free, at least, of the flies that would veil it in summer—if a horse died in hot weather with its feedbag on, the sound of squealing meant rats at the ready—until he was speeding up the wide steps of City Hall. This was his favorite place, better than the Pacific Garden Mission, far more pleasant than the rear door of the Harrison Street Police Station, where he was in danger of being discovered and hauled in himself. The building, a whole block of it, was a hulk, pillared halfway up its façade, dignified and ugly. The doors were too heavy, like safes. They were worse than that school, barred with lead, unwelcoming. He struggled. But then came a blast of warm air and, cold-strafed, he breathed it in. Gratitude, gratitude! He was poor but he was nimble.

And the endless dark river of men—mostly men, rumpled and redolent—found it worth their while to rise if they were still lying down, and flock, hope-struck, around him. On punishing winter nights, by the hundreds, in vests, in shirtsleeves, cheeks striped from sleep on a hard surface, they lay, sat, stood, unacknowledged, unofficial guests of the city of Chicago.

A few were dark-skinned. Some spoke languages Asher heard only as music. The first time he saw them he laughed out loud—it was like a parade! They milled, they shifted from foot to foot, sometimes amiably, sometimes irritably; they started fights like small fires that were doused as quickly as they had begun. Most—nearly all—wanted work. A very few, he supposed, were too lazy or too particular or too starved for strength. Desperation bound them and separated them, both. Their shoes gaped, their collars were rubbed raw by the filth of their necks. The pockets of their dusty, shiny-elbowed jackets and shapeless, outworn trousers were empty.

And their stomachs empty too—no pheasant, no praline—because, though the colossal building was hospitable, with its speckled granite floor and its intricate wrought-iron gates, it was so only up to a point. It sheltered them and asked nothing in return except that they not go foraging on the upper levels where official matters took place—there were no soup lines, no dippers of water. "Not enough water in the goddamned stinking river for these poor wretches," Asher had heard one of the clerks say to another early one morning as they shouldered their way through a clot of sleepers. *Wretches, riches,* not a second of silence between.

When he told Chaya how City Hall was being opened as a shelter, she pulled Asher onto her lap and instructed him in her doubts: What if these men, starving, freezing, despairing, rioted instead? What if they set fires, if they stormed the granite havens on Prairie Avenue, on Grand Boulevard and Ashland, and took their vengeance? Chicago had had its fire, thank you. It had had its Haymarket. Its jails were full of the bitter dregs of reprisal and refusal. Far safer to be kind, she told him. "Do you see that, Asher? Do you see?" Magnanimity was a better protector of property, someone had decided, than force; thus the dormitory of the lost.

"Not sympathy?" Asher asked. That softness the pawn man mocked.

"Hardly," his sister answered drily. "They're trying to keep things peaceful."

All the more reason Asher walked among them, trying hard not to breathe their rankness. "Here!"—the green-stoned bracelet. "Look!"—the pocket watch, the pen, and for one crone huddled away from the men in a gray horse blanket, back slumped against a wall under portraits of the city council, the evening bag whose beads clicked like an abacus when she pressed it to her cheek.

He distributed the bounty randomly, with an open hand. "Pawn it. Trade it for supper," he suggested to a man so thin and lined he was like a twig torn from a tree branch. Who would hire him for a day's work? He was a consumptive German named Johannes, a man who had worked until the work ran out, who would take it to his favorite pawn and buy his dwindling way to a month of dinners and a new suit in which he would likely be buried, and soon. "Get yourself some shoes that hide your toes." Once or twice when someone asked furtively where he had gotten this booty he understood why the pawnbroker kept silent. But mostly, they closed their hands around what they chose to see as a gift, a lottery hit, a heavenly reward. They said thank you, made gracious by good fortune.

"Stay safe," murmured a man with leprous fingers who tried to keep them hidden in his pocket. "Have *you* eaten today?"

"I don't need much," Asher said truthfully. "I have to stay small to get into tight corners. Maybe I'll be a jockey when I'm older."

There was almost a gaiety in it. There was surely a sense of power. *Older*, not *bolder*. His mentor was Robin Hood, whom Asher had met in a book he could not allow himself to steal from the shop whose owner, friendly and inviting, did not deserve to be robbed. (Sympathy extended in many directions. Burglary was an exacting business.) Praying it wouldn't be sold, he visited *The Adventures of Robin Hood and His Merry Men* until he had memorized the best parts.

And in the soot-dimmed glow of the lamp on the table, he took instruction in the sad facts: Some people were fat as dog ticks while others sickened and starved; some people slept secure under a lofty quilt while others shivered in lake wind and tried to protect their ears, those tender blossoms, from being eaten by frost. It was all too simple. "None of it is fair," he told his sister, who squeezed him slightly too hard with satisfaction. "You think so too?"

"I do."

"It all needs rearranging."

"True. Do what you can, Ash. Just stay safe."

"Stay safe, play safe. Stray safe."

"It isn't funny."

"Who called it funny?"

"My little echo," she said and closed her very tired eyes. "My dream. My perfect mirror."

MRS. SLANSKY, two floors down, had been housing her daughter Manya in the late months of her pregnancy. Manya's husband, whose permanent occupation seemed to be unemployment, had beaten her one time too often. He had become a drunk by what Chaya, lawyerlike, called *entrapment*: by frequenting the saloons that cleverly provided free lunch with their beer, their whiskey—by learning to like their true product until a bargain had become a thirst. Manya was a narrow-shouldered, huge-eyed, terrified-looking thing to whom Chaya wished she could give lessons in self-defense. But her scrawny body was bulbous now with her fifth child—the others raged through the tiny, dark apartment like penned horses—and if she needed instruction, it was in surviving her labor, not practicing fisticuffs at the hands of an unmarried girl who knew nothing about the tides of marital strife and forgiveness.

Chaya-Libbe woke Asher just before dawn to tell him she was running up to Maxwell Street to get the midwife and would not see him until tonight. His plan for the day was to inject himself into the crush of soft bodies at Marshall Fields's or the Boston Store or perhaps wander through the Palmer House, attentive to possibilities.

It was not so strange to see boys out of school in the year 1893. Shins cracking like icicles in the cold, vagabonds of all ages rattled loose around the city; a whole population slept under bridges, in hallways. They were orphans, they were remnants of homeless families that could not manage to stay together; they were odd lots and broken sizes whose circumstances had failed them and forced them into ingenuity.

So many were employed—self-employed—as runners and couriers and carriers that Asher did not attract much attention. And by now he knew that no matter the decrepitude of his clothing he never looked like a ruffian. He looked like people's sons and grandsons, or the sons and grandsons they dreamed of. When he volunteered among the most burdened and the least able-looking shoppers and travelers, he earned their gratitude along with their nickels for maneuvering their packages for them, tucking them into cabs, walking beside them as they loitered at the counters, holding their purchases, smiling without cease.

Then, creeping them along, crawling them patiently, he managed to insinuate his small boy's fingers into their newly bought goods and remove the smallest items while they were engaged with yet another salesperson. Jewelry, unobtrusive, was best. He would withdraw a pair of gloves (not to be bartered; to be worn) or an ivory comb, a pigskin wallet. The only useless object he had ever lifted was one of those foolish money clips. To give that to one of the men at the mission or at City Hall would be to mock him, unless the man had a bitter sense of humor.

It was at the Palmer House that he got pinched, caught in his tracks
not for stealing but for poaching on the territory of the bellmen, who had
seen him too often and resented his pocketing their gratuities. They had
run him off before; like bad weather, he returned, the little worm with
the quick legs and the pretty face. This morning, hefting the packages of
a dowager home early from spreading her largesse around town, he looked
ready for the picking. He could see nothing around his armload, beneath
which he had to cant backward for balance.

A policeman was alerted by a small, pencil-mustachioed young man in
a red organ-grinder's-monkey jacket and a matching pillbox. Asher was
facing the bank of elevators, holding the old lady's shopping bags with
his back to the lobby. With a shout of warning, something approximating
See here!, he was seized by dark blue arms, searched—flush this day with
a wristwatch studded with diamond chips, a black silk scarf dripping with
fringe, a mink collar glistening with improbable health, given how long the
animal had been dead—and then ungently thrust into a police van to mild
applause from the lobby. The bellman who had called in the constabulary
rushed to assist the dowager, whose packages had tumbled unceremoniously around her feet when that sweet little boy was taken. Such rudeness!
Her eyesight was insufficient for her to have seen what was sequestered in
the child's pockets. She shook her head under its befruited hat. The speed
of events in Chicago was exhausting. Indianapolis was much less upsetting.
She could not wait to check out and go home.

IN THE van, Asher was caught between the desire to charm, which rarely
failed him but did not seem promising just now, and terror at what awaited
him at the stationhouse. Miraculously, he had never before been arrested:
He had been frightened away, had hidden and been hidden, had been
warned, but had never yet been trapped and captured. Hanging around
the pawns, he had heard some formidable characters explain that they had
begun as innocent perpetrators of misdemeanors—clipping bananas off
pushcarts, tussling with the wrong gang—and were now the felons he saw
before him, whom he could (or could not) judge for himself.

"Can you find my sister?" He could barely speak loudly enough to be heard above the clatter of the horses' hooves against the stone blocks of Wabash Avenue. "I have to talk to my sister!" It would not help him to explain that he stole only to give it all away—no one would believe that. What, he begged of himself, panicked, would Robin Hood have done, separated from his Merry Men? Robin had been caught once in a church, betrayed just as he had been, though by a monk, not a monkey—a smile to himself in spite of all. But his band had found and rescued him and put the monk to death most unprettily. How would Chaya find him? His face seemed to erupt in tears; they did not flow from his eyes so much as seep through his skin, everywhere at once. How long would it take for her even to know he was missing? He let himself be a little boy—why not?—and, hemmed in by the walls of the police van which let in a trickle of light only at the top, through mesh, he cried and cried until he had a fierce case of hiccups.

The old policeman riding with him said without menace, "Take a deep breath and hold it as long as you can." When a gigantic hiccup broke through anyway, with a sound like a snapping whip, both of them laughed. "When we get where we're going," the constable said in his brogue, his dewlaps, like a beagle's, quivering with amusement, "we'll get you some water and you can drink it upside down."

"Upside down?" Asher saw himself suspended by his heels, the rest of his larcenous treasure falling from his pockets: small coins, a miniature clock he was saving for himself, two keys to who-knew-what.

"Not to worry, kiddo. I'll show you. It's crazy but it works."

BY THE time the police wagon had got to Harrison Street (Asher was frustrated; he liked to count every turn, keep track of every street crossed, and he could see nothing from where he sat), he had concluded a sweet little deal with the old policeman: everything in his bag and pockets in return for which, a block before Harrison, the wagon pulled over to the curb at Van Buren and, while the guard conducted a conversation about a wobbly wheel with the driver, whose horses lazily turned their heads to watch, he slipped as sinuously as a mink out the rear door, which was unlocked, though not exactly open. Asher still had his bag for another day, empty now, but not for long.

18

ASHER DID not spend every Sunday in the precincts of the privileged, and on those liberated days, Chaya found herself a great deal more alert than she had been before Gregory Stillman insisted his way, so quietly yet so authoritatively, into her sight.

Those Sundays had continued to be the only time, morning and evening, when she was not at work. When she came upon herself in a mirror larger and less murky than Mrs. Gottlieb's, she saw a figure shrinking like an apple too long in the larder and a face gone gray with fatigue. Complaint was a luxury, she understood, but that did not relieve her, it only burdened her with the need to be grateful, and gratitude should not be a duty.

But she was not alone: Hopelessness had begun to spread its stain from one coast to the other; there were rumors of marches of the unemployed in New York, of frozen corpses discovered in every northern city, of robberies increasing and prostitution burgeoning as the sole means of securing a solid room and a warm bed. Had life on the farm been worse or better? She had lost her compass and could not say.

Meanwhile, shrunken or not, she was being wooed.

Later it seemed absurd—then, it did not—that she thought she could and should make their atrocious rooms look sufficiently appetizing to invite Gregory across the threshold.

There was nothing she could do about the regrettable shade of green of their walls—the kind of green that punishes public places, only scuffed and chipped, with an old layer of pink wallpaper unscrolling like parchment here and there—but she whirled around in the half-light before work, trying her best. Since Chaya had never seen Gregory's lodgings, she was, for better or worse, not as embarrassed as she should have been. Of course she assumed he lived in the manner of Asher's hosts: in warm, glowing rooms adorned with objects that demanded (and received) careful dusting, keepsakes fetched back from journeys abroad—wooden elephants, jeweled birds, paisleys for his tables—sets of books in glassed cases, a bed on which a duvet covered lace-tipped bedclothes, an armoire in which hung his lovely, unostentatious tweeds. But she had never seen all that, and so his life remained a stage-set in her mind, unspecific because glimpsed from the last row of the farthest balcony, while hers was all she had and, by main force, she compelled herself not to be so ashamed of it that she could not invite him to visit her there.

When, trying to keep a quaver from her voice, she asked if he would visit her at home, he cast her a look so boyishly pleased she was almost embarrassed for him. It was exhausting to suppress so much curiosity—so much desire—so as not to seem self-indulgent. And now Gregory was nearly on his way. She spent more than she should have for clarion-red tulips—tulips in March!—to place in the middle of the blue cloth, laundered to the thinnest veil, that covered the table. She dusted, futilely, in every corner, and took ammonia to the windows, whose grit clung to their other side, forever immovable; she spread soapsuds on the paint-peeled moldings and left them grayer than they had been.

But on the evening when she expected Gregory's first visit, she forced herself to stop trying to improve what was not improvable and sit, breathing slowly, simply waiting. She heard him climbing their dark stairs, slowing as he came. When she opened the door to his knock he was breathing as hard as a racer. Slim and athletic though he was, the first thing Gregory said, trying not to look burdened, was, "If exercise is a healthy enterprise, my dear, I think you shall live to at least a hundred and ten!" He held out to her, with a melting gaze, a bunch of blue delphiniums that she imagined poking out of the snow like a dozen flags of some unknown country. It was not meant to be a contest, she knew, but her red blossoms paled beside them.

She watched as her poor rooms registered on him and thought she saw him decide to meet the challenge with more good cheer than it deserved. Was this the sign of a sweet and generous man or an unlikely striver attempting sympathy after a pain that could hardly be shared? She watched his eyes light on whatever they could discover on which to lay a compliment or about which to invent a question: Mrs. Gottlieb's portrait, a bit of lace that she had brought from her first home, the modest green plant Asher and Chaya had nurtured for her. She could see how hard he was trying, sure he had come prepared, no matter what he found, to seem at ease.

Mrs. Gottlieb was keeping herself busy in the other room out of courtesy and because, truly, there was so little space. Asher stared at them with an unreadable look. But they were not a page of text, were not numbers on a map—surely they were giving off fumes of longing, with which he was unfamiliar.

Gregory took her, then, to sit with him in a lovely tearoom, across a tiny round marble table. She had decided to be honest about her misgivings. "Could you have imagined how poorly my brother and I are faring? Tell me honestly, if you can."

He paused to ask her what kind of tea she preferred, but she hadn't a clue as to the difference between Assam and Darjeeling. Wasn't tea simply tea? He smiled patiently and ordered for her "Am I surprised?" He had a most winning frown when he was put to thinking hard that made him seem more worried than perplexed. Gregory was clean-shaven; she told herself the skin of his cheeks looked pampered and then she told herself that was not fair. "It isn't that I have never been in rooms like yours, you know."

Chaya looked skeptical. No one in that tea and confectionary shop, she imagined, retired to a dim fourth-floor flat and went to sleep on a train made of wooden chairs. Self-pity made it difficult to appreciate how hard Gregory was trying.

"I am writing a book, Chaya," he said, a declaration that seemed to make him sit up straighter, just as the smell of her exotic tea was rising in her cup. "You must know this if you wish to know me. It is a secret from my family—you'd think it a memoir of my life of crime!" At that, he grew

suddenly merry. Had she as generous a spirit as his, she would have considered what kind of difficult soil he had sprung from, what kind of cost
accrued to such a labor. But truly, helplessly, she was occupied only with
herself. "I dare to call it a work of *prophesy* and, when you see it, I hope
you shall agree." Such an ambition from so modest a man! Did he expect
congratulations? She stared back at him, her face clean of expression.

"It is a consideration of poverty as the necessary outcome of capitalism,
not the incidental. I sit daily in the Newberry Library searching out my
proofs, of which there have been many, even before Herr Marx told us so. I
would rather say it is in the spirit of Tolstoy." He stopped for a breath, his face
pink with conviction, and Chaya thought how her father would adore him.
"But, you see, I am also out and about in rooms *precisely* like yours—they are
my evidence—and so you would have to be living in far worse circumstances
for me to be shocked." Slowly, inhaling with pleasure, he sugared his tea.
"Dismayed for you, dear, but not so astonished as you may fear."

She considered this. "Gregory, I do not want to seal myself off from
everyone more fortunate but—" She tried to read his expression but it
yielded nothing. "I would like to be"—it felt foolish to say this—"to be
happy. But, please understand, I do not have the time!" She looked away
and fixed her eyes on the gauzy white curtains at the windows. Sweet, they
were. Modest. "Not the time and not the light."

Gregory only smiled at what had cost her pain to say. "Then can't we
meet as equal seekers? Can't we try to separate what is temperament
from—what would you call it? Circumstance?"

"You were born to optimism, dear friend. You must not let me infect
you with my confusions."

He would not erase his smile. "But when I met you, Chaya, do you
remember? At the train station? You and Asher were here, you told me,
to make your fortune. Have you so totally abandoned your confidence?"

She had to close her eyes to remember. "I was so innocent, Gregory. I
was so trusting that we would have a life. That we could *make* a life. You
ride with me from Winkler's to Yanowitz's. Would you not abandon your
optimism if you came upstairs to see us at work? I swear my fingers by now
are permanently shaped to hold my cigar knife." She thought for a minute.

"On the farm there was a tree at the edge of the field that was battered by the wind until it was bent over and could never straighten itself. If you can imagine it—I hope I won't offend you—I feel like that tree."

Gregory did not answer. Instead he ordered a square of cake, more shades of chocolate than Chaya thought possible, under a thick lace of whipped cream. She tried not to swoon at the pleasure it gave her with her first forkful. She tried and, with a long sweet sigh of submission, she failed.

AFTER THAT, Gregory began to come bearing gifts: a purse so pretty— beaded with little jet pellets like grains of black rice—that she could not imagine endangering it with use. A shawl of the most intricate lace, the light blue of babies' layettes, more fragile than that whipped cream. She laughed each time he brought her one of these baubles because, highly destructible and costly, they were so impractical when what she needed (though hardly expected him to provide) were shoes and sturdy undergar- ments. "Do you expect me to wear this to my work?" she asked when he put in her hands a belt held together by a fastener shaped like a golden heart. "Are you mocking me and the life I lead?" She did not like to be ungrateful but she found herself on the edge of anger.

"How could I mock you?" His earnestness! "Your life is genuine. Mine is a shadow, to which I am trying to give substance." He laughed and whispered, so close to her ear that her short hairs quivered. "The real truth is that your anger is heroic. These little gifts are only sweetmeats. Don't you think you deserve a spot of sugar now and then? I know you do. You have said as much." She felt his breath against her neck, moist and utterly soundless. "I am trying to remind you that there are also other lives to be led."

"Sugar. Hmm." She cinched the belt around her narrow waist. "And how am I supposed to attain those?" She was forced to ask this, though she had begun to realize what was happening, and to be helpless against it. He was going to fatten her on sweetmeats, one by one.

Gregory, she had discovered, was truly his family's odd man out. He had trained in the law but refused to practice it. His father and his brother, Ned, were "with" a bank and "in" manufacturing, he told her, those prep- ositions peculiarly vague, as if there were something nefarious to hide about such connections. Clearly there was, but only to someone to whom great financial success at the expense of the less successful—the only way it could happen, he assured her—was shameful. One of his uncles was a much-respected priest at an uptown Episcopal church; another was chaplain at Yale University, a name familiar to her only distantly. She did not know what she did not know, and *knew* it—how could anyone even measure what was not there? It would take the rest of her life—if she was lucky—to discover how little she knew.

The first time Gregory kissed Chaya, it was just beside her ear, a gentle, oblique touching of his lips to the skin that astounded her by what it taught her of the connection between the distant outposts of her body, which had never before reported their existence. She had not realized she was *electric*.

They were standing in the utter darkness outside Mrs. Gottlieb's door, where the gaslight illuminated nothing. It was silent inside. Her landlady would be asleep. Her brother would likely be reading at the table, in the shade of whichever flowers Gregory had brought that evening. But even if Asher had heard them and sat staring at the rustling they made, her coat pressed against Gregory's luscious cape, snowy boots against the floor, he could not see them through the door, where Gregory had pulled her to him to pursue his instruction in the way sympathy—or was it concern? curiosity?—can turn, all of them turn, to body. She could feel her blood cresting through places he was nowhere near touching, and her nipples had not been so awake since they were new. If he hadn't pressed her against something—the wall? the door?—she was sure she'd have fallen.

She had never felt anyone's lips against hers, had never imagined how they could be both soft and hard, urgent, and that hers would open and want to take in—how disgusting this would have been if she'd thought about it ahead of time—a tongue. But—innocence had its virtues—she had not.

How, she asked herself when, finally, Gregory kissed her fingertips and tiptoed down the creaky stairs and she lay herself down on her train of chairs, could she have lived so long and known so little.

———

"WE ARE going," Gregory announced to Chaya one Sunday in April, "to meet someone you will find exceedingly interesting."

"May I bring Asher, then?" She hated the abjectness of needing to ask. Between the things she did not know and the things she was afraid to do, she sometimes felt like a child herself.

But Gregory was wonderfully natural with her brother; he simply treated him as the adult he seemed, irregularly, to be. "Would you like to come for a ride and a visit with us?" he asked in his ordinary voice, bending his head down—he was very tall—but not stooping as if Asher were a domestic pet. Chaya respected him for the respect he showed by troubling to ask what was self-evident.

Asher, grinning, jammed on his cap.

They sat behind the horses' heads, feeling the sweetness of the breeze which she thought they had rightly earned for bearing months of murderous winds. The horses did not have very far to go—around a corner or two and then up Halsted well less than a mile. They stopped before the most dilapidated shack, slathered with signs for a circus that appeared to be on its way to town, and, irregularly lettered, GROCERY and FRUITS in the window, a distinctly unpromising offer. An empty cart stood before the door, hunched to one side where a wheel was missing. "Gregory?" Chaya ventured, confused.

"No, Chaya look on the opposite side!" He had a way of leaning closer to her when he laughed, which was more unsettling than she was sure he imagined.

Across from the weary shack was a brick house, quite clean, with white posts like minor pillars, and a pretty cupola. It was by far the most elegant house, as far as she could tell, for miles around. "This," Gregory announced with a kind of intimate pride, "is called Hull-House. I want you to meet its proprietor." He swung them down from the carriage. "There are a host of reasons for you to meet Miss Addams, but chiefly, she will be an inoculant before you meet my parents."

Again Chaya felt herself borne along on a tide stronger than she was. She had the sense that she was being conveyed out of her life—a life she despised but knew—into another that she dared not try to imagine, nor was certain she deserved.

Given such a lurch of surprise, it was a wonder she could say her name when she was greeted at the door by Miss Jane Addams, who did not yet have the entourage she would gather in time. She was, for a while longer, simply herself, young, hungry, and unassuming.

"Ah, Gregory!" She took his hand into both of hers. "You are as good as your word. You have brought your young lady."

Chaya had been spoken of. She had been promised. Her knees sagged against each other with fearful confusion.

As the morning wore on, she began to realize that she was not expected to have heard of Miss Addams or of her "settlement house," since she was quite new to it, and was only at the beginning of her influence in this neighborhood, which was more or less Chaya's own. The parlor was warm and comfortably furnished, dark in spite of its long windows, its wooden moldings insistent, its carpets intricately flowered. In its later years it would be teeming and hugely significant. They were, as it turned out, seeing a glorious adult in its infancy.

Miss Addams was a small, light-eyed woman, her plain brown hair wisped into a bun that leaked ringlets, and she held her head slightly to one side, as if she were constantly on the verge of making an inquiry, and—how unlikely!—coyly. She also had the most penetrating concentration Chaya had ever been party to; everyone she knew then seemed permanently distracted, the consequence of too many tasks in too short a day. But Miss Addams—who was busier than most but deeply, richly calm—did not ever trade one object of her concentration for another. When she was attending to you she was perhaps more fully present than you were yourself.

She catechized Chaya—"That is Chaya or Chaya-Libbe? Which do you prefer?"—though gently and sympathetically, about her work: what it consisted of and what it demanded of her soul. "Do you know," she said, pouring out amber tea and passing it to her, "you have at least one day of the week when you ought to come over here and meet with a group—to sing or to take part in a play. Or you could learn pottery, or cook! We have a lovely kitchen."

"You have the spirit of a saleswoman."

"Except that you may leave your purse at home!" Miss Addams answered rather gaily for someone as earnest as she. Though she was quite young—Chaya, not experienced at guessing such things, imagined she was not much over thirty—she had the air of an aunt about her, a perpetual nurturer who made others both subject and object, while she, committed to movement, was not a proper noun so much as a verb. "Here, do have some of this." She held out a plate of eggy pastry to Asher, who was sitting with uncharacteristic patience. "This is Christopsomo, a bread one of our Greek friends brought to us for Easter." He took a piece, leaving a trail of crumbs sufficient for Hansel and Gretel to follow home, while he wandered off to count the rooms; for all she knew, and prayed he would refrain, to count the silver. "Do you have books?" he came back to ask his hostess bluntly, with a frown of doubt between his eyes. There were a few volumes piled on a desk but Asher was too voracious for those to impress him.

"Do you read yet, dear?"

Gregory, who had sat patiently to the side while his friend and Chaya investigated one another, winked at her. "This is a boy to reckon with. This boy is ready to join the faculty of the new university. We must tell Dr. Harper about him."

Miss Addams laughed, but Asher met Gregory's compliment and her amusement stonily. "What university is that?"

"There is a new institution being built to the south, called the University of Chicago. But, dear—"

He raised one sweet, sharply etched eyebrow, unintimidated.

She was looking him over with great interest. "Have you begun yet at your primary school?"

Asher returned an exaggeratedly long sigh that betrayed the wishful arrogance of uncivilized genius. "I may not bother with that at all. Chaya took me, but we may just not—"

"Asher!" Perhaps she was too abject before this stranger, but Chaya felt she had to defend her own intentions. "What do you have in mind for yourself? Have you lost count of your age?"

He only glared at her, betrayed, but did not answer.

Miss Addams, turning from her brother's impudence, recited for them such a menu of Hull-House's activities that Chaya was exhausted simply hearing them named. "And all this is without cost?"

"Without cost to you, Chaya." She had a bit of trouble with the guttural in the name—such a pure, country Illinoisan, she was—but Chaya was quite accustomed to that. "We are supported by generous patrons who—"

"My family, for example, launders its money here until it is immaculate," Gregory interrupted, with a bitter edge she hadn't heard before. "On the one hand, they think I'm mad for giving it my time and effort, but they have followed their friends in unburdening some of their guilt by contributing to keep Miss Addams's charges out of their neighborhoods."

"Gregory." Miss Addams shook her head as if he had proved yet again that he was incorrigible.

"No, truly. You know their motives are mixed when it comes to their generosity. It's cash on the barrelhead that buys them their virtue."

She gave him a mischievous look. "I cannot choose to inquire too deeply into their motives. But they *could* give their money to less worthy causes, you know—or to the racetrack. Or keep it to themselves, for that matter. Credit where it's due."

Gregory gazed back at her tolerantly. "All of us trim our desire for purity, don't we. All of us use each other, for better or worse."

Miss Addams returned her cup to her saucer, still unfazed. "I didn't realize you were quite so cynical," she said with an inflection that put him securely in the corner, and turned to Chaya. "You must be sure to take some of this cake home for Asher. And you must bring yourself back as soon as you are able."

They were dismissed, so that Miss Addams could get back to her work which, Chaya began to suspect, did not allow her even this one day off: They had been an hour's work themselves but she had not hurried them by so much as a second. The only part of the visit that hovered just at the edge of disturbance concerned its purpose. Was Miss Addams on display for her sake or had she been brought to her for Gregory's as proof of his democratic commitment? Asher sat between the two of them as they wound their way back to Liberty Street, clutching a piece of the Christopsomo bread that Miss Addams's cook had neatly wrapped for him.

"Asher, would you mind leaving us here for a bit?" Gregory asked amiably when they pulled up to the house. He took off so quickly she knew he was grateful to be dismissed.

"Chaya-Libbe Shaderowsky." Gregory, having finally gotten beyond "Shadow," said the name with scrupulous care, as if he were a cat stepping into a flowerpot and out again. He leaned close and took her hands into his. "I think I love you. I really do think I love you."

He did not ask if she loved him. And she felt a little thrill shock its way through her, not of pleasure but of fear.

THAT EVENING, as he sat in the basin on the floor near the stove, while Chaya was sponging his back, Asher said soberly, "That was a nice lady, the one who gave us cake."

"She is, yes. An important one, too."

"What makes somebody important?"

She had to think a long moment before she tried to answer. "I—she tries to make people's lives better. She does everything she can to help."

He nodded and wriggled a bit under her hands. "Dry my back. What kind of everything?"

"People who are poor need so many things, Ash. You know that." Apparently he didn't think himself one of them. "They need food and a house to live in and they need work to do so that they can take care of themselves."

"I'd like to be important like that some day. Poor people should steal everything extra that rich people have. That's what Robin Hood did." He jabbed with his index finger as if it were a gun. "That's what I'd do." Chaya blotted the bumpy knuckles of his back and ruffled his dark wet hair that needed cutting, and felt, for the second time that day, fear like a chill run its fingers down her own spine.

———

SHE HAD not expected it: Gregory invited her to his parents' house—or, rather, issued an order cloaked as a request. She was discovering that good manners were devious. Insistence could be gentle but still command; the price of refusal was not exactly stated, but one would have to have been blind and deaf not to recognize the urgency behind the proposal.

It might have been that he simply could not comprehend what it would cost her to smile and say, "Certainly," when he put forth, as casually as he would have to a woman who had dwelled all her life in his world, "My parents are giving a dinner in honor of the organizers of the Columbian Exposition to which they would very much like to have you, Chaya. May I tell them you will join us?"

This in her parlor, with its complaining wooden floorboards and coal-stove smudges on the walls. He had never yet taken Chaya to a public restaurant, unless it was that tearoom or the rathskeller in the park where people shouted out their orders at the bar and shared rough tables chummily with strangers. Last time they were there, a lout of a young man had spilled beer on her dress and hadn't so much as apologized. She could only fancy that she was not worthy of showing among his company, which made her, then, his shameful indulgence, a cut above an immoral one, yet too déclassée for Prairie Avenue.

She was as light-headed at his invitation as she had been that winter night when her work—her life—had overwhelmed her. The room tilted, her vision was splattered with spots. Images flipped before her like the pages of those little books that mimic animation, one by one cascading down to make a moving scene: his mother's and father's faces, though she had never seen them. Or if not their faces, then a space darkened by each of them, cameo-like, filled with the sense of their intimidating presence, in full dress. Her empty closet, its pathetic dearth. Her abused, urine-yellow hands and her accent—her inferior, hissing *th*, nearly but not quite gone, her *w*'s with a tinge of a *v* in them, her collapsed vowels. Her frayed chemise, as though they might see its ragged edges. Her ignorance so deep she understood again that she did not even know what she did not know. If only she were bold enough not to care.

"I cannot, Gregory. Please!"

"Chaya, you can. You *must*." He enveloped her, always that woolen embrace. He smelled of woodsmoke and pipe smoke.

"I will only look stupid," she began. "I will—"

"But you will not." The way he held her, she could hardly breathe. "I have told them about you, that you are beautiful and good—"

"And poor as a beggar? I hope you told them that. Gray as a mouse, badly schooled, and stupid." And a Jewess, perhaps above all. How much must he hate them to want to bring an alien trailing her Yiddish accent into their house?

"Chaya."

"What would you have me do, roll a stogie for them, Gregory, to show that I can do something tolerably well? Must I spell out this impossibility for you in detail?"

He held both her hands, and tightly. "Why do you demean yourself this way? Why do you advertise what you are not? Have you ever taken stock of what you are? This is not becoming, you know. There are those who deserve your pity far more than you do. It begins to be—" He sighed, hard. "Self-indulgent."

"Not becoming," she muttered. "Becoming what?" Trying to encourage her, why did he have to make her despise herself so?

"Do you know Shakespeare's *Othello*?"

She was beyond patience by now. "Of course I do not. You are mocking me again. Where do you think I've spent the past years—at *Yale University*?"

He ignored her sarcasm. He had a habit of plunging his head like a horse bucking to remove the hair that hung like a low-hanging branch against his forehead. He did that now so that he could keep a fierce hold on her hands. "Desdemona loves Othello, who has been a great general, a brave man. She says, 'I love him for the dangers he has passed.'"

She looked at him critically.

"May I not love you precisely because you have *not* spent your years at Yale University—and yet you are the woman you are."

With great difficulty, she did not ask him to flatter her by describing that woman. Instead, she backed away and assured him she would think more about his invitation, but that he should not press her on it. She saw the surprise, which became affront, in his face. "I have been known to run away from"—she had to search for the word, which she had never had occasion to use and whose vowels she could not quite separate—"coercion," she warned him, which was not meant to sound as coquettish as she feared it did. She was remembering Fraydl's nephew and the prospect of marriage to a reptile which, if only Gregory knew it, was what had brought her to his city.

So this was the test those young women in Mrs. Humphry Ward's novels were put to. A pity she had read and not believed them so long ago.

MRS. GOTTLIEB could not fail to wonder what implausible connection Gregory and Chaya were entertaining. That evening over their soup, thin but consoling, Chaya laid out her trepidations. "He doesn't love me for myself, he loves me for everything I don't have. He hasn't known anyone who's as different from him as I am." She seemed, as she spoke, to be discovering a way to think about this. "That's as bad as loving someone for all she *does* have."

"He loves *you*, Chaya. Forget this what you have, what you don't have, what kind of *narishkayt* is that. I can see he is a tender man." At this her eyes filled: Nachman was with her, proof that a good man's memory could outlast the years.

"I worry," Chaya told her. "I wonder if the prince loved Cinderella because he plucked her out of the ashes, not in spite of it. Because she was her terrible sisters' servant while he was riding around the forests on the castle grounds and going to parties and drinking champagne and— whatever things they do at the castle. That would make a man feel much better about himself."

Whether or not Mrs. Gottlieb knew who Cinderella was Chaya couldn't tell. But her scruples were lost on the widow, who had a simple standard. "Chaya, do you want to spend the rest of your life, day and night, sorting tobacco? That's better than living over there in a big house with servants to pick up after you?" She was smiling with benign tolerance for Chaya's *narishkayt*. "I know a seamstress who said her missus wouldn't even bend down to pick up a pin. She did it and she was happy to do it because she had so much work, the most gorgeous fabrics you ever saw, making such beautiful dresses." Her landlady was at the table, for once sitting down and not busying herself all around the kitchen. She blew on her soup gently. "You'll excuse me but the truth is, he would have to be a terrible man—a man who beats his wife, or maybe he cheats on her with other women, God forbid—to make it so hard to take your little brother and your two old *schmattes* you have hanging there, and your thin old jacket that lets the cold bite through—and go let yourself learn how to be a real lady."

"And then have to be grateful forever."

Mrs. Gottlieb laughed, a sound Chaya had rarely heard. "Listen to you, Chaya, darling. So what's wrong with grateful? He gives you what to thank him for, you thank him. Is that so hard?"

She was becoming impatient with Chaya, as Chaya's mother would have been. Who else could she irritate with her hesitations?

"And then there's my *yingele!*" She sighed in Asher's direction. He was sitting across the room on one of the chairs that were Chaya's bed, holding down the pages of his dictionary with his elbows. "You can throw away this boy's life for some maybes, some principles? Darling haven't you learned yet, principles cost money? They're expensive. The ten commandments, all right—I would never turn my back on those, you know that, and nobody's asking you to steal or kill nobody. But this is a polite young man—"

"Not Jewish," Chaya reminded her slyly. "His uncle is a *priest.*"

"Where did that come from all of a sudden? Socialists don't care about that. I know what you think about the Jewish business, you're loyal but, you'll pardon me, not too loyal. Have I ever seen you in *shul?*" She smiled slyly back. "Chaya-Libbe. Why do I have to take his side when every girl in Chicago would give anything for a look from those eyes? Here is this fine fellow and he's inviting you home to meet his family. He wants to give you and your brother a future, and he isn't afraid his family should see you. What could be simpler?"

A great many things could be. She mistrusted him and she mistrusted her mistrust.

"One more thing," Mrs. Gottlieb said, pushing back from the table, getting ready to stand up. She had lost weight during her long siege but she was still a solid woman in her plaid apron. "I hope you'll forgive me for this."

"Please."

"You talk about all the things you don't have, you're coming from Liberty Street, you don't have no education, you don't this, you don't that—"

"Yes?"

"So I have to ask you, darling, and you know I don't like to hurt your feelings. But you do a good job running yourself down like your worst enemy. After such a bad advertisement on yourself—tell me, my foolish girl, who do you think you are that this wonderful man isn't good enough for you, that you should throw him away like this." She was blushing at her daring. "You asked me, I told you."

Chaya hugged her landlady tight by way of absolution and let her go to attend to the dishes. When her words came back to Chaya, as they would with alarming frequency, she heard them not as a challenge to her unwarranted conceit but in all their straightforward clarity: Who *did* she think she was? She had not the first idea how to answer.

19

SO: THIS was the time to investigate something that had been nipping at him since the day Miss Jane Addams mentioned it—there was a university growing south of the city. There would be a million books there. There would be professors who might have astounding things to say. He talked his way onto an ice wagon where he huddled beside the driver, feeling the breeze flow over him like cool water. From where they rode, he could see the lake, which was still too miraculous to believe. Way was it not called an ocean, along with the five major and—how many minor seas were there? Today, gray-brown as weathered iron, it beat angrily against the shore, but shattered like breaking glass as it fell back. What would it be like to be cast into such water? He knew the order of the English kings and the genus and species of more animals than he would see in his lifetime, he knew bits and pieces of a dozen languages, but he couldn't swim. This was an oversight he would have to repair when the weather warmed.

"IS THAT the university?" Asher asked the ice wagon driver as they neared a huge clearing.

"That's the Exposition," the man told him. "That's the big fair. Couple of months ago, you wouldn't have believed this, it was something like a swamp, all dunes and marsh and mess." He looked in all directions, where Asher saw half-finished buildings, a horizonful of men working in groups, lifting and swirling and heaving like the builders of the pyramids, uncountable. "They'll never get it up when they say, but they might just die trying."

"Oh, let me down right here!" Asher cried. "This is something to see!"

He stood in the cold and watched men dragging timbers across what remained of the snow. He watched teams of bundled workers raise giant frames of wood, fix them in place, cover them with a skin of hemp and plaster and then—much later, not all in a day—decorate them like frosting a cake. White and more white, they dazzled when the sun shone. The men hoisted statues of women as straight up-and-down as corpses, covered with what looked like stone, white, heavy, who held the roof of one building on their heads. They wore long narrow dresses that hung in soft folds, and stared ahead as if they were under a spell. Dozens of men on ladders and hoists hung angels and made fancy ruffles at the top of pillars. He knew those shapes: Doric, Ionic, Corinthian.

THE FIRST day, he tried to bring them a piece of wood that lay near him, to help, and was yelled at. Finally he was content to watch from a distance. Men swarmed, intent as ants, though not in straight lines. Every thing on earth, big and little, could be rearranged, could change shape, could become something huge and seamless. They were making the hugest buildings in the world. Maybe he would be a workman when he was bigger. This was heaven!

He snuck as close as he could before voices shouted at him again, "Boy! Move away! Go back!" This was heaven.

Later, a cold rain came down so thick it was hard to see. They worked wet, they worked dry, they called out orders to each other and lifted their feet from the soup of slimy ground onto the slick new sidewalks and, at the end of the day, only when it was full dark, some of them went inside their house across the street, a long, low, wooden building no one had bothered to paint, and warmed themselves by the stove.

He stood in the doorway. How could he not.

"Hey, look there! Is that somebody's boy? Come in out of the cold, boy. You look drownded."

No one claimed him. He was mute with respect.

"You're a little one," called out a man with water drops shining in his mustache, merry not mad. It was ice melting. "Did you come to sign up with us? 'Cause all the jobs are gone!"

They laughed and took him in. They were a good lot. Some, far from home, said they missed their sons, who were younger or older or the same age as he. They ate tough beef and potatoes, offered him beer, were surprised that he seemed to be able to read, which some of them could not do. Those who could enjoyed finding harder and harder things for him to show off—first, the newspaper, then a book called *Mechanics of Solid Frame Construction*. Someone had a Bible. He opened it anywhere and didn't hesitate, pronounced hard names like Jehoshaphat and Zerubbabel without sounding them out. "Abinadab. Zuar. Issachar and Zebulun. Zelophehad." He liked the *z*s The syllables tickled.

Reluctantly, he went home to his sister but came back in the morning, slipping, free, between legs on the horsecar, and then another and another morning. No one on that old farm could do the things these men did. Everything they built came out even. Nothing they stood up collapsed, nothing was crooked or sagging.

He was their mascot. They called him "Imp" and "Genie."

Sometimes he remembered he had come south to see the university. That could wait: Weren't universities usually very old? A few weeks, a few months older, it would still be worth the trip. This city they were building was the most exciting thing he had ever happened upon. When it opened—the men in the bunkhouse promised thousands and thousands of visitors, arriving by land and by sea from everywhere in the world—he could be Robin Hood of Chicago again, with a whole new population to devil and undo.

20

WHEN SHE heard Gregory making his way up the stairs, trepidation made Chaya so tired, so very, very tired, that she wanted only to crawl onto her bed of chairs and cover her head with her quilt.

True to his promise, he carried a very large box, which he placed with such care on the kitchen table that she thought it might be breakable. Left to her own devices, whom could she afford to patronize but the peddlers' wagons and the cheap shops along Jefferson Street, whose slick fabrics and bulging seams would give away their provenance. Without a word she loosened the tape that held it safely shut and removed the top of the box and saw that he had brought her a dress swaddled in enough paper to wrap all the fish in the market. But she refused to speak.

Poor Gregory, he would be right if he were offended. Nor did she like very much the ungrateful person his insistence was forcing her to become. He watched her in identical silence, only his fingers twitching with impatience. His eyes, the eyes she loved, burned with anger that she should consider it an indignity to accept something so beautiful from his hands.

She had begun to move in a trance impenetrable by rational thought.

And the dress was lovely, of course, a sort of purple with a reddish tinge. Finally he forced himself to speak. "I believe this is what is called magenta." He looked to Mrs. Gottlieb as if she could be of help. "I thought it would complement your complexion." *Magenta.* The word was new to Chaya, and beguiling. It sounded like a country in South

America. The fabric was a burnished shot silk, modestly high-necked and simply, girlishly, draped. It would almost fit, though without having taken her measure, the amplitude of its bosom made her smile at her suitor's wishful inattention. If she were to wear it, she would be grateful that the hem was a trifle too long so that no one would glimpse her boots, which were the only ones she had, so worn they resisted any shine. Somehow it would be too shameful to point them out to Gregory; there was something intimate about her feet, though she could not have said why. And they were one detail too many for him to notice.

Finally she managed to mumble without inflection, "Thank you, Gregory, this is very—magenta, yes. It is beautiful."

How could she blame him for looking at her with such perplexity? "One would think I had brought you the dress you would wear to the guillotine, Chaya. I see that you are no friend to my intentions, which causes me to wonder if—"

But, in a muddle of principle and desire which, like chemicals that should not be combined, threw up a fog she could not see through, she came to huddle in his arms. She looked over his shoulder whose tweed bristled against her chin, and saw those parental cameos glaring at each of them, first at her, then at him.

"My dear girl," he was saying, "I am not trying to distress you. But you seem not to have any capacity for—" Chaya could see him searching for the word, and waited with great curiosity to hear what it was she lacked. "For pleasure."

Holding the dress before her, she felt its suppleness as if it were made of woven grasses.

But weep she did when, after Gregory had gone, Asher asked her, "Chaya, why did he bring you that dress? It looks like it's for somebody—" And he stopped there and looked away.

"For somebody what?"

"Else. The kind of person we hate at the parties. You know what I mean." He looked at her with a ferocity she had not seen before.

They had watched a cook named Darlene beat her head with a serving spoon in frustration at Harry Carter's soirée when Mrs. Carter shouted that she had allowed the crème anglaise to separate but had served it anyway. Together, they had cringed and tried to send waves of sympathy across the kitchen to make certain the cook knew that they were not *them*, they were *her*. "That is not fair, Asher," she responded. "I am not your 'somebody else.' That is too simple." Her loyalties, so much like his, divided like one of Darlene's wetted knives through butter.

WITH GREAT relish, Mrs. Gottlieb tucked and prodded, and decorated her old hat into unrecognizability—a skill Chaya had not imagined for her—with scraps made into satin lilacs that flopped against each other in profusion, white and lavender, spiced with a bit of purple saved from the excesses of the dress.

"You could just as soon go naked if you don't have a gorgeous hat." Mrs. Gottlieb seemed to eat the word *gorgeous*. She smacked her lips around it.

To complete the impersonation, Chaya borrowed a perfect pair of long kid gloves that felt all too much like tobacco leaves, except that they were off-white, fastened with a pearl. Mrs. Gottlieb had worn them on her wedding day, they were half a century old, and when she tenderly unwrapped them from tissue that crumbled in her hands Chaya knew that she was being entrusted with her landlady's highest hopes.

SHE HADN'T dared tell them that, along with his presentation of the dress, Gregory had renamed her just in time for the occasion as if that, too, were a gift: "Chaya-Libbe would be"—a delicate hesitation—"a trifle hard for people to say, I think. They consider themselves sophisticated but they have had so little traffic with—"

Her heart seemed to turn over in her chest. She stared at him. "With?"

"Well, dear, for all their travels, their grand tours, I fear they would stumble over anything they consider—exotic. Off their well-worn track. So what would you think if we took the first letters—*C* and *L*—and put them together to make a thoroughly comprehensible, easy-to-say new name? Just for them. You can be Ceil. My sweetest, what do you think?" He seemed to comb her face for a response but she understood that, however sincerely he believed he was giving her a choice, only one answer would be acceptable.

What would her mother have thought, who had named her for her own mother, whom she had lost just before Chaya was born? She knew that what her mother had wanted for her was safety. Even her mistakes—oh, Shimmie!—were meant to seal her against need. Which meant that her mother would want what Mrs. Gottlieb wanted for her. Would it be worth giving up her name to have it? It was shameful but, her thoughts ragged and unkempt, she said nothing.

CHAYA AND Asher lived on a wooden street: houses, stairs, paving blocks, a turn to the left, a turn to the right, just north of where the great fire had begun only twenty years before—a neighborhood made of tinder. Not far away, probably less than a mile, all of Prairie Avenue seemed to have been quarried. It was a fortress of stone: brick, granite, sandstone, slate. She lived amidst refuse so ubiquitous it had become as natural to her as a field of blowing wheat.

The driver of their victoria, when they arrived and were dispatched two houses from the corner of Prairie and Twenty-Sixth Street, bent to pluck from the curbstone a lone scrap of paper that must have escaped some guest's purse or pocket; perhaps it was even the invitation to the evening's gala. Having retrieved it, he held it hidden from them like something shameful, balled in his gloved hand, with a look of profound distaste that bitterly amused her.

The houses were turreted and gabled, built right to the street and much too stony. There was so little green, here where they could have seeded parks right to the door if they had been inclined to! Here and there a house was wrapped with a porch, its floorboards shiny under fresh paint—those were the ones that reminded her of Wisconsin; they were not impervious citadels, not true city houses. Gregory's, fenced with pointy black iron spikes, was hewn of faceted gray stone, like a giant carved out of rock; it was not very inviting. But it glowed with lamplight that fell like gold dust from its windows.

One of the futile subjects of her lecture to herself while she dressed and pomaded her hair had been that she would not spend the evening out of sorts. She would not begrudge Gregory and his family their good fortune (though, she lectured herself, there was nothing to force her to think their house beautiful). Somewhere in Torah the rich were said to be reaping the reward for having lived virtuously—it did not stipulate how—which implied that the poor were being punished for their own shortcomings. Hideous, hideous, to be castigated by He who supposedly made you for being the way He made you.

She was not as overwhelmed by the opulence of this boulevard as she would have been had she not by now spent those peculiar Sundays when, as hired help, Asher showed off the wonders of his mind. She knew they looked to the owners of those houses like geese among swans and to the maids and butlers like swans among geese.

What, then, she had to wonder, would she be tonight with Gregory as her stalwart champion, the blunt noses of her unshineable boots poking out from behind her hem. When, inevitably, she tripped climbing the wide stone stairs, he saved her—grabbed her arm with a surprised little exclamation and righted her before she could fall. "Don't be nervous," he whispered, but she could hear the tension behind his consolation. *Why didn't you bring me shoes?* she wanted to hiss at him, knowing herself already too dependent. *If I am to be the curiosity of the evening, where are my glass slippers? Can't you see the scandalous secret I am hiding beneath my skirts?*

GREGORY'S MOTHER, whose name was Faith, was the first of the Stillmans to instruct her in the discretion that separated her class from Chaya's. She was not at all formidable, at least as far as Chaya could tell. Tall, fair, rather fragile, but with a determined—clenched—jawline, she had the apologetic posture of one of those girls who never made peace with looming above her friends. Her neck was so long she had bound it up in what looked like a yard of shirred blue taffeta, as if it were a wound. She held out to Chaya a languid hand accompanied by an equally languid smile, meant either to set her at ease or to inform her that what she thought of Chaya hardly mattered, so incidental was she to the conduct of this family. She wanted to ask Gregory if his mother was lazy or shy—or perhaps, she thought meanly, under such medication for nerves that she seemed rather to possess none. Instead she vowed to watch her as she responded to others who presumably did matter to her, and to study that jaw to see if it ever relaxed.

His father was more what she would have expected: indifferent in a way that she took to be habitual in one whose professional life must have taxed him more than his children's friendships. He had a ring of sleek white hair the texture of a short-furred dog, combed vigorously downward around a smooth bald head, and a slender nose built somewhat on the lines of Gregory's, only more aggressive, more prow-like. But he also had cheerful side-whiskers that consisted of a good deal more hair than what remained around his head. Unless she were to press, if she became his son's bride, for some unseemly item of finance that would affect the Stillman exchequer, Chaya decided she would not have a difficult time with Mr. Edward Stillman. He was otherwise occupied.

And so, having been introduced to the two of them she relaxed, though like a cat asleep, with one eye open. Gregory, who seemed younger and more deferential than she had ever seen him, looked pleased by her performance, such as it was. She suspected that his parents would hardly raise their voices were the ceiling to begin to crumble above their heads. If she were to accept Gregory's terms, she would have to learn a whole new vocabulary to speak the language of their emotions. Thinking of her own family—and they perhaps the quietest of the histrionic crew of the Fields of Zion—she could only smile imagining the wedding, if there was to be one, her father in a top hat, her mother without her apron.

But she was not finished with the introductions. She and Gregory were standing tight together at a punch bowl of alarming size—she could imagine bathing a baby in its cut-glass bottom—when Gregory turned, having handed her a glass, and said in an artificially hearty voice, "Why, Ned, there you are!" as if he had been searching for his brother without luck.

Here was one Stillman on whom, Chaya could see at half a glance, gentility imposed no inhibitions. He had his mother's height, only powerfully girded, and, above a spiny mustache, his father's nose, which looked on him like a scimitar, sharp and imposing. "I was told I could meet my brother's—ehh—"

She smiled and took his hand which—why was she not surprised?—closed upon hers with just enough force to be painful. His face was perfectly square.

"Gregory's Israelitish maiden. I have heard about you," Ned told her without confiding a single encouraging adjective.

"Have you." She tried not to assess him too openly, the way he was assessing her, head to invisible toe, curious without apology. Or worse: curious as a challenge.

"You are—" He smiled. "You have—I should enjoy hearing the tang you have brought from your native country. Which is—?"

"Pardon me?" was all she could manage. The *tang*?

"Of your native tongue. I understand it has left you with the most charming accent, of a sort we rarely encounter on our street. I wonder if I could isolate it if I were to hear it."

"Ned!" Gregory began, but she wanted no one's defense.

"Perhaps," Chaya suggested, "your circle of friends is not wide enough. And now if you will excuse me, since I am so rare, I doubt that we have anything of interest to say to each other." Exactly how had she constructed such a sentence? She had spoken like a character in a book. She placed her brimming punch cup on the table with a thud sharp enough to turn a few heads and did not back away, which would have been craven, but turned her back as sharply as she could manage, knees quivering so fiercely she was surprised she couldn't hear them clacking. It was Ned Stillman's mouth, beneath his whisk-broom of a mustache, that opened in surprise, and then Gregory was following her as she crossed the room to the hallway in search of a quiet place to compose herself.

"Your brother is a boor," she said against his chest. "If I had a better vocabulary in this language I speak with such a *tang*, I am certain I could find a more fitting word." She had never felt so powerful in her life, though she recognized that she had made an enemy she would regret. Perhaps the weight of a vigorous antagonist increased one's strength.

"I am so sorry, Chaya, so sorry. He did insult you, didn't he." He smoothed the hair she had so carefully made complicated for the evening, scattering pins everywhere. "It is never exactly what Ned says, you know, it is what he manages to *imply* … You should not have had to defend yourself against his execrable manners."

She had seen the first faint glimmering of Gregory's need to stand at a distance from his family, and it softened her, to his advantage. "Have I just witnessed an exhibition of why it is you love me?" she dared to suggest. "So that your brother can despise you for it?"

Gregory gave a harsh, one-note laugh. "He needs no fresh reasons to despise me. But I believe I can outdo him in hostility. I love you for yourself and I hate him for *him*self—my feelings are quite distinct." His face was still reddened with high feeling. "Everything you distrust only proves to me your earnestness, my darling girl, though you don't make it easy on a fellow. I can see that you try to see the bright side of so much but I wish you spent less time in—what to call it?" He looked into the middle distance. "Regret. Your dwelling place, that, as if your refusals will save the world. And then along comes something that truly is awful—if only it didn't but, you know, it will and you must see how you haven't saved anything, you have only missed out on so much."

She listened to him in silence. This was not the time to be lectured.

"And my brother most probably takes the prize for awfulness. I swear he should be kept in a cage. But you were so fierce and honest with him. I think he is not accustomed to being talked back to. I love it that you pinned his ears back!"

For his testimonial, she brought her face to his and murmured, "But how can you love a woman who doesn't make you laugh?"

He appraised her carefully to see if she was serious. His laugh, finally, was perhaps more public than it would have been had they been alone. "I suppose no one can do everything, my dear. But look, you have just proved yourself wrong!"

Chaya hoped everyone in the room could see their dark heads touching.

They stood quietly for a while, breathing hard against each other. Which, she wondered, would she prefer in the end, the openness of Ned Stillman's disrespect or the covert suspicion she was certain lay beneath his parents' apparent indifference? Look what their rebel child had dragged in from Immigrant Alley, after all. Why should they trust a woman whose hand, when they took it, was coarsened by work and—except for the lovely beaded bag she carried—dangerously empty?

THE REMAINDER of the evening she devoted to silence. Silence, when she went on strike against coercion, had preserved her at the farm. Now it would be her university; she would attend, like her schoolgirl self, conversations between those who knew more than she—which encompassed nearly all those in parlor, dining room and library, both men and women and possibly even the tall, gaunt dog who was brought in on a golden leash and walked through to the kitchen. "Bertha's borzoi," someone whispered with a tolerant smile. "She will clean the plates for Cook"—and would thus eat far better than Asher and Mrs. Gottlieb, at home tonight at their blue-checked table.

She overheard intriguing fragments—how much more would the Exposition cost than had been estimated—a great, great deal. How difficult the long winter had made its construction. How vindictive were the mayors of the cities that had vied with Chicago to be granted the Fair and lost out—the newspapers of St. Louis beat a drum tattoo of editorial sniping; a private citizen, identity unknown, of Washington, DC (which a Mr. Tollier said could not by any stretch of the imagination be called a city when all knew that it was merely a government compound), had instigated a campaign whereby the postal station which received shipments meant for exhibit was bombarded with the leaky carcasses of dead birds, opossums, every manner of small stinking corpse. A racket of a laugh went up at this story. "It takes one to send one!" declared a man with a head as bald as a darning egg, and lifted his glass in salute. "To Chicago, onward into the future!"

Chaya stood on the outskirts of a discussion of the preopening ceremony of the Exposition, which had apparently taken place downtown in the fabulous Auditorium Building last autumn—yet another milestone that had passed her by. Her stupor had been deeper than she had realized. Her friends at work, Sara, Stuka and a few others, took vicarious satisfaction at hearing stories of the doings about town that they could not aspire to attend, a satisfaction like religion, it seemed to her, in the convenience of the comfort it offered: That which you could not have, instead of making you bitter, became an ideal at which you worshipped. She was turned too fully inward to take much notice of what thrilled them: Chicago had remained, for her, the wound she licked, the missing city.

Now—so strange she could have been dreaming—she stood in the center of a room crowded with the owners of the celebrated buildings downtown, the men who faithfully went every day to work at the Board of Trade just as she went to Winkler's. Pullman, who lived just down the street, went south to his model city or north to the office from which he ruled. Marshall Field walked, for the sake of his health, to his grand new store on State Street or to the warehouse that glowered like the Great Wall of China. (Gregory had taken her past it one time, identifying the buildings up and down the avenues as though they were old family friends.) John Glessner lived in an armed fortress for fear of attack by inflamed workers. "You know about Haymarket," Gregory prodded, "the bomb, the riot. Bad luck to him, he built his house just in time to feel the fire of all that rage." It was no wonder the man, "in" hardware, employer of hundreds, was taking no chances. He looked to live in a bunker with a tiny mouse-door in front, carriages routed to the rear where they could be vetted by a guard.

The dresses of the women who stood beside Chaya, the wives of these men, cost more than her handiwork brought her in a year. (*Oh, tedious*, she told herself. This was becoming too old a refrain.) (But, sang a contrapuntal voice, woe unto her if ever she forgot it.) She could see from where she stood a silvery gown edged with some sort of fur that was also silver—what but a slaughtered shepherd dog might look like that? A *wolf*? It sprang from collar and sleeve, at neck and wrist, as vital as if it were alive. This was dazzling, but not flattering to the woman inside the pelt, whose pallid skin was less vibrant than her unique ornamentation.

Before her, a very heavy woman stood upholstered in sufficient green satin to cover a divan; no corset could be so formidable as to contain her, but she was pink cheeked as a babe and appeared quite satisfied with herself: her jowls were positively sculpted and did not shake. The table was sunk in treasure, lemon tarts, sweet aspics, a chocolate supreme around which gushed out-of-season strawberries, all the way down the room, displayed upon cream-colored lace. The spread was glorious in its abundance, restored by a watchful servant each time a dish was nearly depleted. She regarded it queasily with a combination of lust and nausea, but this woman dove in heartily and appeared almost methodically to sample everything. Chaya envied her the simplicity of her need, whose satisfaction waited silently at her beck, like prey.

While she stood asking herself too many questions, wading through a swamp of uncertainties, Gregory came quietly to her side and urged into her mouth a dainty bar of praline rimmed with coconut—she guessed it was coconut, though she had never tasted it—and delicately brushed its stiff white crumbs from her lips.

Gregory knew what she was thinking—she would grant him that: He knew. But, subversive, he bit into a mammoth strawberry painted with bitter chocolate and slid the other half into her mouth, which she found so stirring it felt like something one should not feel in public. He removed his fingers excruciatingly slowly and sucked the chocolate from them, fixing Chaya's eyes the whole time. It was ludicrous and provocative at one and the same time. He was playing with her. As if this were a game of tennis, she felt herself too callow a partner to know how to return his serve. The ungracious plodder in her wanted to object, "I know how to feed myself!" and turn away. The realist in her, more honest, knew she could not afford to. The sybarite (a word she would not have recognized) wished she could sink against this solid man's shoulder and plead for more.

"All this will go on with you or without you, Chaya, whether you approve or not."

She looked at him in full earnest, unsmiling, ungrateful, feeling her foot inching its way toward his trap.

"Oh my dear, what are we to do with you?" Gregory said and raised her fingers to his lips. "You are very hard on everyone. They expend all this effort to impress and it only turns you grim. What has become of the laughter we practiced just a few minutes ago?"

AROUND MIDNIGHT, a path seemed to part the crowd, and in strode Mrs. Bertha Palmer, whose fame had reached so far that even Chaya in her recalcitrance knew who she was. It was impossible not to feel the force of her presence, though Chaya could not tell if it was her celebrity that made a bubble around her or the magnificence of the woman herself. Truly, she had never seen such skin—she seemed iridescent; she made Chaya want to touch her cheek, which would feel—clichés tended to rise around her in a gentle tide—like a flower petal. No: Like a tobacco leaf, she amended to herself, as if her own life were given value by its usefulness as metaphor. Prime. Her hair, upon a head held very straight without stiffness, was wound higher than she could imagine hair to be capable of without courting ignominious collapse, and around her neck were wound strands and more stands of pearls, less brilliant than that skin. What kind of childhood must precede such confidence, such profound health? No wonder her husband, who had met her when she was a child—thirteen she was, a schoolgirl—no wonder he vowed to wait for her majority, and did. Chaya could not imagine a queen with more regal presence.

She had crossed a line. For better or worse, she saw as she stood a modest distance from this woman, in the lee of her faint perfume (more tart than sweet), that to choose poverty and a cold bed in the face of what Gregory held out to her would take a perverse and stubborn heart bent on self-defeat. She was halfway to being kidnapped from her class. But she had not shared Mrs. Palmer's childhood, the ponies, the peonies, the lessons in elocution and dancing, and she would not try to share her adult life. Here was a Lady Bountiful who shed good works like the aura of her toilette, but from on high.

Gregory had told her that Mrs. Palmer's house, a palace on upper Lake Shore Drive for which the shore itself had been remodeled, possessed no doorknobs on the outer side of the doors. One passed through many layers of servants, at her bidding, to find one's way in—how much geography, water the east of it, had been appropriated to please her!—to her Spanish music room, her Flemish Renaissance library, her Turkish parlor and Moorish bedroom of ebony and gold. High up on her rooftop stretched her enormous ballroom and a picture gallery that rivaled the Uffizi; clearly, had Mr. Palmer been able to work a satisfactory arrangement he would have brought down a star or two for her. And so, visitors sent their cards through a phalanx of maids and butlers and social secretaries to beg entry. Chaya imagined it a long walk to the center of her being. How many were allowed the journey? Her husband, surely? Her children? How many contraries could exist in a single soul? If only Gregory could tell her that.

A commotion was rippling through the room, at the farthest end. It seemed that Mrs. Palmer's dog, Napoleon, had gotten loose and come through the swinging kitchen door, ambled down the long butler's hall and broken into the dining room, which caused a gasp to issue forth, as if there were a fistfight or a guest overcome by apoplexy and fallen to the ground. Conversations ceased; everyone turned to look at him.

He was like the dog Chaya and Asher had glimpsed at the railway station on the day they arrived, a being suffused with the same confidence and conviction as its owner. The seal of a kingdom. Chaya had no names for dogs—this one had the sheen and color of melted chocolate lightened, perhaps, with a dash of milk, and his legs were so slender it was hard to believe they could hold him up. She had never noticed how acute a dog's face could be: Long, pointed, assessing, dismissing, he turned his head to survey the crowd, and the crowd looked back silently, challenged. Chaya found him enthralling and more than a bit frightening.

Then—how could this be?—the creature loped forward and, his aim precise as an arrow's, stopped before her and stood looking up as if she were his benefactor, whom he adored.

Chaya let escape a syllable of surprise and, invited, reached down to feel the silken swatch between the animal's ears. He met her eyes and, apparently satisfied, folded those ears intricately, to demonstrate that he was not on guard in her presence but, rather, at rest. She touched him tentatively, but the dog seemed to approve of the way her hand felt on his head and, with awesome grace—how could a dog possess such dignity?—he bent his long, attenuated legs and sat serenely at her feet, alert but perfectly still.

"See how he enjoys your touch! How absolutely lovely!" Mrs. Palmer, speaking quietly only to Chaya, lay upon her a long unsmiling gaze as if she were measuring her for a dress or—Chaya cringed—for employment. "Well, my dear, you certainly do resemble a maiden in a tapestry, feeding a deer in the forest." Chaya, more still than the dog, had ceased to breathe.

"You must know those tales in which a maid in the scullery is actually a princess in disguise? You appear to have that perfect, delicate touch. And Napoleon's judgment is unerring." Mrs. Palmer patted the dog once on its glittering head, a signal to unbend, stand and accompany her. Obedient, he did so without a backward glance. So much for adoration. She stopped for a few words here, a few more there, inclining her head with interest, vigorously nodding, but never disturbing her ornately sculpted hair. The dog trotted on before her, his nails leaving tiny dents in the carpet.

Chaya assumed she had received a compliment, but comments dropped from the heavens, she decided, become ambiguous when they enter the ordinary atmosphere. She had been anointed perhaps, but as royalty or as a servant? The woman had perceived her situation without even wondering who she was.

Somehow, for better or worse, she felt the moment seal her into the life of the room. Like a fairy godmother, she had given Chaya to her future. Across the laden table, Gregory was silently, discreetly applauding.

2 1

IT WAS all light! The Fair, blazing up beside the lake, was the closest she'd ever come to imagining a heaven.

A shock of sun ignited white temples that must dwarf any that still stood in the world. It reflected off the water that lapped their shores, off lagoons, off extravagant fountains that fractured the air around them with shards of rainbow. Bridges arced the water. A statue of dozens of striving figures with oars raised glowed golden—who had ever seen such gold! Could it be real?

Because she rose and dressed before dawn, and descended the stairs through channels of soot and coal- and oil-blackened hallways as if she were going into a mine; because she had left her work for months now after dark and felt her way up those stairs again, her pupils must have atrophied, like a broken camera fixed wide, and still without sufficient light. Even the few places where electricity attempted to hold back the dark remained laughably in shadow. At Gregory's parents' house, she had stood watching the delicate filaments of dozens of bulbs flicker under clear glass, but the light they gave, despite everything, was feeble.

These buildings—pillared, domed, adorned with goddesses, with angels, with everything but the devil himself—could not possibly be made of wood and metal, simple sheds, but that was what everyone claimed. They were to be seen, not touched. Whatever lay underneath was slathered with an ephemeral mix of nothing, stiffened a little by something, and yet it looked, from here, like marble. How could this be? The sphinx could hardly be more solid! Chaya stood rapt where they had stepped out of their carriage, shivering in spite of the heat.

Gregory had already visited the fairgrounds. All winter, thousands of the impatient had actually paid good money to irritate the workers by wading around. getting underfoot while they were slogging through mud to raise the frames of these buildings, or paint them, or hoist these sculpted ornaments. Asher had spent time here but he kept entirely to himself what he saw. "This!" Gregory breathed. "None of those skeletons promised anything like this. A sidewalk that moves! Isn't it too glorious?" The roof of the Fine Arts Building was supported on the heads of serene goddesses in tunics all in a row. Angels lighted on the red-and-gold square of the Transportation Building like butterflies. Where one arm of a building protruded this way, a balancing arm stretched in the other direction. Gigantic, all of it, and everything balanced, symmetrical, *rational*.

In six months it would be gone, or so they said. Still, the Fair was like the sky splashed with stars, humbling because those who gazed at it were so small, because they lived such trivial lives, and those lives must end. She was not used to thinking *we* about anything but wages and fair or unfair dealing, but the scale of this glowing festival awed her. It was for them to dream on, they who possessed so little.

She wished she could be alone with her astonishment. She understood her brother's silence. This was an ecstasy she refused to relinquish to discussion. Who said she could not be happy!

THEY HURRIED, finally, to the place where Gregory had promised to meet his family. From a distance Chaya could pick his mother from the crowd, her hat commandingly high above those of the other women. She gave Gregory her cheek to kiss, and nodded at Chaya with a slow enveloping gaze she was most likely not aware of. If an evaluation of her worth depended on the cut of her wardrobe, Chaya should simply wish him well and walk to the edge of the pier and leap. "I am pleased you could join us." The voice was neutral, transparent as air which must, Chaya thought, have taken monumental self-control. Then, as if in afterthought, Mrs.

Stillman took her hand, but the sentence had simply stopped—she did not attempt Chaya's name, with its uncomfortable guttural. Apparently *Ceil* had not taken hold.

Watching her, straining for sympathy, Chaya imagined that she might be seeing in Faith Stillman a shy and private woman whose social duties put her constantly on display, in need of the correct response—perhaps a woman uncomfortable with her excess height or her wan, freckled face and nearly invisible eyelashes with which she was forced to greet lovelier specimens, or with the insufficient influence she had had on her way-ward son, this defector to the sins of socialism. In another life, Gregory's mother's labor to seem comfortable might have made an ally of her. But this was not that life. Mrs. Stillman, she knew, wished Chaya were other or—far better—nonexistent but, subdued by the rigors of politesse, which protects as it dissimulates, would make no show of her disappointment.

Lallie, Gregory's sister, was twenty years old and everything her class demanded: quiet but assured, dressed in a manner that flattered while it did nothing to excite any particular curiosity—in a pink cotton today, with a ruffle at the hem quite worthy, Chaya thought, of a window in need of a summer curtain. Her strawberry blonde hair carefully disheveled around a bow that flapped like a butterfly, she showed the feminine version of Gregory's face, even-featured, large-eyed—their dark blue eyes were the color of the water on a fair day, as if it were reflected there. They had the same generous mouth and a chin that bore the light press of a finger like the fluted edge of a pie. It was a family of strong faces. She smiled at her brother's friend enigmatically. If you are going to submit every gesture to an inquisition, Chaya told herself, that is another reason to walk away and be done with this. Perhaps her smile was only a smile, without intent, enigmatic or otherwise.

"Where is Father?" Gregory was looking all around. "Did he not come with you?"

"Your father discovered someone he knew—imagine, in a crowd this size," Mrs. Stillman answered, sighing, "and I believe they have gone off together to visit the one building in which we have no interest—machinery! They say it is the largest building in the world."

"Well, that only means more room for objects in which we have no interest! But the states, Mother." Lallie. "Believe me, you have even less interest in South Dakota or West Virginia or Utah. Why do they have such things? Are we really to care who grows flax or where the Mormons practice their peculiarities?"

Her mother ignored her. "Now, I have been here before, but where would you like to begin? This is simply too overwhelming."

"I want to stay until evening, Mother, when the lights come on!" Lallie seized her mother's hands like a child. "They say it uses more electric bulbs than any city in the world!"

They walked slowly into it, then, Gregory holding Chaya's hand ostentatiously. The bridge they crossed was guarded by elks, as though real animals had been put under a spell that had turned them to stone. Turrets rose from unlikely places like the round building unromantically called Fisheries; a dozen spires pointed up from the shrine to Electricity as if it were a Spanish church multiplied; the Illinois Building, flying flags, lay beneath a dome like the capitol in Washington. Numbers rolled proudly off every tongue, as exact as they were absurd: forty thousand panes of glass here, twenty-seven tons of machinery there. An ugly black cannon so heavy Chaya couldn't imagine how the floor could support it. Bigger, faster, more elaborate, turbines chuffed, and a giant crane that had been used to build the very place where they were standing swung screaming families up and around and let them down dizzy. They saw a cheese that dwarfed the state of Wisconsin, guarded by earnest men in suits too heavy for the heat who did not seem to think their treasure absurd. Wouldn't Asher love this! He would know how many pounds of pressure each machine supplied; he would understand what torque meant, and how the telautograph worked, that sent a copy of one's handwriting a distance, wholly out of sight—she surely didn't. He had nearly choked on the excitement of his first sight of Chicago—*this* would send him into an ecstasy beyond enduring. Chaya imagined him everywhere.

They poked their heads into the Children's House, where the advertisement promised the newest methods of rearing practiced on boys and girls whose mothers had delivered them so that they could enjoy a day of rest protected from maternal distraction. Some of the boys hung from rings, upside down, like bats. Chaya inspected their small faces, imagining her brother safely among them instead of practicing petty larceny everywhere he touched down.

They must have walked ten miles—these women were intrepid. When they stopped for a meal at a restaurant shadowed by palms, Lallie tried gamely to engage Chaya in conversation—"What do you think will happen to these buildings when it rains?" and "Have you tried that molasses kind of thing, it sticks to your fingers, it's called Cracker something? With a *j*. Jacks! Do you know what that means, *Jacks*?"—but the single thing they appeared to have in common was Gregory. "Usually," Lallie said, "we are in New Hampshire by now—our house is near the Glessners, you know. They summer at the Rocks and we are at White Pines, which is no farther than you can throw a pebble. But the Fair! Mother was one of the Lady Managers, you know—with Mrs. Palmer—and so we had no choice but to visit. After all, this is her handiwork!" She did like to prattle, even to the point of breathlessness. "We were here on opening day—not that we could come close enough to see a single thing, there were so many people, and they always seemed to be in front of me! I wish I was tall like Mother."

Lallie was a sweet, enthusiastic girl, Chaya decided, whose best and worst quality was her refusal to be critical—what must that feel like?—but she was trying, generously, to bridge the distance between them.

Because Venetian pillars were less intimidating than Greek or Roman the Women's Building achieved a confectionary lightness that had been purposeful but only brought down upon it the derision of the powerful. Or so Mrs. Stillman acknowledged. "A very young woman—quite a lovely girl—won our competition to design it, but she was not well-treated in the end, and was not as well paid, I'm afraid, as the male architects. A pity. She left us in a fit of anger, which may have been deserved." She was silent a moment. "I believe she was—they say she"—Mrs. Stillman looked around as if for permission to continue—"broke down." Her cheeks had colored at this candor. "A pity, really."

"Did anyone object, on her behalf?" Chaya dared herself to ask. She kept her face equable so as not to alarm.

But Mrs. Stillman only gazed at her as if the question were too taxing to penetrate.

The young woman's delicate creation sat at the farthest end of the court, set off from the "major" buildings partly by choice and partly by default. But women loved it and, Faith Stillman swore, came and came again. "So indeed," she said, giving her head a little shake as if the unpleasantness were settled, "she should be very happy to see how successful her efforts turned out to be. I hope she knows it."

As if to prove her point, Gregory's father, who had joined them for ten minutes, hurried off again with his friend to investigate the suitably masculine: Forestry, it was, and Mines. No wonder the advertisements promised something for everyone! The party wandered through his wife's handiwork, since it was she and the other women—"A bouquet picked from all across the nation!" she called them—who had planned it. (A bouquet?! But she appeared to be in earnest.) "The battles! The vituperation and scandal-mongering! Should we compete with the boys and their toys, or did we want our own domain, where some gentility might be honored? We were not always ladies, I'm afraid, pleading our case with the men. But neither were they gentlemen." Mrs. Stillman reflected a moment. "Or with each other, for that matter." Long and light, with an airy feel, the building housed an assemblage of every kind of lace and quilt and picture made of unlikely objects—a bust composed of thimbles! A cradle made like a mosaic of dried rose petals! *Some people,* Chaya did not say aloud, *have more time than taste.*

Surveying the rooms of lovingly arranged crafts, though, she could feel her awe began to ebb. Where, she wondered, laboring to smile, were the landscapes carved out of tobacco leaves that they at shops like Winkler's and Yanowitz's might create during their fifteen-minute dinner break? Where were the tributes to the seamstresses who could no longer see to work? Perhaps she was simply weary from too much stimulation. Like the habit of Chicago's weather, her mood had clouded.

"Is it not the most gorgeous thing?" Lallie trilled. Gregory was watching Chaya with care. He could tell she was wary of this celebration of the decorative and the trivial. She knew what he was thinking: Possibly she was going to be more trouble to him than she was worth, caviling at every-thing she saw. She wanted to be—how she wanted to be!—overwhelmed by these glass cases dedicated to women's crafts, women's eye for loveliness, women's essential love of texture, color, shape. This was a fairyland built by busy hands; these projects most probably shed pride and pleasure on the hard-worked women who accomplished them before their children woke, or after they had been tucked in to sleep. She imagined they were heartened at seeing their pretty things chosen to be shown to the world.

But—Chaya sighed—she was never good at a party. She smiled vaguely back at Lallie, who understood so little she would likely remain radiant in a snowstorm.

By the time they emerged into the splash of sunlight and the Court of Honor lay over her shoulder, she was filled with awe. Such things as this were possible! Nearly overnight they had achieved a perfect bubble of a world, thousands and thousands of dollars' worth of shimmering bubble, and yet Liberty Street remained. No rats ran here. No garbage spilled onto the walks and heaped at the corners, steaming and stinking. They had hired a special police force. They had constructed an invisible river of sewers. They had hired street sweepers who plied the paths before and behind. But look where the backs and shoulders who had built it were going home to sleep! Follow a street sweeper home and see where he hung his uniform and where he rested his head. What was the differ-ence, she seethed, between a lovely diversion and a brutal lie? Yet—Miss Addams would surely insist—beauty was beauty and if the Fair increased the weight of beauty in the world, she would bless it.

Gregory's mother leaned toward him and, to judge by the inclination of her chin, was inquiring why Chaya looked perturbed. She could hear nothing of the conversation, but saw that the expression on Mrs. Stillman's face combined impatience with a touch of amusement. Chaya looked away. Would anyone believe she was repelled by every grand thing, and did not want it for herself?

When she and Gregory found their way to the train station—they had decided to return by a different route, just to try it out—"You are a gloomy girl again," Gregory whispered, trying to lift her chin so that she would look at his beguiling face. They were being pressed upon by a solid mass of exhausted fairgoers, who held each other up by their sheer, sweating mass.

"If you were as good a Socialist as you claim to be, you would understand why I am gloomy." She felt him flinch. He patted his forehead with a handkerchief whiter than anything Chaya had ever owned. She took note of this and held it against him. He had not the first idea of what it cost to have nothing. "You are always so full of excuses. 'This would be here whether you approve of it or not,' you said, do you remember? At your parents' party? How will anything change if you *forgive* it all the time?"

He stood his ground. "Can't you take this for what it intends to be, Gloomy Girl? There is, I think, a kind of vanity in that. The Fair is meant to lift people's burdens for a few hours. Isn't that enough?"

Enough if they can afford the time and the ticket. ' No, it is not enough. It is an elixir administered by a"—she had to search for the word—"a charlatan. It is not nearly enough."

BUT IN spite of her righteous anger, she could not stay away: There was too much to learn from it, and she had no education. For one thing, she studied the paintings in the Palace of Fine Arts. She could hardly tell the famous painters from the unknown, but there were a few whom Gregory told her to look out for—Winslow Homer, who painted fishermen in fog and gales, John Sargent, whose ladies might have attended the Stillmans' soirée, and someone whose name amused her—Whistler—whose women were long and undulating in shape and somehow mysterious. But there were many she simply enjoyed, and many more by more women than she had realized dared take up brush and paint. Most of the painters and sculptors had studied in Europe. Mary Cassatt had taken her brilliance abroad and brought it back again.

There was less religion than she would have expected, but these were Americans, and many seemed to find it more fitting to render modest scenes peopled with characters she could recognize: some boys training a dog, a humble couple being married in bright yellow sunlight, a scene at Castle Garden of a worn-looking mother seated on a trunk, holding close her infant, while above her head hung a sign that appeared to be setting forth rules of some kind—rules before welcome. And one, which roused in her a surprising lurch of feeling, a perfectly detailed scene showing glass-blowers at a long table littered with equipment; they were attentive, sleeves rolled, an appreciative light upon their faces. She liked that a great deal.

Then, though it was horribly sentimental, she stood in a moist-eyed Sunday crowd and sighed before what looked to be the most popular painting in the Fair. It was made by someone named Thomas Hovenden and was called "Breaking Home Ties." A mother in her homely house, in the long white apron every woman knew so well, surrounded by many anonymous figures and a dog—an unfancy one—at respectful attention, has placed her hands on the shoulders of her son, who is going forth into the world, leaving all this behind forever. He is holding his hat and he is looking slightly over her head, eager to be gone, while she is eager to keep him. Such a calculated scene this was, but Chaya stood among those others as teary as Mr. Hovenden must have hoped. As he had intended, she saw her most and her least beloved sitting together in the common room at the Fields of Zion, those brave and foolish souls, and remembered her desperation to be done with them. She had tried not to see this scene with her mother in the middle of it, but here she was in the selfsame apron, sober and resigned, though her daughter had denied her the chance to say goodbye. Chaya would never know if they missed her as his imaginary family would miss this imaginary boy. Maybe they had said Kaddish for her because she was dead to them. She let her tears flow freely, her relief and her punishment.

She stayed one night, alone, to see the Court of Honor illuminated. As the lights came on over the water—all in a single flash, not gradually but with the push of a button or the pull of a lever—she was kidnapped back to her first awe at the ingenuity—the genius—that had flung a skein of magnificence across an otherwise unredeemed swamp. Thousands of glowing stars, it looked to be, and the grand basin silvered over as though snow had fallen and moonlight grown impossibly bright across it. It was not easy to begrudge the world such a spectacle.

In truth, one of the causes of her return was that even Miss Addams had rebuked her for her ungracious attitude. She believed in art and music, in the crafts displayed by the women who utilized such skill and patience, in the broad net of new knowledge cast by such affairs as the Exposition. She called it "democratic" and told Chaya (firmly but kindly, as usual) that she might try to moderate her resentments. She carried children to the Fair; she carried their parents, some of whom spoke no English. "But they have their eyes," she insisted to Chaya. "This spectacle needs no language to insinuate itself. You must try to be more flexible, dear. Use your anger to change what merits changing but learn to celebrate what is worthy of celebration."

Chaya bowed her head in deference. Still, she could not apologize to Gregory. He and Miss Addams might be right but however awkwardly she had launched the imprecise weapon of her convictions, she remained convinced that she was right as well.

22

THE FAIR was perfect. When the crowds were thick—on opening day all of Chicago was there, seething, swaying, standing still—he could fiddle in their pockets and never be felt. The President spoke—"magnificent," "future," "together," and many silences in which to receive applause. Asher's fingers twitched like fish at the bottom of the tank. Crowds made him greedy; he imagined—delicately, silently—picking their pockets clean. He knew when the listeners were bored. They coughed and shuffled; he could feel their knees shiver. When they applauded they rose to the balls of their feet.

Then it was over. He could see that President Cleveland had removed his tall black hat to speak. Now he replaced it on his head and, with two large men on either side who looked like they could crush him if they happened to fall on him, left the podium. The crowd surged like water in a dish, then surged back again. For one bad minute, Asher thought he would drown.

HE NEVER knew who suggested him—the building man called "Foreman" or one of the rich people who gave the parties he used to work at? No one told him. Only one day, just after the Fair had opened—all the rubble was gone (*rubble* should be the name of a game, such a funny sound), the dirt between the walks was finally dry and thick with plants, and clean water ran in the canals—while he was standing on a bridge counting the tops of all the buildings (one list for domes, one for steeples, one for turrets, glorious, glorious!), a man he had never seen, almost a boy only wearing a man's clothes and a bowler, came so close he threw shadow over him and asked Asher if he could speak with him. No one had ever asked his permission to speak.

"I've heard you know everything," the man said. He had eyebrows that turned up at the corners like some men's mustaches and sharp eyes that looked like they already knew what you were thinking. "Is that true?" He held out a tin of mints and Asher took two.

"Almost everything."

"Do you think fast? Are you good at answering questions?"

"I don't know. Ask me one." The mint exploded in his mouth like a gulp of cool water.

The man, who had said his name was Bloom (which was silly because that was what a flower did and he was no flower), thought for a minute. "Who discovered America?"

"Oh, what is this Exposition called." Asher sounded weary. "Ask me a real question."

"Well—" The man was looking around at what he told Asher was called the Midway. He seemed to own it. "Do you know what Cairo is the capital of?"

A sign in the distance said STREET IN CAIRO. Was there a trick that made the answer more complicated than Egypt? He was safe because *why* was a question he was rarely asked.

The man wiped his forehead with the back of his sleeve. It seemed to be summer already. "Son, would you like to make some really good money?"

Now there, at least, was a question worth answering.

He had not been able to go home since Opening Day. New sights came at him like lightning flashes. His stomach churned with the need to hurry, to see it all. Chai would skin him when she found him. He had been sleeping in a different building every night, afraid to bed down outside where he could be seen—first Agriculture, then that very long one with the paintings, and now, one by one, Germany, Norway, Pennsylvania, which had in its center a map of the United States made of pickles. He was tempted to remove a whole green pickle but feared it might all fall in. Instead, tentatively, he dug his index fingernail into a little cuke, bright green and lumpy like an alligator; it was hard, shellacked over with something transparent. No wonder he couldn't smell pickle. Disappointing. He found the tower of oranges, thirty-five feet of it, a skin of shiny globes whose pores showed them to be real. He had to trust the number; he wasn't counting that high.

Then there were the States. A few had made buildings that looked just like houses back home, low and wooden. One night he tried something Japanese called Ho-o-den whose roof swooped down like a skirt. He could probably continue doing that, there were so many and it was easy to hide from the guards, who didn't seem to look at anything very carefully. They certainly never bent down and looked under or behind the places he found, where crouching was easy.

But food was sometimes hard to find because they were bundling the garbage carefully and taking it away. He tried to get to it when they first brought it out the back doors of the restaurants, before the wagon came to remove it, but he had to move fast when it was still light. Sometimes men, who must be as hungry as he, were there before him, jumping on the bags and boxes of rinds and crusts like rats before he could get to them.

One night the lights came on over the water—he wished he could count them, the separate lights that made a cascade, but he would be an old man by the time he got to the end—and he dived under a hedge because he thought he would be seen with a rag of grilled meat in his fist. The meat dripped gravy, and bits of green stuck to it and stained his shirt, which was already a map of splotches. Although he was sometimes hungry, he was never afraid.

"I wonder if you *truly* know the Midway." The man Bloom drew a wide arc with his arm toward the distant swatch of mismatched buildings that ran off perpendicular to where they stood. "See, it's the place where the fun truly happens. This over here is all American fancy-pants but, sonny, the whole wide world's over there! There's so much beer on the Midway you could drown in it."

Asher wondered what was wrong with fancy pants but he stayed quiet.

"You never dreamed of it all, one thing after another—I've got Irish,

African, Austrian. Go Turkish. I've got Lapland, you ever heard of Lapland? Don't ask me where it is but nobody here ever heard of it. I just got a shipment of llamas, you know the ones with the long necks, the snobby-looking ones with the long eyelashes? Like beautiful girls. You name it, I've probably got it!" His smile turned on and off but in general he seemed very pleased with himself. "That dome, the blue one, you see it? Color of the Mediterranean. The Moorish Palace. You can actually go in and pray, face down on the carpet. Our Moslems do it five times a day."

"Are you trying to sell me something?" Asher asked. "Am I supposed to care about the beer?"

"No, no, I'm sorry, little guy. I get carried away, this is so—well, never mind. Look. All you would have to do is sit in a chair—we'd get you a big comfortable chair—and answer questions people ask you. You don't have to—" The man looked at him very hard, though not meanly. "This probably won't feel like work to you, sport. This will just keep your mind sharp. Keep the blade from getting rusty."

Asher considered. "Would I get food?" He could hear his stomach talking right now.

"Anything you want. Ice cream. The works. A lot of things you never ate before."

He laughed. "I never ate most things." At one of those Prairie Avenue parties he heard a man say he ate snails. He tried to imagine that, but the idea of swallowing slime and shell made him feel sick.

"Can you get yourself here every morning?"

Asher was still laughing. Ice cream would be very good—he could rarely afford it. "I live close. Can I have another candy?'

This Bloom gave him the whole tin and shook his hand, seriously and firmly, the way people shake men's hands. "We have a deal. Meet me here at nine tomorrow and we'll set you up like a king."

That would not be easy with no way to guess what time it was. He would get up with the sun and wait right here. Maybe he should tell his sister. Maybe not.

"Did you ever see real Africans?" Mr. Bloom was squinting down the path at a clutch of very dark men and women milling in front of the

Dahomeyan village, who seemed to be half naked. "Those folks know how to dress for the heat!" He rumpled Asher's hair. "Get a good sleep tonight, Captain, so you'll have all your wits tomorrow. You're going to be a celebrity." He started to walk away, then stopped. "Your name is what again?"

"Asher."

"No, your *sur*name."

Asher began to tell him, but an itch came over him that no one would do well with Shaderowsky.

"Shadow," he told his new employer. "What's in a name." A rose by any name, he began to himself, spooling it out, and smiled. He was the rose and this man was the bloom. They would make a good team. And he would have ice cream.

ASK HIM ANYTHING! 8-YEAR-OLD WONDER WILL ASTONISH YOU!!

Eight-year-old?! He was small but not that small. But business, he supposed, was business and if they could get away with it, who—whom?— did it hurt.

The chair swallowed him. It had a high back and high arms that made him feel even smaller than he was and Mr. Bloom had had it painted gold. It still smelled of something like liquor that he thought was called *varnish*. Large rocks, painted the color of jewels, ruby, sapphire, lapis—Asher had swallowed a list, his precious and his semiprecious—were pasted above and around him so that they would look embedded. He was supposed to be a prince. His throne sat, high on a platform, between Old Vienna, which was something like a castle, and the best, most ticklish name, Zoopraxographical, where he had sneaked in to see some photographs that showed how animals ran and even how an almost-naked man moved his legs, the same picture again and again with little changes that made him seem to be moving and finally took him up across a hurdle and down again very, very gradually. He was going to steal back to that again, it was the best thing in the Fair.

Mr. Bloom had met him with two surprises. One was a bag that contained his breakfast, the first of the things he had never before tasted. He reached in and pulled out a mass of sticky little krobs, sweet and quick to melt when he put a handful in his mouth. This was something new, born at the Fair, called Cracker Jacks, and he could have eaten twice the bag. Cracker Jacks was a good name—it sounded like it tasted.

The second was an armful of bright-colored clothes. "I'm sure they'll fit," Mr. Bloom told him. "You can just slip them over your own things. These are ample."

Ample, sample, trample. What did he look like? He wanted badly to know. (Why was it *badly*? Was there a *goodly*?) A pasha, he thought. Good for a genie. Puffy purple pants and a red velvet vest embroidered with shiny thread. There was a crown made of something stiff that was not gold, but he took it right off, it felt silly and it was hot. Bulbous—another word he liked. (Words, their sounds, not their meanings, were the best joke.) It was good that no one he ran with in the alleys could see him.

"We shall have to get you some shoes, dear Mr. Shadow," his friend said. "Those"—he nodded toward Asher's toes, which showed through disintegrating leather like pale little Cracker Jacks—"will not do for a prince."

"Why am I a prince? Princes don't know all the things I know."

"Hey!" Mr. Bloom said and his face went red. "Who asks the questions here?"

HE SAT back in the shade of his throne. There was someone Mr. Bloom called a *barker*—like a dog?—who shouted at people as they walked by, promising the mighty feats of mind this boy would perform. "The boy's name is Shadow, although he's very bright. A prize if you stump him!" He hoped the questions would be interesting but mostly they were not. Erie, Huron, Michigan, Superior, and—he quickly learned to pause for effect so that the asker would think he was stymied—Ontario! Atlantic, Pacific, Indian, Arctic. No, not Antarctic. Genesis, Exodus, Leviticus, Deuteronomy, Numbers. Matthew, Mark, Luke, and John. He supposed people would not ask questions they couldn't answer themselves. On the first day there were forty-seven of them, eight children. They weren't very smart. It was enough to put him to sleep. Words flowed through his brain; he tongued them, waiting for the chance to exercise them: *systolic*, *diastolic, apostolic, diatonic, dialectic, electric. Sluice, juice, sauce, souse. Symmetry, scimitar, cemetery.*

If he concentrated, he could change people's faces into slabs of shape and color. There were nineteen rolling cars—if someone asked him what they were called, he would not have known, but he did see that men pushed them, which did not look comfortable in the heat. Many languages swirled the air, German, Polish, Greek? They were like music, sharp or smooth but without sense. Food smells mixed like noise.

People trifled with him. "What kind of fruit does Aunt Sally bake into her apple pie?" "What kind of cheese is the man in the moon?" He gave them shaming looks but they laughed and moved on. There were two sets of identical twins and a dwarf. Only one person—a man in a white suit who asked him to name the owner of the horse that had won the most races this year at Washington Park—claimed the victor's purse. It was a booklet of admission tickets to the other attractions on the Midway. He felt no regret for not knowing the answer to such a useless question, a question with no future to it. Mr. Bloom could afford to give those away. Asher yawned six times and dozed twice between customers.

He had logicked this out: If his Chaya was going to marry that slippery rich man with the smooth jackets, the checkered cape, and the pink hands—he did not like those soft palms, those long delicate fingers, or the friendly voice you could use to soothe your dog—he knew what he needed to do. He would bring home enough money so that she would not have to go with any man. He knew—she had said—that all she wanted was to find a better house for them with real beds in it, give him warm dinners made of fine foods, dress him in warm woolen clothes, buy new shoes for him, for herself. (His toes were sore from hitting the street. He'd have thought Gregory might notice and bring him new ones the way he had brought Chaya that dress but his glance was—no surprise—only on Cinderella.) If he wanted the university, she would send him to an academy and ready him. Mrs. Gottlieb would come with them.

He would find the money, earn it or steal it—stealing was so easy, it made him ripple with pleasure every time he hid, in the bottom of his one untorn pocket or his sack, what he had taken from someone who didn't need it, someone who had an endless supply of everything. Winter was over; there were no more poor people sleeping in City Hall who deserved it. He could keep it, bring it home, let her see it; then he could take it to pawn. Robin Hood feathers his own nest. It was the best game of all. She would not see him until he had a little pile of fortune for her, like the pasha whose glittery clothes he was wearing. He knew he could do anything; he had wriggled like a cat through every opening.

When he closed his eyes at night, it was the soft curve of her cheek that he saw, round like the edge of the earth. Her nose was as small as a thumb. Her hair was his dark blanket. No Gregory Stillman could steal her—*Still-man, Steal-man*—away from him. No Steal-man would make her as happy as he could.

WHEN HE was tired of sitting and being stared at, he leaped off his throne—a big step down—and took off like a rabbit. No one could make him work when he didn't want to work. The Dahomeyans were milling, a mahogany forest. Hagenbeck's wild animals made jungle noises that came sailing right out over the wall and you could smell their stink, like pins in your nose. Who said bad smells were bad? What if you called them good? Across the road, quite close, that new university was only a few gray buildings, very plain beside the clamor and color of the show. Quiet was built into their heavy stone. On the other side, just outside the Fair, every night a man named Buffalo Bill (from the city in New York State or a herder of animals otherwise known as bison?) was throwing a rope in a dirt circle and riding on a black horse to the whoopy noise of cheering. Dressed in hides, a woman named Annie Oakley shot at birds that dropped from the sky in pieces, like broken flower pots.

He had saved for last the thing he most wanted to see up close, not the half-naked ladies wriggling their bellies, not Hagenbeck's giraffes and elephants. It was that magic wheel built by a man named George Ferris. For this he needed fifty cents; he could not inch his way onto it, sneaking. It was the tallest thing he had ever seen, firm on its metal legs but delicate, like a toy you could build with sticks and watch fall. It was more air than anything. How did it stand? There were thirty-five railroad cars hanging in a circle, wooden, glassed-in, shining. They barely swayed. Carefully—he was looking straight up at it—they moved up, up, over the top, down again. The space between them didn't change, they didn't bunch up or tear loose the way he feared they would. Children shrieked, and possibly adults, once a woman fainted, but they were all safe, flying—dangling in emptiness!—and setting slowly down.

He had no twenty-five cents, let alone fifty, but he could shuck his fancy costume, stow it behind his throne, and stand wailing beside the ticket counter, howling that he had lost his quarters, had dropped them in the crowd, and now he would never get to ride. "Little boy," a white-haired gentleman asked him, bending down to engage his eyes. He had eyebrows like scrub brushes. "What has happened? Where are your parents?"

This was the first of his inventions. He was here with his sister, who had left him alone to ride while she went to the police office with the Columbian Guard to report that her money had been stolen from her closed purse. He was here with a distant uncle who had abandoned him, perhaps to go in to see Little Egypt because she seemed to be all he could talk about, her "danse du ventre" that he would never encounter in Boise, Idaho. (It would never have occurred to him to pronounce it *Boy-z*. He knew some French: *Bwahz*.) He waved his hands helplessly and charmed a crowd. The first time he collected a dollar, donated twenty-five cents at a time by sympathetic motherly and fatherly hands who seemed to enjoy helping him, and one girl his own age dressed in many layers of lace like a decorated cake, who timidly came toward him to drop a ticket in his palm and pull her hand back fast as if he were one of Hagenbeck's jabbering beasts.

He had heard from Chaya's "sweetheart" that eighty percent of Chicago came from some other country. Who would even bother to doubt him? Gibberish, more amusing, would do, salted with Yiddish and bits of anything else he had picked up along the way. Even Elizabethan English baffled people, if he said it very fast. He got himself a heavy pocket.

But, helpless to resist, he spent it all on this ecstasy. A conductor in a uniform who rode in every car called out the names of the buildings below. He could not imagine sitting down. The seats turned to one side and then the other. Face to the window, trying each side, he was rapt. They lurched to a stop while others climbed off, climbed on. Then they started again, two circuits to a ticket. It was not about words. Words stopped up there. Roofs, more complicated than he had imagined from the ground (towers, doors, stripes of black tar where repairs made random designs). Streets slicing through dark brick, through grass, the winding cement lanes of the Fair, hedged and flowered. That sidewalk that moved very slowly like water creeping forward while people, amazed, stood and were carried along, stone-still. To the south the repeated silver sluice of many train tracks, and then, east, the lake! The endless lake, so big he felt his knees buckle at the sight of it, more serene than sky. Each time he went up, it was different, flowing lapis to turquoise, once or twice a gray-brown the color of dirt, edged with white ruffles. It was flat as solid earth or roiled with anger, a furious sea-god blowing down at it. Once, at sundown, the horizon turned to flame.

No wonder: Looking up, wasn't he closer to the sun? His breath caught in his narrow chest—could people live as high, as far from the earth as this, without catching fire? Icarus fell in flames. But he wasn't doing the flying here, he was safe in Ferris's machine, and there was glass, sometimes clear, sometimes smudged, between him and the glowing open blue of the sky. Nothing was ever like this swooping rise and fall, a pressure as if someone had placed a hand at the back of his head. He had to force his mouth tight closed or he would cry out. This was the first time he wasn't driven to count or name or alphabetize what he was seeing for the comfort it gave him, sopping up his energy to keep it from spilling over. This was what God saw, looking down on creation, all of it at once, an intricate geometry, so calm, so orderly, so clean and small, and he—all the people on the wheel with him—smaller than a point on a line. At home, he remembered, they raised a little glass and drank, *l'chaim*, to life. Here it was, finally. To life, to life, to life!

He had heard from Mr. Bloom that the Fair was going to be here only for a short time. Then what? It would disappear, he said. But Asher looked north, looked south and east and west, and then at the latticework of his castle in the sky as it made its slow circuit, and knew that everything he could see would stay exactly where it was. It was hard—rock, brick, wood, too heavy to move. The wheel was rooted in earth, miles and miles down. Those stone goddesses held a building on their heads. The bridges were solid enough to hold hundreds of people who weighed thousands of pounds. The water was deep. On the wooded island, orioles slashed the air, and tanagers, and plain little sparrows too; at night he heard crickets scraping out their country voices. He had forgotten crickets. The great wheel turned patiently, like the earth, keeping time, never slow, never hurried. He needed to assure Mr. Bloom: It would be there forever, all of it, like the Sphinx or the Parthenon.

WHEN BIG Dog, the barker, who was also the ticket taker, was engaged in deep conversation with a pretty—he supposed pretty—young woman in pink and white who twirled her parasol first clockwise, then counterclockwise, trying to drill a hole in the air, Asher placed himself, smiling amiably, close to the money tin. The barker, who wore a bowler, a shimmering vest, and a huge polka-dotted bow tie, had turned and was pointing down the Midway and the woman was squinting alongside him, ready, even though he looked preposterous, to take some kind of advice. Asher's hand darted out, scooped up what could fit in his palm, and was gone by the time the barker turned back in his direction. The voluminous gold pants—pantaloons—of the pasha's outfit were perfect for secreting almost anything. When the barker discovered his loss, he staggered a moment and asked Asher if he'd seen anything.

"I saw a lot of things—three rolling cars, a Turkish palanquin with two brown-skinned women in it, a feeble old man in a wheelchair that was being pushed by a monkey. I saw, I think they were sisters, nine of them, all dressed up in matching yellow dresses, but each hat had a different color ribbon. I saw—"

"Shadow, pal, you talk too much. Did you see somebody with his fingers in the till?" The barker picked up his hat, wiped his whole sweating head with a rag, and replaced it.

Asher looked at him blankly. *Till. Until?* Soil was tilled. The barker was shaking the box; a few left-behind coins clanked against each other dully. "Didn't see anyone near it." True. Words could mean many things, but he would not lie.

The barker looked in every direction at once, his eyes flitting like swallows.

Picking coins out of people's pockets was better. He pushed through the thickest crowds which, every minute of the day, seemed to be cheering and hooting at one of the dancing girls, veils on, veils off, as if she were a parade. Her white belly jiggled, ripples on the lake, and her hips made circles while the rest of her stayed totally still. She appeared to have two different bodies, joined in the middle. Why all these men—women too, but mainly men—found this exciting was one of the many mysteries, but it was very convenient. It felt peculiar—a mite too personal—to push his fingers into rear pockets almost right up against someone's warm flesh, but it was like Opening Day, he left with twenty-two dollars and two money clips, four leather wallets which he emptied and left conspicuously in the dust in front of the building so that they might be found, and one lady's reticule that contained nothing but a handkerchief embroidered with the initial *K* and a modest border of yellow roses.

For a few days, until a guard threatened him and appeared to mean it, he approached the most helpless-looking people he could find and offered his services as a guide. A few couples straight from the farm thought this was an accommodation of the Exposition, albeit an odd one. They followed close behind him, listened to his explanations regarding the construction of their state's building—he made certain to find out where they were from and take them directly to it: South Dakota, Tennessee, whichever it was. These constructions looked like real buildings but they were better from afar because up close and inside, they turned out to be shells over simple framework. The only real thing, he thought, was the wheel. You could not fly up in a car made of this thing called "staff," only jute and plaster. How backwards: the flying thing weighed tons. The buildings were no better than cardboard. It made him laugh with superiority, as if the wheel were his own invention. People pooled up around him, listening gratefully. Many tipped him.

One morning, passing the Children's House, he saw a knot of women, noisily distraught, and bored his way into the center of their little circle of pacers and grumblers. They were angry because the nursery was already full and their children would have no place to spend the day except clamoring at their sides.

Asher gave them his most engaging smile. "I will keep them and tell them stories," he offered. "For one dollar each, I will keep them occupied all day."

The women laughed and clicked their teeth. One of them, commanding in a slithery dark blue with a hat that looked alive, said, "My son is older than you are!" and coldly laughed.

"Age," Asher announced, looking up at her, sniffing, "is a coincidence of the alignment of the stars. Can you name the six highest mountains of Asia? Can you itemize the parts of a horse or tell me who Sappho was and where she lived?" Examples of things the woman would not know leaped lightly into his mind like bubbles. They tickled; he had to exercise restraint not to blow them out into the air.

The woman had stopped in her tracks, her hand on her son's shoulder. The boy glared at Asher as if he had been challenged to a fight. "What is your name, young man? Do you work for the Exposition?"

"I do." He was not lying. And he had better get back to work. "My name is Asher Shadow. I will be sitting with your children on the Midway between the Javanese house and the Zoopraxographical building."

"The Zooprax—"

"Ographical. Full of running men and horses leaping hurdles with attention to the action of their legs. Zoopraxographical. I will take good care of your children. You may visit them, if you like. And if you will give me twenty-five cents now—twenty-five for *each*—I will take them on the great Ferris wheel. I promise they will love it."

The women looked at each other in some confusion, but when the one in blue gave him a firm nod, which made the feathers on her crown seem about to fly off—she ushered her boy to his side: "This is Germaine. I will be back for him at three o'clock"—three others followed suit, two quiet little blonde girls who seemed struck dumb by his confidence, and another boy, tiny, probably too young to want to hear his stories. He would think of something. "Everyone hold hands," he instructed. "We are going to be a snake." They wound in and out of the skirts and trouser legs of the crowd, making a hissing sound, and when they arrived at Asher's throne, he gathered them around like his courtiers, and began at the beginning of the *Arabian Nights.*

BUT AT the end of the day, he saw where his booty was going to go.

He was walking near the south gate when a rhythmic chanting filled his ear. It was no song. Dozens of men were walking with signs on a forest of sticks and each sign was painted with fury: NO JOBS NO FAIR! NO WAGES FOR GOOD WORKERS!'

They had built this magnificence. Now—could this be?—they were expected to disappear. Asher, inside, peered out through the fence at them, watched them pace, felt the soles of his feet tingle. They marched back again, right past him, shouting, faces stony with anger. None of his friends from the Barracks was marching, but he could easily imagine those good men here among them.

The sleepers had left City Hall, now that the wind was down, but this was a crueler wind. Jesus was right, though he wasn't supposed to think about Jesus: *The poor ye shall always have with thee.* He ran to the exit where oblivious families strolled licking ice cream cones, chattering, heading home exhausted by pleasure, and joined the marchers, arrowed in between their stamping feet, no sign to carry but a scheme to empty his sack for them: Robin of the Fair.

A fairgoer, standing beside him, pulled off his hat, waved it in triumph, called out, "Fucking unions! Lock 'em all up, fellas!"

But another man, rougher-looking, as though he could have been on that line, spat at his feet. "They ain't union, pal. You don't got a job you don't got no union behind you." He spat again, a bigger gob that quivered on the concrete like something alive. "Those poor suckers are starvin' one by one."

Asher studied him. He had heard Chaya talk about the cigar union, how she and her friends had gotten no help from whatever a union was. Women betrayed, she had said. You have to have power to get any power. His sackful of goodies was too light, too frivolous. *Trivial,* that beautiful word that sounded like a flower. There was nothing he could steal that would give him power.

Still, he tapped one man on the arm and held out a pilfered watch and muttered, "Here, take this and hock it." The man turned on him. Large in the bone but fleshless, red-faced, the man hissed, "What the hell's that for? Can I eat it?"

"No," Asher insisted. "But you can get a little mazuma for it. It's worth—" The man knocked it out of his hand and moved on, scowling. Asher picked up the watch, inspected it to make sure its face wasn't broken, and closed it in his palm.

Then—though he was watching he didn't see them coming—around the clot of men swirled police, their darkness, and where Asher stood he could see arms upraised, which meant batons, their fat sticks, their official sticks coming down on the men's heads. The commotion—shouting, threatening—pulled him toward them, reeled him in too close to the bent backs, bared teeth, curses. It was like standing beside a fire that threatened to escape its circle and singe them all. He stepped back, feeling oddly guilty. Even there he heard the swish of air as a nightstick thrashed down and opened a head. Caught a blood splash on his bare arm and shook it to be sure it wasn't his own. One copper—he used to like the sound of *copper*—flailed at anyone he could reach, waving his arm like he was trying to put out that fire but no, he was fanning it, making it worse. Howls fled upward. Asher didn't know men could scream like that. Steer bellowing in the stockyards, trapped. Then the high screech of a stuck animal. He had seen a pig once, back home, in someone's yard, and it sounded like that having its throat cut. He had been glad they didn't keep pigs.

He watched the men shoved into a police wagon, flung in, tripping over each other, the door slammed hard. A sharp whistle and the wagon was gone with a snarl, its horses kicking up stones.

A few men were left, milling, stamping their feet. They looked insulted not to be taken.

"What? What?" Asher demanded of one of them, pulling at his sleeve, one of the empty-handed left-behinds. "Why were they—"

"No goddamn jobs is what. We got used and they threw us the hell away, that's what."

Asher leaned in. The man, in a scuffed old suit, dusty here, shiny there, and stretched out in the knees, muttered on and Asher tried to make sense of it. "How did you get used?" *Used?* They were still here.

But they were the builders! They were the men in the bunkhouse, men who filled in the swamp, who made the Fair out of wood and staff, plastered the faces of the buildings, laid the paths, planted the thousand trees, proud of their work, they had told him. Satisfied, for all it had tuckered them out. For this they had gotten themselves beaten? For wanting to use those ropy arms, those backs that never tired? He looked for the man who had found him first and brought him into the bunkhouse, who loved to hear him read from the Bible, but no one seemed to remember him. That meant there must be a lot of hardworking men who had been forgotten.

Someone was shouting about a meeting tonight. "We're organizing, we're not goin' away like fuckin' sheep!" A thin stream of blood trickled down his cheek. He took off his cap and thrust it like the stick he didn't have. "They want us to disappear. You don't throw men away like rubbish. You don't take their labor like it comes free and just turn your back."

Asher peered up at him and the man goggled his eyes, mocking. "What."

"What? Nothing. I only—"

"Count yourself lucky, kiddo. You don't need a job. Just wait and see what's waitin' for you when you do! Ought to rot, the whole damn lot of 'em."

Asher shuddered and stood as tall as he could manage. "Can I come to the meeting? Tonight?"

The man looked him over and laughed one hurt burst. "What the hell, why not? 295 Division, upstairs. Come one, come all, all hands on deck. You get yourself there, we might even have cookies."

HE FOUND 295 Division the way he found his way everywhere: walked, stole a ride on a trolley, no longer afraid to dangle off the back, mouth open to the breeze. Dodged foot traffic, horse traffic. Distance was never a problem, it was a voyage, and a hundred things amazed him on the way: three men in red capes who stopped in the middle of the street to stand on their hands and walk, their capes fallen over their heads. A horse gone wild, dancing—it looked like dancing—front legs raking at the sky. A load of lumber fallen off a wagon, splayed across the street. He went around it. A dozen men—eleven, actually—assaulting the ground with picks and shovels, all dressed alike in what might be prison uniforms. They were singing or—he listened carefully, cocking an ear—grunting out a rhythm. So much happening at once, he was going to live forever!

There was an upholstery shop at 295 Division, with a fat mustard-colored sofa and a matching chair crowding its window. Voices came down to him; the meeting had started. He took the stairs by twos, tiptoed in and found a seat on the aisle nearest the door. Hot room, low ceiling, so many men—he counted forty-four plus a large, tan sleeping dog—given to muttering to one another without lowering their voices. The speakers poured forth heated words and pounded the table. One smashed it so hard with his fist the dog jumped to his feet and looked around alarmed. Laughter, a stroking from above and the dog subsided. "A good hard knock might calm you down like that," someone shouted to the flustered speaker.

Their words sailed past Asher, most of them, but some he caught: *Socialists* shared everything and did not believe in disruption but in something called *evolution*. "People need to learn, they need to be led to understand." *Anarchists* refused what was offered, would not be bought, would not compromise, that filthiest of words. (Words could be filthy? Asher saw books with soiled pages, rucked up, dirt-stained.) "Revolution, not evolution!" Only the lily-livered gave in. He tried to imagine liver—he saw it stretched out on a plate—with lilies growing from it. Silliness from adult men.

A very tall, very thin young man, afloat in a long black overcoat, with some kind of accent deeper than his own, began softly and ended up shouting, "And the church! The Romish church, the Protestants in all their useless variety! The church keeps us in bondage! How can the world not see it, how the blind lead the blind, the apologists make excuses and meanwhile our children starve!" Asher wanted an explanation but could not ask.

Who was apologizing, and for what? His mouth tasted like road dust. He was used to learning from books—books with clean pages—not from all those syllables rushing forward so fast in this ragged assortment of voices. Anyone could tell they were bitter, though, all of them, because they didn't have work to do. Or they were paid in pennies while the rich wallowed in their palaces. He knew: His sister needed two jobs or they would be living on the street. Some of them wanted to make an army to march on—who? That was never clear. "Capitalism is the tyrant!"

But where, where would they find it to wrestle it to the ground? Asher closed his eyes and thought as hard as he could. The parties he worked at, Sundays. The fresh flowers in silver bowls and whipped-up cream and books in the library so clean because they had never been touched. The crowds of visitors at the Fair, spreading around their coins by the handful, like farmers seeding their fields. What they called *capitalism*, wasn't it everywhere? How could they live without it? But the capital was in Springfield, what did that have to do with all this ruckus?

He blinked with effort. All he knew was that their fury gave off heat, a kind of roiling, something like motion. Men stood and clapped and sat and murmured to their neighbors, not polite, not too nice to disagree. They were desperate. That was a word he knew and liked: It had *despair* in it, or almost. Chaya used that word, or used to. It meant, *We are drowning, we are dying.* He and Chaya were not dying any more but that made him feel a kind of shame. He had, they both had, gone blind and deaf to their dying.

The last man to speak was large, he looked like he could move boulders. He had been taken by the police at the gate to the Fair! Asher felt a thrill at that. The man's head was bandaged, one of his eyes flamed with blood. He shouted, hoarse-voiced, "Many words begin with a *d*—there's *disaster*, right, boys?" A sort of cheer, not gleeful. "There's *debt*. It's debt that devours us and never so much as today." He waited for another round of enthusiasm. "And there's *death*, y'know. There's always death, they give it out like medicine on a goddamn spoon. But I have a different *d* word, fellas."

"What?" the whole room clamored. "What's the word?"

"*Defiance*! We will defy our masters. We will defy the bastards who want us to keep our mouths shut. Well, down with 'em, I say. Into the lake with the bloody lot of 'em and we'll stand on the moving sidewalk we built—*we* built it, remember that!—and we'll watch 'em sink." The sound of all those men clapping sounded like wind, like rain, a great storm breaking. But he did not say how they would muster the bastards into the lake. And there were no cookies.

The meeting done, no one seemed to notice Asher. He wanted to ask a hundred questions but he was too small, he was invisible, lost between their milling bodies and the chairs pushed crooked from their rows, and, disappointed, he went down the stairs and out. Started the walk home—it was dark now—vowing to find some books to help him make sense of the *-ists* and the *-isms*, Socialist and Anarchist, Marxist and—why had someone hooted at this?—something called a Social Democrat. So he was a Proletariat? Everyone had nodded at that word. It did not seem to be something you had to join up for. He wished he had dared to tell the bandaged man that he had been there, had seen him clubbed and kneed and shoved into the police wagon howling, that it had made the bloodied man a hero. So rarely afraid to speak up, tonight Asher was too awed to say a word.

23

GREGORY HAD a surprise for her. "This will please you, I think, Chaya. Just you wait!" He handed her up to a seat in a hack and told the cabman to go a few blocks north and another few west. Like her own block, the houses here were sad wooden fronts sagging, brick fronts grimy, chipped and unadorned. What a decadent city this was. It was a rigged game, whether one chose to play or not. There ought to come a huge wave off the lake to drown it all, sinners and saints and especially the ones who owned their souls, to even the score.

"Here," Gregory called to the driver, and the horse stopped as suddenly as if his nose had hit a wall. Chaya saw a plain brick building, three stories tall, its front stoop and cornices half fallen in, most of its windows gaping uncovered. She followed Gregory into its murky hallway, where the rankling smell of mildew mixed with the residue of some cooking disaster that must have charred the bottom out of a good-sized pot.

Then, after a long climb, with an exclamation of triumph, he managed, by feel alone, to find the keyhole, and with a click and a push, the door opened and he made a bow of welcome. "Dear lady, my new abode."

Oh, Gregory. Her eyes welcomed the light, though the windows were shadowed with old grime. In that light she saw a room as worn and decrepit as Mrs. Gottlieb's parlor, but rescued, incongruously, by a few furnishings he must have carted from home: a solid, shining, mahogany breakfront with silver drawer-pulls, two commodious leather chairs in a luscious forest green, a round table with the scalloped feet of a lion. On a scuffed pine dresser, a nicked enamel pitcher, a nicked enamel bowl. Such effort to abandon his fate, which would not abandon him! Such desperation to belong. She was embarrassed for him.

He was as proud as a poor man who had moved up to better rooms. They were passing each other, Chaya saw, bitterly amused, one rising while the other fell.

Gregory bounced gently on the bed like a boy, grinning. Lifted a dented kettle he might have bought from a junkman on Maxwell Street, then remembered he had no water unless he went downstairs to pump it. Only the pile of papers and the shiny maroon pen on the table betrayed his difference from his neighbors. He didn't ask her what she thought about it, only combed her face for a response. Had he known her true opinion, he'd have been more surprised than he was when she came into his arms as if to congratulate him.

How strange that she found this folly endearing—that he could be so earnest and so entirely wrong. He was no prince after all. He was more flawed, he was more human, and, it seemed, he needed her approval more than he needed his comfort. How vulnerable he felt when she took his head to her breast and cradled it there against her long file of buttons, which ground themselves into his sweet cheek.

He unfastened those buttons very slowly, concentrating, his fingers too big to slip them easily through the little loops that held them. She should be raising her arms to embrace him, should be caressing his dark head, his neck, his shoulders that suddenly seemed wide and looming, helping him out of his own complex clothing as he was relieving her of her multiple layers of skirting. He stopped to press his lips to every limb he bared, but she stood inert as the heavy green pitcher on the ledge behind him. This is, she did not quite think but felt, panicked, what I am not allowed until—unless!—he is my husband. This is what they warn us against, doing what we are doing. His fingertips, warm palm of his hand, tongue inside her mouth as if it were her own, this time no surprise. She stood in a pile of undergarments, her feet catching in the folds, ruining them with her shoes.

Then—his bed stretched behind them, a shore too far to be reached—he laid her down. Every part of him pressed against her as if they had never been meant to be separate, and he was somehow on her, in her, none of him rough and raw but amazingly smooth, for all his force. She let herself be stunned. Naked, he was so young, so oddly delicate. There were hollows where his neck met his chest. Bony legs—boy legs—twined with hers. His fingers trembled, touching her. She couldn't believe how much she wanted to take him into her.

She had not realized how curious she had been about what the whole world found so compelling that men killed to have it, forced women to lie down for it against their will, that kingdoms rose and fell with the movement of flank against flank—they were only thighs, after all, hairy and hairless; her breasts tipped the color and shape of almonds in their skins, not lush enough to fill his hands; flat belly against flatter; and then, in the dark, the places she hardly dared name. Lying beside Gregory finally, in the deep shelter of his arm, she recognized how hungry she had been, not to feel what she had felt—astonishment and pain and finally the dark swell of something like an itch she could not touch or even find while he fell away from her, damp, breathless, shrunken—but to know what she knew now. Still, the great world-mystery was not quite solved: There must be more to it than this baring of what is never seen, and then that tearing, and a gasp, his gasp, like the pain of mayhem wrung from him. Later she would know. Now she would sleep, and Gregory too, his breath subsiding.

My impoverished lover—lover, my fool!—will we have to line up together at the Pacific Mission for our dinner, thin gruel and a stale roll? She hoped he would not be laughed at too harshly while he pursued this foolishness. She kissed his temple, on which the comma of dark hair she loved lay stuck to his damp skin. It would be all right soon enough: Let him pump his water in the yard on a chill December morning, carry his nostril-filling bowl down two flights, sloshing high against its sides, and if he put his foot down wrong in the dark, into his hands and onto the immaculate knee of those tan trousers he had folded so neatly today. Such guilt! Such good intentions! He would never last as a pauper, and when he failed at it—when he reverted—she knew she would be relieved.

ASHER STAYED away, and stayed, and stayed.

Misery and exhilaration swept Chaya as if she were swimming through changing currents in a pond. It would do no good to look for him, she knew, because she had done that before and Asher was a tomcat—for many months he had been vaulting fences, lunging down alleyways like a chased thief, running below everyone's vision, stealing to put the world right. He knew the grip-cars, he knew the horse cars: The city was far more his playground than hers. But he had come home at night; when she returned from her job at the buckeye, she had kissed him in his sleep. All she could do now was worry and wait.

One evening a rumor passed along the street that a small boy had been killed nearby at one of the many deadly crossings of train with street traffic. These were the times when four or five such catastrophes might occur in a day, most frequently involving the young and, to themselves, invincible, who believed they could outrace anything on wheels.

Chaya ran to the precinct house and threw herself upon the police officer in charge. He was a large Irishman with eyebrows as furry as chenille and hands the size of dust mops who, unfortunately for himself, had been standing at the door looking morosely out at the rain. He caught her full weight against his chest, which was, painfully for her, armored with double rows of buttons, and soothed her gently, an amazing kindness in a man so mountainous. Calmly, he reassured her that the boy had actually not been a child but a diminutive Chinaman, probably, to judge by his clothing, here to work at the Exposition, whose builders seemed a congress of every nation in the world. Only then did her breathing return to a normal rhythm that could sustain her. But though he wasn't hers, who, she wondered miserably, would there be, so far from home, to claim the poor man's body or even to know his fate and mourn for him, however the Chinese people mourned? She was very susceptible to feeling just then.

The policeman asked her for a description of her missing boy. He seemed as sympathetic as one could wish. What would she say?

Ten-year-old prodigy. Dark-haired. White-skinned. Small-boned. Delicate-featured. Sometimes clean. Smarter than you are. Reads. Calculates. Possesses a memory of inhuman capacity. Indeterminate commitment to the rules of civil law: steals modestly. Sleeps where necessary. Lies when expedient. Unforgiving when angered. Circumcised. Answers to Asher, though may not answer at all. Please return to grieving sister.

"STILL GONE, the little bounder!" Sara said, clicking her teeth. They were leaving work; it was still light outside, which shocked Chaya every time, as though it were an aberration. "I've had times I've wished my brother would disappear, but I didn't really mean it. But Chaya, he'll be all right out there. He is quicker than anyone who might want to do him harm, you must know that. He will sneak through any fence."

They walked together a while, melancholy, agreeing that life was so unpredictable they felt like bits of branch spun round in a river, helpless. "Should I be spending all my time searching for him?" Chaya begged of her friend. "I think that I shouldn't be so happy with Gregory right now. It makes me feel selfish."

Sara's freckles had vanished, these days, under a light veil of powder. She had grown up and had grown pretty since her fireman, Joe Scully, had come into her life. She wore her hair in a womanish roll with a becoming fringe. "You don't even deserve an answer to that. You are doing what you can. You have too much conscience and it does you no good, nor Asher either."

Chaya made herself change the subject to the only thing Sara cared about these days. "How are things with Joe?"

"Oh, my father has begun to object to him," her friend said, almost gaily. "He told me a fireman is as bad as a gambler, and I'll lose him to a burning house some day. But I said, 'Then I'm a gambler too and I'll take my chances on him!'" She laughed. "If we had to get everybody's blessing, do you think there'd ever be any new babies made? How do you think the world goes round?" She was going to be contented, Chaya could see, because—if her luck held—she would make her own path. Sara had only agreed with her about how helpless they were, buffeted in the stream, because she wanted to oblige her in her misery.

She couldn't remember how the world went round, in fact. Asher gone, it had stopped for her and she feared it might never start up again. She was the guilty one, who—thank Gregory, thank her unsanctioned distraction—had allowed her sister-concentration to lapse. "You will be out of your father's house soon," she told Sara, hugging her goodbye when her crowded car pulled up beside them.

"You will come to the wedding and I will finally meet your Gregory!"

A flush of something that had no name—a brew of fear and embarrassment, perhaps—warmed her cheeks. She sighed. "And you will meet Gregory."

And what would *her* father say—pray God or if not God, good fortune— were he to meet her beautiful suitor? A *landsman* in spirit? A big-hearted, helplessly devoted servant of decency? Or would he see a wealthy, coddled son of the ruling class, a cousin-once-removed of the Czar? A *goy*, uncircumcised. Would he think his daughter had gained a world or had given one away?

SHE HAD asked Gregory if she might see what he was so diligently writing, his chair pulled up close to the window for the bleak Chicago light, but he refused her. "When it is farther along," he promised. "When it is a clearer expression of what I hope to say." Pretending to be abject, feigning anger, nipping at his ear—nothing she did prevailed against his obstinacy.

She stayed away a while and then begged him again, but he was resolute. Was it terrible, then, one evening when she was awaiting his return from a meeting with Miss Addams's benefactors, to go to his desk and very carefully, barely breathing, pull out the brown pebbled leather book whose pages he worked at so faithfully?

Perhaps it was terrible, but she did it nonetheless. She opened the covers, trembling, and read standing, as though the appearance of casualness would cancel her transgression. Asher stole objects, solid material possessions which cost their owners dearly; she was, she reasoned, a thief of nothing but words, robbing him invisibly, leaving no scar, not even a fingerprint. If you loved someone, it was your obligation, if he would not enlighten you, to follow where he went each day.

But her reward—that would take a while to calculate. *Oh, Gregory!* She felt the same disappointment scored with relief that had entangled her when he so proudly showed off these poor-man's rooms. His need so overpowered his natural endowments that (this was the saving paradox) she felt a burden lifted, even as she patronized his innocence. For here was the inescapable fact: His writing was dutiful, speckled with numbers, fierce, at times, with his passion for change, for what he called *betterment*, by way of the sacrifice of those least likely to hear him. The word *capital* recurred and recurred never to be praised; the socialism he had studied at the identical fount at which her father had drunk showed itself full of fury but fatally dry without faces, hands, bodies to give it blood. Gregory's words lay heavy, inert, like bread made of deficient yeast, wholesome but unappealing. She could not imagine anyone willingly raising it to his lips. He was saving himself, she supposed, but who would follow?

It was surely not easy to write convincingly of the insults and indignities she had borne, she and her neighbors and long-lost family. Perhaps there were some who could do it: She had heard Miss Addams speak, and she had a remarkable talent for giving body to the spirit that moved within her. She had met and nurtured so many actual *people*! But Gregory's was all conjecture; it was abstract, its assertions theoretical. Those were not words she knew very well; she only recognized, in these earnest pages, what was missing. Chaya narrowed her eyes to call forth his eager face, the warmth of his eyes on hers, the peculiar way he fixed her gaze, challenging her to look away as if willing her to stare back, to recognize his avidity, would be enough to hold her fast. His writing was exactly like that. It was shaped by the force of his *wanting*. She suspected that his pages fell in some parched place halfway between scholarship and sermon, though she recognized that she knew nothing of either. They would not—this she trusted—make the bones rise and dance, or the dust sing. The abandoned would stay lost.

But she could love him better for that. What was wrong with her, she dared to wonder, that every time she found Gregory wanting, he became more dear to her? His vulnerabilities must be some kind of recompense. He had, and could not leave behind, his breeding, his education and financial comfort, even his beauty—she did find him beautiful, from head to foot and, with irresistible pleasure, in between—and then he had his humbling decency, his wish that he could give it all back and gladly go bare. To be so competitive embarrassed her. But (voices jangled at each other as she stood beside his desk listening for his key in the lock) competition was not the precise word for this welling tenderness, this desire to protect him from his defects. Did she think she deserved a monopoly on neediness? Was it arrogant to want to level the ground between them?

Oh, loving someone was not simple! Those novels her teacher pressed upon her at school, though they pitted very dissimilar suitors against each other, each to represent a different world, still did not begin to hint at such confusions. Asher should have taught her some of love's complexities, the endless shifting of power. She was more experienced but he was the brilliant one; she was steady and competent; he was the happy one, the one with wings. But this man, this man—his regrets and appetites and insistences, and all he did not suspect about his failings, made it impossible to deny him. Every inch of stature he lost made it easier for her not to crane her neck to look up but, instead, to gaze levelly into this face and find his richly blooded, willing lips and kiss them, strength for strength, passion for passion.

When, a few hours later, Gregory lowered himself into bed beside her, he did it slowly and delicately, as if it were a rowboat in danger of tipping, because he was a considerate man and did not want to disturb her. Chaya, awake, her eyes closed, did not fail to take note of that.

CHAYA AND Gregory stood, hands joined, looking out over the lake just before evening. The sun was so deep a red that, had it been a painting, she'd have thought it a wishful fantasy. A perfect ball, edges precise, it was dropping toward the western horizon with surprising speed. To the east, its colors, reflected, lay across the water: The entire sky was aflame.

"Hard to believe," Gregory whispered, "that *we* are moving and not the sun."

This she had heard, but she wished she had had the education that could explain such an unlikeliness. Who was responsible for such a discovery? Copernicus? Galileo? Not to know such a thing was to enter the world unready.

The surface of the lake was cut a thousand times by tiny waves as if a boat had gently stirred the water, and the sun, moving or not, was casting red-orange fire across it. One long moment, hot to the eye, and flame rippled across the restless surface, burning the tips of the little waves.

"Gregory," Chaya murmured against the rough shoulder of his overcoat. "You cannot imagine how happy I am."

Gregory laughed. "That doesn't sound like you, my sweet. Aren't you obliged to count the people over on the west side who are never free to see the lake?"

"No, today I am not the center of the world." She put her face against his, coquettish, to be kissed. "Today the sun belongs to everyone. Fire is—" She sighed and considered. "A mystery. Like music, I think. Nobody owns it." Gregory's hair was glossed pale with reflected light. The man she loved gave off a modest glow. She stared until it was quenched. "And that," she announced, "is all the philosophy I have!"

Chaya watched darkness seep out of the sky and take away the water. "Today I am nothing but grateful."

"I WOULD prefer a small wedding," Chaya told him, knowing she was defending herself from scrutiny and possession by his family's tastes. More to the point, weddings were said to be the obligation of the bride, and on this ancient rock her little ship was snagged and splintered. She was not prepared to suggest a rabbi to officiate (she wished she dared, and then looked away from her cowardice).

But the more she thought of her wedding day, not to say her marriage itself, the more she longed for her family. Not in a single stroke but gradually she seemed to have revised her memory of what she had thought her mother's abandonment: Had she not wanted to keep Chaya safe, hadn't she thought she was securing her and keeping her close? There were too many contradictions to settle the question; she only knew what she had felt but now, flickeringly, regretted: that her life did not include her Mama and Papa and her darling brood. Surely they had to be there with her. They could pay not a penny toward the wedding and she would not apologize, no matter what tradition demanded. There would be no way to make them comfortable, since she was barely so herself, but they would be with her. She would claim her true self, swallow her misgivings, and be proud.

About the modest wedding, "I concur," Gregory told her amicably. "Though I will have to fight our first skirmish with my mother over that. Not a skirmish, actually—I suspect it will be a serious battle with cannon and artillery. But I should be quite as relieved as you if we were to keep this simple." Clearly it would not be his first encounter with his parents' displeasure. He had, quite pointedly, not discussed with her their response to his announcement of the engagement. As yet, no invitation to meet with them privately had been forthcoming; no public notice had been paid. Anticipating no such occurrence, news reporters were not bent double at the keyhole listening for a story.

Chaya tried to imagine anger among such tightly controlled, tastefully silent people. Possibly they simply stopped speaking? Or they might use sarcasm, say terrible things, induce him to be ashamed of her. Ned she could imagine being cruel, but her parents-in-law-to-be would have some other means of showing their disapproval. Lovemaking was only one of the new languages she would have to master.

Then there was the question of where they would live and, even sooner, of how Chaya should conduct her affairs before the marriage. She was not yet the beneficiary of Gregory's wealth. (Whether, living where he lived, he was any longer its beneficiary was an interesting question she dared not raise.) If she were to leave her work, she would seem a kept woman. Not seem: *be*, especially now that Gregory was receiving some return of virtue on his investment. The deeper problem—that she could not abandon her servitude without feeling traitorous—she refused to confront. Conscience, as Mrs. Gottlieb had warned her, was not only costly but its moral dilemmas were debilitating, and with Asher gone, she had hardly the strength to wake each morning.

And then, and then again and again . . . her Mama and Papa, her Dvorele and Yakov, her Beryle, her Yitzhak, her Masha. Were they all to come to Chicago, at least for the nuptials? She could not even dare ask if, exhausted by failure, they were ready to emigrate, this time not to a new country but to a new city. They should not have to become her husband's burden. It was time for her to make a visit. She had added inches to her brothers and sisters in her imagination, filled out their bodies, deepened their voices, at least a bit.

Her eyes grew redder every day she went to work without Asher. Her friends asked where their little Reader had disappeared to but all she could do was shake her head and shrug.

Until one Monday morning, a woman she did not know well, one of the Italians who conveyed warmth without much language, called out to her as she was arranging her tools—like a surgeon, she laid out knife, clippers, paste pot, rag in their exact places before she could begin—"Your brother—I seen him! He so *bello*—so beauty!"

"What? Where did you see him?" Chaya had leapt up and rushed across the room where she nearly knocked over the woman's desk. "You're sure it was Asher?"

"Sure, sure I sure." He was at the Fair, she managed to say. He was a prince.

"A *prince*?"

"Si! *Bellissimo!* People come, they laughing. They love!"

She threw herself upon Winkler's mercy, pleaded for the morning off without penalty. This took an explanation that was difficult to make credible: that the Reader who had sat daily entertaining his serfs had no fixed address, that he was a wild boy, and lost. It was easier for Chaya to say all this—incriminating, peculiar, perhaps damning—because she knew that she was going to tell Winkler very soon that she was finished with his shop for good and all. A tide of guilt washed over her at the thought: So this is what it feels like to leave desperation behind. To have privileges. To have immunity from reprisal. Well, maybe Sara could stop working too. What kind of wages did firemen make?

She fled as if she were being pursued, up the quaking wooden stairs to the Alley L, which took her to Sixty-Third Street, and down and, scraping in her purse for the fee, she half walked, half ran in and across the endless Exposition grounds until she came to the long confusing swathe of the Midway. It was too early for the crowds to have arrived; she had had to wait, in fact, for the ticket takers to open their little windows and set out their huge circles of tickets. Now she was going to have to calm herself and walk slowly and peer with concentration at every one of these unlikely entertainments. It was more of a soup than a carnival: The Indians sat beside the Orientals who sat beside the Dahomeyans, some of them moving around and talking, agitated, others morosely stationary on rugs and chairs. Perhaps when the masses of visitors showed up it was less artificial and depressing. Exhibits need viewers.

Her heart beat so hard she wondered if a woman her age could expire from excitement, and—if she saw him there, somehow a prince, whatever that meant—from joy.

24

HOW THEY had left Christa. How they stole away in a wagon, hidden between milk jugs, and he was carried around by the train conductor while she sat stock-still at the window: Asher remembered almost nothing of it, so much had overwhelmed him since. He could hardly stay in his seat now. The train was so much faster, grander, than the Ls around town. "It's thicker!" he called out to them. "It's tough. The Alley L is a chicken and this is a bull."

"If you don't remember riding to Chicago," Gregory prodded, "what do you remember of your old home?"

Asher hesitated. "Home?" He had run up and down the aisle a few times. "What's the difference between a home and a house?"

Gregory stared back at him. He often stared like that, nothing to say. Did he speak a different language? Meanwhile, what an idea, moving inside something bigger that was also moving! It was like the earth rotating while it traveled around the sun. "Watch!" Asher cried again and again, though his sister had lost patience. She thought there was nothing to see.

But he stopped for Gregory's question. "I don't know if I remember a house or a home. I'll remember when I see it." His eyes flickered with doubt. "Is it a park? The farm. Or a—where there are different animals? Something zoological?"

"Wherever did you get such ideas?" his sister asked him. "I'm surprised you don't remember more. You already knew so much when we left."

He shook his head under the neat haircut she had paid for, first ever not by her hand. "Knowing goes forward, remembering goes back. I'm not so good at that."

She was always surprised to discover that his genius had rules. She thought he had broken every tether.

"Will I know my mother and father?" He was swaying in the aisle as the train swayed, a dance. He exaggerated the movement.

That stung her. How could he not know them? "Oh, I hope so, dear. They will be very hurt if you don't remember them."

He escaped up the aisle again. "I won't lie if I don't."

"I'm sure he won't," Chaya murmured to Gregory. "He does terrible things—I believe he would steal from his grandmother if she happened to be rich—well, and if she wasn't buried in Ekaterinoslav!"

Asher was stopping at every seat and making a mental chart of destinations: three for Galleon, one for Sturgis; a large family with two boys—twins near his age, with whom he played eye tag—were en route to Columbia City. A man in a funny white suit—he said it was a sailor suit—was going all the way to Door County up at the top of the state. (He saw a door at the county line that the train would have to pass through, very big, wooden, with panels and a knob. Huge. How fine!)

How far was it between the stations? How fast were they traveling? When another train passed them, he held his breath—was their speed doubled? Halved? Surely something happened between the two trains, but what? They shook at its passing and a roaring noise rushed in. It wasn't enough to memorize some things; that didn't work for everything.

There were so few people in the fields as they swept past, it all seemed horizon. Green, brown, green, green, yellow. Squares and lines, hedges and stands of unidentifiable light-killing trees and in the distance, farmhouses with and without porches. A small girl in a blue dress stood still and waved at him when he finally made himself sit and look out. Maybe people were waving all the way along and he hadn't seen them. She was surrounded by brown cows, dark as rocks in the field. He waved at her, already wistful that she was grabbed back into distance.

Asher could not imagine Gregory on a farm. What little he could call

to mind with Chaya's help (dust? mud?) would soil the man's perfect cuffs.
Chaya laughed, a nervous little laugh, and told him Gregory had insisted
on coming home with them because, she said shyly, he loved her and must
know where she began.

"You didn't begin there. Are we going to Zhitomir?"

She told him that wasn't the point. Gregory had even convinced her
not to warn her parents of the visit, even if she'd known how to. "Let me
have an unposed portrait, not a stiff one, everyone in their Sunday best."

"Our best is on Saturday," Asher rebuked him coolly. What did he know
of them? And why did Chai seem so different with Gregory? That tinkly
laugh was someone else's.

The station in Christa was almost familiar, brick and limestone, fancy,
with a castle turret on one side. He liked its friendly shape.

But down at ground level, the world slowed. He watched Gregory walk
to the end of the platform to find them a hack. Asher had never seen him
at such a distance—every movement was smoothed by confidence—the
way he raised his arm, the words he spoke. The soles of Gregory's shoes
seemed to walk an inch off the ground. No wonder Chaya was in his
vest pocket.

Did he remember Main Street? Not much of it—one shop called
Doreen's Mercantile, under a yellow awning—that was, or was not, where
he first felt the kleptomaniacal itch in his fingers. "I used to get you ribbons
there!" he called out to Chaya. "Didn't I?" She nodded but did not look
happy at the thought. Was the town rich or poor? It was hard to tell, it was
so *plain* compared to Chicago. It was like a simple painting—he had seen
a whole house of paintings at the Fair, had slept in it one night in a long
hall full of golden frames and slickened scenes that glowed when the light
hit them just right. You could see where the paintbrush had licked them.
Christa was like the kind of painting that showed one thing at a time, not
a scene that went back and back. There were trees up and down the street,
dark ones, light ones, nudged by the breeze—in Chicago you had to go to
a park to see so much leafage, so much greenery (*greenery, scenery*)—but
here there were only a few streets and behind them you could see where
the fields began, so soon! A narrow place. Most of the roads that veered off

the main street were dirt: ridged, wrinkled, lumpy. Wagons tipped to this side and that, waddling as they went.

The pied horse that pulled them out of town was a careful walker. He took his time like an old man picking his way. Chaya and Gregory were quiet, holding on to each other's hands. Everything about them was secret now. Turned to each other, they kept him out. Asher stayed busy looking for something familiar, anything. Erased, those years—or he would remember when they were in the farmyard, because that was where Chaya said he had lived most of his time.

Then came a fence, uneven, collapsing in places, fallen into tall weeds, and a break in the fence, and the horse took the opening and pulled them in. Gregory pulled bills from his pocket—he had a silver mazuma clip!— and paid the cabman, who looked him up and down as if he were one of the savages at the Fair. Then he shook the reins with a little shout, neatly turned his horse and vanished.

25

CHAYA KEPT her eyes closed through most of the trip, though she was much too agitated to sleep. She was trying to remember the girl who had accidentally stolen her brother and escaped the Fields of Zion. When she'd told Asher that she was marrying Gregory he only looked at her in silence and blinked as if the words were not sound but a light that shocked his eyes. She tried to reassure him that her love for him would not, would *never* change but, he said, with a weariness that alarmed her, "You are going over to *them*, Chai. You hate them and they hate you. You *know* it."

"But Gregory is one of us, Ash. He is giving over his life to the same people we are!" She knew Asher had been spending time with his down-and-outers, coming home late from their incessant meetings, which he said little about. She was not sure that, so occupied with saving the world, he understood that men and women shared something beyond the economic, even the social. He was a little slow where that was concerned, hadn't quite awakened yet to the convex and concave fit of bodies, and of sympathies that went nameless. When she saw the way he turned away from her without a single word of congratulation, she thought, *You have lost him now. You have surely lost your first and deepest love.* But she vowed that they, together, she and Gregory, would bring him around.

Dreaming, she kept herself busy from Dearborn Station until they arrived in Christa. It was as though everything had already happened.

They would be met by the children, who would shriek with delight when it came clear who it was, returned. She could call up the smell exactly: sour, ashy, burnt-over, raw earth, and something green that she pulled up and tasted without danger. Sorrel, clover. Mrs. Gottlieb made sorrel soup; she said it grew all over where she was a girl. And Gregory standing back modestly, watching them, showing a helpless little smile. They would be speaking Yiddish.

Then, out of the distance, with a high cry, her mother would come rushing forward and smother Asher against her. (Chaya, gracious, would allow him the first embrace.) The size of her mother would be so familiar, her long legs, her large feet. She looked strong. Her eyes, a *goyishe* blue, would be more tired than they had been before. She had no smell but sweat and yeast, a little bit of yeast: probably she had been baking. Children would pile on him—Dvorele, Yakov, Binyomin, Masha, bony, short-haired boys and her sisters in faded spriggy skirts, with high-pitched voices. They'd grind against Asher, screaming his name, reaching for him. One brother—Beryle, probably, who had always been the liveliest—would punch him in the arm in greeting. Asher, they would be surprised to learn, was used to being famous. Many crowds had surrounded him before, imagine!—the cigar women, the Sunday partygoers, the hungry who had no homes except, on the coldest nights, City Hall, and the fairgoers, of course, the ones who paid actual money to converse with him!—but none of them *touched* him. She knew he did not like to be touched by strangers and would wish they were not pawing him now. But he would work hard at saying nothing, shaking no one off. It took self-control he didn't know he had. She would be proud of him. Her boy.

Their father, Mama might say, was in town buying feed. Asher's hesitation met some small hesitation from her—she seemed happy to have him—them—there, but she had a kind of reserve behind her smile. She still looked afraid of Asher. It pricked Chaya; always had. It was cold water and not a warm bath. Not what you expected of a mother.

Then Chaya would introduce Gregory, in a language Gregory could only nod at. She would gesture to him, to Asher, to the farmyard. She saw Mama look at Gregory with her head slanted, the way she had seen Mrs.

Gottlieb evaluate something, a mop or a dress she was thinking of buying from a pushcart on the street, figuring out whether it was as good a deal as she was being told. Did she have no English at all?

Enough to say, "Thank you, is good, yes," and then cover her eyes, embarrassed, like a girl. When she took down her hands, she would begin, shyly, to beam at Gregory, the smile moving every part of her face.

CHAYA WAS prepared for the Fields of Zion to be as worn and colorless as she remembered: unpainted buildings, missing slats on the sides of the coop through which she could see a deep darkness, a scrabbled dooryard humped with clots of dried grass. But all that would be suddenly irrelevant, the fabric of her life, like a torn seam, cauterized by the heat of her return. The people moving across the yard would be warm, real, and clamorous. The women who had come out of the kitchen would stand in a ragged ring around her, as if they were too dazzled to come closer. Fraydl would hold her apron to her face, to stifle her emotion.

The brim of her hat tight against the plush of the train seat, Chaya saw it behind her eyes and it gave her such pleasure she tightened her hands into fists, impatient: how she would go to her mother like a child, relieved to be held against her as she had never been before. Her mother, that cool woman, crooning *Chayele, meyne tokhter, Chayele,* wet-cheeked, rocking with her. She was not angry, she was not about to scold. The winters fell away, Chaya's abused, tobacco-stained fingers, the silence of Mrs. Gottlieb's long sleep, the search for her brother. She kept her eyes clenched against everything but this rocking.

Then she remembered Gregory. As if she had awakened from a stolen sleep, she would look frantically around for him and then find him. Would see—perfect, perfect!—how the children had seized his hands, the bigger ones fitted under his arms, and were dragging him from one side to the other of the dooryard, showing him the chickens who would not stay in their house at laying time, and who fled at their approach, introducing him to a horse she had never before seen, white as an albino, charmless but sturdy. The horse would have a brown tail that rotated lazily, like fingers skimming through water, first this way, then that, unhurried. The horse, barrel-bellied, would look at her calmly, as if he knew her and was not surprised to see her.

Asher, her dream-Asher, had disappeared. Always and forever the cat in him would render no explanations and beg no leave. He was most likely in the woods, exploring, or running through the cornfield. Discovering the pond, none of its purposes (swimming hole, *mikve*) visible just now.

Set free by her mother (who would be thicker than she remembered, but with a far lovelier face, the forthright face of an aging girl), Chaya would go to claim her fiancé. "Are you surviving all this enthusiasm? If you would like me to call them off—"

By now, sweating the way she only saw him sweat when they lay together, exhausted, in his bed. "It takes an effort to be friendly," he would whisper, "when one can only grunt and smile. Don't they go to school?"

"I don't know. But I know nobody speaks any English out here. Only in town." Seen up close, Gregory would seem, as he always did, to be made of some wholly different stuff than everything, everyone in the scruffy dooryard. He was so clean, so unblemished. His pores had never closed around this incessant floating layer of dust. His hands seemed impervious to dirt, doomed to stay clean even after Dvorele proudly thrust into them an egg, possibly leaking, and stuck all over with straw. His woolens did not chafe into wrinkles. His shoes were dulled, but it would only take a cloth to renew their gleam.

By now, her father would have returned with Zanvel and a wagonful of seed bags, and he would be so flustered at seeing her—who could have predicted it?—that he would give her a perfunctory greeting and quickly turn back to unload his cargo. She hoped he was so overcome with emotion that he could not let her see it, but his scowl was not promising.

She would go in search of Asher, futilely calling his name, and when she returns alone, she will strip Gregory to his shirtsleeves, collar undone, receiving the huge, shapeless sacks from her father, who counts aloud as he hands them off the wagon: "*Finf. Zeks. Zibn.*" She sees Gregory sling them over the shoulder of his striped shirt and carry them, straining, to the side of the barn, where he stacks them in a teetering pile. One sack slumps sideways to the ground and she watches him struggle to get a handhold on its shapeless girth. *You are deeply good, my love. You are rich with effort. Now, who will be more impressed with your willingness, my family, or me, or your own sweet self?*

The train had stopped at Sturgis. She opened her eyes to watch a family descend onto the platform, where they were greeted with embraces, the children swept up gaily by their grandparents. She closed her eyes again, to continue her dream, which she could do because she was not asleep.

WHEN, FINALLY, they sit down to supper, sadder than Mrs. Gottlieb's worn and shabby rooms, what they will see is the cracked, unmatching china bought cheap, some delicate, from some downtown lady's elegant dining room, some intended for farmers, thick as their workhorse, all of it crazed with use and permanently stained. She remembered bowls of whatever happened to be in season in the garden, which in some months was not quite sufficient, bolstered by bread, endless, boring, stomach-filling sourdough. "Dunk it," their mothers had coaxed the children. "Take that gravy on it, you'll like it. Here, push the bread around a little. You see?" They did dunk, but they could not make themselves like it.

But this was August and today the table would bloom—why not?— with squash and beans, vivid greens and the first young beets, with a few roasted chickens on the side, meager and still whole but golden and shiny as varnished wood. Colors would glow, textures make a carnival of contrasts—she could not remember such a bountiful spread, but why not create one? With luck and good weather, it could actually befall them.

Pesye, thrilled by his presence, would very likely put Gregory at the head of the table. "*Shah, shah!*" she'd scold, waving her hand at him when he protested, as if he were a disobedient child. The men would applaud. Chaya tried to suppress her cynicism about such large gestures of generosity from someone she knew to be small and suspicious. Would Pesye see in Gregory a benefactor for the farm, or merely—merely!—a handsome, gracious, mysterious suitor for one of their own, their prodigal returned with a glamorous catch? For all her pious chauvinism, perhaps not only a gentleman but a *goy*? Pesye's eyes would still and forever be tiny as raisins in her doughy face. When she smiled they disappeared entirely, and she would smile more this day than Chaya remembered having seen in her lifetime.

But their English would be a problem, wouldn't it? Always, the men managed better than the women because they were the ones abroad in the world, bartering, negotiating, selling what they did not keep. Through their attempted questions Gregory would nod and maintain a not-quite-convincing expression of interest and concern. When Zanvel arrived at the necessary moment, and asked him, "What is your line of work? What you are doing for a living?" he would take a long contemplative swallow of water. (Their water was gorgeous, Chaya had to admit: clean well water unlike anything the city could provide.) She waited, apprehensive.

"I am—writing a book." He would say this like a slightly guilty boy, uncertain whether he should be proud or ashamed. (Or was this only her skepticism at work?)

"A book! Like Tolstoy!" Chaya pictured her mother transfixed behind him, where she was dishing out a stew of summer squash and early turnips, smooth and sharp-smelling.

"Not—exactly." Modestly. "I am trying—"

Oh dear. The color would pour upward from his collar to his hairline. His jacket was hanging on the back of his chair, a swathe of subtle, winy browns.

"I am trying to write about—how unfair it is that workers are so—" She, if asked, would say *abused*. "Oppressed." That was a word they would recognize.

That was the word, in fact, or rather the idea, that would finally bring Father to respectful attention. He'd have been slouched, looking darkly at the two of them. He would have asked no questions, volunteered no answers, would only seem, whether jealously or simply disapprovingly, to be measuring the distance between the child he had loved and the woman who had returned a stranger.

Since she was painting the picture, she could, by force of her own need, happen to be turned to her father in his chair near the end of the table when Gregory lay the words *labor* and *oppressed* side by side in the same sentence, to see his expression relax like someone putting a painful burden down, like Gregory unscrewing his face as he lowered those heavy feed sacks to the grass. It was Gregory's vocation—futile, she thought, another well-intentioned folly, all right, but pure in intention—that would impress Avrahm Shaderowsky, socialist manqué. He would not wink at Chaya, not being a winking man, but would widen his dark eyes a fraction as if to show her he had been light-struck—*enlightened*—and she would pause with her spoon halfway to her mouth. They'd have finished the squash and turnips and be on to a lovely custard, spun of the two things they always had in plenty, courtesy of the renegade chickens and the hard-working cows, and she would widen her eyes back at him, surprised, relieved. Content.

She had seen it and so—*dear Lord, please, please*—so let it be.

IT WOULD not be easy to estimate the morale of the community, and to judge by the condition of the buildings, how the farmers—that still seemed an absurd word for them—were faring. Little would appear to have changed. Even though the garden was yielding and there might be a bit of stringy meat at the table, it was a good guess that they would not have become comfortable, let alone prosperous.

Shimmie, that terrible fate she had blessedly escaped, had probably stayed; had (wouldn't this be logical?) set his colorless eyes on the next girl down the line, and wed her. Gittl would run forward to embrace Chaya when first she arrived, but her stomach, round as an apronful of tomatoes, would prevent her from coming very close. Shimmie, hairline already in retreat, leaving frail wisps which made him more ghostly still, would be one of those men who shadowed his wife, either because he was too smitten to leave her side or because he saw her pregnancy as a perilous state that rendered her helpless. She imagined herself behind one of those thin wooden walls in the tiny room they'd have been assigned. They would not have built the houses they had dreamed of. There would only be space for the baby-making bed and a trunk, perhaps, to hold what few valuables they owned between them, and a quilt or a featherbed for winter. The devout couples had the larger rooms, to accommodate two beds to make tolerable the weeks of the month when husband and wife were to stay separate.

She could not avoid the image of Shimmie's head beside her on the pillow, and worse, his head the least of it. This was worth a sigh of relief: She replaced him with Gregory stretched, tan and taut, across his beautiful bed with its ornate headboard carved like a bower (another incongruous detail in his poor-man's rooms), saw all the marvels of his body through which he patiently guided her, so perfect, so complex, so assertive, annihilating the guilt she should have felt for being there with him.

But enough. Good luck to her old friend Gittl (if Gittl it was) who whispered, blushing, that she thought she might be carrying twins. It was unseemly for Chaya to imagine how they had come to be, twined around each other in that thrusting globe of a stomach. Beside him on the scratchy plush train seat, she searched for Gregory's hand, and the bone-strength of his fingers, squeezing hers, stirred her quite ignobly as if, right there on the Chicago and Northwestern, he had cradled her breast in his warm palm.

THE HACKMAN let them down in the grassless dooryard between the barn and the Commons and drove away. Chaya turned slowly, facing the buildings, facing the garden, facing the rumpled road they had arrived on, waiting for the children she had called forth in her dream. She heard no voices. No horse, old or new, grazed beyond the fence. No chickens scuffled the ground between the weeds and flapped their feathers with the sound of a shuffled deck of cards.

A long silence. And longer still.

"Chai?" Asher asked finally, very quietly. He slipped his hand into hers. Gregory was standing, hands on his hips, lips slightly parted.

There was such an air of absence, of removal, that it felt the way it had once when a tornado passed only a few miles away: an airlessness that made it hard to breathe. It was not simply silence, as though they were occupied elsewhere. It was a hollowed-out stillness, an emptiness that still held the shape of what had vanished. Pale grass, thick unmoving grass, lay across the yard as if it had always grown there, clotted. Where there had been one, there was no path.

It was absolute as death.

Gregory slipped his arm delicately around her waist. "Chaya?" He said her name softly as if he were waking her. "Do you have any idea—"

For that he received only a look from her. *Why does crisis make us stupid?*

She walked slowly forward, the way she would in a real dream, not in the fantasy she had so indulged on the train, elbow on the windowsill, leaning smiling against her hand. The Commons door was open wide; blowing leaves had scattered their way across the floor like fallen birds. No tables, no chairs. No woodstove. The crockery was gone, both thick and thin. Everything had vanished, and, except for the leaves that must have gotten in later, some good wife had swept one last time with punishing rigor. After her abandonment, Mrs. Gottlieb had sunk into her long sleep and Chaya could feel just such a torpor rising in her chest, softening her legs at the knee. There was no place to sit herself down, though, unless it was the floor. Nothing remained onto which she could sink, close to the ground like a mourner on a box sitting *shiva*, grieving.

"What should I have expected?" Her husk of a voice. "Even if they had wanted to tell us—Asher—" She looked at both her boys. It was her fault, her pride. She had waited to bring them her perfect life. She had not thought of them enough, and when she did, it was without pity. "Even if they forgave us, how would they know where to find us?"

"Were we hiding?" Asher asked, turning his eyes up to hers. His innocence was a punishment.

She had to think about that. "No, not really. But the city—you know how it covers you up." Snow in your tracks. Grass on your grave. When she left them, she was flying free, and because she could have flown back to the nest at any moment, she never doubted she could wait until she was ready. She had never thought escape could work both ways.

But they had left not so much as a shred of paper, a stick stuck through a message, a map incised in the barn wall—not any hint at all, in case she came looking. Now she was an orphan.

CHAYA WALKED off to the right of the long unplanted rows, through milkweed and spiny, tangled grasses, far out into the field. Asher ran beside her, quiet as an animal, and Gregory followed at a distance that betokened respect. The rusted gate of the little graveyard hung crooked, from one hinge. How could they have left their dead, few though they were? She had trouble moving the gate and when Gregory stepped forward to help, its single rusted hinge crumbled so that he was left holding it, its grillwork yellow-green with lichen.

Her panic had subsided in the long walk from the barnyard, but it returned as she scanned the stones. Infant Sorele's grave was overwhelmed with weeds and—"Oh!" Chaya breathed. Beside it, a newer one! On a flat, gray stone, hand-cut, her brother's name—בּעריל—and the year of his death without a month or day. Last year. It was not possible. It could not be, her scampering, mischievous, chattering little brother beneath the soil. But the dirt was more freshly turned than it was on the old graves, she could see that. Ruined flower petals, orange and yellow, were faintly visible in the dirt (though the pious ones would never adorn a burial with anything live. It was one of the arguments between factions, but always the antagonists pulled back because no one would argue hard in the face of a fresh death). She sank to the ground and cried for her brother—next to her Asher, Beryle had been her favorite, the one with the most spirit and the sweetest mouth. Everything about him was slightly awry, from the cowlick that stood straight up like a cock's comb to the space between his teeth to his big puppy feet that forever got in each other's way. Could he have sickened or—more likely, given his temperament—might he have perished in an accident? He was the child who would leap from the highest rock, stay longest in the pond, dangle from the rafters in the barn. When would this have happened? תרבב told her nothing. How could she not have felt such a cataclysm a hundred miles away? And where, oh where, in their grief, had they gone? How could they have left him here, so alone?

Now, rising, she saw that the single row of graves had multiplied. There was the beginning of a second row, two small anonymous stones, just large rocks from the field—for infants. And there—ah, no, another with no stone, but clearly a tamped-down, recently filled-in mound. *Who? Who?* She reviewed their faces, which were suddenly too dear to be borne; saw the shapes their bodies made, their vulnerable bodies. Her mother, her father might be here, too freshly dead to be marked, or so fragilely marked that their names had blown away or been seized by an animal. There were foxes in this field. There were deer, raccoons, every kind of life sweeping across the hill and through the graveyard, fence or no fence. She stared at the dirt, which gave no sign. Zanvel, Itzhak, Fraydl, Uri, Pesye, anyone at all.

Gregory, supporting her on their way back to the road, could say nothing. None of this was his. Though it had been hers she had defaulted on it, and now, bankrupt, she was owed nothing. No explanation; not even a name.

"Back in town," he finally said, "people will know where they have gone." But they had been such a lonely outpost, would anyone have known them well enough to have heard their plans? He could never understand how solitary they were. He could not begin to imagine their otherness.

There was no carriage to take them back down. Asher offered to run ahead and find someone with a wagon. Chaya watched him calculating, that little catch in his eyes when he was looking inside his own limitless head. If he came upon a horse and carriage anywhere along the way, or a hay wagon, he would talk someone into bringing him up here with it. If there was no one in sight, she was sure he would simply annex it as his own and learn, quickly, how to curb the horse.

But before she could restrain him in the tone she knew he hated, he was gone, jackrabbit raising a fog of dust. He would have a long way to go before he found a farm.

Asher had not returned by the time they arrived on Christa's Main Street, peppered with dirt, their feet burning with pain. He was leaning nonchalantly against the window of the newspaper office, having finished polling every shopkeeper and a friendly man at the post office window as well. "They told me where the school is. I went over there, too, but no one was there. Is that where I would have studied?"

Chaya was nearly prostrate with thirst and exhaustion. "Yes, I suppose you would have, if we had stayed. You could have taught there, probably, as well as the teacher!"

The start thing Asher had learned was: Debts. What little the Fields of Zion had had they sold, months ago, at auction, but the debts had hardly been touched when the sun went down. They didn't own that farm, as the man at the post office knew, so they could not sell it to recover as much as a dollar. And then—so many farms ended this way—they had simply disappeared. Possibly, the man at the livery stable said, they had not really snuck away. Only they kept so much to themselves, people never did see that much of them except when they came into town to market, where they had creditors but not friends. But they might not have run away at all, just cleared out, finished—that depended on how you looked at it. No one had any idea where they went, or if they stayed together or scattered. Such removals were not uncommon these days.

Asher had left Doreen's Mercantile for last, because Chaya might like to see it again. He sniffed around, trying to remember if it was, indeed, the place where he had discovered the convenience of gently removing and secreting what he wanted. The woman behind the counter must have assumed they were creditors. *So that is how much I have changed,* Chaya thought, numb. Was it her dress, her hat, her carriage? Two years in the city and she had become anonymous!

The proprietress was wearing a blue taffeta with ornate black frogs sealing up the front, considerably too dressy for her situation, which advertised that she had airs and thought she deserved them. She leaned a bosom shaped like a goosedown pillow across her counter and said, chiefly to Gregory, "It would be like Jews to run away from the money they owed."

He widened his eyes, about to object, but she went on without pause and with considerable relish. Those people thought they were too good for the English language. She had heard that they bred with each other, sisters and brothers, fathers and daughters. Many strange things happened up there, and then they had some diphtheria that probably came from a sick cow or something dirty they should have cleaned up, and some thought there was the chance they had passed it on in the milk they sold. Doreen, personally, was glad they were gone.

Chaya took a moment to ask herself if she had heard correctly. "I am—I was—one of those people you have just insulted. Good people." She said this with deadly calm, her face flooded with blood. Gregory laid a restraining hand on her arm, which she looked at as if it belonged to a stranger.

"Your lies are stupid and dangerous." Her mouth had filled, somehow, with sand. "If the others on this street have the kind of vile imagination you do, I can see how they would not have found friends to help them in their need."

Her words seemed to come from a stranger as well, she who had so hated the farm, who had so dismissed Christa as a place for victims of no ambition. But she could hardly see, now, through her rage, which became a veil that mottled everything, light and dark, before her.

The woman in blue muttered something, not an apology, only the defense that she had not known to whom she was speaking. She took a large step backwards as if Chaya, wronged, might be dangerous. But Chaya was already stumbling over the threshold and out into the warm late afternoon which, as the sun began to pale, smelled wantonly of petunias. Such sweetness felt corrupt just then. She wanted to be alone, not to think but to wail. They could have gone anywhere—could even be in Chicago, for all anyone knew. Was it diphtheria that had killed Beryle and the others whose names were not recorded, that wretched choking disease that made children wish to die rather than suffocate?

Was Gregory's family, now, the only one she had? The questions were too exhausting. All she wanted to do was sleep.

26

THEY WERE on the train again. He listened to its clacking. Could you count the times they passed over a tie? Too, too many all the miles to Chicago—that would be like counting stars.

Chaya woke up and took his hand and asked him what he remembered about Beryle.

The farm was so distant—he thought of time as space. If he could see it, it was real. What Chaya remembered was invisible. And who. She was sad now because she let in too many old, done facts and they seemed to hurt her.

"I don't remember him at all. Or much else from then."

"Beryle was your brother," she scolded. "Your little brother. How can you not feel—"

"I can't *see* him. Do you have a picture? What did he look like? I might recognize him."

His sister drew away from him, folding her skirts tight around her.

"Everything is new," he told her. "Everything real is right in front of me where I can touch it."

She sighed. "Asher, what do you see when you are reading? You love words so much, I think you love them more than you love people. What do they mean to you? You can't touch them."

He had to think about that. He stared into his hand, at its folds and the lines that ran off in all directions. Today was so hot they were wet and shiny. Little rivers. "But they—they touch *me*. I like the way they feel in my mouth. They keep me busy. And they're full of things that happen right where I can see them."

Chaya was staring at him as if she'd never seen him before.

You can't touch a lot of things, he thought. Music! Fire! He had learned a beautiful word the other day—what was he reading? Some poet whose name he'd forgotten. He had learned it just in time because that's what they were: *ineffable.*

"When I'm reading, they leap around in my mouth. The syllables."

"The syllables." She was still not smiling. Did she know what a syllable was?

"Just listen. It's a part of a word. It makes a single sound. *Sill-a-bull.* That's three syllables. When you say it, it feels so funny!" He could feel his tongue behind his teeth, alive, ready to move. His lips made shapes to contain what his voice wanted. But her face worried him.

She sighed again. She was still too much of a sigher.

He smiled and shrugged. "Doesn't it?"

"CHAI," HE said to her one morning before she left for work. "Would you do something for me?" He could see she was feeling the need to placate him—*play* and *cater*—because he would not forgive her for Gregory.

"Do what, darling?" She looked too eager: he knew she would do anything he asked.

"Come to a meeting with me? Meet my men."

"Your men. You think of them as yours? I'm not sure what you mean."

"You'll see."

"I'd have to take an evening off work."

"Play sick. Tell him you're contagious. What can he do to you? You're about to quit." *You're going to be a lady,* he didn't say. "Let Yanowitz find himself another slave."

She was thinking about it, eyes wide, trying to see what he meant. "Can I bring Gregory?"

"No, you can't bring Gregory! They would laugh him out of the room." He would be shamed, bringing that fop (a new word, as harsh as it sounded. *Fopppp*).

She did not look happy.

"Are you afraid to do anything without him?"

"I'll see, Asher. I have to—"

"Have to what? Do you need his permission?"

She narrowed her eyes at him. "I hardly recognize you these days, little brother, do you know that?" Tears balanced on her lashes but did not fall.

"Do you know what *ditto* means? Ditto, ditto, big sister. The same to you."

She fisted her hands as if she might raise them against him. "I will not go anywhere Gregory is not welcome, Ash. I'm sorry. He is giving— trying to give—his life to our struggle and I do not intend to banish him because he—"

She hesitated long enough for him to take courage. "He what? What is he giving? You can smell his money on him, he's like an actor playing a part, he's—"

"Enough, Asher. That is more than enough." She turned away from him to finish buttoning the shirt she wore for work and finally those tears brimmed over and streaked the face he used to think beautiful.

27

SHE COULD not talk about Gregory with Gregory. She could not ask Sara
what she meant when she said she loved her Joe. Mrs. Gottlieb saw nothing
but salvation by bank account. Miss Addams was brave and brilliant but
she was not truly Chaya's friend, her equal. Her family was missing and
her brother thought her a traitor. Ungrateful, self-pitying girl, what had
she done to herself? In her confusion, furious at everyone, she stabbed at
a tobacco leaf that was resisting her, muttering, "Stupid thing, what is
wrong with you!" and, sloppy, sliced her thumb so deeply she watched the
blood pour over her little table like spilled wine. Pain for a reason, that
was better. Pain that made her cry out and call for help. She watched the
women rush to find what she needed and was comforted. They thought she
was brave, letting them bind her up without a whimper but it felt good to
look away from her invisible misery for a few minutes of sanctioned pity.

That evening, because she could not go to Yanowitz's with her hand
bound like a paw, Gregory took her to the opera, where she sat surrounded
by the people she was going to live beside forever. The women smelled
of too much perfume; for some reason they wanted to be taken for roses.
The men seemed to her hulked in their seats. Down the row, one of them
snored gently until his wife gave him a vicious poke.

She put her head back and stared like a child. The round cornice at the
front of the hall was a glory; it was lush and golden and for once she did
not resist it. Listening as she had never done, she could feel her breathing

slow and deepen. No words, or at least no words she could understand: The story was called *Il Trovatore*. A war was raging somewhere but there was time for soaring tributes to love unlike any she could imagine; there was a mourning mother and a gypsy witch, a fire and a glowing anvil to beat upon, and a chorus of dancers both lovely and absurd, who padded around on the wooden stage with an indoor sound that was nothing like feet on soil. The words flowed right over her, incomprehensible, but the music made her hold her breath. She drifted and drifted.

So, Chaya thought—Miss Addams was right: There was a space so far from ordinary life it could not be compared to anything else. It was beyond translation. As he had when they stood at the side of the lake watching the sun's reflection swelling and breaking, Gregory took her hand and held it, delighted at her delight. She was not sure she liked it that he derived so much pleasure from watching her discoveries, as if he were a parent and she a child. But was that any reason she should deny herself a lifetime of music? Was there any reason for anything? She had never been drunk but she was drunk there in her seat, wholly irresponsible, allowing herself, once again, to be at peace.

THEN BACK to earth: Gregory's mother asked for an audience with her. That was not what he called it when he told her, and Chaya was sure Mrs. Stillman did not think of it that way, but she felt summoned, with no possible escape. "She wants to know you a bit, my sweet," he said to her as placatingly as he could manage, though he surely knew the request would make her quail. "You know she is as diffident as you are." Chaya—surely to goad him with her helplessness—stiffened her back and said, "What does *diffident* mean?"

He appraised her coolly. "You don't have to know what it means to imagine how difficult this is for her. I simply think she is a little bit like you. She is not demonstrative, like Ned. Or negative. Nor is she indifferent, like my father. I'm certain she will be as terrified as you but you—" He sighed, deflated. "This will be good for both of you even if it feels like medicine going down. You are going to be friends for a long time, you know. You might as well begin now."

They met on neutral territory, at a restaurant on State Street, neither in his mother's neighborhood nor Chaya's. Faith Stillman came toward her smiling, color high on her pale cheeks, and, mouth dry, Chaya nodded and followed her to their seats. It was, of course, a Sunday, because Chaya had no time for such pleasantries on a workday; there were families all around, noisy and full of motion. The room was as big as a cow barn, high-ceilinged, and every voice seemed to echo.

Before she spoke, Faith Stillman looked down at her hands, which she had clasped in her lap. "I am—thank you for coming today. I—" She fixed her eyes on the table ahead of them where a small boy was banging his spoon on his plate and being ignored. That seemed easier than looking straight at Chaya. "I first—I would like to call you by whatever name you—prefer. Gregory refers to you as Ceil but you—I don't—"

This was, somehow, her way of acknowledging that Chaya might not be exactly who she was said to be. "Thank you for asking" was the best Chaya could manage until she could calculate what answer would honor her thoughtfulness. "I am—I have always been Chaya-Libbe, though the Libbe part most often disappears, it makes the name so long. The Ceil is—" If she could not be truthful, why was she here? She allowed herself a modest wince. "I understand that Gregory worries that I would have to hear people mispronounce it but—" She would not acknowledge that what concerned him was how it identified her as a "Jewess." Instead she gave him credit he did not deserve. "I really don't mind how people say it, though. With or without the difficulty, that is my name." She gave as challenging a look as she could. "As Faith is yours."

"Oh, yes. Faith was my grandmother's name, though I must say I remember very little evidence that she placed much faith in anything. Her religion. Her husband who was—" She laughed, mischievous. "Well, let us never mind that."

The menus had arrived and Chaya was confronted with a dozen choices she could hardly picture. What decorated the tables at the Stillmans' or the parties that Asher and she worked was beautifully nameless, picturesque but anonymous. She blindly ordered some sort of steak.

Faith Stillman plunged, then, so courageously Chaya nearly dropped her water glass. "You can eat the meat, then? That is not, um, what I think is—kosher? Special to your faith?"

She laughed, though Chaya supposed her daring was not funny to her. "Oh, many—I am not—I do not follow—yes, I can eat the meat. There are many of us who do not follow the—" They were, and more credit to them, getting right down to it. "The traditions. In many ways. Though we respect them. Some practice them, some do not." How would her dear apostate father have answered? Chaya shrugged as if the question meant nothing to her, but she understood that Gregory's mother needed to know how far outside her experience she fell, and how far this unfamiliar young woman might divert her son.

Faith Stillman, fanning herself delicately with her hand, claimed that she was eating as little as possible so she might fit into a dress she had bought for a wedding. She ordered an elaborate salad and Chaya was left thinking, *Wedding, wedding, isn't that why we are here?* Hadn't he told her?

But she had reminded herself as well. "And now you two . . ."

Chaya sat up straighter. "We two appear to be on the way to joining ourselves, yes, for the future, I suppose you would say." She looked at her future mother-in-law, terrified to know whether she would oppose her outright or undermine her gently.

"Chaya." She managed the *ch* as gamely as she could. "I—you need to know, first, that I trust my son utterly in all things." She smiled. "Or should I say, nearly all things. No one has perfect judgment, wouldn't you agree?" That confiding color, and a spray of freckles, rose on her cheeks again, an alternation of pallor and blush. She was not made for keeping her feelings secret. "Therefore, his having chosen you speaks all I need to hear. He has never been—irresponsible—in his relationships. Like some." She might as well have named names. Astounding. "And I thoroughly—I dare to say thoroughly though that may speak only to my limited experience—I understand that you have weathered many—ah—changes in fortune very quickly."

Their food was set before them, Chaya's with the admonition to keep her hands away from her heated plate. She stared at her steak, swimming in pale blood, as if it might begin to dance. *Here it comes*, she thought. *Here come her qualms and refusals.*

"I so respect what you have had to master," her future mother-in-law said to her, picked up her fork, and held it still. Her hand was shaking. "It must be extremely—challenging—to have learned a new language and new—what?—new ways of doing things."

All Chaya could do was smile vaguely, look encouraging, and wonder, *Does she think I come from deepest Africa or the provinces of China?*

But that was not her point. "My own life has been—what you would call—bounded. Chaya. I—when I was a child I walked in the footsteps that had already been walked in, you see, and my feet fitted perfectly. I did not deviate. Nor, I suppose, has my Lallie. We have been—obedient." She was looking into the distance. "Or no, that makes us sound like trained poodles. Let us say, obliging. We have accepted the terms offered us."

Again Chaya said nothing to interrupt. Is every life a fabric of compromises, then? Warp what you love, weft what you must tolerate, an imperfect weave, however strong and lovely it might look?

"Sometimes it was not easy. I was tall, quite tall at an early age, and that was exceedingly uncomfortable. A girl is not supposed to—well, you may imagine. And I was—I was called *goose neck* all the years of my childhood." Her hand went to the high pleated collar that covered her neck as she said this, as if in sympathy. Her pile of greens lay untouched. "Otherwise, let me say, I was not generally at ease but I did not dare go my own way." She was smiling sadly. "And so I want you to know that I have great admiration for your—" She sighed. "What would you call it?"

This was not a rhetorical question; apparently she hoped for an answer. Was she as guileless as she seemed, so steeped in regret? Or should Chaya be suspicious that she wanted to trap her into admitting that she had vaulted herself up a steep precipice, using her son for a foothold? That her accomplishment was securing the Stillman fortune to save herself? Oh, naïf! Oh, cynic! This was a momentous choice and she dangled between the two. She stalled by cutting into her steak and watching its juices meander in little streams across her plate. "Gregory is. . . ," she began. "I had no expectation when I came to Chicago with my brother that I would be—" Be what? What had she been? "I was for a long time very lonely, Mrs. Stillman. My situation was a bad one. A grim one. But mostly, I would say, I was just—alone and cold. I was—many times I wondered if I had made a mistake coming here, away from my family, away from everything I knew. I would not wish anyone to be so—" She wanted to say *untouched* but she did not dare.

She had not breathed since she began.

"He is such a good man, Gregory. He is kind and he—I think he is trying not to follow in the footsteps that were laid out for him." She wanted to say, *And so he is your son,* but that felt like a raw attempt to plead for her favor. "And so he keeps me warm. I don't know what else to say. I had not intended it." Then, surprising herself, she asked, suddenly urgent, "What was he like as a boy, Mrs. Stillman? I wish I could imagine him before we met."

"Ah, what was he like." Gregory's mother closed her eyes to contemplate the matter and then spoke slowly, sorting out her reflections as if she had never thought about them before. "You—I think the most important thing you must know about Gregory is that when he was little he was his brother Ned's shadow. Ned was born strong and of a, what I would call, a contentious nature. He was never gentle. He was not given to conciliation. And he was not considerate of his little brother, who followed him around like a puppy." She did not look happy, remembering. "Gregory had a tender soul, a sweetness that brought out the sweetness in everyone except Ned. Oh dear, he bore insult again and again, he was mocked for his softness. He was—how shall I say it? He was made of such a different texture, you could feel it if you touched them both." She shook her head. "Ned mocked him for being so endlessly hopeful that they would be friends—and it was vain to try to protect him." Again, she was looking into the middle distance, away from Chaya but, to her credit, not away from her question. "Therefore I would say that when Gregory was old enough to come into his own a bit—to make his own judgments, to see how Ned's words and actions were hurtful and how unnatural it was for him to emulate such—" She let the sentence dwindle, unfinished, while Chaya worked at grasping what *emulate* might mean. Mrs. Stillman finally managed, "I need to assure you that Ned is not always what he seems, he has his—he is passionate, he is intense and goes at everything full tilt. I do not want him to seem a cartoon, you know." She sighed. "They are both my sons. But I do believe my boy did everything he could to mark a distance from his brother." She looked at Chaya, then, with far too much implication. "In everything."

Chaya was not glad to hear herself so used. But—sometimes second thought was kinder than first—that was too proud. She winced to think how harshly she had judged Gregory. There was sufficient pain to go around.

"You know, of course, that Gregory's father—and his brother, it goes without saying—they are concerned that you are—"

"You needn't put it delicately. I know what they think I am. What I want." And Chaya knew from this most amazing conversation that if—*if*—this ally could do anything to calm their hostility it would be very covert, very subtle, and it might not succeed.

"Gregory may already have warned you that they are not kindly disposed toward—"

It was obvious that she stopped herself; she could not, Chaya understood, say *you.*

It felt rude to chew while she listened to something so weighty but she thought her meat and her pale, golden potatoes kept her from flying off, unmoored, toward the ceiling. The voices around them had disappeared.

"I worry that my husband is considering"—Faith Stillman had gone alarmingly pale—"cutting Gregory off if he proceeds with . . . that is such an ancient ploy I told him I was disappointed that he would follow such a tired sort of vengeance." She pantomimed a yawn and smiled at her audacity. "But he has so little—relationship—with his son that he can't, like the rest of us, you know, maneuver—manipulate—his behavior. He can't, you understand, withhold—" She had the habit of looking ruefully resigned. "This is all he has for punishment, Chaya. His holdings. His balance at the bank." She held her hands out, empty. "I wished at the least, as I said, for some originality in his threat. Talk about following in ancient footsteps!" That pained smile again. It made her eyes apologetic. "I suppose I shouldn't speak this way, but, my dear, you are going to be one of us." Truly! "It is appalling but, going back many years, the Stillmans have tended to treat each generation the way they treated their dogs, they have gotten their heirs to heel by yanking hard on their collars. And so my Edward and my Ned are simply doing what they consider their legacy. They consider themselves—protectors."

Gregory had told Chaya no such thing. But she enjoyed her lie. "Yes, he has shared that fear with me, Mrs. Stillman. But it does not seem to have daunted him much. I don't think his first thought has ever been his—" What an alien word! She could hardly say it. "His inheritance." Those books Miss Singlet had given her, those heroines deprived of fortunes— she saluted Miss Austen and—she had a new word: the Austen *emulators*!—with her own small smile. What would Gregory's mother think if she knew Chaya's hesitations, her nervy vacillation about accepting the comforts of his class? Would she look ungrateful or braver still were she to confess? Oh, she would confuse matters mightily!

But this challenge could not go unanswered. "As for me, I can only repeat that I never sought anyone's fortune and—please believe this even if it seems unlikely—I might very well be relieved if we were not to be—not to have that wealth to—" She came right up against her own confusions and there was her Asher drilling her with his furious eyes. "It would, to be honest, be simpler if we were without it."

"Which simply confirms my admiration for both of you. Though you are young and may not appreciate the difficulties of doing without."

Chaya could only laugh, with a kind of gaiety, at the absurdity of that. "Oh, Mrs. Stillman, I believe I would be an experienced guide at doing without."

She ignored Chaya's impiety. Perhaps she was embarrassed. "Well, you and your brother will bring some—variety—into our little lives, that is certain. And the more you confound them the better, though you must expect that you will bear as many insults as my dear boy bore."

I will have him. The thought washed over Chaya like a warming light. *Even if I am a pretext for his goodness, I will have her son for her sake as well as my own.*

Those islands of pink had returned to Faith Stillman's cheeks. "I hope we shall be able to meet your brother some time soon. Asher, isn't it?" She said it as if he were a cinder. "Gregory tells me he is remarkable." She seemed almost jolly. "Now let us pay some attention to our plates before they come to remove them!"

28

ASHER KNEW the word boycott. *Boy-caught.* He considered it but he could not *not* come to Chai's wedding, a boy caught by loyalty and traps of memory: her light hand on his back when they first lay down at Mrs. Gottlieb's. Her tweaking his cap to set it right. Her pleading face and her startled face, all her faces turned to him. He wanted to shout, *No, no, don't go with him!* He wanted to shout, *Traitor!* But he could not betray her in front of that family of Steal-man's, stiff and silent, the more disapproving the more silent. He could not protect her but he could not run out on her either.

He had never seen a wedding, at least not one that he could remember, so he could not compare this one—Chaya and Gregory in the parlor of Miss Addams's house, surrounded by smilers and weepers—to any other. Miss Gates, who also lived there, had set him to helping drag in baskets crammed with fall flowers, deep reds, yellows, oranges, small separate sunsets, which they set on every ledge and surface. The cat was permitted to attend. She sat patiently, Sphinx position, in the space between the bride and groom and—was it called an audience? They sat like viewers at an entertainment but did not applaud.

Chaya, wearing a white dress with tiny flowers caught in the weave, gazed out at them with a lost face, picturing, he knew without asking, her mother and father, her missing brothers and sisters. She looked hollow. If someone knocked against her where she walked, a piece of her might break off and shatter.

Gregory's parents, instead, came in and sat themselves, looking as if it was all happening somewhere else. His mother's cheeks might have been wet. His brother Ned smirked, in black, shirt and all, like a minister without a collar. He had two daughters, or the same daughter big and small, who couldn't sit still. Lallie fussed and fussed with the belt of her layered pink dress, which she seemed unhappy with, unbuckling it, buckling it again. It took all her attention. Each of them seemed separate, like a portrait in a gold frame. That was what was strange about them—they looked as if they never touched. Only Ned's wife, whose hat looked like a serving tray heaped with edibles, kept slapping viciously at her children's knees and elbows to keep them from twitching, from bouncing and pinching each other.

A dark suit, his first, had arrived for Asher, hidden under a fog of tissue in a box with a scrawl of fancy silvery writing on top. It scratched his knees and felt like a nipping animal around his ankles. Chaya had held up one finger to warn him he could not refuse to wear it, but he didn't open his eyes at the mirror because he knew he would not recognize himself. He was coming to this day as someone else. He remembered when Chaya wore that plummy dress Gregory gave her and it made her a lady. He had been a pasha at the Fair, soft fabric flapping around the tops of his boots. How could that happen—what you put on wasn't your skin, only a different shape and color, different texture, but you were changed and never to be found again. Everyone in masquerade! *What if we could walk around without clothes? Naked, could we be changed so easily? Who might we be if we were not quite ourselves?*

THE OTHERS who lived in the house, this Hull of a House, came quietly downstairs. There were two not-young women, soft-skinned, soft-haired, who might be sisters, who smiled constantly and asked after everyone's health, and a very lively young man who rubbed his hands together impatiently, ready to begin whatever was coming next. There was a man with a monocle, professorish, whom Asher planned to talk to if he could. His teeth were yellow the way Chaya's fingertips became when she rolled too many tobacco leaves in a day. The cook came in from the kitchen in her white apron and hovered in the doorway to watch.

But there were scant others. Seventeen, including the cook. He had heard Gregory's sister say it was a scandal to be married in such a place— *such?* What was *such?*—but at least their friends were spared the spectacle. (People wore spectacles. Miss Addams and Miss Gates, Gregory's father and that hawk-faced bother Ned. How could a wedding be a spectacle?) Oh, Sara from the cigar floor was sitting near the back, and Stuka with her jolly curls—they were holding each other's hands with excitement—and Mrs. Gottlieb, crying quietly into a handkerchief he had filched for her from the Exposition. (*Filched*—word full of crunch that would exercise the mouth of anyone who said it!) She had found a grand dress somewhere, a blue-gray shiny as a steel pistol, and had done something to her hair that made her look like a woman one might see downtown, browsing in a shop window. Another masquerade. Before she sat down, she clutched Asher to her. She was happy and she was sad: They would not be coming back to her house, except as guests.

She was speaking into his hair—he couldn't tell if she wanted him to hear and answer or just listen. "And you can't even tell she's a Jew, the *kallah*." She tsk'd, shook her head and tsk'd again. "No *chuppah*, there won't be a word, not a blessing. She gave it all over to him." She squeezed him a little; it almost hurt.

Asher, impatient said, "You loved him. You wanted her to marry all this." He waved his hand at the roomful of *goyim*. That word he heard often enough from Mrs. Gottlieb. That and *yenem*—hostilely, them. *Yenem* was ugly but he loved the word *alien*, the liquid sound of it and the drama, and here she was in Alienland where in her ordinary life she would never have set a foot.

Two frail-looking women were sawing at a violin and a cello, first a droopy melody and then something gay and a little marchlike, repeated and repeated while Gregory came forward and, alone, Chaya walked the short distance to stand before him. Her face still looked blank to Asher, neither sad nor happy. More likely frightened, and she should be. But she would never tell him what she was feeling any more. He knew she would not trust him to be kind.

Everything was hushed. This was what Chaya called *good taste* now.

Asher preferred riot. When he was asked to carry in the wedding ring Gregory had placed in his hand, he walked with rare care to the front of the room where Miss Addams was in charge of "joining them" in the basketed flower garden they had constructed. There were her spectacles slipping down her nose the way they always did. She wore her regular clothes, something between a brown and a black with a reluctant little gush of lace at the throat, and a shawl full of curlicues to be fancy.

"I am, I know, not the ideal person to unite two loving people in marriage because I have not myself had the pleasure of such a union. But what I believe to be more important is what I understand of the force of unity in the face of many difficulties." She smiled benignly out at what was, for the moment, her congregation and asked what made it possible for two people who had been strangers—utter strangers going their own ways!—to meet by chance and regard each other with curiosity. What made it possible to discover that they were walking toward the same horizon, step by step around obstacles, into unknown avenues, both of them leaving behind the narrowness of their separate histories. Asher heard a rustling where Gregory's mother sat. She was having trouble sitting still, her face twitching with affront. He imagined that Chaya missed their mother today, but when he taxed his own memory, he could not see her.

What made it possible, Miss Addams went on because those weren't really questions, was imagination, the daring to imagine a different future. Then came a cascade of all they hoped for together, and in her voice they became a whole army brigade, overthrowing this and obliterating that and Asher thought about the men on Division Street and looked around him at the silks and the velvets and the stiff collars and the disapproving faces and he thought, Maybe Chaya has wriggled out of her past but won't it take more than imagination to put aside the comforts that keep that Steal-man soft?

Miss Addams insisted you could take having too much and use it, spread it like a balm, for the people who have too little and by believing it, like the prophets of a new, blended religion, this charmed couple would prevail, holding hands the whole time. She was right, she probably didn't know much about love—neither did he—but the woman couldn't miss an opportunity to spread her gospel even among these nonbelievers. She smiled at them with the warmth of a small fire you could warm your hands over, and was silent. Then came a snort from the vicinity of the groom's family, this time, from beneath some mustache, a very masculine thump of derision. It was amazing the bunch of them had not pushed their way out or shouted down their hostess, who beamed at them with—was it really?—innocence.

Asher was so rapt he forgot it was time to hand the wedding ring to Gregory. "Ash!" his sister whispered, a fierce awakening, and he fumbled it and it fell onto the carpet, which was complicated by entwined Persian flowers. The cat, intrigued by the glint of gold, leaped up and began circling it for the kill, and then they were allowed to laugh. Chaya sagged against Gregory, pricked by the laughing so that the terrible bloating air of all this properness fizzed out and, thanks to his clumsy fingers, he recognized her again.

Then—where had he come from?—a man with a camera shot off a fierce explosion of light. Miss Addams stared at him sternly and said, "If you please, sir, you will exit as rapidly as you entered, and by the same door. And I do not want to see the result of that intrusion folded on my table tomorrow morning." The man raised one hand to say, but not mean, "Pardon me, madam," and backed out. A wind of murmuring went up: The *Tribune*? The *Times*? The *Herald*? Were his sister and Gregory so famous that someone would write a story about this wedding and put that picture at the top? Who would want to see it? Because it was a "scandal"? Was the man with the camera like the bad witch at the christening banquet for Sleeping Beauty? Was he the uninvited?

After all the words, the new Mr. and Mrs. Stillman went out onto the porch and, from there, stepped into a victoria garlanded with yellow and blue flowers, a yolk-yellow bow at the rear like the bow on the fanny of a girl. They looked dazed, riding on a flood of cheering and clapping, and rode away for a ceremonial tour of the city. Why the clapping? They had not *done* anything.

It took one cross look from Mrs. Gottlieb to keep Asher from leaping in between them. Chaya had told him once how he was weaned: "*Shoyn.*"

Finished. Their unsentimental mother. Some things echoed: finished again. She didn't remember if he had cried. This time, dry-eyed, slouched against one of the porch pillars watching them go, he wanted to kick Gregory or kick the horse or the wheels of the carriage. Kick something until he hurt it and it hurt back. He wondered if it was time for him to learn to smoke.

AND NOW what would be changed? He and Chaya had walked down the stairs at Mrs. Gottlieb's, trying not to trip and fall, carrying the little they owned, and now they would live "for a little while," Chaya promised him, upstairs at Hull-House. She called this a compromise because she had not liked the rooms Gregory lived in—"You would not have liked them either, Asher, I promise you"—and neither of them wished to rent, let alone buy, the sort of house Gregory's parents foresaw for them, armored in stone, all echoing halls and slippery floors, the kind where Asher had performed so many Sunday afternoons. He would sleep in his own room now, small— she said *cozy*—down at the far end of the hall. Usually it housed a maid.

"Housed?" he challenged. "That is too small to be a house. I hope the maid was no bigger than I am. She would have to live bending over." He could see she felt guilty for leaving him. He didn't argue.

This was what being married meant, then—you left your brother to go and sleep in a high wide bed with someone you hadn't even known a blink or two ago. But there was one thought he could hide in. It didn't make him less lonely but if he could leave himself out of it, it seemed a good thing: If people were only their real selves without the masquerade of their clothes, then she and her husband could at least see each other truly. He knew (he had heard in his alley and had seen in one particular book he should not have been looking at) that married meant sometimes being naked. He was happy for her, then, but—he thought about this as he shook the wrinkles out of his new pants and hung his jacket shakily from a hanger—he could not pretend to be happy for himself.

29

THEIR MODEST honeymoon finished—no European grand tour but (Asher in tow) a few weeks at White Pines, Gregory's family's New Hampshire summer house, which was not grand, praise be, but rustic in what she did not recognize as the common affectation of the wealthy: simple, aged furniture, worn upholstery, musty books on the shelves (enough to keep her brother satisfied), mysterious sporting equipment in every closet and an obligatory moose's head glowering from the wall above the stone fireplace—Chaya woke to confusion.

Every day but Sundays, for so long she shuddered to contemplate, she had hurried out of her bed—she had exchanged her train of chairs some months ago for a cot that felt like bones loosely bound by a thin layer of flesh—and washed in chill or heat, dressed with memorized movements, arranged her unsleek hair without ever seeing it, dabbed her mouth with tea that had not steeped long enough and a round of bread, and gone.

She knew every inflection of Chicago dawn, different in each season—cool purple turning gold; tranced a dull fog-gray so many days, locked under cloud, or pearly with snow about to let down as if the sky were a trapdoor that silently, invisibly opened. The rising light was almost something she could touch, so frail, such magic in its endless changes, its creep and recoil and opening up. It was the medium everything lived in, like water in the sea. Only when she arrived at Winkler's would the dawn be frank and full and then she had to stifle it, climbing the stairs into deadening gaslight. A dozen women from the south and the west poured forth from the trolley alongside her, and climbed the stairs with a clatter like an army in boots.

Today there was no need to leap from her bed, whose light sheet lay across her like another layer of air. Gregory slept turned from her, deep in some dream, miles away, out on a lake, perhaps, or up on a mountain. She dressed slowly, taking time to adjust her new shirtwaist, which would need breaking in to be wearable. She twisted her hair; disapproved. It had looked so lovely for the wedding, lilies of the valley securely pinned, after a kind of attention she never had time or occasion to give it; had as many minutes as she needed, now, to brush it and rearrange it, pin up an escaped curl, fasten a black velvet choker at her neck, Miss Addams's gift, a cameo with an anonymous profile in ivory facing whatever she might like to imagine. She looked at her face and saw, at leisure, no one she knew: a woman carefully arranged, ornamented, ready to begin her life again, safe, replete. Spoken for. Renamed.

Gregory slept on, little gusts of breath rising from his pillow. Asher she would not disturb. His door, at the end of the hall, was still closed. She hoped he was relishing the chance to be alone. When she put him to sleep last night, he was surrounded by towers of books. Then down the long stairway silently, on the carpet runner that ate footsteps. She could feel the sun warming her shoulders. In the kitchen, faces awaited her, cheerful, serene.

Breakfast in Miss Addams's wide, bright kitchen: a blue bowl of orange marmalade, heaped glowing like chunks of amber; fresh ruddy tomatoes and fleshy cheese, sweating slightly, in banked slices; a glory of bread with crust that crackled at the touch. Eggs whipped into a pale froth by Cook, and poured with a hiss onto the griddle, then spread in a perfect, self-contained circle. Amazing, Chaya thought idly, to keep from thinking anything else, that eggs know how to make a shape like that, like something seamed, and keep it. They must be the most disciplined of foods. Look, their edges are secure!

"I have cinnamon buns," Cook told Chaya, raising a blackened muffin tin like a celebratory glass. "Dear, you should have one, they came out perfect this morning, just for you!" Cook had a face round as a clock, and her colorless hair stood straight up from her forehead like a cock's comb. Her skin always looked slightly floured.

What had she done to deserve the peace of this table, those clean blue-checked curtains, the long cabinets behind which stood every size and shape of bowl, stacked and ready for filling. That giant woodstove with its paws of polished chrome in which the cat was, just then, contemplating her face, then slowly, luxuriously, raising a leg to wash her cheek. She made a lapping sound, as if she were drinking milk.

Chaya had trouble swallowing the lovely crumbs; soft though they were, her throat was tight and dry, unaccustomed. Didn't Sara and Stuka deserve this early morning sweetness?

"You don't like it, then?" Cook prodded. She was all pride where her offerings were concerned. Hands joined before her chest as if in prayer, she looked pierced with disappointment.

"Oh, I do! I'm not—" Explaining would sound ungrateful. The buns were a gift. If she were able to think into tomorrow, she would know she could not go on feeling this way. One could not be eaten by such foolish guilt forever before it became a self-indulgence—Gregory had called it her vanity—but that would be worse, like putting a death behind her. By now she'd have finished two packs of stogies, tightly wrapped and tucked in the little box she kept on her right, next to the paste pot. The sound of gossip, jaggedly accented, would surround her, syncopated by the tap of the packets as the girls finished them off and stored them. The girls, the women, the grand-mothers, who had wished her well and would—she hoped—miss her too.

Cook and Miss Gates with her sharp nose and her eyepiece that dangled like something broken over her chest, one of the Schumacher ladies, and perhaps at any moment Miss Addams herself (though she had undoubt-edly eaten already and was at her desk in the study, attacking the day's demands)—all of them clucked with sympathy, or were careful not to cluck, for the bride disappointed by her marriage.

CHAYA BEGGED Miss Addams to put her to work. She had told her how peculiar it was not to go to her factory. She felt, she said, as if she had left her leg in a trap, escaping.

"Yes, of course. But that would be unseemly, wouldn't it? To report to the factory now, as the wife of Gregory Stillman. And you have no need—"

"Yes, I agree, it would." She wasn't entirely sure what *unseemly* meant but she could imagine her mother-in-law's expression at the idea of her persisting at her cigar bench. She had already been subjected to advice about the best way to remove the nicotine from her fingers. Vinegar would do it, a generous soaking draught that rankled like smelling salts. "And I can't pretend to like being bound to the work. It was very unpleasant."

"You look unconvinced, Chaya."

Whenever she spoke with Miss Addams with her slightly tilting head, Chaya felt her own head balancing in the opposite direction. It was, she supposed, a sort of sympathetic compensation.

"I feel—disloyal. I know that's foolish. There isn't a one of us who wouldn't leave if she could. Just say goodbye and never come back."

Miss Addams always looked as if she understood, though the more frequently she used that frown of pained comprehension the less Chaya thought it should be trusted. It was, she knew, an arrogant prejudice to feel even the most creeping superiority but she could do little to shake it off. This heroic woman did her best but, like Gregory, she lacked the feel of labor in her own hands. She worked hard for the attention of her donors— it was expensive to rescue so many lives, to feed this furnace of enterprise and optimism—but that was work in the presence of laden tables, of sherry and claret, of men in smoking jackets shaking one's hand earnestly at the top of the stairs and promising a check. She had never had to be abject before a Winkler or a Yanowitz. Saying goodbye, without explanation, to her two gruff employers had given Chaya greater pleasure than anything she had done in a very long time. Though she didn't think they cared much—Winkler shrugged his sweaty bulk as if he'd been overcome by a hiccup and Yanowitz muttered about how hard it would be to find a better employer—it was more thrilling, she told no one, than the spreading joy she felt receiving Miss Addams's blessing at her wedding.

What Miss Addams did for the neighborhood, those hundreds and more hundreds whose lives she sweetened, she did *for* them. One had to be a little beneath her, or a lot. She would never condescend; still, one had to need. Certainly there was plenty of that to go around. But where, Chaya wondered, very much alone with her double knowledge, did it leave her?

Gregory sat, daily, at a small elegant desk under a dormer or at the lovely library, writing his book. He still would not show it to her, which was just as well; having stolen that stultifying preview she was afraid to read more.

As for Asher, he had called the trip to New Hampshire his "vacation," and had happily gone back to the Midway, from which he continued to bring home gifts like a cat depositing mice and birds at her feet. She could not hurt him by reminding him that she no longer needed these sweet-meats. Gregory thought Asher, jealous, was courting her; she worried less about his psyche than at the more immediate possibility that his collar would be grasped one day by a constable's hand for appropriating, at will, anything he found amusing. Like the little gifts he had fingered into his sack at Doreen's shop in Christa, the presentations were minor: a peacock feather, a fan edged in black Spanish lace, a bar of soap engraved with the body of an elephant, and, once, a plaster globe the size of a melon with Chicago denoted by a giant golden star that seemed to have fallen on the Midwest from some galaxy. She would never succeed in disabusing him of his belief that if he could manage to get something into his pocket, of great value or none at all, he had earned it.

"I recall that Gregory said you have a particular love for reading." Chaya and her benefactress were moving—Miss Addams rarely stood still—through a corridor, between overseeing the distribution of milk to infants who lacked it and the establishment of three Italian women at spinning wheels where they were to create thread for an exhibition of native crafts and national pride. The women, who wore aprons as though they were planning to cook and not spin, walked backwards before their benefactor as she approached, dipping their heads with respect; they looked like boats being tugged clear of a looming ship.

Though the day's particulars changed endlessly, Hull-House was always teeming. The many languages that flew through its rooms made a sort of song that did not trouble Chaya because the cigar shop floor had been like that, open to so many who were still at home only in their native tongues. Their attempt at English syllables made no sense if she didn't concentrate, and only a little when she did. Miss Addams had learned a fraction of everything from Italian to Hungarian, though most of it emerged sounding alike. She spoke an odd, effortful poly-language ineluctably of middle America. Mostly she used it for soothing.

They were in the neighborhood nursery now, where Miss Addams had scooped up a squalling baby in a huge dingy bonnet that must recently have belonged to an older sister; it slid comically down over the girl's round black eyes. "There, you funny thing," Miss Addams said amiably, lifting the brim and making a face. The child quieted and pulled the hat back down with a wheezy laugh.

"Would you like to be the leader of a group that will talk about books? Or perhaps plays?" The baby was flirting, slapping at her, and she was flirting back.

Each of them held an infant now. Chaya's twisted in her arms like the house cat, who did not like to be handled. "How do these people—the ones who come here—have time to be reading books?" It still took some daring for her to raise a challenge.

Miss Addams produced her slow unexcited smile. "For some, it is the best part of their day, to read a few pages and dream. Don't assume our friends here are only laboring machines. You mustn't do that to them." Every response she made seemed to be a gentle rebuke. Did the woman never doubt? Did she hesitate or regret or wish she could call back something she had done? More likely, she would repent what had been left undone, but that was not the same. Asher had said, on the train to Christa, that he could not look backward, only forward. In their different ways, they had that in common.

Chaya tried to imagine the disheveled, discouraged suitors for Miss Addams's succor sitting with an open book across their knees. They must be better organized than she. Or hungrier, or quicker. They must live in some kingdom where the light was good. Chaya wished she had come here while she was working; had submitted herself to this place where she'd have been on the taking rather than the giving side. She had not stored up enough to be prepared to give back very much. She still needed filling up, but Mrs. Gregory Stillman could not ask for that.

30

IT WAS true: The Fair was closing, and soon. They meant it, though even when he stood with the men he had refused to believe. Glory would revert to swamp. Thousands of separate showings of dear particulars, tangible and eye-filling. Another week and then—no way to imagine it. Once something was, how could it not be? Maybe the strikers' families would swoop down and claim it: He could see them set up between the Music Hall and the Casino. Children running the aisles, riding the golden Statue of the Republic, flicking on the lights, silver streaming down across the water, across the toothed silhouettes of the roofs, and off, and on again, everyone carrying off treasures no one suddenly wanted, ivory this and olive-wood that, silkworms, blown glass, oranges and lemons from the indoor grove. Wives cooking beef and biscuits on the hulking industrial stoves in the Machinery Hall, setting out feasts in the restaurants. Sleeping in the Midway tents, swimming in the lagoons. When winter came, huddling warm inside.

What a gift it could be. The men, out of work, out of hope, had been waning, thinner by the week, unshaven, eyes desperate as if someone were chasing them all the time. They had marched for a while, then gave it up, came back now and then, outside the gates, to raise their furious signs and shout, but no one was listening. Asher had heard his barker complain that once the Midway shuttered, he would never find work. "The city's shot. It's gonna close up tight. Unless you got an in someplace, otherwise—" He slashed with the side of his hand right under his chin. "Duck your head and keep it down. It's all over the world is what I heard. Riots coming."

The crowds thickened near the end, the laggardly and the penny-squeez-ers finally flushed out. "Now or never!" Big Dog cried out as the throngs poured down the asphalt. Asher shrugged when that crazy little Mr. Bloom walked up, spinning his bowler on one finger. Stopped, inquired. He still came around, checking. He made his acts behave, put out better than their best. He called it "Control of Quality," though what was he going to do this late in their lives? Close the exhibits that weren't performing? Fire them? The Esquimaux were accused of having lazed off, lying around in phlegmatic heaps like puppies in their heavy fur coats. One or two were said to have died of the heat, though he thought that a vicious rumor. The Dahomeyans complained all the time; they were probably not hot enough! Asher had no demands. He made eight dollars a week, not counting what petty larceny put in his pockets, and a little sugar out of the till when Big Dog wasn't looking. He was content.

"Last chance to challenge our Knight of Knowledge, our Pasha of Pertinacity! Throw something at him—any question in the world—and see if it knocks him down!" Big Dog paced, forever wiping his brow, sing-songed, flung back his arm to point at his Titan of Trivialities. His Imam of Inanities, his Prince of Particulars. (Asher could not get enough of his names, he felt the way a petted dog must feel.)

For weeks, the crowds seethed. Chicago Day was like a dare: He couldn't see through shoulders and hats to the far end of the Midway. On Jubilee Day, after wrangling over whether they had been consulted enough about the Fair, after anger and refusals—he had read a whole little pam-phlet called *The Reason Why the Colored American Is Not in the World's Columbian Exposition* and he could see why, few as they were most days, they were aggrieved—and then forgiveness or at least compromise, hun-dreds of spiffed-up Negroes crowded the walkways, keener than he had ever seen them, men with shiny buttons and mirrory shoes, women sailing under floating garden hats, children wound around their legs, celebrating, spending money he didn't know they had. What a fine-looking crowd they made, proud and straight and every shade of skin from luscious dark like pith of mahogany, lightening, lightening all the way to the color of Italian people he had seen, or Mexicans. They could ask me questions about anything to do with being colored, Asher thought but had no one to say it to, and I would surrender and be sorry about it. But few stopped. Many went to see the Africans. Some peeked in at the Street in Cairo. What did they think, seeing their brothers and sisters on display like that, stared at and silent? He wished he could ask but he was afraid of accidentally insulting them by asking the wrong questions.

The last days were ticking away. Some mornings, when business went nil, he concentrated on geometry, the buildings all peaks, angles, circularity, negative and positive space. Memorize them. Chew them down like daily bread before they disappear into—what? Smoke? A flat horizon? Into memory, like a person you have loved who dies. He would never be good at remembering.

There were official pictures, photographs, which—lovely!—meant writing with light. But they were silent, they were gray, flat, soulless. He had a collection of color postal cards and souvenirs, from a glass globe that contained a Peristyle the size of a man's thumb, to a set of silver Columbian spoons, to a wooden wheel with cars that looked like tiny harmonicas that swung from hinges like the actual thing—none of them purchased. But they were a sad nothing, a nullity, a mockery, compared to the living thing, which was an organism as complex, Asher believed, as the human body. Other days he counted the preponderance of blue or purple in the middle distance, or the number of unfamiliar languages that floated by. Nothing would ever be as interesting again. The circus? A carnival? Something that taught nothing and packed up and moved on, unfolded from trunks and boxes and then folded back down again? They had no weight, no beauty, only clamor. Sawdust and hurdy-gurdy. Even if he found himself a place at the university, those grave gray towers, new but made to look ancient, poking up oblivious to this stampede just across the Midway Plaisance, he would never live in such a whirl again—order and disorder, mind and matter, Robin, Pasha—or know such joy.

HE HAD no right to feel cheated but he did. There was no last day of the Fair. Instead, there was a funeral.

The city was like a person hit over the head with a plank. Shock. Two days before the Fair was to end, a madman had walked right into the mayor's house—knocked on the door, shown in by a servant who now threatened to do away with herself, and who could blame her. Stood in the hallway a moment waiting until Carter Harrison could oblige the stranger by consenting to see him; became impatient and entered the parlor where the mayor sat in his bathrobe and, in return for his courtesy, shot him an uncounted number of times with a pistol. Then the intruder, a newsstand man named Eugene Prendergast who seemed to think the mayor had promised to make him something called "corporation counsel," whatever thing that was, let himself out, shooting back at the mayor's butler as he ran, and went to the stationhouse and turned himself in. He was not repentant: The mayor had refused to answer his letters, attesting to his claims to the position. What should he have expected?

Asher had seen the mayor twice, once making a hero turn around Clark Street, flapping that hat of his—a grand man straight as a general in the saddle, gliding in sunny confidence through the crowds who loved him. The other time was at the Fair. Was his horse bigger than everyone else's—it was certainly the shiniest bay he had ever seen, suggesting that some groom had lacquered his haunches and dusted him daily—or did his generous spirit enlarge the man?

IMAGINE BEING the cause of such mayhem. Hundreds of thousands in the streets, mass weeping, helpless anger. The murderer must have a headful of cobwebs. Black hung down the fronts of buildings—where did they find such bolts of black and run them up so quickly? Instruments, deep and throaty, sent out grieving music. Strangers spoke, embraced. Suddenly everyone loved the mayor. The flash of the gun had made him Abraham Lincoln. His opponents silenced each other with praise.

Asher sat on a stool in the kitchen at Hull-House. Before the news, he had been awake with excitement half the night, planning his goodbyes to his throne, to Big Dog, to the uniformed Columbian Guard who had

never caught him with his hand in any pocket; he had perfected devious-
ness on their inefficient watch. There was going to be a parade, a gorgeous
showing, three cheers for Chicago in fireworks, ending with a fiery flag
in the sky.

Instead, "Maybe you'll go to 'is hanging," Cook suggested. "They ought
to do it right on the steps at City Hall. It'd make us feel a fair bit better."
Though she had most likely never given much thought to the mayor, violence had plunged her into an unforgiving mood. "One madman and he
does us all in." She shook her gray head so long it looked like a tic. "So
you're out of work now, little man."

He sighed. "I was going to be out of work anyway. But I didn't get to
say goodbye. Why couldn't he have done it a day or two later?"

"Ah, you're more sentimental for yourself than for that fine man
gone? Well." She shook water off her hands, fast, like a wet dog. "So
you're planning to miss going to your job every day like a regular workin'
man." She had no inkling what he had been doing, and a good thing or
she would have pestered him with questions just to ruffle him. "Why
don't you just go on down and say your own farewell, private? No one'll
keep you out, will they?"

He looked at her, round-eyed. An idea—the infinitesimal corner of
an idea—started up as if Cook had breathed it at him directly. He hated
his stuffy room up at the end of the hall. Hated Chaya for saying good-
night to him and closing the door to her room every night to be alone
with Gregory. Hated the ladies in the parlor, Miss Starr, Miss Smith, and
the preachy Miss Addams and her friends who were always improving
things and suggesting cures and running in every direction and not being
depressed. He knew he ought to like her, respect her—she cared, after
all, for the failing, the blighted, the starving, every bit as much as he did.
Probably that was why he found her so galling. Asher did not like the
word *should*, let alone the word *must*. He resented being the subject of a
kingdom. A queendom. Too many people gathered around Miss Addams's
skirts, looking docile as cows with admiration. One hour, he had counted
fastidiously, he watched her speak with thirty-two different people.

The strikers and the men without work would join him, or they would not. He was going to move his operation down there again, not now but soon, the way it was at the very beginning. He wanted to thank Cook for the idea but keeping quiet was safer if he didn't want to be stopped. He sat rocking on his stool. "Did you know they are going to have seventeen horses at the funeral, and a whole extra set of pallbearers, and a black horse?" Asher sat with his elbows on his knees, hunched like an old man. "His own horse is out of work too. Wrong color."

She gave him a long wary look. "I don't know where you heard all that so quick, we only just heard the terrible news. You're probably just making that up. But anyway, I should think it could be so," she said, bending over the oven and, hand on her aching back, straightening slowly. "If ever there was a use for black, poor man, this is it, isn't it."

31

EACH MORNING when Chaya—Ceil Stillman, now, a name she would barely recognize if she heard it called across the room—walked down the carpeted stairs, joy seemed to come forward to meet her. Hull-House faced east, and though its long front windows were narrow, the rising sun penetrated sufficiently to make her want to shout her rapture. She could feel as much as hear and smell the activity in the kitchen; the air was lightly cinnamoned, and the cat, luxurious in her dark fur, would come to the bottom stair and tuck herself daintily down to wait for her. At the Fields of Zion, they had had a barn cat, or rather the cat had the run of their rats, their chipmunks. It seemed there existed a hierarchy among four-footed creatures too: Miss Addams's cat, Sophia (named for Tolstoy's dutiful wife), lived a cosseted life in which she did not have to hunt her breakfast any more than Chaya did.

She had been doing just as the persuasive Miss Addams had suggested, since such moral force made one feel craven for denying her: A dictionary by her side, she led a group in the reading of great books, which, hardly a step ahead of her charges, she herself had first to discover. But for all that she enjoyed the discussions and liked her students—Miss Addams referred to them as "your women" as if Chaya had created them—she was not comfortable on Halsted Street. The settlement house was a great heart beating with conviction—passion, even—and she respected everything about it. But two things beat in her an opposing rhythm. One was that Asher was keeping himself distant, as though her married state frightened him, or warned him off; as if Gregory owned her now, and would not share. He moped, he read, he kept to his room and would hardly speak to her; as she had waxed, so had he waned. She was constantly preoccupied, searching for a way to lure him to her. Nor was she entirely certain he was welcome here since he was technically, if not intellectually, a child, and other boarders with children had had to make other arrangements for them.

Her book class was a cluster of shy immigrants—two young men irregularly, which tended to mean that their employment had given out—who were making their way laboriously, like horses lumbering through deep water, into *Romeo and Juliet.* They liked it best when she read to them; sorting out the words themselves was terribly difficult but their enthusiasm reminded her of her own when she was called a "scholar" at the school house in Christa.

One woman, Demetria, who sat with her infant in her lap, nodded when Chaya told them that the lovers were, in truth, young adolescents, apparently intended to be thirteen or fourteen. "Oh, yes, in my village we have brides that age of Juliet. Younger!" she whispered proudly. "But they no speak like this one. Never!"

"Have you ever seen a Greek play?" Chaya asked, fully knowing the futility of the question. Neither had she.

"What plays are those?" Her baby was grabbing at Demetria's book, trying to crumple its pages.

"Oh, they aren't very happy, the Greek plays I know. Only tragedies."

"Nothing about village like mine? Is called Nakia."

Chaya had to demur. Surely she didn't know the names of all the Greek plays that existed; it was Asher who had told her about them, blood in his eye—about the blindings and the murders, the becalmed ships, the woman who killed her own children and the one who was forced to drag her son from a cave and take him to be slaughtered for vengeance's sake. She had wondered just what kind of place this Greece must be, to emerge in any-one's dreams the way those stories had overcome their authors. Poisoned minds. Like stories from the Bible, was this true history? Did they make it up or had all that gruesomeness actually happened? The teacher needed a teacher. Gregory might know, that was the kind of thing he'd have learned at university. She vowed to use her newfound time to read them, as many as she could find—Hull-House had a modest library now, too sweet a consolation to believe. And if they were performed at a theater, she could finally afford time and a ticket.

But on the day she sat down with *Medea* she found herself unable to concentrate, as if an attack of influenza were descending upon her; the words floated as incomprehensibly as islands of ink on the page.

The chill of winter had begun to inch its way toward the city. What, she wondered in her distraction, had become of the white ermine muff Gregory had given her? Could she have left it in the coatroom at Winkler's? That seemed as good a guess as any, but as she started for the door in her lovely warm coat—how much more bearable the weather had become!— she realized that her usual route to work had been from Mrs. Gottlieb's. She had no idea how to negotiate her way to the trolley from here.

But she had money in her purse.

It still astonished her to open the little black snap-bag in which bills lay folded around one another, coins clinking alongside, spilling out when she was not careful. Gregory had simply handed them to her without a word, and had kissed, rather paternally, the top of her head.

The exchange felt almost illicit—spending money for having done what? She had once heard a woman ranting from a soapbox on a down-town corner, disheveled and apparently bitter about her state, accusing married women of being no better than kept, of trading the favors of their bodies for worldly sustenance. She railed about their inability to vote, their banishment from the ranks of power, their abject weakness when offered the shelter of a man's name and bank account. People seemed to hurry their steps as they passed the woman, as if she were dangerous. Her anger was so scattered that Chaya had dismissed what she had understood.

But she found herself, now, ruffled by a faint breeze of sympathy when she opened her reticule and closed her hand around a clot of paper that would buy her a comfortable ride to Winkler's. Gregory would say she had too many qualms.

She went out onto Halsted Street where she was greeted by a stiff wind, raised her hand, trying not to be tentative, and a one-horse cab stopped for her. It was a wonder, if not precisely a delight. She sat very straight, self-conscious before no spectator, and looked everywhere at once as if looking preoccupied might make her less conspicuous.

Chaya might have changed but Winkler's had not: It hulked as plain and dour as ever on its corner. The long flight of stairs, in spite of all its use, was still and forever dusty, and the huge room on the second floor lay before her like a lake tinged with some green light-eating scum. She stood in the doorway just out of view, halfway between shame and regret. The spreading sadness in her chest had no name, really. They would think she'd come to gloat. Her new coat was dark purple, heavy—when she put it on the first time she remembered the sweat where Mrs. Gottlieb worked, the weight of the fabric of coats just such as this dragging them down to the floor, too exhausting for the women to lift. It was a royal sort of color, cut and assembled with complexity—more costly to its maker than its wearer. And her hat—her hat, though simple, was piled with autumn flowers, golden chrysanthemums and burnished leaves. The secret to style, she had always suspected, was understatement. But didn't her friends here, who would go home to grimness, deserve their frequent election of showy colors and artificial flash at the neck, at the wrist?

She stood in the doorway too self-conscious to go in empty-handed and demand Sara's attention, and Stuka's, Yudita's, Nicolina's. She had not come to be envied but to be forgiven.

When two men lumbered down the stairs carrying a table, she had to move out of the way, into the stogie room. The rank smell of tobacco and perspiration shocked her as it had her first day on the floor. "Look!" someone called out. "Chaya!"

They were not free to swarm around her until their break. She hadn't forgotten; she had tried to time her appearance with their dinnertime. When they were finally free to rise from their benches, in an instant she was swamped. It was worse than embarrassing. A little gypsy-dark worker, someone she'd never seen before—perhaps her replacement—stroked her sleeve appreciatively, as if it were alive. Another woman, older, Slovenian,

Chaya remembered, her fair hair under a plaid bandanna, tried to remove her hat so that she could inspect the flowers more closely. "Please!" Chaya murmured, her fingers twitching at the strangeness of it all. She was afraid to sound impatient. They must be desperate for someone to give them hope, she thought, stricken *if they have to make a heroine of me!*

Sara embraced her, smiling at the fuss; Stuka was gone, home to nurse her mother, who was dying slowly and, for Stuka who could not leave her to come to work, expensively. What was left were ranks of tired-looking women and a few girls too young to deserve this labor, eager for someone to admire with little provocation. Apparently they did not mind envying her. She gave them hope—had she not appeared in that newspaper under the headline CINDERELLA WEDDING? That was not why she had come. But if her muff had been left on the coatroom shelf months ago, someone who admired it had taken it home. Use it well. Frowning, she reflected—and felt such a flush of guilt she knew she would have to kill it before it killed her—*Gregory, if I ask him, will surely buy me another.*

"WHAT ARE we going to do with you?" she asked Asher that afternoon, having returned from Winkler's more confused than when she'd set out. She had not expected to find him in his room in the middle of the day, but there he was, wearing a face that told her he was hiding something.

"Nothing!" But his eyes were furtive.

"Are you going somewhere? Are you leaving your room these days?"

When he shook his head, looking away as he did so, she thought, *I have lost him. I am not his friend any more.* Even his movements were cribbed and tight.

"My soul, come here, will you please." She reached for him—touching him would restore them to each other. But he gave off a new kind of dignity that enclosed him in an ice-block of privacy. Was it that he was growing up, or had she broken their tie by loving Gregory? "Please, Asher. Talk to me. What are you thinking? You are doing nothing with your"—why not?—" your brilliance."

He gave her a long, demanding look. He was going to make her labor.

"Please sit here with me." She patted the bed beside her.

"I'm not the cat. You can get her to curl up there when you want her, but I am not a household pet."

She laughed. "Try getting the cat to do anything. This is the first time I've known your powers of observation to be inaccurate."

Nothing. The intensity that made him so searingly present could withdraw him into absolute nullity. She thought of her refusals, back at the farm, how she'd learned you could erase yourself. "You are trying to make a point, I recognize that. And your point seems to ignore the fact that you now have the means to do"—she cast about—"anything in the world you want to do."

Asher bored. Or rather, feigning boredom. He showed her a parody of a world-weary man, eyelids half lowered, an advertisement for indifference.

She ignored the insult. "You could attend the university. I am quite certain you could induce them to accept you in spite of your age and lack of schooling." She smiled encouragingly and felt the smile returned to her unappreciated. "Or even because of it."

He gave her a scrap of smile. "Do you think they would like to *study* me?"

She took the bait. "They might! Wouldn't that be interesting!"

Asher was pacing, but only because the room was small and gave him no place to go where he had not just been. He was still a compact boy, but he looked compellingly large in that space. "No, it would not be interesting. I told you I am not a pet, nor am I a specimen. Mendel tried to breed tailless rats. A terrible idea to do that purposely."

She was losing patience. "Ash, this does not sound like you."

Along with the new wardrobe she had forced upon him, warm jacket to solid boots, he seemed to have a new repertoire of faces to express disgust and impatience. He must be under the influence of someone whose scowl—her own?—he had learned to emulate. It dragged his bow-shaped mouth down on one side, which made even his small nose slightly crooked, which in turn made his ears look huge. Or had she done that to his ears by imposing that harsh, practical, good-boy's haircut on him? "What is bothering you, my sweet? Why won't you tell me?" He could allow it to grow back and obliterate the memory of being shorn like a sheep. "Are you missing the Fair?"

He stopped pacing. "I am missing everything."

"Ah. Missing being hungry? Being cold? Being left at home when I went to my work? All these things?" She listened to the litany herself, with an inward blush. "I think we have a way, both of us, of becoming too attached to our habits. Even the uncomfortable ones."

But he glowered at her so acutely that she could feel where the skewer of his gaze entered, his eye to her eye. She had to look away. Once she had called him her mirror. He had breathed her air. She'd been certain he dreamed her dreams.

Where was their orphaned loyalty, each to the other? She would not say, *Asher, I feel that too,* because, little skeptic, he would think she was only consoling him.

32

YOU HAD to see the guards before they saw you and duck into shadow. Easy. The men they had hired to keep watch over what was left were slow and lazy, because who cared about it any more? The Exposition was rubbish—crumpled, thrown away, deserted, dead. No, dying piecemeal, not deserted, but all its life, now, was destruction. Dismemberment. Rememberment. Dross. He had come south once and stopped in his tracks at the sight of it attacked, unhinged. It was going back to swamp. Portions of the moving sidewalk that led from the harbor were already under water, the dry sections upthrust like something trying not to drown.

Assembling had been slower work than wrecking: They weren't dismembering it yet but it had begun to decay. Only the exhibits were coming down. The framing, the slathering of all that staff—huge tubs of hemp and plaster—the shaping into curves and cornices, and then the spray of its whitening, none of that was built to last, and winter was having its way with it. A different set of people (better dressed than the builders!) had uncrated, arranged and positioned and stowed and placed some of the wonders, delicately, behind glass, while others lugged, by the ton, the glittering machinery, turning it, walking away to look and judge, coming back to change the angle, putting shoulders to it, turning it ten degrees. Pronouncing it perfect. Again and again and again: Calibration. Celebration. Desolation now.

Cart horses, dray horses of all sizes, colors, and conditions, stood everywhere, stolid, tolerant, waiting for their loads. Then, leaning forward against the weight, they towed it, all of it, dozens and dozens of them dotting the paths. Traffic. Wagons, sledges, lorries, clogging the walk-ways, tugging, hauling, some piled, sloppy, as if everything were suddenly garbage, some carefully stacked. Boxes, bags, trunks, padding. All those paintings. All those pickles, those prunes, those clocks and gears, clever moving machine parts, returned to sender. The buildings were being abandoned, timbers, dented metal, floorboards, and the sludge of white skin that covered it all, huge chunks and clots of it, jagged, useless. The horses were themselves an exhibit, aimed north toward the city or south toward the dumps, to the train stations, the ships, and gone, goodbye as if it had never been whole. Or never been.

They knew it would come to this when they built it. What kind of special place in Hell—he had read Dante, shivering—awaited men who constructed beauty, knowing they would empty it of purpose a few months later? A strange and ghastly place, he hoped, because they had no right to create something alive and then wantonly destroy it. "Like flies to wanton boys are we to the gods, they kill us for their sport!" The Fair had had a heartbeat, now extinguished by the wanton boys. Want, want, want on, want none. It had been a hoax, not meant to be mistaken for real; a bubble, a bauble, to pacify the crowd when everything else was falling down and men were starving, children dying, businesses collapsing. A jewel in a slag heap and even that snatched back.

Pulling apart that beautiful body, casting its limbs, its organs in every direction—it was the first thing since forever that made Asher cry. He had climbed the façade of the Electricity Building, small feet easily accommodated in its declivities, and skipped up into the tower (minus its bulbs) to look down on the emptied buildings. Whole sides of Machinery and Fisheries were falling in. The wind blew through half the States. Transportation, with its beautiful golden arch, sagged like something melting. The blue dome of the Moorish Palace let in the real blue of the sky. Cannibals, stripping away flesh. One hundred twenty-two buildings. Exhibits beyond even his count. The Midway a ghost town, its long straight avenues strewn with refuse, carried and dropped by dogs and once—Asher watched, astounded—a fox who meandered by unafraid. The dray horses and their wagon loads were so heavy, some strained till they stumbled. Here and there they capsized, falling with a whinny and the shout of the drover. Everything spilled out and Asher, spiteful, cheered to himself. One dingy white horse, when his knees buckled, let everything in his wagon slide into the lagoon, slowly, smoothly, and, after a burp of surprise, whatever it had been, the water healed over it. Some, more lightly loaded, went steady as ants bearing leaves in their mouths. Christa, Wisconsin, had been nothing to him. Now, his glorious city left to rot, he was dispossessed.

CHAYA SAID she was looking for a suitable place for them, their own, as if that would make much difference. "You told me Gregory has rooms," he said like an accusation. "Why are we here and not there?" She answered by wrinkling her nose as if she smelled something loathsome, which he had never seen her do.

He lay on his stomach in his little room reading the seventeenth-century poets; admired their language—that George Herbert made designs with his words, altars and wings, and modestly admitted to his faults. "Love bade me welcome: yet my soul drew back, / Guilty of dust and sin." Calmed himself, wondered what exactly they meant by *God* and *sin*. Was he a sinner? (Helpless to resist, he had pocketed the palm-sized book from the bookstore he thought of as his own.) He was bent on rearranging unfairness. Chaya told him that was good. Was that a good thing or a bad thing, spreading around what separated people so deeply that some ate foie gras and some died of starvation? He was not about to ask anyone. Miss Gates, who lived down the hall, wore a silver cross but he didn't think he'd like her answer. His sister was not the one to talk to any more, though she pelted him with questions. Gregory he would never speak to, unless the roof was blazing. And then there were the Ists, whose meetings he had tired of: They seemed to prefer talking to acting. Talk was like the cotton candy at the Fair—it filled your mouth and then it disappeared.

This house was too full of women, plus a few men who looked like ministers, prissy and soft-handed—though what did he know, really, of ministers that he should think he could recognize one on sight. They wanted him neat and he wasn't and wouldn't be. They wanted him stock-still and lost in a crowd. Children came to the kindergarten, caged birds offering their wings to be clipped in return for light and warm things to drink, and toys. They fell upon the toys like starved animals on carrion. Anyone who asked what he was doing with his days—they did, casually, something he'd heard called "making conversation"—received his most withering stare.

But misery tired him out too much to run the alleys. Too much mourning to move. Too much mooning. Mornings he heard his sister's door open—as good at hearing as the cat—and hated her. She was already dressed in her body's disguise, new colors, pleats and plats, loving them, and glided downstairs looking full, never hungry any more. Gregory (not accustomed to working-girl hours) came later, bounded down the steps, whistling. Whistling always meant you had what you wanted. You couldn't get it by whistling It meant you already had it.

EARLY DECEMBER, snow receding, he went back down to Sixty-Third Street, climbed the fence, and there was a colony of men casting shadows on the icy lawns, ducking behind the skeletons of buildings. Walking in the open. Once he saw a guard warming his hands beside them over a fire they had built—wood lay everywhere, flung tinder, kindling enough for a thousand fires. That was one guard who didn't care why he was there—he could have been one of them except for the luck of knowing the right person who knew the right person who gave him the job. Mostly, though, they hid when the guards walked by. What were the uniforms keeping watch over? A corpse. *Once a copse*, Asher thought, fresh from his English poets. *Now a corpse. Who copes? Cops.*

He counted: He had seen twenty-four men—no women—and how many more they must have been. Clots of checkered shirts, bleak jackets, worn uniforms, filthy gloveless hands, they slept inside the buildings, under the bridges, one or two in every abandoned restaurant, on the floor, across the benches that hadn't been taken out yet. The buildings were falling, stripped by winter to their frames like arks of bone. The air smelled burnt. And the great wheel, the gorgeous circle—what were they going to do with the wheel? The stairs to its entrance were deserted, a fine red velvet rope across the landing as if it were the way to the Opera House, and up above the cars gigantic as Pullman's coaches swung in the late fall wind, creaking. Nightmare.

Asher ran like a rabbit from group to group, hoping to meet someone he knew. The grounds seemed even larger in disarray. He had read about Atlantis: Soon it would all be underneath the lake. Another civilization would find mysterious bits—silver spoons, walnuts, incandescent light-wire, water-logged lace. How would they understand the wild combinations of large and small, stationary and moving, soft and solid, on this island, this thousand acres?

Near the end of his second visit he ran right into the standing lap of a man who crowed, "It's Jehoshaphat! Hell, where're your legs takin' you so fast?"

Here was one of the best of the men he had met at the Barracks when the Fair was being born, not disintegrating. His name was Donlan and he had loved to make Asher do the hard names in the Bible; while the others called him Genie, he was Donlan's Jehoshaphat and nothing else.

"Well, look at us, would you!" He slapped Asher hard between his shoulders, as hard as if he'd been a man, and a big one. "You got yourself a nice coat there! Who'd you get that off of?"

He had forgotten Chai had bought him a roomy, warm jacket, gray, with a knitted collar that closed snug under his chin, and sound shoes, and made him thank Gregory for it. He shrugged.

"Come on around the campfire, meet my friends." He was always gracious, always introducing him like a full-grown comrade. Asher wished Donlan had seen him on his throne, in his vest and pantaloons. He'd really have respected him then.

The men sat in a rough circle.

"Asher Shadow," he told them in his public voice. "I used to work here, on the Midway."

There was not a job between the lot of them. There was bitterness and coughing, there were names named—Pullman-may-he-rot, assemblymen and congressmen, the mayor (the dead one and the live one, no love lost on him), and their friends Bathhouse Coughlin and Hinky Dink Kenna—"I hate to call my own people scum but there it is," Donlan said, his jaw set hard—and a whole skein of cheaters and grafters, protectors and accomplices whose pockets were lined with gold, who served the interests of every group but their own.

"The interests?" Asher asked. "What are those? Something interesting?"

Why did they laugh at that? "The interesting part," his friend Donlan said, so amused he beat his thigh with his fist, "is how they shake people down for the money and what they get in return. It's diabolic, it is!"

Asher decided he could not penetrate this particular line of talk. Were these Socialists or Anarchists or Proletarians? He still got the words confused. All he understood he could see for himself: Chicago was on its knees and these good-hearted souls were starved as beggars but wanted nothing to do with begging; they felt themselves cheated; they had taken refuge here—refuge in the refuse!—because it was a place to hide and not be alone. They were not trying to escape from work; work had escaped them. "Alls we want, you know," Donlan said to him earnestly, "is a chance to use our hands, that's what we're good at. We couldn't even get none of this work—" Nasty glance over his shoulder at the emptying clattering on behind them. Wild neigh of a horse objecting to the whip or the ton of machinery it had to pull. "They could hire us when they get ready to clear those buildings away. But no. We could put 'em up good and fast, snowed on, rained on, pissed on, but you know, when it comes to tearing it down, the crew don't need so many hands. And they got their friends, and their friends' friends, and out we go on our asses." A wink at Asher. "Scuse me, son. I don't want to give you the idea I got a dirty mouth. Our noble behinds."

Asher looked them over with care. "Did I ever meet up with any of you at City Hall last winter?" Had he ever put anything valuable in their hands and waved away a thank you?

"Ah, last winter we was busy down here. Coldest bastard winter in the history of man—woops, there I go again. What a mouth on me!—but we had work. Remember the Barracks? You could get warm in there. Three squares, too." Donlan wasn't as looming as he looked at first. His shoulders leaned in; he stooped around himself like someone protecting his chest and middle. He might have been keeping warm. His skin was ruddy with the wind, and the tip of his nose was wet. Everyone's was, dripping, icing their mustaches.

MOST OF the men Asher met came from some other place—Chicago meant work—and now they were like dogs that had found a place without too many fleas to lie down in, and didn't think it was worth leaving for uncertain destinations. When they spoke about their families they got a soft, unfocused look in their eye that was different from their ordinary stony one, or the one that flamed with fury.

Didn't they know that the children they were describing no longer looked like the ones they remembered? They'd have grown out of who they used to be, just the way Asher had. What if some were sick, or worse? If somebody died back in Wisconsin or Indiana or Pennsylvania—a few somebodies—like his own brother Beryle, how would they hear the news? The Wooded Isle or the snowy lawn beside the Electricity Building was no address. Donlan talked about his boy, Joe V., who could do anything with his hands, making things, fixing things. "He's a little genius, he is." He forced a small sound through his teeth, a cross between hopelessness and impatience. His face, when he spoke of his son, was lit with pleasure and doused with a dark suspicion, all at the same time. Asher tried to imagine his own father talking about him somewhere, his genius son who could do nothing with his hands but everything with his head. Who would he be telling that to? And where would that be?

"I can't go home to him, though," Donlan was saying. "If I ain't got work, why should I be another hungry mouth? Last I heard they was at her folks in Ohio and the whole lot was half starved."

"Joe V. too?"

Donlan threw a rock into the distance, nothing to hit. "Him too." He winced at something sharp. "Horses out there keep on dying, nothing in the feed bag, you notice that? Men all along the highway, stone cold, not a thing in their feed bag neither. I seen one of them. A couple." He did not look at Asher when he said this.

A man named Waldo. who had a wooden leg like a pirate in a book he loved called *Peg-Leg*, said, "I helped burn up one of them. Ground was too hard to bury him, we drug him off the road and made a pyre and we lit a match and wished him a quick ride to heaven.' He wiped his nose with the back of his sleeve. The cold was making it bleed; he held his nostrils together with his dirty fingers. Waldo was the same one who told Asher how to cook horse meat and not think about where it came from. "Anyways," he reassured them, "the old boy's dead already, so he don't know. It wasn't disrespectful."

"But the man at the side of the road that you burned up—you wouldn't eat him."

Waldo shook his head, insulted. "Don't you know the difference between a horse and a man? We ain't cannibals yet, boy." He sniffed. "I'd rather eat tree bark."

Another man. Marco, who always seemed to be shouting, instructed him in the best way to rob gardens when the time was ripe. Asher wished he could tell him he knew more about robbery than anyone here had ever dreamed of, but he zipped his mouth like a purse and was proud of his control. Bakitis, who wore a tattered scarf that he told Asher was a shred of the Greek flag, muttered something about blood. They seethed and teemed, sat, stood, paced, all the time planning—imagining without plans—vengeance. Fire, mostly. That was the easiest to accomplish and the most satisfying to think of, eating up profits, worrying the vultures at the insurance companies. Maybe even gorging on the bastards who were starving them. "That fire before, in '71, that wasn't nothing compared to what we could do if we picked our targets."

"We could burn out Pullman." Marco yelled, no secret. "How come nobody's gone down there and done that? That hotel he named for that fat daughter of his? Flash—*shoosh*! There goes Florence!" He rubbed his hands together, warming them on the thought.

Donlan sneered. "They got guards. Mac. You don't just traipse in and set fire to the draperies and walk away."

"Why the hell not? You got matches, ain't you?"

"Because they're expecting you is why. You think they can't figure out the likes of you? You want to go to jail, that sounds like a good plan. Least that would keep you warm."

Asher listened, heard desperation, asked himself what good his books or all that back-and-forth debating on Division Street could do a hungry man whose children were withering out of his sight. Or in it. His hunger at Mrs. Gottlieb's was never this bad. He had a roof. He had a table piled with his booty: Shakespeare, Sophocles. George Herbert and John Donne who said, "No man is an island." Revolution you could close between covers.

Unseen. Invisible. Lost. They were lost, the Shadows. Abandoned. No, not both of them. Chaya, traitor that she was, seemed to be found. Mrs. Ceil Stillman behind her door with her whistling fool.

He stared into the fire they had made. Hemmed into a narrow space, it shot above the rim of the metal refuse can. Refuse. Re-fuse. Why was it called that? It held all the things people refused? Nothing but flame now, hot sparks rising into the snow-gray air. It wouldn't do enough good to find objects the men could pawn. What besides jewelry could he deliver into their hands that would help them when what they really wanted was work? Robin Hood was failing at his undoable duty.

But it was all he could think of. "I could go to some—" He didn't want to say *parties* to these men, it felt immoral. "I know some places I could go and get some—" This was not something to discuss. His old booty bag had hung too long on his bedpost; it was time to fill it. He was surprised that more of them had not become thieves. "I steal from them." He tried to sound ordinary, not too proud. No preening.

"That's good," Donlan said, "but it don't change nothing."

Asher blushed, feeling small, as if copping jewelry was for children.

"You're up against big-time thieves, Jehoshaphat, not hot little hands." The city's elected officials were clean-hands robbers, Donlan muttered, they never had to touch a single object that cast a shadow. They signed papers, they shook hands, they talked about the price of wheat and silver, about international trade and something called tariffs and they let neighborhood bosses alone. There was such a thing as an alderman—Asher puzzled: an alder was a tree—and that's who let the garbage rise and the houses fall and all they showed to their districts was their lard-fat naked rear. None of it seemed real to him but apparently a lot of money changed hands without actually filling anyone's palm with weight or heft. It was exactly what Asher heard at his meetings, the one thing all the Ists agreed on: *The bastards did it legal.* Donlan rubbed his hands together to work up some warm. "Saloon we go to when we got a couple a coins? They get shook down all the time, no escape if they want to keep their business." Victims hung by their heels, being bounced until coins fell out of their pockets—Asher imagined it—and men in uniform doing the shaking.

"What if—" He was thinking fast. Not even thinking. Feeling welled up in him, a heavy wave. "Batter my heart," he had read and his heart was battered now. "What if I could get some jobs—a dozen, maybe—at a factory I know. Could you do—just heavy work, like you did here?"

Donlan widened his eyes. "You know somebody—"

"I think I do. I do. But he's a hard"—he tried it—"bastard." The word made him feel taller. "But maybe I can shame him into doing a decent thing one time. He's sort of in my family."

Marco called out, "Why the hell not, kid. You got a little opening, drive a ramrod right through it." Whatever a ramrod was.

33

GREGORY'S SISTER Lallie sent a note to Chaya inviting her on a shopping expedition. This form of indoors hunting and gathering, it appeared, was an approved profession for a young woman of marriageable age who had not yet bowed her head beneath the yoke of housekeeping or—this would without a doubt be her sister-in-law's future—of keeping her own servants. Servants, Lallie had informed her, were as demanding of attention as any other occupation and for this pleasure one earned nothing but, rather, paid, and dearly.

Chaya, between Greek tragedies, had been reading what she could find in Gregory's small library about socialism, and thinking gravely about her father and his blighted ideals. Where, in what slum of what city, was his spirit being ground down at this moment? Marshall Field's block-square emporium seemed too much an altar to covetousness for her to want to worship at it, but she so much hoped to cultivate her new family that she agreed to come. If they were to be rudely "cut off" by Gregory's father—an expression as violent as its intention—he had not made his threat real and so she had not been enjoined to exercise economy. Rather, Gregory was pleased that she was to spend the afternoon with his sister.

Lallie, in any event, seemed, like a bubble, to float above sullying earthly concerns like the reorganization of capital or the desirability of the single tax. Her cheeks that seemed to stay perpetually pink, she had an endearing way of capturing her bottom lip with her top in mock embarrassment as if she were always doing things she hadn't intended. Today's invitation demonstrated her generosity: By including Chaya in her concentration on the niceties of personal decoration, she was granting her an honorary normalcy. Possibly Lallie hardly noticed the differences between them. Having dreamed, as a girl, of a wardrobe dense with ball gowns, Chaya thought those should have been *her* preoccupations but as Chaya-turned-Ceil, she had bought only enough new dresses and appurtenances to be appropriate to most occasions. She spent her vanity on little that was visible; she only wished not to stand out as inadequate or, worse, superior by refusing to engage. Still, she sensed that it was politic to allow herself to seem Gregory's sister's playmate.

And so, prepared for her favorite sport, Lallie laid out the itinerary this day: new shoes of a kind—buckled like those of the Puritans—she had seen on a friend's feet (though she fretted proudly that her own shoe size was so small there might be no such shoe to fit her), and perhaps a silk dressing gown to take with her on a weekend excursion to the Michigan home of a distant cousin (though this was not the season for silk). But practical things irritated her, and surely flannel would not make for an uplifting mood. She had in mind something in robin's-egg blue. "Is there nothing you are in need of?" she demanded lightly of Chaya. The possibility seemed incomprehensible. "If it isn't too impertinent to ask, are you assured that you have nightclothes elegant enough to make an enticing entrance when you—ah—" She sucked in that lip to suggest the naughtiness of the question—"retire?"

Chaya could only smile at this implication, remembering Lallie's brother's short sojourn on Madison Street in those pathetic rooms furnished with Maxwell Street cast-offs. Were she to appear at their bedside in the sort of frippery favored by Lallie, all whipped-cream lace, loosely tied ribbons and exotic rippling color, his ardor would cool quicker than she could wink (if she were, like Lallie, a winker). For Gregory, flannel would do.

The sisters-in-law debarked from their hack directly in front of Field's, which commanded an entire square block, and entered its brightly lit aisles. Lallie could not know why Chaya stood still, breath held, face red, when she confronted a salesgirl leaning across her counter. Comfortably plump and girdled, the young woman had a defiant pompadour that rose from her forehead like a dark cliff, and a smile falsely ingratiating.

Breath released, Chaya allowed herself the deep satisfaction, then, of someone who has crossed a divide. She had changed the balance, clad as she now was in her lovely nubbled blue woolen coat, its soft fur collar dyed to match, and her feather-heavy hat. How sad, how superficial, that they bought her the respect she had so painfully failed to elicit when she came a beggar for employment. Little do you know, she wished she could say to the salesgirl, that I am the poor woman for whom you had, and proudly showed, contempt, turning up your pert nose and gesturing me to spare you a sight so crude. You were one generation ahead of me, that was all.

She would not allow herself to gloat but she saw it for what it was, another masquerade, the willing capitalist "consumer" at play. Humbled, embarrassed, she held her tongue and obliged her sister-in-law by acquiring two shirtwaists as giddy with lace as an antimacassar on an armchair, a dressing gown whose watery colors changed as she moved, and—to indulge Lallie's lascivious fantasies that Chaya was certain concerned her own future romance more than Chaya and her brother's—a very minimal black gown suspended from straps frail as spider web, in which to sleep or—they shared a knowing giggle—defer sleep. She handed over its price vowing never to wear it, as if that would absolve her.

Lallie was not satisfied with the shoes on display, which she deemed too practical, fit only for a housewife, so onward they were to forge, to the Boston Store. They hailed a hack directly in front of Field's and had just begun their trip when they heard a commotion a few blocks north on State Street. A dark shape was approaching with what seemed the inevitability of an ocean wave. It was wider than the street, and before it all traffic, all pedestrian movement, fled to the clotted sidewalk. With an oath from the driver, their carriage pressed itself against the curbstone.

"Oh, the strikers!" Lallie whispered, as if the word were too shameful to say full voice. "Or, I should say, the men without employment. I suppose they aren't strikers if they have no work to stay away from! What do they expect we can do for them?" She looked mildly exasperated. Chaya stared at the mass as it came closer, straining after their words. It was difficult to make out what the men were chanting, but the very size and solidity of the march were astounding. It was a black cloud that rolled across the day, obliterating all else for her. Police on their glowing, monumental horses walked behind and beside them, as threatening as the marchers them- selves, over whom they towered. The way they flanked the chanting men they seemed to be shutting a door on them, separating them from their spectators, containing their force with a larger force barely contained. The legs of their mounts moved like pistons. The horses, like their riders, were nervous, primed for action.

Chaya stood shamefaced before them, the large bills Gregory had put in her hand this morning burning in her purse with an unholy light. The men carried signs that said FOOD! They said WE WANT WORK! They had not striven to be clever. Fists thrust upward, they thronged forward earnestly, though not in step. Someone carried a flag. No one smiled.

"Come, Chaya," Lallie prodded. "Watching them is no help to anyone, it is only meant to depress us. We have work to do, too." She pushed open the door and they were taken into the buttered golden light, from which they would emerge in a few hours scented, themselves, with an inescap- able fragrance that marked them as surely as the men and the horses were marked with their respective odors. She had never in her life felt so shamed, and more so for her silence.

Home, what she would remember of her day with Lallie was the dark shadow of the buildings through which the men had marched. Joe Slivka, a worn and battered neighbor of Mrs. Gottlieb's, had told her, once, how cattle poured through the chute at the stockyards where he worked up to his ankles in blood. Noisy and ragged they went, shoulder to haunch, on their way to death. And here were ranks and ranks of two-footed cattle, feeling, thinking—organized, brave and hopeful, really, not willing to be cattle— but just as doomed. Who owned the buildings they marched between? Who owned the mayor? The Stock Exchange that had failed? The banks that foreclosed on debts without mercy? Who owned the Nineteenth Ward, her Ward, where it seemed as difficult to remove the garbage as it was to stop the wind over the lake? Whatever their names, she knew she had stood at the

Stillmans' table between their corseted, silk-clad wives, hesitating between a lemon tart and a napoleon.

What was the good of it, finally, this sitting in a warm and friendly room speaking of Oedipus and Othello, whose troubles seemed quaint beside the stench and contagion that pressed against their walls? Speaking of their pain was not easy, those two self-blinded old men, but yet it was not difficult enough. Conscience was a throbbing nerve; Miss Addams suffered it but would not yield. When Chaya plucked at it like the string of a mandolin—Mrs. Gottlieb's Nachman had left his instrument, which Asher had loved to finger—a deep note emerged, vibrating a music that felt red to her, dark red, the color of Joe Slivka's blood-sodden boots. Marrying Gregory had assuaged nothing.

One of the inhabitants of Hull-House, who had been away but had just reappeared, was a woman named Florence Kelley. They sometimes referred to her as Mrs. Wischnewetsky, a name that apparently attached to a regrettable marital lapse she had recently overcome, with the encumbrance of three of Wischnewetsky's children as a reminder. The three young ones, two boys and a girl, though they were neither obstreperous nor disrespectful, could not live with their mother at Hull-House, where some lines of prohibition, though not many, were drawn; instead, they boarded in one of the green suburbs. They visited their mother often, but were not welcome to stay. By whatever cost-accounting system she used, their mother found their absence a necessary cost to pay in order to pursue her work.

Mrs. Kelley-Wischnewetsky, a socialist like Gregory, was so fierce that Chaya was put off by her the first time they met. Large, handsome as a man, with hooded eyes and sensual lips, she spent the first two courses at dinner raging, though no one was refuting her. She had causes, and anyone could realize they were good ones—reducing the servitude of women and children in factories and, invisibly, in sweatshops, and the deadly length of the workday for both. Chaya, easily brought back to the smell and feel of her cigar bench, sank in her seat under the weight of full recall. Her fingers twitched, her nostrils, summoning up the thick sweet-sour air, withered in self-defense.

They were seated at dinner in the long wooden dining room, where Cook was laying out steaming bowls of turnip and shepherd's pie. Chaya, intrigued by Mrs. Kelley (or was it Wischnewetsky?) and her denunciation of the soullessness of employers, offered her own testimony, shyly. "But you see, there are a lot of pieceworkers like myself who had no choice but to work day and night, otherwise we could never have paid our rent!"

Clearly, Mrs. K-W—who could be blamed for simplifying her allegiances?—knew this territory well, but, like Gregory, it was unlikely she had lived it firsthand.

"What did you work at?" Mrs. K-W asked abruptly. as if she were interviewing Chaya for yet another position. She did not much seem to value the niceties that usually accompanied her class.

Chaya, trying not to be cowed, took a tiny bite of turnip for fortification and explained how she had dragged herself through the double shift, long hours at Winkler's, evenings at Yanowitz's buckeye. "Those were the days," she confided, "quite recent days, actually"—and she looked at Gregory who was listening, rapt—"when I saw no sun early or late. I was a cigar-making machine, and if I had any mind at all. it was in total eclipse."

"You see! You are only proving my conviction, dear!" the older woman said triumphantly, as if her misery had been the result of Chaya's own foolishness. "If your hours had been restricted—and only our eight-hour law can hold them in check, trust no employer to restrain himself—some other young woman could have had the other part of your employment, do you not see?"

Chaya saw, but she also remembered the trivial weight of the coins that slipped from the envelope into her hand on payday. She was intrigued watching Mrs. K-W, who, though much more vociferous, seemed entirely at ease and affectionate with Miss Addams: Who was this vivid, outspoken, upper-class sympathizer, who cared more about her convictions than about her dinner which sat hardening before her, barely touched, while she played, with relish, a long scale, hitting every kind of note from disgust and disappointment to a searing, contemptuous fury?

What was most wonderful about her was that, for all her righteous anger—or perhaps fueled by it—the woman seemed to crackle with hope and optimism as if they were an electric current. Miss Addams, though always busy, was quietly and efficiently so; she seemed positively tranquil beside Florence Kelley-Wischnewetsky, who was full-voiced and turbulent and who, Chaya thought with regret, had not much approved of her in her innocent victimhood.

BUT SHE was mistaken. The very next evening, Mrs. K-W tapped her on the arm as she was taking her seat at the dinner table. Chaya felt frail as a child beside her.

"Mrs. Stillman—"

The name was camouflage, alien and absurd.

"Do you think we might have a word?"

And so they talked, unceremoniously standing in the doorway, and Chaya, both flattered and terrified, allowed herself to be pressed into an army of "reformers"—what chutzpah in the word!—from which she knew, by instinct, there would never be release. Surely Miss Addams had alerted her friend to Chaya's hunger to be of use.

First she was treated to a lesson in the two meanings of the word *determined*. "Either one's life is *determined*—hunger, disease, desperation—because the forces of greed and self-interest are aligned against one, or one lives a life *determined* to overcome those forces. I make this sound simple. It is not simple. There are, in this city, sixty-six thousand employers and I have twelve inspectors. But it is possible, if one finds a place to plant one's feet." Chaya nodded dumbly. So she was "one." But had she not, as a worker, always been faceless, countable by number, not by name?

All it meant, her recruiter told her without hesitating to see if she understood that she was being pressed to join Mrs. K-W's righteous army, was that she would go out with a pen and notebook to study the sweats, the sort of hellhole Yanowitz had run in his own rooms. She would have to talk her way in—admittedly a daunting challenge—and then she would observe, and assign numbers and checkmarks to a variety of categories. "Indoor toilet? *Functioning* indoor toilet? One does not guarantee the other, believe me. Ventilation? Light? Type of power if it is a garment shop— foot? Steam? Gender and ages of the workers?" Mrs. K-W ticked them off with a terrible dispassion, though when she spoke her color rose as if she were facing a furnace. "You will find little boys in the can factories with unbound bloody hands. You will see children roasting before ovens to make crackers like the ones we ate with our dinner. The list, as you no doubt know from your own experience, is nothing if not a description of the circles of hell." She seemed almost to take satisfaction from having so exhaustively organized the potential horrors. But, it seemed, the law to limit hours and ages, which she had fought for with the ferocity of an angered mother bear, made it illegal for owners to deny her access. That would be her shield.

"But will I be safe?" Chaya asked. "Won't they be—" She stopped to imagine herself being chased from doorways, threatened with weapons. She knew men like Yanowitz.

"Angry? Indeed. Resistant? Only as far as you allow them to be. Will it be dangerous?"

"Yes?" Chaya realized she had been standing on her tiptoes, which did not enlarge her voice.

"Yes, it may be. And you are a—what shall I say?—a slight and inexperienced young woman. Obviously." She gave a little half sniff that sounded like disdain. "But I sense, Mrs. Stillman, that your anger may be equal to theirs, and we might as well tap it. It will be healthy for you to turn it to some use besides regret." Mrs. K-W's dark-eyed gaze was unwavering, like one of the massive golden statues at the Exposition that stared into the distance as if it were the future and she had been fashioned to command it.

34

CHAYA DARED find herself disappointed that, for the first thirty days, Mrs. K-W assigned her no more than clerical duty, but she'd have been terrified to venture into what they called "the field." Having lived at the Fields of Zion, when she heard that word she still pictured meadows bounded by wooden fences.

At the end of each day when the twelve inspectors returned to the office—which was just downwind of Hull-House, quite nearby—she inscribed their notes in a giant ledger. Every inscription attested to such pain that even the bare inked notations could restore the seen: The factory whose windows were painted black not only to forestall observation but, she assumed, to punish its workers. The boy of no discernible age, operating in no familiar language, whose clothing stank of excrement. The girl beaten by the owner with a stick for sewing a bad seam and then, having caught her finger in her machine, fined for bleeding on the garment.

On and on it went, the litany of inhumane employers and fearful workers, spiced all too frequently by threats to the inspectors, their notebooks confiscated, and one who was actually thrown down a flight of stairs. Mrs. K-W sued on her behalf, though she was hardly surprised to win nothing but an editorial rebuke for her "socialistic attempts to curb and fetter the rights of capital." "The *Tribune*," her mentor told Chaya wearily, "was founded on two principles from which it does not waver. They should decorate its masthead: 'Know where the money is, follow where it leads, and never apologize.'" She could be quite merry in spite of all. "'And where it does not lead, find out who is abandoned.' Which sound like invitations to reform but actually describe the way to the plutocrats' fortunes, which will, with their assistance, be left undisturbed." Her smile conveyed no pleasure. "Oh, Mrs. Stillman, I should be better at my numbers, shouldn't I? I suppose that makes three principles, a suitably asymmetrical number. The holy trinity of our age!"

Chaya wondered if serving as one of Mrs. K-W's inspectors was too easy, a kind of atonement. She didn't think she was gloating; quite the opposite, she was only willing to lend her weight to the balance. She went out a few times with a Mrs. Donaldson, a rather formidable lady in a hat so heavy with adornment that she was amazed the woman could hold her head up but who stared down the floor bosses in a way Chaya could hardly imagine emulating.

Another time she accompanied a very slight young man named Doster who reminded her a bit of Gregory in that he was lovely to look at and polished in manner, but who seemed daunted by his task. "I have been here before," he confided as they made their shaky way up a long external stairway on Wells Street, "and this supervisor boxed my ears with a rolled-up newspaper." She stared at him, embarrassed. "Of course I am prevented from raising a hand, except to defend myself. But I was tempted to lay him out right there beside his mangle." Chaya was sure it did him good to envision such a victory but she doubted he could have executed it; his assailant must have carried three times his weight. "The girls on the floor just looked away, they turned their heads." He spread his hands wide and she could see that his nails were bitten to the quick. "It is a grim task, reporting what we see, my dear. Are you certain you want to do it?"

She assured him she did, though she cowered mightily inside. How she wished Gregory were volunteering his whole self like this young man, instead of summarizing purgatory from a distance, even at the cost of his very clean fingernails. "I can only hope my best is good enough," she assured Mr. Doster. Just to hear herself say it she told him, "I have done some hard things myself but this will be, I think, a test of a different kind."

THE FIRST week she was nauseated much of the time from the combined stench of perspiration (they were called sweatshops for a reason), fish and fried onions from lunch pails, the air dense with fabric finish, and the stink of scorch thick across it all. The pressers' steam raised a cloud that sucked every breath of air from the small rooms, and the hiss that flew out obliterated half of every sentence. Cigar-making had been a party compared with the manufacture of clothing, any kind from winter's to summer's to the miscellany's between.

The first evening, returned from her investigations, she immersed herself in the copper bathtub in the room at the end of the hall where green plants flourished on the washstand because the air was damp. The filth of what she had walked through would not wash off; she understood that. How, how could one human commit such sins against another? It was a naïve question but there was something almost comforting about asking it, as though some time there would have to come an answer.

"AH," MRS. Kelley-Wischnewetsky had said to her when she returned to the office undone, "may you never become immune to your disgust. May you stay inconsolable." Was that a blessing or a curse? Nothing she had lived with at Mrs. Gottlieb's had prepared her for the lurch of piss and occasional vomit, of dead dog in the street and spoiled food in the kitchens of the apartments she passed, and the front-room shops where workers spent their days. Mrs. Gottlieb's—orderly, maintained with pride, childless—had she but known it, was a palace.

That first night, exhausted though she was, she thrust herself thirstily against Gregory as if she had spent the day crossing the desert on her knees. His body was what she needed, live, taut, healthy. He smelled so good, so fresh and untainted. He had the sweet neck of a boy and the hard chest of a man, and nothing in his life had begun to ruin him. Everything about him, and their bed, their crisp sheets, the lamplight in which they made soft shadows, was clean. She lay beside him shuddering with relief, opened herself to him as if his healthy body could save her, worried, at the same time, that her sudden ardor would offend him.

Could you exchange your disgust for the body's pleasure? Death for life? Could dismal reality be an aphrodisiac? She remembered reading somewhere (and being shocked) about a woman who had made love rapturously after the death of her mother, because that way she could assert their terrible difference: She was still alive. She made love to Gregory for the sake of hope. The worse her daily rounds, the more miserable the indictments that went into her pebbled notebook and thence into the ledger, the more she needed to be touched by immaculate hands, and was ashamed. If ever she stopped feeling such shame, she would know she had lost herself, for whatever small thing that was worth.

As she drifted off into the shallows of sleep, it occurred to Chaya, vaguely, an idea with the timid imprint that water might make, that everything anyone did was a sort of exchange. Needing the buoyancy of passion in a clean place to erase the day's darkness. Escaping from one reality into another—wasn't that, in some way she was too tired to explain to herself, why Gregory loved her? Why, when all was said and done—in spite of his failure to be a "natural socialist!"—she loved him? The thing that led the lives of the poor into their deaths was that they did not change, minute to minute or year to year.

That was an abstraction she made so that she could sleep. But what she had seen that day was nothing theoretical: She had been sent to check on a woman who was said to have absented herself from work because she was sick and—the shadow of Mrs. Gottlieb's shop, emptied by typhoid, loomed over her—they needed to know what caused her affliction for fear she might have brought smallpox to the factory floor, or tuberculosis. She readily allowed Chaya into her apartment, which was horribly strewn with anything one might dare name: crusted dishes, undergarments sagging over the back of a chair, a pail to catch what must have dripped from a leaking roof. There was even a dog, so mangy its back was bare, a sickly pink. The woman was young, with very fair hair not loose but pulled harshly back, punishingly so; she might have been pretty if she had not been so sallow and forlorn. "You have a baby," Chaya ventured, which she supposed sounded like an accusation. "No, no baby.' Vehemently. "Me only." Chaya insisted, it was in her notes, and she took it upon herself to move through the apartment, touching more than she'd have liked to and listening hard, and that was when she heard a weak mewing. A cat amidst all this wreckage? A cat with that dog lying there watching her?

No cat, though. She listened hard and, on the odd chance, pulled open the closed door of a closet and there was the baby, lying on a shelf like a package awaiting delivery. He was snuffling and flailing in his stained little shirt, frail hair plastered to his head, and when she touched his forehead he was burning. His mother cried out to her and, had Chaya not gathered him up and held him against her own chest, she'd have taken the woman into her arms and wept with her. She remembered Mr. Doster saying that they were forbidden to make physical contact with their "subjects" and she thought how vicious she would seem if she took the baby from its mother and insisted she follow, because she could suddenly see that the girl—she was really just a girl—was burning too.

And so she reported what became an "incident," not a mother moored in pain, and never heard anything of what came of that. Of *them*. Had she betrayed or saved them? Wasn't that the worst of what separated them one from another? That there was a system, an attempt to make some order out of chaos, but it was not sensitive enough to hear the voices of the souls it hoped to serve?

It hardly surprised her that she awoke one morning having dreamt she was standing on a bridge at the great white Fair, and when she turned full front she was serenely smiling though she had no arms.

35

NEXT IN the round of party-givers came Gregory's brother Ned, Chaya's least favorite relative. Precisely because Gregory hated him, she explained to Asher, he had no choice but to attend. Asher failed to understand this, but he took a deep, edgy breath and offered himself up to share her sacrifice. On the night of the party, he smiled, he dressed up in the suit he had worn to her wedding and a tweed cap he was instructed to remove at the door. He ought to have alarmed her with his sudden willingness but she was elsewhere, lost in herself.

Ned greeted them—later for the gritting, the grilling and gutting—at the door. He was gracious in his own house, his square cheeks pink with health, or, perhaps, alcohol. "*There* is the boy we so rarely encounter these days!" Sour-sweet with whiskey and cigars, his breath smelled combustible, so soon, before all the carriages had even pulled up close to the door. He clapped Asher between his shoulders, just where, Asher thought, the guillotine would once have fallen. Heads falling into baskets like cabbages. Blood flying out, staining the knees of the executioner. This man, Ned Stillman, made him see violence. Was it his rough voice curdled to coyness? "To what do we owe the honor of your presence, iddle kiddo?"

"I am your brother-in-law," Asher grimly reminded him. It took an effort not to leap at the man's throat. "Don't you remember, I come with the bride?" *I'm here to skim your rooms of their fancies,* he did not say. *To pocket what I can of yours, to poke and pilfer. Idale kiddo.* "Do you have some chocolate?" he asked, because they would expect such a question from a boy with a wide collar spread like white wings, gull wings, over his chest.

No one had much to say to him, child that they still saw, and he leaned in on their chatter: whom they had seen at the opera looking worryingly pale, fogbound Venice to which someone had sailed in harrowing weather, and London more crowded than ever but oh, the gorgeous feast at the house of—whoever—in Highgate.

Ned cursed at the unions that were stripping him of his fortune. He raised his voice with each pronouncement, as if the striking men might hear him and "Desist!" he shouted, smiling as if he'd made a joke. "What will it take to get to them to desist! Nightsticks are not sufficient. A little state-sanctified brutality might be in order." His guests hummed their approval. "A few smashed heads might do the trick." Raised their glasses. Concurred.

Gregory, holding tight to Chaya's arm, called out, "Ned, don't you think that a bit extreme? Do we really need blood in the streets to make you happy?"

"Oh, you are tedious, Gregory. You and your soft, floppy heart. You would give over the city to the lazy and unclean. To the jabbering class. How did it happen that you became bewitched by those people? I think we have a family in common, but one would never know it."

The Steel-man only glared at his brother. And Chaya did not dare speak in this company. *You see!* Asher wanted to shout. *You see! You see where you've brought us!*

"I happen to share the opinion of Medill and his legions, whose editorial stance is that this city will not prosper unless we keep well separated the men who build and sacrifice and those who leech upon us only to spend their days with their elbows on the nearest bar."

"*Sacrifice?*" Gregory's voice got away from him, Asher thought, the way he himself sounded these days when, unpredictably, his voice broke.

Ned's face was turning violet. "Do not make me out the villain here, Gregory. If you are so aghast at what I call sacrifice, I would appreciate it if you did not enjoy the sweetmeats from my table, which are prepared by a cook whom I pay, on linens my washerwoman bleaches, whom I must pay, in a house kept warm with a mountain of coal for which I must also pay. How do you think an evening like this comes to be? Just who should underwrite it?"

For this Gregory was prepared. "If making a party seems to you such a sacrifice, Ned, I fail to see why you let yourself be so put upon. And what does all that have to do with the fact that with your assent there are thousands of men in this city who have no roof over their heads, who have no food for their children? Please tell me, what is the equation here?"

"My assent? Do not presume to lay the blame on me, if you please, for the fecklessness of those roofless men." Asher had never seen anyone sniff and raise his chin as if he smelled something foul, but here the man stood. If he'd had a cane he'd have shaken it. "Sentimentalist, get yourself another whiskey and let us leave this for now. I will make certain that I do not trouble you to attend the next time we invite our friends for a convivial evening." Ned turned his back as sharply as a soldier and left Gregory standing shielding Chaya. It was the first time Asher felt so much as a cinder of sympathy for him.

HE WANDERED the rooms upstairs, fingering the flowers of that wretched man's wealth, slipping them into his sack (which everyone assumed was filled with books. He had one book, today, at the bottom, but mostly had vacant space in which to drop his discoveries). Men like Ned kept no money loose; there must be a safe or a strongbox somewhere. On the library walls, above dusty Dickens, Gibbon, Scott, pictures of hulking men kept silenced watch. The architect who'd built the house, a man named Richardson, large as a house himself, dead of it all too soon. A familiar face above a checkered cape—the mayor! Harrison the ambushed! He had been a friend of Ned Stillman? Crooked like the rest, and, could be, shot for it, no matter what they said of the crazed assassin? Was the mayor's son, his successor, any more honest? They were a gang of take-and-hide, get-and-keep-everythings. He closed his hand around a pen, golden, filigreed, and dropped it in his sack, where it bounced against a brass inkwell (inkless). *Donlan, for you. Write to your son with it.*

"Asher, may we bother you to come down to us and perform your party game?" Gregory stood behind him smiling, framed in the doorway, unsuspicious. He always had an inviting, hopeful look. How could the man spend his time cataloguing the sins of the boodlers and bleeders and look so clean and cheerful? "So many people remember when you answered questions in their parlors. Would you come and be their amusement, and then we'll have cake." His voice turned down at the end of the sentence; it was not a request.

Asher manufactured a smile. He would pay up. It would buy him the look of innocence; his perfect·book-memory was like perfect pitch. "Greenland." "The House of Tudor." He tried not to yawn. "Cosimo de' Medici." "The French Congo." They were so easily satisfied. He sat up straight, still small on his plush-padded chair, his head below its upper curve, and pretended to strain at recalling facts that he tossed like coins to an organ-grinder's monkey. Soon his deepening voice would turn reliable and he would be too old to amaze them.

Dismissed, the chocolate of his reward carefully licked off his hands—his host and hostess smiled at him as he darted a lizard tongue between his fingers—he went upstairs again to the pleasures of burgling.

He was holding a silver watch in his palm, studying the slow, patient movement of the second hand when, poking into his thoughts like something slipped under a door, it occurred to him that, finally, this was the moment to produce what he had promised. Pocketing goodies made him feel like he was evening the score but—Donlan was right—a mountain of hockshop tickets wouldn't change anything. What those men needed were paychecks, for their bellies and their self-respect. He pulled out the stem of the silver watch and turned it as fast as he could and watched the minutes fly by, and then the hours. He could feel the blood coursing through the soles of his feet, feel it prickling his palms. He pushed the stem back in, a sharp little click, replaced it on its shelf, and headed for the stairs.

ASHER LURKED around the table, whose array of sweets had dwindled under the onslaught of guests who were not too polite to ignore their appetites. He found a strawberry in a shiny chocolate shell, tongued it cautiously so as not to finish it too quickly to use it as a prop, and stood himself, like it or not beside Ned, whose posture was that of a palace guard. It was unlikely the man knew how much Asher despised him—so rich in self-regard, why would he suspect such a thing? "May I ask a favor of you, my—" My what? Dear man? Friend? Brother-in-law? He left the sentence unfinished. "I wonder—"

"Not half so much as I wonder at you, my little man. How is it your brain retains so many abstruse facts when most of us can barely manage to remember where we have left the keys to our front doors?"

Ab Struse. He would have to look that up. This admiration, Asher thought, was an astonishing attempt at ingratiation on the part of the man he so reviled. Whatever the reason for it—a desire to draw a distinction between him and his sister?—it was an opening. Here came the ramrod Marco had suggested. (He'd looked that up too. He knew a metaphor when one came round.)

"May I ask a favor?" he repeated. "Sir." That was the word he'd needed. Ned looked benignly down at him. "I am—I have—I don't know how many men you employ at your factory but could you possibly make use of a few more?" He tried as abject a smile as he could but forbade himself to say *please*.

Ned laughed and put his hand too familiarly on Asher's shoulder. "And why would you be making such a request, if I may ask, a young fellow like you whose hands are still soft, and may they stay so. You are fortunate that you can leave the punishing work to your elders. Have you become a junior member of an employment agency?"

It was not amusing enough to deserve that laugh. "I have—some friends—a dozen or so—who are very skilled at heavy labor, who are in need of work and they would be—" He forced himself to look directly into Ned's forbiddingly pale blue eyes to telegraph soul-to-soul. Assuming the man possessed one.

"As if *skilled* and *heavy labor* belong side by side, my boy!" His brother-in-law blinked at the humor of the idea as if its naïveté assaulted his very eyes. "And why would I take on this cadre of talented laborers? Because, you understand if I were in need of help, I would know where to find it." Now he seemed to have fixed his gaze on Chaya, who stood close beside her husband beneath a painting too dark, from where he stood, to decipher. Asher recognized the ploy of seeming to be fascinated by something so as to have a place to hide discomfort; the paintings were all too murky and ill lit to reward much attention.

Before Asher could hazard a reason—why indeed should the man be magnanimous?—Ned squeezed his arm and pronounced, "I do think I might arrange to take them. A gift to you, because you are a brother of sorts, aren't you. If you will send them over early next week I can find something for them. Tell them to ask for me when they come around." He gave Asher an abstracted smile, the kind that did not reach his eyes. "I believe I may owe your sister a bit of—well, let us leave it at that. Be certain to tell her, will you? Just as you suggested, iddle kiddo, let us call it a favor. For the sake of"—he sighed heavily—"family."

36

A PARTY at the Stillmans'. She felt as if she had emerged from a burrow into the light of day; the brightness stung her eyes. Sweet things, laid out like elegant merchandise, made her gag. At the least, she had a moment with her brother. "Thank you for coming, Asher. We are doing our best, aren't we—to be family."

Asher stared at her as if the word were unfamiliar to him. "Did I have a choice? Anyway, these people aren't my family. Do you think they are yours?"

Her eyes had burned when she told him what she was doing for Mrs. K-W. "And what are you doing with your days now, Ash? You should be at the university."

He'd smiled cryptically. "I am *near* the university. That should be good enough." His wild streak had become nearly the whole of him. "What, precisely—" She was smitten with guilt—she had been elsewhere. While she'd pondered her marriage and her new vocation, she had been guilty of neglect.

He gave her an oddly vicious grin. Who knew what mischief animated it? "I am making some plans. I am going to surprise you." He'd been growing; she had hardly noticed. Or it was his tweed suit, cut exactly like an adult's, that reminded her that he was not her *ketzele* any more. More tomcat that pussycat. "The last time we were here, did you hear brother Ned spitting on the workers he likes to put out of their jobs? 'Lazy as niggers,' he said. 'Why do I owe them a paycheck? They come late, they get sick—I had two die on me last week.'" He grimaced and, had he had not been in a carpeted room with no spittoon in sight, she was certain he'd have spat. And there was more to come: Gregory and his brother had an awful encounter, Ned at the top of his lungs, Gregory with restraint, which she was sure Ned heard as cowardice. She stayed as far from the two of them as she could for as long as they were compelled to stay. She studied the paintings, which were de rigueur for such a house. Hung high, they were dark and dense with men grappling like wrestlers. Out of the shadows in the largest, a swan hovered, menacing, above a young woman in a toga who cowered beneath his wings and turned her face away. Chaya found that more alarming than inviting, but, trapped, she busied herself with them as if she were in a museum, or back at the Fair.

Gregory's mother floated by, inspecting her son's guests' glasses. "Please, *please*, avail yourselves of the punch bowl. That is pure champagne, with green grapes to connote blossoms, and it is just calling out for your attention!"

"She thinks she's amusing," Asher whispered. "I think she's ridiculous. Blossoms!"

Given their little history of confiding, Chaya felt more than halfway kindly toward her mother-in-law. She tried to imagine Faith Stillman without her lovely gray dress, its apron of lace over silk fine as a spider web; without her careful coif and the luscious earrings that swayed when she harangued them. Her necklace suspended a single ruby like a drop of blood that sat like something intimate against the fabric that covered her hollow collarbones. Her coloring was so pale—Lallie had surely gotten the improved version—that had she been one of the women who kneaded a treadle in a sweat—without makeup, minus the clothing she chose carefully to disguise the length of her neck—she'd have faded, all freckles and pallor. Chaya felt protective of her, but she had no way to express it.

IT WAS, as it turned out, not moral revulsion that had made Chaya queasy at the dessert table. She was both thrilled and panicked to discover herself pregnant, a possibility she had not much thought about. At the Madison

Street rooms, Gregory had promised her he was "taking care of—" and he had waved his hand vaguely. He hadn't told her that, safely married, he might have stopped taking care. She was stunned at what had happened without her suspecting, let alone willing it—the glory of it! While she had been intent on pleasures newly found, a force larger than she was securing a place for her in a long, an infinite, line. She had trouble believing it, but when she felt her waist and discovered it slightly widened, and touched her breasts only to discover a tenderness that was very nearly an itch, she was silenced. Oh, she wished her mother were with her! How thrilled she would be.

A child, then. Fine. Better than fine. But *now*, when she'd just got her useful life in order? She could, she supposed, bring her child along with her when she made her inquisitorial rounds. Otherwise (and how could it be otherwise?) she would become yet another mother who gave over the care of her child to a surrogate. How complicated it was, all of it, and into this welter of confusion, like it or not, she was going to cast yet another soul and allow herself to be joyful.

37

CHAYA WAS grateful the first time she felt truly, unignorably sick: Shouldn't the creation of a new human demand one's full attention, and, along with delight, even some sacrifice of comfort? Shouldn't it announce its presence—invisible, mysterious—by hinting at the visible, unmysterious changes to come? When she found herself unable to sit in a room where coffee was being brewed or fish unwrapped, she was satisfied that the baby-making mechanism was grinding away efficiently, thrumming like a benign machine with no off switch. Gregory, though not happy to see Chaya miserable, was proud, nonetheless, of his part in making her so.

Her condition also thrust her a step closer to the mothers served by Hull-House. They came forward with advice of all kinds, from the sorts of horrific potions she should be imbibing to give her baby strength— vinegar, sauerkraut juice, emulsion of eel—to the necessity of sleeping with her head facing true east. Least welcome was the discreet suggestion that she and her husband sleep separately and that she not yield to his seductions for fear of damaging her child. "Remind him," she was advised, "that it is his child as well." Then again, in perfect contradiction, came the assurance by a Sicilian mother of seven that when her labor began, she should indulge in a "feast of love" with her husband to ease the baby's arrival.

She thanked the ladies and, touched, discarded their suggestions.

Gregory was working at finding a house of their own and she would soon, she was both pleased and sorry to realize, be on her own and missing her mother, whose advice would likely be less exotic.

But on the first morning after Miss Addams's own doctor confirmed her state, and after she had settled her mutinying stomach with soda crackers and carbonated water, she discovered a fount of unwelcome advice in her own bed.

"Where are you going. love?" Gregory asked her, propped on his elbow. Last night they had ignored the warning against disturbing the babe with their lovemaking; the covers were still wonderfully disarranged.

She was fastening her skirt at her waist, by now almost sufficiently widened to need the buttons moved.

"Where am I going?" she echoed. "Why, to work, Gregory. Today I have a list to attend to on the far west side. I didn't know there were even houses out that way."

He sat fully upright. "But you don't intend to continue Mrs. Kelley's business in your current state!" He was rumpled, his hair at angles she thought particularly adorable. She sat herself on the edge of the bed and smoothed them down with a placating hand.

"But of course I do! Why would I stop?"

Gregory gave her a look of pure incredulity.

"Chaya! You yourself have talked about the contagion in those places. You called them cesspools! Do I need to make a list for you? Do you recall? Typhus? Diphtheria? Smallpox? Are you *mad*?"

She stood and put her hands on her hips the way she had seen people do, for emphasis, though it made her feel as if she were onstage. "No, I am not mad. But neither am I a coward."

"You have a new responsibility now. You are—"

"I know what I have and what I am. Or will be. But darling—" She was bent on keeping her voice low and respectful. "Those contagions can fall upon me anyway, whether I am bearing a child or no! Why is it more dangerous now?"

Gregory looked around the room as if he might find someone to argue to, since her sanity was hardly to be trusted.

"You are no longer responsible for your own health and safety, must I really remind you? Must your zeal render you *this* irresponsible?"

She was trying hard to understand. She knew that he was earnest and afraid—she even knew that, looked at one way, he was correct and she was tempting fate—but still his argument fell flat. "No one protects the women who work in those places when they are in what you refer to as my 'state.'" She said this as quietly and calmly as she could.

"Ah, Ceil. Chaya!" He could almost accomplish the throat-clearing consonant. "Will you always regret that you are no longer helpless? Is that to be your lifelong melody? 'Let me live no better than the lowest'?"

And so they wrestled, and Chaya was made to question whether she thought herself indispensable, whether she was resisting Gregory's control over her actions, whether she could, in fact, survive her responsibility if something terrible happened to the child she was carrying. Gregory insisted that, of all men, he would not dream of standing between his wife and the needs of her constituents, but did he have no right to protect the child who was every bit as much his as it was hers? "Chaya." Conciliatory, her name like a hand patting her head. He was out of his pajamas and into his day's working clothes, suspenders fastened, shoes tied. His shirt collar stayed unbuttoned because he worked here at his desk, at home. "I have a thought, dear."

She was standing at the door, preparing to bolt.

"Shall we ask Miss Addams to mediate for us?"

Miss Addams, as it happened, was not happy to be consulted. "There are a good many things I know, my friends. More than is good, my doctor tells me, for my equilibrium. But I must say that while I excel at weighing human and political burdens, I have had no experience of how one comports oneself in a marriage."

"But the dangers?" Gregory was eager to ignore her neutrality. "Don't you think these—these pest-houses—could be a disaster? You don't need a spouse to appreciate that where contagious disease rages—"

"Pest-houses! Rages!" Chaya, impatient. "Gregory! Don't be carried away! Doesn't that simply tell you how badly these victims need a witness?" She could feel herself quiver with vehemence.

"No one person is so necessary that she cannot find someone else to do her work under such circumstances."

"Oh, thank you very much. Here I have finally found a way to be useful in the world, to be something other than a part in a machine for the profit of greedy men, and you demean it."

"My darling, really, you surprise me. Is this the imbalance of emotions that is said to accompany pregnancy?"

"Please, children, please desist." Miss Addams waved them out of her sight. "I am beginning to feel myself cast as Solomon the judge before the two women at war over one baby. Except that I cannot say which of you is the true parent." She was faintly smiling. "Has Florence Kelley weighed in on this matter?"

Gregory smiled as triumphantly as a poker player with a full house. "Florence Kelley is, today, in her role as Mrs. Wischnewetsky, mother of her children. She is in Winnetka this morning, visiting with them where they stay."

"That," said Chaya, "has no bearing on this situation. Do you expect to impress me that she loves her children? Do you think I fail to love my"—she folded her arms protectively across her stomach—"my almost-child?" She gave Gregory exactly the smile he had given her. "Now, if you will excuse me, I am late for my work." Again, she felt herself onstage, prettily if figuratively stamping her foot. Gregory had taken her to see Ibsen's astonishing play *A Doll's House* just last Saturday evening. She did not wish she had a door to slam, but she felt the rip of Nora's anger. She gave Miss Addams a nod of thanks, placed a very quick kiss on Gregory's rough cheek—he had not yet shaved, so eager had he been to catch Miss Addams at breakfast—and went to collect her coat, place her hat on her head without appearing to hurry, and, hand quivering, tuck into her purse the black notebook in which she would record the day's atrocities.

CHAYA WAS so furious at Gregory that she trembled as she walked. Her legs could hardly support her. Standing, leaning against a fence, she thought she must look like Hannah in the Book of Samuel when the priest thinks she is drunk, but she is only—only!—engulfed in grief.

She arrived at her first assignment, a top-floor uniform-makers' shop—could it be that the dark blue of the Chicago police force emerged in crates from such shameful rooms? Street level was occupied by a narrow, shabby fish store whose sawdust lay all around its door, damp and trampled, and the hall and stairs were rank with the stink of it.

A handkerchief would seem a flag of disgust; she held her hand over her nose. Could she dare take this stench home in the folds of her dress, on the soles of her shoes? Even without her morning queasiness, this foulness would scourge her nostrils and make her gag. She had to stop and breathe in once, twice, containing herself, before she continued climbing the stairs.

Her knock was answered by a woman, not much older than herself, so bent that her back was parallel to the floor. Chaya entered humbly. No matter what she thought of the owners, she could never bluster in, threatening and vengeful, like the Law, for fear of humiliating the victims, who were already helpless and ashamed. Nor could she tell them she had been one of them, or nearly so, as if anyone might share her good fortune; that seemed cruel by yet another degree.

She tried to speak to the hunched woman, whose chest nearly touched her knees, but she only answered incomprehensibly in—Polish perhaps, or Bohemian. Then a man came forward, who seemed slightly demented—his eyes flew around the room, far above her head, and his fingers fluttered like insects around a light. But speech was hardly necessary; she saw what she had come to see: Nine people breathing repellent air, two bare bulbs, one of which flickered irregularly, a special torture. They worked in silence, which might be habitual, might be for her benefit. There was no owner present, no overseer, and no available English. They were like souls marooned on an island.

Then the man who had seemed so angry startled her by careening toward her and pulling at her sleeve. "What you got, lady, we no work?" He tugged and tugged until she was sure the cloth would tear. "You say! You tell! What you got for us?" He brought his face so close to hers she could smell his breath; his eyes were the palest blue, but their whites were flooded red.

It was the question Chaya could not answer, the awful challenge that made Mrs. K-W's work both noble and ignoble at the same moment. If you pulled one thread in this terrible economy of souls, would the whole fabric come undone? She had arrived a savior but stumbled down the stairs and into the light a villain with no knowledge of economic laws, the cause and effect of markets. The hard facts were Gregory's territory but that made them no more useful than her sympathy.

GREGORY'S MOTHER and Lallie, lacking other employment, were prepared to hover over Chaya as if she were their ailing child. She was not to raise her arms, she was to submit to daily bedrest, she was to drink a quart of milk each and every day. "I shall bring you whipped cream treats," Lallie promised, "and think of how they are going straight to the bones of the little one. And to its tiny teeth. Oh, the heaven of it!" She pretended to swoon. "Have you ever thought that everything we women do—primping and putting on our nicest costumes, and dotting our wrists with scent—all of it, in the end, is solely intended to lead us to childbed!" She nodded at her own insight. I sometimes think this is the only thing men are good for! And we must work so hard to entice them."

She pouted prettily—things had not gone well for her recently in her courtship by a blond midshipman who had somehow gotten landlocked here, near a lake and a river but nothing resembling a sea. After a good deal of dancing and laughing, he had expressed a wish to return to a vessel out of New York called the *Otterbein.* That sounded suspiciously foreign to Lallie and she announced that if she ever found herself beside it, she would kick it hard in its steel-and-rivets side. "What is a side called, on a ship? A flank?" She turned to Chaya petulantly. "There's fore and aft and—you came here from Europe on a ship, didn't you? You must know"

ASIDE FROM the natural tiredness she was cautioned to expect in her state, she had to acknowledge when she allowed herself an extra hour or two of sleep that she had been exhausted for years, deeply, dangerously tired. And what benefited her would certainly benefit her child. Lallie put a lilac-wreathed card into her hands that read:

Empty your mind of every care.
A nest of pleasant thoughts prepare.
Your child will feed on your content,
Nor follow where your worries went.

Once she would have thought such a message banal, but perhaps during pregnancy the brain did soften along with the pelvic bones. She thanked Lallie, nearly overcome, and promised herself that she would obey the injunction. She had a mind in need of emptying.

WHEN, DISCOURAGED, she came to tell Gregory she had decided to stay at home and be, for once, indulged—would try to be of help keeping Mrs. K-W's voluminous documents in order—futile, too futile—he opened his arms and pulled her to him gently: She was to be treated with exquisite care. She was not to be upset. Henceforward she was—he did not say this because it was understood—not to be made love to, even though her radiance made her irresistible. *No wonder men strayed while their wives' bellies grew,* she thought but would never utter.

One rogue idea demanded suppression, in spite of how attractive this cosseting sounded—that no one she had ever known before her marriage had had the leisure, let alone the means, to withdraw from the world to be worshipped, and look! Their children—most of them—survived. They dropped their babies in the field, they birthed them in miserable beds and barns, on pallets, in open air. Her aunt Minke was delivered of twins in a sledge, in deep snow, halfway between Slutsk and Maripolsky. Her mother had given birth to seven without a single comfort. And on the ship that brought them to America, a very young girl produced a large-headed, large-voiced baby in the dark of night, crying that she had not even known she was with child.

But every one of them would choose her lovely bed, if only they could, would they not, and the grave attention of Faith Stillman's doctor? Eyelet lace and two down pillows. A tall glass of pulpless orange juice, its sides beading because it was so perfectly chilled. Hanging on the armoire, now, on a padded hanger, a spring-green maternity frock, gift from Lallie, who appeared to have given herself an excuse to shop for three. Chaya was hardly in need of the voluminous dress yet but its promise gave her a kind of pleasure she had never felt before: that she was in step with all natural events, all the earth's fulfillment. She liked to think back to her first sight of Gregory, valise in hand, all kind concern, and then envision him above her in their bed, his bare boy's shoulders, the tendons of his neck straining with the effort it took, the thrust and release, that brought her to this moment, palms flat across her stomach, lucky woman, feeling for a first twitch of movement.

Except, except ... If the baby were a boy, heir to the Stillman name, could he (did she care ask?) be circumcised? Her child, girl or boy, would be such a stranger to the world she had left behind, it would truly grow up on another continent.

Gregory came upon her once, bent singing softly to her baby who turned, still imperceptibly, to her rhythms. She wished he had not looked at her with such perplexity but it took him a moment to realize that she was—of course, of course—singing in Yiddish.

38

"ASHER," CHAYA called to him as he bounded up the stairs. He was chilled from his afternoon with the men at the fairgrounds, happy to tell them about Ned Stillman's promise but rageful because as he'd made his way toward the exit, he had glanced back over his shoulder and caught sight of the poor, stilled, useless wheel against the sky—*defunct, defect, defeat,* words and words and empty words rattling around in his head like marbles—all these living things stripped bare, skinned. Skeletons.

He could see that Chaya had been waiting for him. "I have something wonderful to tell you, love. Come, let's go up to your room." They sat on his bed and his sister took his hand, spread his fingers, traced the lines on his palm like the veins on a leaf. "You need to know, darling, we are going to be leaving Hull-House."

"I don't care." Shrugged. Took back his hand. "I never wanted to live here."

"Don't you care why we are leaving? We are going to have our own house."

Shrugged again. Her business. "I thought you didn't want a house. Isn't Gregory a socialist?"

She looked more familiar laughing. "This has only been a fine convenience, being here with all these good people for a while, so that we didn't have to think, didn't have to decide anything about the future. But no one says a socialist can't live decently. Not ostentatiously, of course."

She raised her eyes to the modest room, its fine-checked curtains, its eaves. "But believing that all men deserve a fair wage doesn't make it a sin to have what you need."

"Have you fallen out with Miss Addams?" Would anyone dare?

Chaya put her hand to the front of her dress and held it there, flat. "No, dear, not at all. Only, you see, we'll be needing more room. More privacy." She took a deep breath. She was climbing something steep. "Gregory and I—we—are going to have a baby."

He stared. It was there beneath her hand. She was warming it with her palm. True, then, she had been as far away as she'd seemed, disappearing into this. He felt himself dimming in her sight, going pale and out of focus, and not his fault. Gregory's fault. Hers.

"This will be so lovely, Ash—the baby will be yours too. You'll have someone you can play with, you can teach to read. You'll be Uncle Asher!"

Iddle kiddo

He wanted to ask exactly how that baby got inside, under her dress. His books assumed he knew already but he did not exactly, the mechanics of it, and there was no one to ask. Too late for that. Some of the boys and men, when he ran the alleys a long time ago, would mutter things and thrust their bodies, move and twitch, and laugh about who they "had" and who they "did," but what were they having and what were they doing? "Will you name it after Father or Mother?" He knew that much, the son for a *kaddish.*

He might have smashed her in the stomach, to judge by her face. "We don't—I don't believe they are dead, Asher. To use their names—they would have to be dead." She hugged herself, the not-quite-flat front of her.

Lost, strayed, stolen wasn't good enough. Nothing but dead would count. She looked stricken. Struck. Sick.

His sister was becoming one of them, girly-women who sat like birds on a fence, useless, twittering, battening—fattening—on party food and gossip. No more work, the shirker, growing that stomach sucked all her energy. Blotted the juice of her, left her dry. No more anger, that he could tell. She was too calm, quiet like something stunned, under a blanket. Her face had changed too: cheeks he wanted to poke to deflate, and a vague darkness around her mouth, not quite solid, like the smut inside a lamp. And worst, her eyes looking past him. Was it the future she was combing, that far horizon, because it would have her child in it? Searching out its destiny, making it promises?

She seemed uninterested in his fate any more. She asked sisterly questions but without conviction. (*Conviction*: that was what you got for committing a crime. *Commitment* meant caring about something, or being sent to an asylum! Language was a trickster. Where did the rules come from?)

She and Gregory had found a house to move to, no babies at Hell-House. There would be a room for him—"Walls made for books!" (cheerful, a chin-chuck)—and, down the hall, a nursery. Hickory, dickory, dockery, nursery, hearse-ery. Mercy, Chaya! He said it into his pillow. Didn't know what it meant, but he knew she had failed him, who was here *first*: Mercy, Chaya, and be done.

Behind his closed eyes he saw the shadow of his sister leaving him, going down to Gregory and Miss Addams and supper.

39

GREGORY, WITH his family's help, found them a lovely, almost-new house in Lincoln Park, blessedly not too near his parents. It had a rounded brick corner—a "turret," which sounded a bit too castle-like to Chaya—that would demand an equally rounded upholstered something to sit on. Every house on Deming Place had some distinguishing feature—Gregory proudly reported that there were no two façades alike. They had a stained glass window above the porch, a design of crisscrossing shoots of lavender and green; the neighbors lived beneath guardian gryphons, metallic lampstands, filigree awnings. One had a preposterous fountain that, if the wind was blowing, doused anyone who passed in a haze of water.

Chaya was amazed at how much attention it took to choose the most trivial details for the new house. Did it—should it—really matter what her doorknobs would look like? Or, less importantly, her drawer pulls? Large or small? Pewter or brass? Carved or embossed? She remembered the drawer that had been Asher's cradle until his arms and legs battered its sides when he turned in his sleep. There had been one shaky porcelain drawer pull against its faded wood. Did it matter one iota to the world?

Gregory, it turned out, had very precise expectations in these matters of décor. When she shrugged, she could see him flush with disappointment. "One needs to be exacting about what may seem petty details, darling, because the whole, you know, is composed of a thousand choices that must agree with one another or the effect will be"—he considered—"chaotic."

He had challenged her when she asked what difference it made whether they pulled open their drawers with glass or pewter and he had looked at her impatiently. "Necessity is a hard standard, wouldn't you agree? Would there be any art at all if we were to use that as a yardstick? What is necessary besides food and roof and—" She would not have called it a leer but rather a look of pleasure at the gentle swell that was now visible beneath Chaya's dress. "No music, then. No paintings. Not even the books you adore, if you are going to be so absolute." He laughed. "My darling, I think we may have to bring Miss Addams back into the argument again. I believe she is the only one who can soothe your ascetic side."

She said nothing. Instead she concentrated on emptying her face of disapproval.

"I'd have thought," Gregory continued, and she could see the effort it took to keep his voice gentle, "I'd have thought that your first house would have excited you, Chaya."

So she was once again a girl raised from the cinders, ungrateful.

He was more agitated than she had seen him. "Must you make an interest in décor into a moral judgment? A moral failure? How do you think these lovely homes you have visited lately were constituted? With care, darling. With forethought."

"You have the better eye, Gregory, that's all I intend. Truly, you have had a lifetime of"—what would be the least hurtful word, and the most accurate?—"feasting on beautiful objects. You are like someone who eats delicacies and savors their taste and I am, I suppose, still merely eating to survive. I'm sorry if I fail you there." She was afraid to look at him but kept her eyes cast down with an abjectness that burned in her throat. When that was too painful, she raised them. "So please, dear, enjoy the pleasure of indulging these great decisions for both of us. I am going up to have a nap."

She went slowly up the stairs thinking of a new word she had learned that very week: It was *prig*. What, she had asked, did it mean exactly? "One who is self-righteous," Miss Addams had told her. "Or arrogant, perhaps. One who thinks himself—herself—rather more pure of heart than another and is, ah, I suppose you might say, stiffened by it." She smiled, one eyebrow critically raised. "Oh my, I hope I haven't accidentally described myself."

"Never!" Chaya assured her. "You can laugh at yourself, which is more than I can do."

Prig then, Chaya should not have mocked those household decisions, she scolded herself. Gregory did not deserve sarcasm for what might be her blindness. She resolved to apologize but first, quite sincerely, she needed to sleep.

ONE THING more, an accoutrement to their house, which she neither expected nor approved. They had not fully moved themselves in, they were establishing the order of the rooms when, at the top of the stairs, out of what felt to her like nowhere because her presence was a surprise, there came their newly arrived maid Colleen to ask if she would enjoy a cup of tea. Chaya told her as gently as she could that she would not but she seethed at the need to speak with a single soul just then.

When they married, Gregory promised they would not have servants and the question never arose until they left the simplicities of Hull-House. Though he told her he wanted to protect her, especially in her current state, from the need for menial labor, she feared he meant that he liked things done as a maid would do them. Life is short: Chaya would not have dreamt of ironing their sheets. He had got the serving maid for her for her birthday, like another gift in a box, prettily wrapped. She hated to offend him by saying she did not, did not, want her. "Her name is Colleen," he had said, "but sometimes servants are renamed, if that does not please you."

She, who would not become Ceil, had looked at him very long and hard, her husband who allegedly walked the same road she did. "She is not a horse," she told him. "Nor is she a slave. How could you dream of renaming her?"

He had shrugged. "My grandmother had a woman named Stevie, which she thought barbaric, and so she became Sarah. Informally rechristened, you could say. She didn't appear to mind."

How difficult it was for him—for both of them—to give up their habits.

Every family Gregory knew had "help." "Do you think she would rather have no employment?" he asked guilelessly. "Or be indentured in one of those factories you abhor?" Again, the best she could manage was to try not to judge him, in return for which she had to trust that he would do the same for her.

40

HE HAD done his good deed for Donlan and eleven of his friends—not grand enough to induce a swagger but still an achievement that made Asher's face go warm with pleasure. It had been an exertion.

But, after a week of satisfaction just short of gloating, when he took himself down to the fairgrounds (which he had begun to think of as the Burial Grounds) there was Donlan, there were Waldo, Marco, Bakitis, and an assortment of others, sitting around fire in a basket and, tiring of that, wandering aimlessly between the stripped bones of the buildings.

When he heard what had happened he felt a dry fury, his mouth parched into silence. They had worked at Ned Stillman's factory a week, been given their wages fair and square, and dismissed. "Out the door same way we come in," Marco snapped, scraping his gloveless hands together the way he'd have squashed an insect. "Pretty nice boiler works too. Some handsome machines. Everything workin' full tilt. They're not starvin' over there but we're back where we started."

"Worse," threw in Waldo. "Puts you back worse than you was. No explanation neither." His face was pink with cold, which made him look feverish. "Guy in a nice white shirt and collar comes and says, 'So long, fellas. You can get your pay envelope over by that window and don't count the pennies, it's all there.' Not even a thanks or a sorry." He spit at his own feet. "Guess your friend or what was he, your uncle, didn't think you'd ever find out."

Or, Asher thought, he didn't care. Or—this was hard—he did. Only a nasty man would play a trick like that, as if it was a game. He could see that Donlan didn't want to complain in case his feelings would be hurt. They were not just bruised but bleeding. Meddling, he had made things worse. Whenever he ran and fell—when he was little, he would race around the fields until he tripped and all the air got flattened out of him—that was what this felt like. When you got older, most likely a punch to the gut would do it. No breath. Lights popping behind his lids. "Rat bastard," was all he could say, feeling how limited was his vocabulary of insults. "Jesus Christ!" The worst of curses wasn't good enough. He would apologize, though—did and was told he didn't need to be forgiven, he'd done his best. He kicked the basket full of fire and kicked it again until it rocked and nearly fell over. Couldn't cry before his men, he was no child, but all the way home, running partway to work off the energy of anger, swinging onto the Alley L, tumbling off before the fare collector got to him, he boiled with fury. The iddle kiddo was going to make the man—the liar, the hypocrite, the bully—dearly pay.

He was lucky to arrive at Hull-House when he did: later, and Chaya and Gregory would have been gone. The last of their belongings stood heaped in a wagon box behind two splotchy workaday horses, guarded by the driver while they were saying long goodbyes inside. He supposed he'd have found out their new whereabouts easily enough, courtesy of Miss Addams, but—he wavered, faint at the thought—they would have gone on without him. Had they searched for him? Hadn't they cared that he was not there with them? Without closing his eyes the farm loomed, deadened, deserted. Turn your back and the world disperses. While he sat like a cur in the dark they would have departed. That set him trembling.

By the time his sister came out on the porch, saw him and, with a little shriek, came running, he had made himself look nonchalant—the word like a slouch, that lovely *non-sha-laahhnttt*—leaning against the wagon as if she had kept him waiting.

41

GREGORY BROUGHT home a scrap of the news and gave it to Chaya as she was pinning up the last curtain hem in the nursery. It was a Sunday and he had been with his parents for an early breakfast, from which her condition blessedly exempted her. He told them she was sleeping.

"Should we be surprised," he began dryly, and stood tight against her back to press her to him.

She laughed—"Gregory, I have pins in my mouth! Do you want me to swallow them?"—and pulled free. "What should not surprise us?"

"He's fired them all. Ned. A week and they are out the door."

"Oh, no! Asher's men?"

Asher had been strutting like their old barnyard rooster.

"Every one of them. Turned out onto the street, and no apology either."

"Ned was with you?"

"No, the hypocrite's in church this morning. You know, he gives his wife that little present to show off with—the family pew. Father told me. He thought it exceedingly amusing, the whole thing. 'That child's little divertissement,' he called it. He likes to refer to Asher as the 'self-appointed hobo.'"

Chaya sat, her legs suddenly too weak to hold her. Whatever was a *divertissement*? And did it matter? "So much for good faith. Of course there was no way to *compel* him, but those men must have felt themselves without choice to let themselves be led by—" She shook her head. The little *meshiach*. The baby Moses.

The nursery would be simply furnished but full of color, to tickle the eye. May she (she secretly prayed for a girl) be spared genius. May he (though a healthy boy would be satisfactory) be glorious and ordinary, unburdened by the weight of too much facility, too much confidence. May her child be spared too much longing.

Asher was up in his new room, unpacking books. They had never spoken about his devotion to what was left of the Fair; somehow his dignity demanded that it simply be accepted as a fact, like weather, like a passing fever. To tell him this would be cruel. Not to tell him would be patronizing.

She found him asleep on the floor between the leaning towers of his stolen library, stretched out, at ease, with his old German dictionary under his hand. She sat for a long time and watched his breath rise and fall, poor half-fledged pigeon, and tried a dozen sentences to see if there were a single one she might plausibly utter that would contain admiration, pity, and anger in equal draughts. Her brother-in-law Ned Stillman was not one jot less heartless than his power allowed him to be, nor did he possess sufficient imagination to know how to be different. But she was the messenger this morning, and because she knew Asher to be immoderate in his need, she was the first one he would hate.

But she could not read him. When she told him what she had learned of Ned's perfidy, he narrowed his eyes to sullen slashes as if he were searching out something visible but very distant, and said in a cold voice, "Oh, I already knew that. And he is going to pay for it."

"Asher? My sweet?" How could she not reach to touch him.

"Don't call me that. I am not *sweet*." He was still on the floor, his knees pulled up before him, dark stockings bunched around his ankles.

"You did a kind thing. And brave—it was brave of you. Almost as if you were a one-man union!" She hadn't quite thought of it that way before.

He would not engage her glance.

"But you can see, this is all so much more complicated than one person can solve. Even a heroic person. You are like—you are trying to be an entire fire brigade, Asher, but no one can put out every fire alone." She was trying to be gentle, but he did need to hear this admonition. "I'm afraid, dear, that there is a huge—an abyss, really—between our wills and our power."

He did not really seem to be listening. Something in his face, his skin, or perhaps it was the air around him, did not resonate.

"I thought that every single day when I went off to make my catalog of those hellish sweats for Mrs. Kelley. If willing alone could shut them down . . ."

He sighed and clicked his tongue against his teeth. "We aren't poor any more. Your will and your power got you Gregory."

She had to think about that for a long minute; it seemed harsh to remind him that it was Gregory's house in which he had just been sleeping. "No, actually, Asher, that is not the way it happened. *His* power, perhaps. My—" She had no word she liked for that exchange of wills. "You make it sound as if I struck a calculated bargain, and that is not fair and it is not so."

Her brother only smiled, with a vacancy that showed he was humoring her.

"All I can say is that I am so sorry. Your friends deserved better. But Ned Stillman is a hard man, and if he has a conscience, it is not available for everyday use. Now—" She turned from him to the splay of books in which he sat. "Can I help you with these?"

He continued to consider her in silence, as if the dense, peculiar life had been sucked out of him. "I thought you mustn't lift anything." Mired, slow, like a boy at the edge of sleep.

"Oh, Ash, one book at a time! I am sturdier than that."

He fixed his gaze on the front of her dress, where a modest curve was just beginning to disturb her buttons. "What do you think it looks like now? Is it bigger than"—he looked around, then at his own hand, which was clenched as if against pain—"my thumb?"

"Oh, yes!" This jollity felt like a conversation in another language. "They say it is shaped something like a seahorse, can you imagine that? A tiny curled-up thing just floating in a kind of ocean. And, of course, it is no 'it,' it is by now a 'he' or a 'she' or . . . well, that is too mysterious even to try to imagine."

But Asher looked no less burdened. He continued to stare, his forehead creased above his eyebrows, those tender dashes. It was impossible for Chaya to guess whether he was regarding the past and what he had tried and failed to accomplish, and why, or was straining forward toward what would come, what he might compel—try to compel—to happen after today.

"I shall have Gregory find someone to build some lovely shelves for your books," she told him, hopelessly. "And if you would like a desk—"

"Some big pillows," Asher said, gesturing around him. "The Moroccans and Tunisians and the Turks—I especially liked the Turks—at the Fair, they all sat on fat pillows. Close to the earth. I don't like chairs, they seem—"

"Chairs? What do you mean?"

"Shaky. You can't trust them."

"Asher." The sound of him concerned her: *Shaky* was indeed the word for his face, his voice, his toes, which had begun to twitch the way a dog runs in its sleep.

"They fail you. Sometimes they come crashing down. I want some cushions covered with, you know what I mean—those carpets they use. Like gardens, all twined up." He laughed. "Wool gardens. Made of knot flowers! Are they or are they knot?"

She thought it would help her, if not him, if she could put her arms around him, assure him he was not as alone as he looked.

"Aren't you going to laugh?"

The best she could do was stretch her lips wide. "Knot flowers! Funny." Barricaded by a blue Longinus, by a dark green split-spined Marvell and, maroon, Rumi in translation, her boy stayed flat on the bare floor, out of her reach.

42

LETHARGY. BEAUTIFUL sound. Why wasn't it a girl's name? *Lethargy.*
A lullaby. And he had been tranced like a baby sung to sleep until, when
the setting sun gilded his new room through its curtainless windows, his
sister long gone back to her smug busyness, he woke decided. Some invisible machine had threshed this out while he slept, discovered an action
to match his anger. He knew what he was going to do, knew it with such
urgency it was as strong as anything his body wanted. He sat on the floor
watching his hands and arms turn to gold. How, now, to make it happen?

Asher riffled through the faces of the men who shared his furies, the
shiverers at the Fair, the Ists ranged around the steamy room on Division
and, with a puff of relief, came upon the one he would speak to. The man,
always in the front row of the Anarchists' side, was barrel-bellied, his hair
a no-color between blond and gray. He was amused-looking behind a wiry
beard: If he were a painted portrait it would be called *The Contented Man.*
But Dietrich was the most discontented man in any room and he was famous
for it. He swore he had lost more jobs than anyone in Chicago. "I am a
very good machinist. The best. Only my mouth condemns me." He smiled
when he spoke, the way the serpent must have smiled: What he said was
seditious. (Asher went to his lexicon for that.) "The fire next time must
purify their hearts. They may blame it on a cow if they like, or vandals, or
on an angry God. But *we* should be the ones responsible. *We* will cauterize
this city, this nation, with the heat of our righteousness!" *Cauterize!* Not

caution; not *caught*. The man was doubling his vocabulary. "We have been too cowed"—*cowed*?!—"by the hysteria after Haymarket. For years now we have not dared to rock or shock or overturn so much as a vegetable wagon. Cowards! Hypocrites! When are we going to remember the strength in spreading terror?" He spat out the word *terror* with such guttural force Asher could feel how it must have scraped his throat, emerging.

So it was straight to Dietrich that he went. Bent down at his hairy ear and told him his hope, his plan. Dietrich nodded slowly, in his own unhurried rhythm, beard scraping the top of his chest. Took a long look at him (how itchy to be scrutinized; to be, like it or not, assessed! He had been raked by a thousand eyes in his celebrity, but all that felt ancient now. Felt trivial, to be a child ventriloquist). "Yes, my little foot soldier," the old man said in his scratchy accent. He hugged his belly the way, these days, Chaya was touching hers. Lovingly. "I think I can teach you a few things." Think was *sink*. The things were *sings*. His other language had left smudges, like Yiddish but not quite. "If I tell you what you will need, can you get it? You have ways?"

Yes.

"If I tell you how to assemble this thing, you are sure you know to follow the directions?"

Yes.

"Tell me." Tenderly, in case it was a secret that had to be cajoled out of him. "Is someone helping you with this, my good little man?"

No. No, no.

"This you are sure?"

"This I am sure. Of. Sure of it."

"You are alone?"

Asher sighed, impatient. "I am alone."

Dietrich stirred, his weight sandbagging him to his seat. "Come, then, with me elsewhere. We shall discuss this where there are not around so many thirsty ears."

He thrust a puffy hand at Asher who, gasping with effort, hauled him up, then ducked out of his way for fear Dietrich's belly might tip the old man forward and crush him flat.

"You know Most?"

Asher shrugged. "Most? Most what?"

"No, no, Johann Most."

Asher looked all around him as if someone were there to be introduced. "Does he come to the meetings?"

"No, no, he is a leader when it comes to sabotage. For this he has undergone prison, has suffered—great pains. He has made a book about revolution, very good, very important. The science of revolutionary warfare." He said *revolutionary* with a flourish, his voice rising. "You read, yes?"

Asher laughed. "I get by."

"Then you should find it. Swallow it down, good medicine. It would make you strong."

He nodded, thinking, Hurry on up, old man. I'm not reading, I'm *doing*. Finally.

"All right, now you listen to me. Most, I trust him, he does not believe in dynamite, it is too dangerous for most people. You he would certainly advise against it. All you would do, you would blow off those little hands of yours first thing." He took hold of Asher's wrist roughly, turned it up and back as if he were measuring its strength.

"But—"

"But lucky there are easier things." *Easier sings*, Dietrich said, which made Asher smile. Songs were the last things that would survive his vengeance. No one would be singing when he was done. "Nitroglycerin. Guncotton, this you have heard about? Fulminating mercury is not so easy to find." He swept his eyes from Asher's head to his scuffed boots as if he were weighing him. "For you we need foolproof. We need something it wouldn't set you on fire, hmm?" He ran his fingers through the pale wilderness of his beard, considering. Amazing that nothing crawled out of it. "Yes, all right. This you can do, no danger. Herr Most would give his approval, A-1."

Asher was surprised—all it came to was a Mason jar stuffed with flannel (so easy to find) for a wick, and a nasty brew of kerosene and something rank, a white powder he could buy from a gardener whose name Dietrich wrote out for him. "Stinks," Dietrich told him, "but who cares, you got a man's work you got to do, is never pretty, am I right?"

Just that, a phosphorous match and, unbottled, his fury. Now, could he throw hard enough with his thin, weak, untried arm? If he stood too close, he could be caught up in flame. Too far and he would make a pretty mess outside, under the window. His men might have helped, and happily, but he would not ask. This was his own to do.

"Good luck, little man," Dietrich said to him and patted him on his tailbone. "Remember, a good revolutionary stays quiet"—he put a gnarled finger to his lips—"even if all goes well. Taking credit will only help if you got an army behind you that can come in and sweep up the results, yah? And you don't got an army." He had never asked why Asher wanted to destroy a boiler works and Asher was relieved that he didn't have to say.

His fire, wild, flaring, had finally banked. His resolve was steady now, hot and glowing like ashes. Ashes, ashes, Asher! He had been named, he understood it now, just for this night. Once Chaya told him a story the pious ones on the farm believed: that we are born knowing everything (all of Torah, that was, because to them Torah was everything) but why could it not mean everything that would ever happen? An angel touches us just above the mouth, in that little runnel hollowed from nose to lip, and as we grow we forget it all. I must have known this once, he thought, walking fast through the night, before the Angel of Forgetfulness touched me. I am remembering that this had to be.

HE WENT to see the factory (STILLMAN STEAM BOILER WORKS + BOILERS. STACKS, COOLERS, DRYERS, LARD TANKS AND PRESSES) on a cold, clear day; ran most of the way, across the river and far to the west. It was huge; long and wide and dark as a dead thing.

Was it, he wondered, the protection of this building and the money he threshed out of it or something bigger, something more like spite or plain mean-heartedness that made men like Ned Stillman hate poor people so, and mock anyone who fought for them? Which came first? Among the Ists, the Capitalists were guilty of ruining lives, you could hardly be let in the door on Division if you didn't believe that, but he wasn't sure he understood why they wanted so much more than they needed, why they were devoted to piling up dollars and houses and jewels and . . . where did it end? Was it for the Good of Mankind, as they liked to say, what Ned Stillman insisted was Natural Law, or what that writer Darwin called the survival of the fittest? Did they deserve to survive? Would it matter if Ned Stillman perished with his factory? Once upon a time (so many stories he had loved began so) he'd have asked Chaya what she thought about this but now, now, she lived in the enemy's camp. She had not meant to abandon him, he knew that, but here he was, disrespected, underestimated. *Yah*, Dietrich had said. Believe what you believe: Abandoned.

The workers were gone, he saw no light inside, no stirrings outside, neither horses nor carriages. Silence. Full darkness. Distant, some kind of bass-voiced horn on the water, and once, so vague he might have imagined it, a rumbling train. The longer Asher stood listening, the deeper the feeling that he was alone and nothing lay before him but a huge lifeless assemblage of bricks and chimneys, spouts and windows, dozens and dozens of windows reflecting back nothing.

Heart smashing against his ribs, he scraped at the edges of one of the windows carefully with the sharp edge of a rock that cut like a diamond. He didn't want the glass falling noisily out. It gave quietly, obediently, cascading down in little bits like a waterfall. Shook the bottle, full to the brim with the vile concoction, knew it was bubbling, it hissed a little, but he couldn't see the bubbles in the dark. Pulled out the cork, struck the match a few times till it flared, dropped in the small flame, waited till it caught, and pushed the plug back down, tight. His arm was so thin, so unmuscled he was ashamed. He stood tiptoe just outside, right in the pool of shattered glass. Drew in one long, stern, punishing breath, no regret, no forgiveness. Pulled his hand back, wrist cocked, and cast his rage as hard as ever he could into the unlit machine room.

Fled, then. His back was to Stillman Steam Boiler Works when it hit but the huge orange light broke above him, throbbing. He heard the concussion—gorgeous!—and even felt its heat leap out like a slap of congratulation between his shoulder blades. He turned, finally, and the sight of the fire behind the windows was beyond words. He breathed that punishing breath out—done, Ned Stillman! Dietrich would be proud of him. He stayed crouched, letting his pulse slow. The dancing light was better than any show. It banked and flared, seemed to die down and then leaped up and out where there was no more window. When, finally, he rose and took off into the blackness toward the street, he heard a scuffling and saw jagged shadows coming toward him fast. He stumbled on the curb, scrambled up and got to his feet just as the arms of a policeman closed around him tight and held him, squirming, biting, kicking, shouting, caught.

43

SHE WAS preparing for bed when Gregory brought the news. She was standing before her mirror thinking that it reminded her, though it was far more elaborate, of the mirror that her mother kept above the single chest they owned in Zhitomir. Its curve was that of a pair of human shoulders, sloping but graceful. She was brushing her hair, slowly, slowly, up, out, down, while her mind wandered afield.

Then, from the doorway, Gregory called out "Chaya, Chaya, come quickly. Your brother has done it this time!"

"'Done it? Done what?"

Her husband's face was startlingly flushed.

"Gregory?"

"He's set off something—a bomb, or some device—in my brother's factory. He has maimed a guard, and possibly he's killed the woman who was cleaning the rooms." She had never seen Gregory at a loss for what to do with his hands. Now all he could do with them was pump them up and down like an agitated child.

She wanted to sink to the floor, a helpless lady fluttering to the carpet in her soft white nightgown, but of course she could not. And there was the baby to protect, to clutch at, to shield. Very deliberately, to keep herself steady, she placed her hairbrush on the cluttered vanity. "What," she asked in a measured way, "are you telling me?" The measure was a sign that she had gone numb. She had not taken a breath since he had called her name.

"Pray she doesn't die, for Asher's sake," Gregory said, not sympatheti-cally but punitively. Had anyone ever uttered words so unnecessary? Instead of praying, she pictured Asher calling to her, shouting her name.

OF COURSE she demanded to see him. Gregory told her to wait for an attorney to accompany her but she could not pace, doing nothing, while he searched (or planned to search, in the morning) for the perfect defender. While he was tending to all that, calmly making a list of potential saviors, she tried to sit still but when that became impossible, she dressed and slipped out of the house and, on foot, headed into the purple hour just as dawn was breaking. By the time she arrived at Harrison Street, the sun was full on the stone face of the stationhouse.

In a room crowded with indifferent faces, men in uniform, men in vests and suits, a few of them confronted her, interrupted her, found she had gone thoroughly—conveniently—blank about the details of her brother's life. There was whispering, papers were filled out, some were stamped, and she was suddenly being spoken to harshly.

"You are his guardian." A man with the eyebrow of a gray caterpillar said this as if he were informing her of something she didn't know. She could see that his job was to provoke.

"My brother—I am his guardian, yes."

"Your husband, Mr. Stillman?" The official looked skeptically at her, most likely surprised to see her here without him.

She had to think for a moment; the marriage was still so new. It was difficult to imagine that she shared responsibility for Asher with her husband. "Yes, of course. Officially, yes. He is Asher's guardian as well." Guardian-in-law—there was no such thing but there should be.

The man took in a large snorting breath as though what he was about to say cost him mightily. "I am afraid you are going to have to spend some time with us, Mrs. Stillman"—the *us* sounded hospitable, as though he were offering her a companionable stay in his own house—"while we determine your culpability in this matter."

"*My* culpability?" She stumbled on the word, which she had never had occasion to say. She could see a bailiff already on his way to her side, the official having smiled viciously at her and then, unsmiling, nodded to him to do his duty. He had arms that strained at his uniform and a neck like a granite pillar.

"To judge whether you are guilty of neglect—he is a minor, after all— or of—" He turned that smile upon her again, unwarranted, sudden as a splash of chilling water. Each time she saw his teeth and then they vanished. His smile was wolfish. "Or of complicity in his crime."

"Those are my only alternatives?" She felt herself standing taller to receive this sentence as if it were a blow. Was he saying that she could she be held responsible for having shaped her brother's conscience?

He swept his eyes up the front of her and slowly down again, assessing her in her brazenness. Her pregnancy was only modestly visible, and just as well. As for her dress, she was used to feeling shame at its inadequacy; since her marriage, she wore fetching outfits that did not feel like her own. But the judgment he was making, she knew, had more to do with her husband's possible power, and that of his family, than of her own comeliness. It was a complicated business: Whom would he most, whom least, offend by taking into custody a possible conspirator in a crime that affected two brothers, the husband of the accused and the proposed victim? The senior Stillmans' neighbors on Prairie Avenue were the kind after whom streets were named.

But he was accustomed to such conflicts—half the criminals in the city sent weepers and mourners to petition on their behalf and he was schooled to ignore them in honor of the wronged parties. "Those are the only two at this moment, yes, missus. I am glad you understand."

Would he apologize and remind Chaya, for civility's sake, that he had no choice? He would not. He nodded to the bailiff, who took her arm roughly as though to demonstrate the inseparability of Law and Force. She should have listened to Gregory and not sneaked out before the sky had brightened and he had roused an advocate to defend her and her Asher. An attorney would never have allowed her to be seized and hurried out the door, and thrown—nearly thrown—inside a pen whose door clanked with the solidity of falling rock.

He loved her for her willfulness, Gregory said. For her zeal. And he despised his brother for his stone-hard heart. But truly, when he comprehended what Asher had done, and when he heard the hidden facts of Asher's life and all she knew of it, acts of piracy he could never imagine, he and his comfortable history, he would never forgive her. She had hoped that, having once loved her, Gregory might have maintained a modicum of human concern for the two of them. The more hours that passed, the more naïve she felt. As if she were a fish too small or unattractive to keep, her good, honest, timid Gregory, irreparably a scion of his family, would surely throw her back.

THE CELL'S stench rivaled that of the stockyards. Was it blood? Was it rotting meat? Was it, more likely, simply too many creatures corralled in a small space, breathing out hopelessness and venom? Their cologne had turned rancid; someone had vomited where the wall met the floor and made an orange cesspool with bubbles like fish eyes on its surface. The noise—chattering, laughter, and a barbaric shrieking probably intended to drive them all mad—was insupportable. Which was, she realized, the very point. Lockup was not a spa. They were, perhaps a dozen of them, held in a single pen.

She swore to herself that she would not be hardened by her encounters with these hard women, that whatever sensitivities she had cultivated with effort would not be worn away by the incivility that surrounded her. Anyway, she had had her vision cleared by her work for Mrs. K-W—she was no virgin. Her cellmates, she imagined, were mostly prostitutes and thieves, and women who had betrayed a trust sufficient to register with the Law, and so she was sympathetic toward most: They were far more needy than she. But it was strange—because she was clean? Because she arrived well-dressed? Or because gossip and the intrusions of news reporters so quickly twigged to her arrival?—it was clear the women saw her as one of *them* rather than one of *us* and muttered at her and kept their distance. It would be far too complicated to instruct them that until quite recently her life had been as bare and pitiful as theirs, her fingernails just as caked with grime.

Chaya stood alone, facing the chipped brick of the wall, and worried about her brother, a child among felons. The men's cells were in the basement, stony, stinking, roiled by shouts of protest, threats of vengeance more potent than those of the women—so she would hear in good time. "Pigged together like herrings in a barrel," one of her cellmates said to no one in particular, bitterly grinning. Here in Chicago, and probably elsewhere, they had no special accommodations for boys—this was worth agitating for; the sort of thing at which Miss Jane Addams and her friends excelled—but at the moment only the discretion of the policeman who brought in a child and then the judge or jury who would sentence him, could separate him from the foulest murderer in the cellblock. They did not care about his age, his motives, or his susceptibility to influence.

Still, she would plead, Asher had a prodigious mind, even an unnatural one. His mental capacity—his intellectual accomplishments—should not be held against him; he was helpless in their grip. Prodigy or not, his crime might make it appear the boy possessed no moral sense of his own, as if it were his single missing part—but she knew that in Asher's case "morality" would need defining. If he was a thief of extravagant daring, she planned to argue, he was a thief for the public good, never for his own advantage! He had preyed on property but property was not alive, like starving men. It could not be betrayed.

But his life of petty thievery, she knew, she would never be sufficiently eloquent to explain if it ever came to light. As for the violence, she suspected that Gregory and his family would assume he was executing what he had learned at her knee. If he had come under pressure from the men whose meetings he had so zealously been attending, who would be held responsible? Her own commitments, of course, were under suspicion by Asher these days, but that was far too subtle to be spoken of. He was a sparrow and they would think him a predator: a hawk, an eagle. Was he an anarchist or just an angry boy?

She pleaded to be allowed to see him, needed to hear him tell her how he had come to this. But, "Female inmates do not fraternize across that line, with our males," she was told by the red-faced matron, twice her height and weight, who spoke to her like someone pinching her softest flesh between her fingers. "That line" was a different floor or two, but no matter.

"Male! I'm speaking of my brother. And he's a boy—a baby!" She could not bear to imagine what he was feeling, abandoned to a cellblock replete with—she had not the strength to imagine.

"No baby gets in here," the matron told her with great certainty, a nurse playing doctor. "They're pimps and gangsters. Bur-ga-lers. Tramps. Your brother's a *felon*, darlin'!" She leaned up against Chaya and dropped poison in her ear. "And felons hang."

Chaya was not a fainting woman, but she made herself swoon, as slowly and gently as she could so as not to jar her child. She heard the other inmates' voices rise around her like a gust of wind or a covey of birds scared up from a bush. When she fainted, she withdrew from their company. It was dark where she went; it was silent. Finally, gratefully, she was alone.

THIS WAS not prison—it was jail, a short-time lockup, which is a sort of door that swings both ways. Mrs. K-W and Miss Addams, whose habit was reflection, not condemnation, might help her to understand in some orderly fashion what she was seeing. But Chaya could not discern on her own a system of oppression where all she understood was that—noisy, grabby, stepping on each other's heels and setting up yowls at the offense— they frightened her. Had she applied her mentors' methods, she could have seen that so many were here only as a rebuke and an inconvenience, based on the unsuccessful estimate that, say, a lady of ill repute would exchange her profession with that of a placid wife at home in her kitchen if only she were harassed a few times more often than her patience could bear. "I'm tired of spendin' every damn weekend in this hole," one woman complained, "like it's gonna make me a saint! I seen that bailiff out on Wabash the other day, window-shoppin' the girls like the rest of 'em."

They were not all coarse: A few, who dallied with the city's most august figures at top-notch houses like Miss Carrie Watson's, were accustomed to oysters and champagne, and wore—like Chaya—beautiful clothes they did not have to pay for. Who knows whom they had to have offended to have lost their protection and ended up in this place? When she spoke about the women who'd been lured to the cribs in the Levee, Mrs. K-W insisted on sympathy: These women lived by a hierarchy as rigid as the military's, or that of the constabulary that watched over them. The girls who worked the street, she said, victims of bad weather and anonymous customers, were the drones; the expensive ladies who walked on thick carpet and took their time with their regular "visitors" were the queen bees. Even behind bars, and spitting mad to be here, you could hardly tell them from society wives.

None of this was Chaya wise enough to understand while she stood quaking and, shamed, tried to turn her back on them. When somehow they heard why she was being detained, they were as scandalized as churchgoing matrons: So she was the sister of a "boy arsonist"—she held dangerous political opinions, while they, as decent as their sainted mothers, held none at all. "But listen," one woman shouted back—she was undoubtedly as young as Chaya but her sweet face was worn, her makeup smudged and patchy. "They could knock down all them factories for all I care, they just make rich men richer." So, they were political after all.

"Yeah, but who'd make your unmentionables, darlin'? The stuff you love don't just fell out of the sky."

"I don't care. More power to that kid, I hope somebody gives him a medal."

FINALLY, AFTER far too long—Chaya took the insult as it was intended—Gregory came, without an attorney, to post bond for her; her little brother was beyond the reach of bail, having been deemed a menace to civilization, if Chicago was said to have such a thing. She was merely accused of being a co-conspirator, and thus, on the assumption that the other half of the conspiracy was penned up in safety, she could be considered disarmed. She desperately did not wish to leave with her boy still in that downstairs dungeon. Gregory, out of patience, led her firmly along the corridor toward the exit.

She wanted to cry out for pity at what Asher must be undergoing in that wretched cell to which they were abandoning him with no defense against the vile men who would tower around him. A clean-haired, clear-faced young boy in crackling new boots, good leather, which would make him appear to be wealthy. Whether they poked and prodded or left him alone, he would be so frightened she could hardly bear to imagine it.

"I should have known," Gregory said to her bitterly as they settled themselves in his brougham, "that in the end you would choose your brother over—" Clearly he wanted to say *me*, but instead chose something less personal but larger: "—your marriage. Does it occur to you there is something unhealthy about that?"

This revision of reality would not do. "I have made no such choice." She could feel the stiffness of her reply in her very posture against the leather seat. "And, may I remind you, you have spoken ill of Ned far more than I have—understandably, since you had the misfortune of growing up beside him." She looked out over the sleek, dark heads of his horses, seething at such willful misunderstanding. "You know what Ned has done, the hurt he has caused. Did you expect no response?"

Gregory still did not look at her but kept his eyes straight ahead. "He set off an explosive, Chaya. He tried to destroy—" He shook his head as if to dislodge the thought. "Are you truly ready to defend such a heinous thing?"

"He is not a thing, he is my brother. I have never asked Asher to do harm to anyone, and certainly not to your brother, whose word is worth less than nothing. Whatever poisons Asher has drunk up have begun as—" She did not know quite what to call them. "Your dear Ned enjoyed humiliating him and his poor friends and you very well know that. He enjoyed making Asher into a little fool." She swallowed hard. Ned's betrayal, his contemptuous, noxious double-dealing—she lacked the vocabulary for such treachery. Gregory, who had the words, had called his brother a buzzard who did not bother to wait until his carrion cooled.

"But a *bomb!* A firebomb, Chaya. Whatever Ned's sins, do you favor anarchy now? Is that what you call just?"

"It was midnight. Ned was safe at home—or, knowing his habits, perhaps in some other place where he ought not to have been."

"Chaya." Gregory put his hand over hers, gently. "What have we come to? Are we truly antagonists now?"

Their headline had read: WEDDING JOINS COUPLE'S SEPARATE WORLDS: SOCIALIST SOCIALITE, JEWISH CINDERELLA CIGAR WORKER JOINED IN HULL-HOUSE CEREMONY, SWEAR COMMON GOAL: ELIMINATE POVERTY, REFORM ECONOMY.

On the story went. It had been a long time before she understood they were being mocked. Now, to account for his coldness, Chaya strained to imagine how it felt to be Gregory, who had cast his lot with her and her ideals—publicly, irrevocably—and, condone them or not, who was going to be held to account for them. Could she not spare some pity for him? But it was only her brother's face that hung before her, more vulnerable than any grown man's.

How far from his past could a man's good character and worthy intentions take him? Out of love and loyalty, how could she defend the indefensible? And who was responsible for seeding another's conscience? There was no one with whom she could speculate about such questions. There was no one unless it was Gregory.

When they arrived at home, they turned their backs and walked away from one another.

AFTER A long interval spent in their half-furnished parlor in silence, knowing she would soon be caught up in a frenzy of testimony, claim and counterclaim, forced to see her boy alone in the docket, beyond her negligent care, she opened the door of their bedroom carefully, as if she were stealing her way out of rather than into it.

Gregory was seated in the lap of his armchair staring straight ahead. He had left carefully unfolded on the side table beside him the *Tribune*, as if to salt her wounds.

MIDNIGHT BLAST INJURES TWO: BOY BOMBER LINKED TO CONSPIRACY.

The maid had brought her incessant gift of tea, which sat ignored beside him. Gregory looked at Chaya without expression.

"Gregory? Darling?" Her voice felt rusty.

A missed heartbeat. How familiar his rhythms were to her, how telling this hesitation. "Yes, Chaya." Usually he smiled when he saw her. This would be, she understood, only a fraction of her punishment.

"What are the things I am permitted to do while I am—under—bond." Saying such a word was so alien that it was as frightening as touching a gun, being forced to pick it up and feel its cold weight in her hand.

He sucked his teeth, which a gentleman never did, and in the insult she heard his disgust. "I would imagine you are at liberty to do more or less as you like. What did you have in mind?"

She shook her head, blank. The question had only been a way to test the coolness of the water that lay between them. "I hadn't anything particular in mind. I only wondered."

He shifted in his chair, whose pillow rose like a blister where his weight had been. Gregory always wore his tie and jacket at home. It made her itch to think of sitting at ease in a tight collar and vest. What a good boy he was. "I wouldn't go out in the street and organize a strike just now, or carry a petition to the mayor, but short of that sort of thing—" He was not looking at her while he spoke. He was pointedly looking at nothing. "And I should stay a good distance from Harrison Street."

She smiled at him wanly—"I think I shall just . . ."—and cast around for something that would not provoke his suspicion. "I shall just go down and walk along the water. The lake, I think, will do me good."

He made no move to join her. "Take a wrap, then. It is colder outside than you might think." He turned away from her and steepled his fingers before him, as final a dismissal as any word he could have said.

44

HE WAS yanked, hustled, pulled along by a very large man whose belly stretched out the front of his tan uniform so that he looked more pregnant than Chai. And he was not being gentle, Asher understood, because he was so rageful: The man was a cop and he had the shirt of a bomber in his fist. There were memories, always memories, in this city, wounds and scars, and who cared if the arsonist hardly came up to his shoulder. He pulled a cell door open and flung Asher in so hard he stumbled and almost fell.

Two men stared at him, one a graybeard, the other young and slender, catlike, which served him well because he was a second-story man, proud of it, who made sure Asher knew in his first ten minutes that he nicked jewelry and vials of morphine and any cash he found lying around, all in the dark. Me too Asher thought but didn't say, but I'll bet you don't give yours away.

The older man was sullen and didn't boast about his crimes. He looked, Asher thought, like a pirate, face rugged, skin tough and stubbled like dead grass. Turned out he didn't have much English, though he grunted a lot to show, or pretend, he understood.

What had he done to land him here? the young man asked. Asher thought they might have been friends under other circumstances—he had a pretty face and a vain look about him but his sharp gaze had nothing vicious in it. Asher suspected the man would be a fancy dresser.

"Oh, I tried to blow up a building," he said as casually as he could.

It occurred to him that he had become two people; one was watching the other from a distance.

"Why the hell d'you do that?" the burglar asked, almost respectfully. He was a pacer, he walked while he talked, circling like a dog readying to lie down.

"I had a grudge." The word was heavy, ugly in his mouth: *Gruh-d-je.* Trudge. Sludge. Judge. "I had what you could call a score to settle."

The young man laughed with delight. "What happened to the building?"

Asher had to say, "Not much. At least I think. I didn't get to see it very well."

"Aw, kid," the burglar said, shaking his head. "I hope you didn't kill nobody."

That was when Asher felt his two selves join again. *Please, please,* he prayed to no one in particular. "The only person I wanted to kill wasn't there."

"You sorry? You could get yourself a hell of a sentence for that, you know."

Asher sighed. He was going to be an uncle soon and because of his grudge, Chai might be alone without her husband. And he'd be here, or worse: wherever they sent people after they were convicted. He felt his two selves separating again, the stupid, reckless one and the one, anger spent, brimming with regret. He sank into silence, slid down the wall to sit on the concrete floor, knees bent in front of him to make a hedge and keep the two men out. Hours, a few more hours, maybe even overnight—he slept—but how could you tell, clangor all around, and shoutings, and vile curses.

And then the guard appeared, a jangle of keys bouncing at his waist, and opened the cell door. "Out with you, fella. Yer goin' home now." He was hurried along the corridor, down some stairs, roughly, and pushed into a windowless room where the warden—he assumed it was the warden—sat behind a battered desk, swiveling, a little left, a little right, in his chair. The guard slammed the door behind him. Nothing they did in this place was delicately done.

"Say hello to yer uncle here, sonny. Yer a lucky kid."

His uncle. Off to the side where he had not seen him stood Ned Stillman in an overcoat with a shining fur collar. "His sister's brother-in-law, to be exact," Ned said to the warden with a wink. "No matter." He turned to Asher. "So aren't you going to say thank you? This isn't a favor every man would do you."

Asher was too stunned to speak.

"Come on, now. We've fixed up your little prank with these boys, and they're willing to send you home with me. Which is very generous, considering."

Asher's face was beginning to redden as if he had been running.

"The only thing I couldn't get them to do—because they're being exceptionally understanding, don't you think—is, they can't wipe it off your slate. It'll be there, kind of like a bit of a scar till you become of age. Nothing too ugly I wouldn't worry, if you keep that little nose clean from here on in. I told the man here, he's so precocious, this boy, he isn't but twelve years old—or is it thirteen now?—and he has a criminal record! What do you say now, Mr. Shadow?"

Mr. Shadow said nothing. He was trying not to cry. This serpent, this *asp*, was taking his triumph from him. Was manhandling his motives. What would he have to do to drag Ned Stillman's name into the muck where it belonged? Really kill someone? This was the way it was done: If you didn't want embarrassing publicity, between gentlemen you could undo anything that happened. If you didn't like to look like you had lost something, you could close your hand and crush it and make it look like a favor. Wink and turn it around and no one would ask any questions. He would throw himself in the lake before he coughed up any thanks.

The machine rooms at the Stillman boiler plant, as it turned out, had suffered something less than annihilation. This Ned explained, grinning, in the two-horse brougham he had parked at the door. It had taken three brooms and a plethora—a plethora!—of dust cloths, frequently replenished, to settle and collect many layers of plaster dust and bruised and broken wood. The gray surfaces of the steel-sided machines nearest the window would be forever pocked. "But, I tell you, Asher, I had to bend down so far to see the pocks I could have licked them if I was hungry." The Bohunk cleaning woman had been terrified into a stupor, all her English gone, but was unhurt, and the watchman had been busy trying the doors to be certain they were locked. "Lucky man was all the way down at the far end of the building, out of range of your"—Ned looked for the best word—"mischief."

Asher wanted to spew the worst words he could, accuse, condemn, humiliate this man, chin sunk in the fur of some slaughtered beauty, but his defeat was total: He was a boy, too young a boy, and could not prevail. He had had his petty victories, bags and bagsful of material goods, valuable trivia he had fingered, fisted, fanned out among his minions to buy them another day. But who was the victim this afternoon, and who the winner? The headline this time would shred his dignity and feed it to the rats in the alley: WUNDERKIND EXPLOSION SAID TO BE VANDALISM: CRIMINAL CHARGES DISMISSED.

So much for the Anarchist conspiracy. Instead, the Ned Stillmans who owned Chicago did what they wanted to, no one could steal a mark on them. He, Asher the child, was nothing but an irritating shadow who had cost this snake a few hours of his time, three brooms, and many dustcloths, frequently replenished.

He looked out over the twitchy ears of the horses that were taking him home. (It was not his home, he wanted to but did not say. He had no other.) Plethora, a plethora of dustcloths. He began a list of words that sang their syllables to him. He knew a Greek word for "angry." *Agriamo*. And one for "calm." *Sungaleiao*. What could be as beautiful as that? Listen! The satisfaction of it! Or was it *Sungaleniao*. Some day he would go to Athens and the Peloponnesus. He would see the Aegean and the Acropolis. He would change his name, Asher-to-Asclepius, and wear a toga that would not itch like these miserable woolen knickers.

45

HOWEVER FINE the neighborhood, with its small grassy yards and its shapely houses stony Italianate, wooden Germanic, they could not see the lake from where they lived. Chaya walked and walked and sat on an icy bench and walked again until she was so chilled she thought her fingers and toes would crack off like frozen twigs. What she felt was like an illness, the kind that made her wish she could sleep until it had done with her. And what kind of damage was this despair wreaking on her baby?

When she opened the front door she found Gregory seated in his slender-legged parlor chair. He looked at her very strangely, as if he hardly recognized her

"What is it?" She was alarmed. "Has something happened?"

"He is upstairs in his room. Sulking."

"What? Who?" Hands still quivering with cold, she had been removing her hat. Now she stood still with her arms upraised, like a woman posing for a Mary Cassatt painting.

"Your baby brother. Who else has a room up there."

"What are you talking about?" His tone was still contemptuous, and she felt herself being teased, the way he compelled her to eke out this information one syllable at a time. "How could he be home? When I was there they wouldn't allow me to see him!"

Gregory was tamping tobacco into his pipe. Chaya thought, *If I have to wait for him to light it, I shall throw something at him.* Lighting up was a slow, contemplative business during which everything stopped—that always gave the smoker an advantage.

He was not looking at her. "Why don't you ask him yourself."

She took to the stairs so quickly she nearly tripped. The scritch of Gregory's match followed her, and his first quick deep puffs to make sure the flame had taken.

Asher's door was closed but not locked, which she took as an invitation. She gave him the respect of a quick knock but she was already inside before he could respond. "Darling boy," she began, to forestall his thinking she was going to berate him.

He came to her in a rush and hid his head against her breast. "Please, Chai, please don't say anything. I've already said everything to myself."

She kissed the top of his head, which still smelled vaguely of that jail cell. Every kind of trapped smoke, mold, and all the putrid things that rise from the common bowl. Or she imagined it so, having come herself from the same pit. Probably he had no smell at all.

"But I won't say I'm sorry. I know how it looks and I know it was—" He flung his hands out to the side as if to show her how empty they were. "Are you going to make me apologize?" He looked, at one and the same time, so young and, in his exhaustion, so old, the first faint shadows like bruises under his eyes—she could see what Asher would look like years from now when, perhaps, he'd have found a better way to work at dismantling his enemies. He took a deep, wavering breath that she thought might have hurt him. "Can you be sorry you did something and not sorry at the same time?"

"Sorry because it was wrong or sorry because it wasn't very"—she looked around at his towers of books, which were his true domain—"effective?"

"No!" Petulant. "Because I got caught. But when you do a—a thing for the revolution—you're supposed to say you did it. You take the credit and the blame. I wanted Ned to know it was me. I wasn't going to hide it."

They were in deep water and she wasn't a swimmer. "It was a lot of things, I'm sure, my sweet. I wonder if you understand all of it." She wished she could say, *I know, I know*: how public hunger met private hunger, and scrambled all her loyalties together, the men at the Fair, the man in her bed. The man who treated her like a child's toy. All that—all she could not say—had been tinder for his flame.

She would have to know before too long if Gregory saw how impossible it was to parse this and be done with it, because Asher was—riding home from the jail, Gregory had said it, and how much dignity it must have cost him—Asher was her first, her original, her unchangeable love.

"You have both done damage," she finally said, "and you both need to be forgiven." Then all she could do was hold her brother while he cried.

46

CHAYA HAD lived all her years without the habit of confiding her sorrows. Looking back, she recognized how she had had no true friends—none, at least, to whom she had opened her heart. Asher was not exactly a friend. At the Fields of Zion, the girls near her age had found her strange. With her books and her refusals, all she had suppressed of words, of judgments, had somehow prickled her skin and made her too spiny to be much loved. At Winkler's, she had had Sara, but Sara, born to be contented, conformed to a different—simpler? luckier?—pattern. Chaya, like it or not, was cut on the bias. There was Gregory, of course, but now he was responsible for the way her throat was clotted with tears so sharp they possessed edges. She felt herself alone in their bed even while he lay, turned away, beside her. What had she done that was so terrible that she drew such punishment from the man who loved her?

SHE CAME into Hull-House one morning to meet with Mrs. K-W, a sheaf of reports under her arm. There was a small office downtown for the staff of factory and sweatshop inspectors, but Miss Addams had, for some reason, requested that they meet here today. Mrs. K-W, seated, looked at Chaya long and hard and ventured, "I hope your baby is not responsible, dear, for causing you to look like a newly docked refugee from the famine." (Her family had become host to an inundation of relatives from Ireland—that was the Kelley part of her—who were still arriving empty-handed, one step ahead of starvation Beside them, refugees from the Ukraine had looked well-fed.)

"Oh, it isn't the baby" she responded, embarrassed. She tightened her hands around the Pumpkin, which could already help to steady her.

Mrs. K-W listened to her confidences respectfully. Her own marriage, Chaya knew by reliable hearsay, had ended with blows struck and struck again. It was unimaginable that anyone dared lay a hand on this formidable woman, but those were the stories; apparently she had been less forbidding in those days. Her husband, this Wischnewetsky, Lazare, had been a Russian-Polish doctor, a Jew, and when he suffered reverses, a violent man.

"Chaya," Mrs. K-W offered. "Do you know how this sounds to someone, you understand, who has had to reconcile herself to far more damage than coldness and—what would you say of Gregory just now?—this sort of vengeful unforgivingness?"

Chaya felt like a child, balling her fist to knuckle the irritation she was not certain she deserved. "No, I don't know." She sighed. "How does it sound?"

Mrs. K-W was in the habit of turning a button between her fingers while she thought. Her dress had more of them than Chaya imagined she had patience for. "I think—I could be terribly wrong, it goes without saying—that your husband wishes *he* had been able to wreak some violence on that dreadful brother of his. Of course, being civilized, he could do no such thing. But when your brother attempted this act of—what would you call it? *Reprisal*?—Gregory was overcome by an overwhelming sense of guilt, as if he had executed it himself. Does that not seem plausible to you?" Mrs. K-W's voice was always emphatic. "And to add to that, the boy was so very daring! Foolhardy, perhaps, but—definitive."

Chaya sat stunned by this circumlocution. If Gregory was secretly grateful to Asher for doing what he could not do himself, why was he so vengeful? She shook her head in confusion. Perhaps one had to have a university education to understand this.

"There is," Mrs. K-W said with some satisfaction, "an alienist named Freud—Sigismund, I believe—who practices abroad—who has recently

advanced some quite intriguing theories that describe peculiar displace-
ments of anger such as the one I propose. I am reading some of his essays—
they will soon, I have heard, become a book available to anyone—because,
as the entire world seems to know, I have myself had a good deal of it to
cope with." She could, by now, give a bitter little laugh at her marital history. "And they are filled with unlikely ideas that, even as they run counter
to logic, seem to make an odd sense." She twirled her button absently,
looking more perplexed than Chaya had ever seen her. "Peculiar, I know,
but they advance, I should call it, a different logic."

She had not felt so inadequate, so uncomprehending, like a child,
for years.

"Think on it, dear. Instead of defending your brother to him, you might
even, gently, suggest to your husband that you understand how complicated
Asher's actions might be for him. Just—drop the idea into his ear and see
if it yields a more sympathetic response."

Chaya nodded at this and thanked her mentor. What worried her was
that the woman who so confidently prescribed this novel attitude had
barely escaped her own marriage intact, pulling her children behind her,
out of the advancing fire of her husband's aggression. Some people seemed
incapable of despair. Or they were simply too busy to let it stop them.

CHAYA AND Mrs. K-W were finishing their work together when Miss
Addams entered the room where their damning documents were spread
across the dining room table. Mrs. K-W was very close to submitting their
findings to Governor Altgeld, who was eager to forge a law to restrain the
rapacious. Chaya was nearly dizzy with the alternation of her fortunes, joy
at this triumph—"Pending," Mrs. K-W cautioned—and fear for her own
household, its sullen man, its sullen boy.

Miss Addams stood beside her, looking purposeful. "Chaya," she inter-
posed quietly, without excitement. "I believe I have some interesting news
for you."

It was a moment she would often try and fail to recover in its innocence,
its ordinariness. "I have had a visit," Miss Addams said with a cryptic smile,
"from someone I think you will want to see."

Chaya stared blankly at her. She was eager to go home to try this new theory on Gregory.

"I asked her to return at ten, just now, because I knew that you and Mrs. Wischnewetsky would be here." Her smile grew broader and more personal. "Will you step into the parlor with me, please."

Perplexed and a trifle irritated, Chaya rose and followed Miss Addams and the vague trail of her morning talcum. They turned the last corner into the dim front room and at its far end, her back to them as she studied a painting of men clutching the sides of a capsized boat—a depressing sight, Chaya had always thought, not expressive of Miss Addams's optimism, unless the men were about to be saved—was the tall, unhealthily gaunt figure of her mother.

She was alone—where were the children?!—and, whether from hunger or emotion, she looked near collapse. Instead, she sagged in her daughter's arms, murmuring the very words Chaya had dreamed when Asher and Gregory and she made their journey back to the farm: "*Meyne tokhter! Meyne sheyne tokhter!*" She placed a tentative hand against Chaya's stomach and closed her eyes with satisfaction.

Miss Addams dipped her head respectfully and left them to each other.

47

"I SEE—" her mother began in the only language they had ever shared—
"the newspapers." She stopped as if to ask if her daughter understood her.

"It's all right, Mother," Chaya told her. Her Yiddish still came easily
though she might have expected it to stir slowly and, so long disused, rip
itself out of her, bearing shreds of skin. "You can speak like always. I hav-
en't forgotten how." Everything she had suppressed was a pebble in her
gullet. "Tell me how you found us."

"Us," her mother said, meditative. "There must be an 'us' or you
wouldn't have this." A glance at the front of Chaya's dress. "A man at your
father's place, he saw a newspaper that said Asher Shadow—it sounded
like Shaderowsky, it sounded like our little *meshugene.* Who else would be
so smart? You should see what they said. The police. Do I have to believe
this boy would try to explode a bomb? An *anarkhista?"*

"It's very complicated. I'll explain it later. You'll see him, you'll see that
he is still the sweet boy you knew." It was a lie, or almost a lie; such words
should burn her lips. "But how did you know to come here?"

"The news—Miss Jane Addams, they asked her, she said this is a good
boy, he wants the best for everybody."

They had sat themselves on the hard horsehair sofa in Miss Addams's
parlor. The business of the house, which rarely halted, seemed to go on
behind a curtain, dimly audible. She and her mother held each other's
hands in silence, laving their faces with concentration. Oh, her mother

was so worn, she had gained—no, lost—more years than the time that had passed. The skin beneath her eyes had been hollowed out, as if the Stillmans' cook had gouged her flesh with the little instrument that scooped out balls of melon. When her mother removed her hat, her ears looked huge, a dog's ears, where they poked out of her graying hair, which could only mean that her face had become pinched and shrunken.

They were living in Cleveland. The farm had broken up last year, everyone scattered, because of a terrible occurrence. She could hardly say it without doubling over with the pain.

She tried and stopped, wiped her flowing eyes, tried again. The milk they had sent off in those cans—the same innocent dull-silver cylinders Chaya had crowded between on her way to the train—had gone off harboring diphtheria, that scourge, that slaughterer. Had taken death to market. And how had they known the tainted milk was theirs, since so many farms contributed to the giant milk company's vat for bottling? Because Beryle, who loved to skim his share out of the pail before it went into the cans, the only one who liked it warm and bubbly, had taken sick. Suddenly, after dinner, after a perfectly normal morning playing in the orchard, his throat had closed, just closed, all black inside, spotted gray-black. Running sores erupted on him everywhere, like bites from some vicious animal, and nothing they could do would stop them. Fraydl, dear Fraydl, gone. Then Fraydl's little Chaike—the same symptoms, but she got better. Masha, her sister, though, was out in the *beys olam*, under a stone, along with her Beryle. And Mutkele, the baby Gittl had by that Shimmie. Taken before the sun set. Why they didn't all perish she could not say. "Because we buried them so fast, it could be. You know, the *goyim* don't put theirs in the ground so quick." She kissed her fingertips. "A little gift."

Mystery solved, those four new, lonely graves accounted for. Such random cruelty that if you believed God was watching, you would abandon Him as He abandoned those children. Quick-footed, noisy Beryle silenced. And Masha, who laughed all the time. She was glad she had never believed.

"Disaster," her mother said, whispering as if she might still be in danger. "We were afraid, it was not safe to stay there. We already auctioned some things before. It was easy to go."

"You ran? You ran away?" She didn't mean it to be a rebuke. Or per-haps—she would sort it out later—she did.

"Better say we escaped. Who knows who would come looking? Blaming? Who knows if we were what they call guilty. I don't know. What is a crime?" She clawed at her daughter's face with her weary eyes. "It could happen to anyone. We kept our cows clean. No one could say—they were healthy." She stopped to count her losses. "First you go, Asher goes, then my little Beryle. For what?"

Chaya felt disembodied, as if she were looking down at herself and her mother from far above. The visible Chaya, she was sure, bore little relation to the one that was listening. None of her guises felt real to her: The child in Zhitomir playing in a shady courtyard. The girl grown sullen on the farm. The exile, fleeing. The breadwinner at her cigar desk, nothing but yellow-stained fingers, palms, moving parts. The woman made love to the first time, secretly, one long sweet afternoon. The bride of an august family. The chastened woman, making a slow peace with her unyielding husband. Or suffering him to make that peace with her. The wife awaiting this child that made an alien shape under her clothes. Where—what—was she among all these? Some creature who pretended to contain all those fragments? All she could do was watch. But she was Asher's sister, always. That was her one fixed pole. She had always been and would always be Asher's sister. Now she would try to be a daughter again.

Strangely—her mother looked almost abashed—they were doing well in Cleveland. "The streets aren't made of gold, but this is what we came here for. What your father promised. This makes sense. I am so glad to be—to look out the window and see streets. Buildings made out of stone! To have neighbors so close. To have a store to buy what we need. And the *goyim*, they don't bother us." She gave Chaya the saddest smile. "You knew. We were not so good at making things."

So she had been right to imagine her mother as miserable as she had been.

"No more pretending to love a cow. The sickness—it didn't surprise me, Chayele. Always there was too much on the farm that could go bad. Things that could get soft when they should be hard, hard when they should be

soft. So much was rotting all the time. I was always waiting for some—"
She closed her eyes against it. "Some plague. Not boils, not darkness, not
frogs. But something. And it befell."

Chaya sighed hard. "There are plagues here too, mother. This city."
It was impossible to convey the decadence she had seen. Where would
she begin?

Her father, through a friend of a friend of a friend, had found work
as a bookbinder for a Yiddish press. A miracle. "These books are—" Her
mother smiled ruefully. "I don't know if you'll like this, Chaya—they are
socialist books. He binds them and also he *reads* them! Your father is so
happy to be angry again. He was not made for the barnyard, keeping the
peace between the hens and the roosters."

She laughed and squeezed her mother's hands. "My husband will be
very happy to have another socialist in the family. He is rather outnum-
bered just now."

Her head spun with the pleasure of sitting face to face with her mother,
forgiven—perhaps forgiven; some day she might hear otherwise—for
abandoning her, and then—when she stood after such concentration, she
was nearly dizzy—of leading her home in a comfortable carriage. No more
bouncing blue wagon to deliver them to their destination muscle-wracked
and bone-sore. She kept her mother's hand in hers.

Gregory was not at home. He was off, she remembered, interviewing
a Reverend Stead, a minister visiting from England who was passionate
about all that ailed Chicago; he had gone out this morning in high spirits
at the prospect. Happy to be angry, her mother had said—oh, Gregory
would adore her father!

Nor was Asher anywhere to be found, but she was accustomed to that.
She walked her mother through the half-furnished rooms of her new
house, seeing them through her astonished eyes. The carpet's rich colors were finer than any planted field's. She had begun to arrange her
new dishes in the sideboard, behind beveled glass. Her mother removed a
sprigged teacup, blue and yellow against white, and turned it tenderly in
her hands. It was almost enough to reconcile Chaya to their loveliness, and
to its expense, how her mother thrilled to what she had achieved. Given

what her mother—her entire family—had survived, could she be blamed for loving this modest opulence, still so alien to her daughter? Finally it was her moment of harvest.

But no Asher presented himself for the best reunion of all. "Well, he will be back," Chaya said as casually as she could, though she knew how unpredictable were his goings and his comings. "He's rather independent, Mother." She sighed, exasperated. Of all the times to be gone. "He is still his own strange and unlikely person. Wait till you see his roomful of books. But he's grown so much, you may not recognize him." His lengthening legs, his flinty elbows and fine-trimmed hair. "Our little man is in long pants now. Let us hope he comes home tonight for dinner."

48

HER MOTHER made it clear: They would not be a burden on Gregory. It was important for her to know they had not come begging.

That had hardly crossed her mind. Instead, she was imagining the room that would some day hold all of them, Shaderowsky and Stillman. It was unkind but irresistible to find the prospect grimly amusing. If Gregory and she, not to mention his parents and brother, ever returned to cordiality, there would come a moment when her Mama and Papa would button themselves into their modest finery, scour the children's faces till they reflected light, put a rein on Yakov, who was given to eruptions of energy and—what to do with Asher? Leave him at home? Throttle Father's politics into silence? He and Gregory could share a wink across the table that wretched capitalism had laid with riches: sugared pecans, foie gras and mousse in silver and pewter and Limoges on lace.

Sometimes she wished Gregory and she had moved to some distant city to start fresh, invisible lives. Perhaps that was the solution: San Francisco, New York, anywhere they could go around all that they could not, here, climb over.

At six, Gregory came through the door breathless with excitement. Chaya watched him enter, cheeks blushing with the cold, eyes still lit with the pleasure of having spent his day warmed at the fire of a man more appalled by Chicago than even he. Reverend Stead of Great Britain, who had come intending only to be a visitor to the Exposition, as an adjunct to his verbal lashings, was compiling a virtual street map of brothels, pawn brokers, and saloons, which he intended to advertise to the world and shake under the noses of the city's officers. Chaya saw Gregory in the front hall stop to remove his coat and hat and, preparing to confront her, quite visibly rearrange his face into hostile blankness. Unsmiling, he entered the parlor where she stood, flushed with pleasure, beside her mother.

Then she was reminded why she loved this man: He could not stay distraught. In spite of all, he knew what was momentous. Unimaginable though it was to her with her qualms and quarrels with herself, affection better suited the lines of his face. (She prayed her baby would inherit its father's temperament.) When she introduced them, every bit of stiffness fell from Gregory like a robe he let drop to the ground. Oh, how, in spite of all, he believed in blood, how he believed in family! Why, then—but she tried to push this aside—could he not grant her Asher, who did not despise her as his brother despised him?

"You are well, and you have traced us to our lair!" His metaphor demanded more than he could guess of her rudimentary English, but Chaya could see that he wanted to embrace her and was only restrained by propriety. He was looking hard at her mother, studying her with his customary intentness.

She could see how pleased this greeting made her mother. But she herself was bewildered. Was she no longer banished for her brother's action?

Perhaps Mrs. K-W was correct about Gregory: He had felt obliged to be unforgiving of the one who had acted on his own deepest desires. And now, to a man inclined to tenderness, here was the important thing to heal them: her lost mother, actual, in their parlor, this tall, broad-shouldered woman with her rumpled face and missing tooth, her plain, worn black dress with its out-of-date sleeves—Chaya was learning of such irrelevancies from Lallie—and her fifty words of English. "*Meyn*—husband—English, have more. But he work." She made a face, squeezing out the words as if they hurt.

Gregory put his hand lightly on her shoulder to reassure her. Then, turning to Chaya, his familiar kind face restored, "Some dinner, dear? Your mother has come such a long way."

It was just as well, she reflected, passing the bowls of boiled potatoes and steamed carrots, sprinkled with raisins to be festive, that Asher was off somewhere tonight, in the event Gregory could not see his way clear to forgive them simultaneously. That would come. He looked relieved, though Chaya could imagine he was frustrated at not being able to tell her about his day with the astounding minister.

Instead, he turned his attention to his mother-in-law and, with Chaya translating, asked her so many questions about her family's life in Cleveland that at last she shyly asked, "And you tell me some things of you?" The gaze she cast about the room—high-ceilinged, trimmed with glistening moldings, and, set into the front door, that colored glass, those lavender flowers and pale green leaves like the windows of some secular church—suggested that she wished she could ask how he came to own a house as fine as this. She seemed uncertain it was permissible to address him as an equal.

But Gregory shrugged away her deference. "My life is much less interesting. I had to marry your daughter to make myself worthy of comment."

The irony was not entirely a happy one but, euphoric, Chaya allowed herself to laugh before she turned the statement into Yiddish and made her mother smile.

49

"WHY YOU not come with me. I riding the train. I go." Bakitis removed his frayed cap to scratch his mown-haired head. He looked without expression at the shiny black louse that was crawling evenly up his finger.

First thought: The train? Who can afford a ticket? Second thought—ah, the poor man's Pullman! Would it be better to run the rails than the alleys? "You would—I could go with you?" Very little flattered him but Asher was so pleased his scalp prickled.

"Kid, you always smarter as me. You help me figure out what's what's."

Bakitis was so honest Asher could love him for it: He called things by their names. "Let me think about it. I'll think fast."

How could he have massed up such a mountain of negatives? He would not cross the street to the university. He would not sit on a cardboard throne again and waste his attention on questions that already had answers. He would not—could not—find work it would pay to do. He would not live on Chaya's husband's inheritance. There was no place here for his strangeness—what if he took his strangeness to new places, if he went out to see what he could not even imagine? Asked a question whose answer was not in a book somewhere. It had never occurred to him.

He loved the names of cities, the kind that didn't describe anything, at least in English: not Middletown or Plainview but Ashtabula, Indianola, Albuquerque, Perth. And there were warmer place than Chicago in January! Better to sleep in blue air than in that boxy room with its heavy door, its

windows framed in oak. Darkness, the smell of soap and furniture polish, the narrowness of the hall, the steepness of the stairs. And that maid
Colleen poking her head around corners, a stranger who picked up what
they dropped, asking what she could do for them in a kick-me voice. All of
it the boundaries of his sister's little life, her safe deliverance. She made too
many curtains that kept the sight of the world outside the windows. She
would grow fat after she expelled that baby, a baby born rich. Already she
was gorging on the milky products out of which it was being constructed.
She was drinking beer and stout to stoke the machinery, and stout she would
be at the end of its assembly. She would never go back to chasing down
the murderers in the sweats. It would be too hard once she had grown soft.
A thrush, someone wrote, it didn't matter where, cannot be an eagle. She
would play cards with Lallie's giggling friends in their rainbowy, ribbony
dresses, and join the board of the symphony or that new sprawled-out Art
Institute uptown and then, liking the first, would have another child, and
sometimes go to read to The Poor, who were growing smaller and smaller in
her sight. He remembered lying on the old piecework quilt that hung down,
at Mrs. Gottlieb's, from Chaya's bed of chairs—how he wrapped himself in
it and how they whispered before they slept, trying to learn what Chicago
would ask of them, and what it would give back. Gone, for better or worse,
that quiet hour when they were both afraid.

From where he had sat himself on the shore of the lagoon, he looked
down at the water. Once Bakitis had threatened to drown himself before
they all starved to nothing. It would probably be yielding at the bottom,
soft under his famished bones. Silty. Silken. Settled. Hopping a train was
a better idea.

Marco came to him, still feverish. "Little guy. Listen." He was sweating
in spite of the frozen air, his cheeks flushed, a makeshift scarf all the way
to his chin, shred of some left-behind cloth that looked like it had been a
banner. "Remember, I wanted to burn out that bastard Pullman?"

"I remember. You and everybody else. You planning to try it?"

"No. But Bakitis tells me you're checking out tomorrow. I'm better, I
come too. I think I will. Be your caboose." He came so close Asher could
smell his fever, like scorched cotton. "You know how to make a firebomb,

ain't I right? You did that boiler factory." His face looked hot, as though his fascination with fire had entered his own body. "That was real good."

Asher nodded. At least someone was grateful. "Yes? And? Therefore?"

"Therefore! You so funny. So. And." Marco seemed to need to think about his connectives. "And so some of us got an idea. How'd you like to leave a little goodbye present to the Exposition here."

In silhouette, they looked like a bear and a cub. The large, dark, bearded man put one arm around the boy's shoulder. It sloped down from so high Asher felt nothing but bony wrist across his back. But it was a comfort, after so long, to be touched any way at all.

"How about you put together another one, a dozen even, however the hell you do it, and we have some fun here. These buildings ain't good for a damn thing now. They all gonna come down soon if they don't fall in first. Wouldn't you like to help them along some? Like, you know, putting down a animal that's dying."

Asher, surprised, stared back.

"Look at it." They were standing across the water from the Court of Honor, so gorgeous, so sullied by neglect. In the falling light, the silvery windows of the Machinery building (exactly twenty on each side) were a long row of blind eyes. The Music Hall was stone silent. "Kill it, kid," Marco whispered. "Damn thing's dying anyway. Like, you know, doing in a horse that's hurting. Why not help it out." He checked Asher for a response but got none. "We show them it ain't nothing but firewood now. Someplace we can warm our hands, 'cause it's cold out here, brother, in case they never noticed. How about a bonfire like you never seen before?"

Marco was crazy—always had been. But still it was something to think about. It wasn't dying, it was dead. The abandoned Exposition stank of uselessness, insulting to anyone who had loved it. Why not a touch of violence as a farewell. You gave us fireworks? Here's some fireworks! Would they even try to save it? Pump water from the lagoon? Why bother?

"A gesture," Asher said. A just jest. Someone might even recognize his signature in the ruins. "I'll show you how to make one. All of us can fire them up together." FIRE AT FAIRGROUNDS! COURT OF HONOR BUILDINGS DESTROYED IN SUSPICIOUS BLAZE. Honor had already been destroyed, if anyone cared. Asher wanted to go inside the ruined hall and lay the blazes himself, for spite, a touch here, a flare there, dragging a torch up the stairs, holding it against the canister long enough for it to catch. Wouldn't it be pretty.

But, "No," Donlan said firmly. "Oh, no. You ain't no flea in a lousy mattress. You stand out here with us. You can be straw boss." A sop. He held Asher against him, inside his mangy coat, one long minute.

THE FLAMES—he tried to calculate but couldn't—probably reached a hundred feet. They spread and leaped, eating the dark. Doubled in the lagoon, they illuminated the whole known world. His handiwork, better, a hundred times better, than Stillman's boilers. When the wind blew, gouts of fire rose and leapt, great flowers of light, all the way to the lake. Asher could hear them sizzle where they landed.

Flamboyant flame. Famed and final. He wished he could torch every building.

They fled before the Law could find them. Like roaches, scattered, hid, or walked between the helpless members of the fire brigade and half the south side, trying to look indifferent. Smiling.

Sparks cascaded down, larger than snowflakes, and where they touched the lagoon, the water pimpled, hissed, sputtered. Ash danced on the surface before it was swamped. The sky, reflected in the water, went seven shades of pink, of orange, of rich rose. Midnight, thanks to him, was full daylight, everyone's face more fevered than Marco's. He hoped each man of the thousand thousand roofless tonight in Chicago saw the unholy light and cheered. This world did not love them. Let it go.

Asher sat alone on the slanted shore of the lake, near the crumbling skeleton of the rolling sidewalk, his back to the fire. In his anger he could, with one huge twist, have broken away from Donlan and immolated himself like some Zoroastrian on a pyre. But he felt purged, pure, just as he'd hoped. Energy surged through his every joint, every connection, electric. He had seen something through to its end, at the least. Had refused to let it fade. The flames, wild and wind-buffeted, had seared away everything but what he needed for the rest of his life. Neither did the world love *him*, he supposed. But—a new thought every minute—how could he dare tell anyone to let it go. Who could say they didn't love it, even hungry, even in pain. *He* did. He had everything to learn, or learn again, this time without words.

50

GREGORY'S PARENTS never came to their house; instead, summoned to appear, they dutifully reported for Sunday dinners and the occasional party. One day it was Gregory alone who was called and he went with the look of a man on his way to the gallows. When he returned, paler than Chaya had ever seen him, it was clear he had been jerked upwards, his body left to dangle over a gaping hole. "They have done it, finally. Done what I'd expected a long time back." He gave her the smile a dead man gives, fixed and cheerless. "I hope you haven't become too attached to this house, my darling. I hope you have not decided to forgive it for being beautiful, because it is gone now." Some unkind satisfaction glittered in his eyes, as if to say *You see?*

All she could think was, *My darling?* Had she been returned to her native state? And so she had been. "Did your mother have anything to say about that?"

"She did not. You would have been disappointed in her. She stood beside him without a word, with her hands clasped as if she was a praying woman. He said he had refrained from acting on my—infidelity to the values of our family—my infidelity!—on her behalf but that his patience with my *straying* was now strained beyond endurance and he was 'cutting me off.' A lovely phrase. I asked if he was accomplishing the surgery with a knife or an axe and he said"—and here Gregory forced his voice down to a basso profundo—"'Laugh if you will but I guarantee you will not find penury amusing.' Such a dramatic vocabulary the man has, for someone so devoid of imagination."

Chaya went to him without words. He took her into his arms and rested his chin on her head, which she took as a small sign of forbearance, for which she supposed she should thank his father and his heavy hand. "He said he was acting without having consulted with Ned because this was not solely about Ned, who is his own man who can take care of his own business." He was warm against her but she could feel how rigidly he was holding himself. "Of course, he lacked the courage to say any of this in your presence." A very deep sigh. "You may have noticed that bigotry does not tend to make a man courageous." He sighed again. "Or subtle."

She could find nothing to say that would not sound inadequate. She was going to have to think hard about what it would mean to give back what she had barely begun to accept as hers. Yet—she would not let herself smile—wasn't it a victory of sorts, not to be rich? Her brother, and she his accomplice, had finally settled the question. Mrs. Gottlieb would be disappointed.

"Chaya, I have some savings. Not a great deal but I promise you will not go back to your cigar bench. At the very least, having failed my father's test of fidelity, you will now have a chance to administer yours"—he laughed joylessly—"and I am certain I will not fail it. We are not being thrown to the wolves." The color was returning to his cheeks. "If they want a demonstration of our principles, they will have one. And just as my father said, this has nothing to do with my sainted brother." Bigotry, as Gregory had said, might not make men courageous but perhaps righteous anger could.

NECESSITY HAS a good name when it comes to its daunting demand that one meet it with invention. She suggested that they might take the occasion to move to Cleveland where her family seemed at home but Gregory, in spite of his father's influence, had a great many friendly connections in the city and Chaya watched how he used them to create a place for himself. So—since intention was all—it was possible after all to use one's friends and acquaintances uncorrupted. Reverend Stead, who had returned to Britain, engaged him on his first journalistic assignment, to continue his reports on Chicago's stupendous failings, which were published abroad to great if hypocritical acclaim. (Because who, in London, could pretend they did not equally excel at debauchery and inequity?) In order to keep the good Reverend abreast of the social and the moral tide of Chicago's least favored populations, Gregory met zealously and often with every kind of leader, religious, legal, and with Chaya's two dear friends, Miss Addams and Mrs. K-W, and from what they told him reflected back the unsurprising news that "sin" remained constant and "reform" stayed a few steps behind the most earnest scourges.

He did not finish his book but Chaya completed it. Revised, she liked to say, and completed it in her own style, bearing witness to the atrocities she had visited for Mrs K-W. She would not have thought of creating such a document but Gregory, passionate and thorough, had laid the foundation and she gratefully built above it, with heavy editing. Somewhere along the way, she picked up the dubious but graphic designation of *muckraker*, which she thought just the kind of word her Asher would have loved to wallow joyfully around in.

Giving up the house was not so difficult; in fact there was a certain satisfaction in finding, with Gregory, what she called a "happy medium" between its unearned grandeur and the exaggerated modesty of those terrible rooms he had pretended to. They found a brick bungalow exactly like the rest of its block, larger inside than it looked, and clean. Its front room was a sun porch, which Chaya filled with ferns and ivy and a birdcage containing a blue budgie smaller than her palm. Undistinguished, the house did not embarrass her the way the Stillmans' excessive bounty had; there was far less shame for her in no longer feeling like the Lady of Someone Else's Manor. They gave Colleen a generous parting gift. At least she had not curtsied when she took it.

And what that reduction in their means made possible was a meeting on equal ground with her darling Sara. One day when the trees were in bloom, they arranged to meet in Lincoln Park to show off their babies and reminisce. Sara and her Joe and little Joe Jr. lived on Francisco, on the far west side across the river, and Chaya was delighted to see that she seemed beatifically happy with husband, child, and the comfortable four rooms they had found, with a little shared yard and a good-sized tree she was already envisioning her son climbing. One of the reasons they met in the park was that Sara most likely believed that Chaya's presence in her freshly papered parlor would diminish the pleasure she took in it. But Chaya had a surprise for Sara: Their new house, she told her friend almost proudly, was not much larger than hers and Joe's.

She had, she supposed, learned the concept from those Greek plays she had struggled through at Miss Addams's of something called *hubris*. Why must everything return in the end to the discrepancy between economic fortunes? Whom you know, how you live, where you spend the hours of your life—she had always understood, but without the experience to prove it, that all those dire separations between people represented nothing innate, not intelligence, certainly not virtue, yet everyone was so defined. *Hubristic*—ugly word but applicable no matter where she looked. She was happy almost beyond words that disinheritance had put the two of them on the equal footing their affection deserved.

"Her name," she told Sara with more solemnity than she intended, pushing back the top of the rattan carriage to give her friend a better view of her sleeping child, "is Beryle. For my little brother."

"That's pretty, Beryle." Sara looked confused. "But your brother—his name is Asher."

Chaya sighed at the length of the story that needed telling. Trying to explain was like embarking on a journey with many milestones to pass before the destination materialized out of the haze of distance. Simply, she refused to believe he was dead. She had been correct about her parents; she knew she was right about Asher, though she could not have justified her optimism. The authorities had never made a definitive ruling on the fire. Arson? Accident? So many vagrants were sequestered on the Exposition grounds, anyone could have set it off with a careless match, an ill-tended cooking fire, a blaze for warmth on a brutal evening. Perhaps they'd have settled it had there been liability claims, but the buildings were officially condemned, which did not elicit the utmost effort from the inspectors.

More conflagrations had followed, massive ones in early summer, though whether one should call them disastrous or inconsequential, who could say? They destroyed nothing of value. If anything, the destruction saved the costs of demolition. Had any lives been lost in the Court of Honor fire? No one could hazard so much as a guess. All that remained was charred, unreadable. There was only this fact, and it was equally illegible as a message: Asher had not been seen after that night.

Chaya told the barest story to her friend, seated on a bench near the pond in the park. Sara was pink-cheeked and healthy-looking in her new motherhood. Both her thin, lank hair and her figure had thickened as she thrived. Her cigar-making days behind her, like Chaya's, she was gratefully devoted to the life she had always believed she was destined for. Her only dissatisfaction concerned the hours her Joe was condemned (she suspected he enjoyed them) to the firehouse. He had not yet encountered anything he would call danger. Sara had become a praying woman, though: Clearly she and Chaya had different standards for danger. "But, Chaya," she said, indignant, "could your boy have been so cruel that he would just—leave— and not let you know where he was going?"

Chaya rocked the carriage in which her baby had begun to stir. She looked straight ahead, at nothing. "Cruel is the word, yes. But if I don't believe that—" The question, or one of the many, was, Could he have hated her so? Hated Gregory? To vanish as if he had been a sheet of paper loosed from one of his beloved books, blown away by the wind? Might he have thought she would dissuade him from leaving? These meditations put strain lines on her face, which Gregory tried to kiss away. But the balm of his lips could not penetrate her grief, and her sense that she and her brother had done to their love, their bond, something gravely wrong. She remembered Asher's alarm, the first time she dressed herself in Gregory's proffered finery, that she looked unfamiliar, too much one of "them." Her glorious boy—she had known it, she had always known it—was too rigidly himself to bend. He belonged to himself and not to others. Not even, apparently, to her.

Miss Addams, when she heard about Asher's sudden departure, had shared her hopefulness. Mrs. K-W, however, whom Chaya had thought incapable of despair, turned out to possess an imagination for disaster. Once

she had confessed to Chaya that she believed parents loved their children—
or needed them, perhaps—more than their children, once grown, loved
them. "And you have been, in a sense, your Asher's mother. Hence"—she
had deeply sighed for both of them—"disposable." Now her face, which
tended toward full disclosure, clouded. "Oh, my dear, with his sense of
injustice, you don't think he would have—intentionally—"

"Never." Adamantly. "He was too—he was—" Beyond her comprehension. But not beyond life.

BERYLE WAS awake now, and crying out to be picked up. Sara touched
her lovely face gently with a fingertip; the baby had Gregory's faceted
lips and Chaya's uncle Dovid's slanted gray eyes. Her gown and hat were
embossed with threads in a sweet seed design. The outfit had come, as a
peace offering of sorts, from Faith and Edward Stillman. One small step
at a time she had been allowed back into the presence of Gregory's family
where, in truth, except for the sake of appearances, she had no desire to
dwell. And there she found that Asher's name had been expunged. Nor was
her night in jail—so strange to recall that she sometimes considered that
she had dreamed it—a shame to which anyone would ever dare allude. (A
shande, it was, a scandal, in her first language. She wished she could say
the much-used word out loud to someone but she did not even murmur it
to her Mama and Papa, for discretion's sake.)

And then there was this: The absoluteness with which her brother and
his name were absent from the room when she brought Beryle to visit
her grandparents had led Chaya once to consider the possibility that the
Stillmans had somehow arranged his disappearance. Had such a heinous
idea ever crossed Gregory's mind? If she dared to voice it, she might as
well pack her belongings and leave the house. The unasked question lay
like a shadow between them.

Before they—she—returned to his parents' presence she had wrung
one concession from Gregory: that if she was not treated with respect,
they would leave Chicago to forge a different life. Would investigate the
city where her parents seemed content or try New York, where they would
enjoy a welcome anonymity. She could see that the prospect hurt him, but,

weighing the pain of losing them, not only wife but daughter, he yielded. Chaya did not think of herself as a hard woman, but some things, she had finally learned, she could not turn away from or negotiate.

And Mrs. K-W was tonic for her. After a proper interval for sympathy, she asked when—not if—Chaya was prepared to return to what she called "actual" work.

She did not know, she had told Mrs. K-W, but she would be back. "A few months, I think. I am nursing so often just now it would be difficult. But I will, I promise you, pick up my notebook again and get on with it. I must—you understand—or I will hate my life, which deserves my gratitude. Please believe me."

Mrs. K-W looked at her levelly. Her alphabet of responses, when it came to commitment, ran from A to C and stopped there firmly. "Try to remember one thing, Chaya, even if the rest eludes you. Our families—we owe them everything we can give. But they are individuals, and individually they often fail us."

"Yes?" She had listened skeptically. "And we fail them."

"But the collective—the distressed to whom no one appears to owe anything—they will always console you. To make the lives of strangers less onerous—"

Is inadequate. Is necessary but not sufficient—that was a new phrase, a judgment like *hubris*, and a useful one. Strangers were not beloved clear-eyed boys constructed of jostling syllables and passionate generosity. Her worthy thief, her wordy Robin. What was it about this country—or these times?—that induced so many people to vanish? Should it be called defiance or hope and restlessness? Was it hope and the promise of relief?

Once, at Winkler's, she had listened to a story so sad she could not see her moving fingers through her tears. Anya's father had separated from her mother when their poverty had become insupportable, and left Belarus when Anya was a young child. Just recently she had heard from a relative that he might be here in Chicago, and after many inquiries she made her way to his cobbler's shop, which was as small and dark as a cave. And there he was, seated over his last, cutting tool in hand, serenely humming. He was grizzled and unkempt, he had grown wretchedly thin and had to bend close over his work to see what he was about, but, though she had not seen him for fifteen years, there was no mistaking him, his hooded eyes, the sharp curve of his nose, his narrow-lipped mouth. Anya was a frail, pallid girl with apologetic eyes at the best of times. She had stood in the doorway of the tiny shop and asked in a timid voice, as if she were reduced again to childhood, if he was Meyer Shkolnitsky and if he had a daughter. "And he looked at me straight. Not a word. He never stopped working, he had a boot in his hands and he never put it down. That was all he had for me. Well, I am no beggar so I didn't say a word, I walked away. I let him be."

The women at their cigar benches gasped. "I know he was frightened I would want something from him. That was his first thought. And then his only thought. That was what his life did to him. So when I came back a few days later to see if he really meant it, the shop was empty."

Was there nothing she could do? her shopmates demanded, wounded themselves.

"But no. For what? What would be the point? My pride? Some things you can't get with a threat. When he's dying, let's see if his boot comes to comfort him."

When Chaya told this story to Gregory, his eyes too clouded with tears, and again she understood that what was most deeply hidden in her husband—his caring, vulnerable self—was hers alone to see.

And, he insisted, my dear, my very dear, no matter what befalls, there will be music. You cannot silence it.

FROM THEN on—forever—Chaya would search the newspapers, beyond reason but not beyond hope, for word of a young prodigy who had solved a vexing problem or invented a machine or, more likely, written a book unlike any before it.

Or she would hear that, excavating around the old fairgrounds to clear the way for a park—one building had been saved but the rest had gone green, to shrub and wind-stroked prairie grass—among the tarnished souvenirs they'd unearthed—the tiny silver spoons, the tarnished emblems of celebration—they had found bones, long ones and short, entangled with a belt buckle, a few workaday buttons, the all-but-devoured brim of a cap.

Unless, one morning, she would reach for the mail that lay stacked on the glowing mahogany table in the hall, that table with its clever delicate legs, and find a letter from her brother. No one could impersonate him. No one could guess what he would find worth telling her.

Chaya. Chaya-Libbe. Sister.

This California has 5 major cities, mostly with Spanish names—San, San, San. A ragged rocky coastline of ocean (not lake) where you mostly can't swim. It is called Pacific but it is not peaceful for a minute, it should be called Martial (il mare, si?). The opera house in San Francisco is nicer than the one in Chicago. It has more boxes and more gilt (not gold!) on the balconies. I am almost 5 feet tall and I have let my hair grow as long as a girl just to confuse people. I have 184 books and keep them in the order of the alphabet. There are not so many poor starvers out here, everyone believes they will turn a corner and discover they are rich. It is not so old and not so cold and the light is brighter everywhere. Also, it is all hills. Every green place smells of something called eucalyptus leaves that are strong and cutting. Breathing it feels like cold air in my nose. You hardly need a coat here, a jacket is good enough and there is a whole season just for rain. Fog, too. Fog, fog, and fog, but then it gets clear and you can see down to the water from the top of your street. There are snails on the ground sometimes, disgusting to step on. There are many Chinese people because we are facing Asia (and possibly other Asians as well but I can't tell), and fishing boats in the harbor. I can pick up fish every day and cook it. Sometimes I put breading on it. I almost forgot the seals! Nothing is shinier, noisier, slipperier (slippery word). They look just like the rocks they lie on. Then suddenly a seal-rock will slide into the water! You would like them. What did you name your baby?

Your brother,
Asher

ACKNOWLEDGMENTS

Bottomless thanks to my first readers, critics and enthusiasts both: Carolyn Alessio, Susan Bielstein, Rona Brown, Janet Burroway, Rob Cohen, Marv Hoffman, Ben Kintisch, Elinor Langer, Natania Rosenfeld, Bobbi Samuels, Sharon Solwitz, and Meg Wolitzer. Also to Tsivia Cohen, Maggie Kast, Garnett Kilberg-Cohen, Peggy Shinner, and Sandi Wisenberg for Sunday afternoons around the table.

An extra helping of gratitude to Mike Levine for fanning an uncertain flame, to Sarah Gorham for appreciating its heat, and to Edith Milton for her loyal and lucid attentiveness across the years.

ROSELLEN BROWN is the author of the novels *Civil Wars, Half a Heart, Tender Mercies, Before and After*, and six other books. Her stories have appeared frequently in *O. Henry Prize Stories, Best American Short Stories,* and *Best Short Stories of the Century*. She received an award in literature from the American Academy of Arts and Letters and fellowships from the Guggenheim Foundation, the Ingram Merrill Foundation, the Bunting Institute, and the Howard Foundation, as well as two grants from the National Endowment for the Arts. In 1984, she was selected as one of *Ms. Magazine*'s "12 Women of the Year." *Some Deaths in the Delta* was a National Council on the Arts prize selection and *Civil Wars* won the 1984 Janet Kafka Prize for the best novel by an American woman. She now teaches in the MFA in Writing Program at the School of the Art Institute of Chicago and lives in Mr. Obama's neighborhood, overlooking Lake Michigan.

SARABANDE BOOKS is a nonprofit literary press located in Louisville, KY. Founded in 1994 to champion poetry, short fiction, and essay, we are committed to creating lasting editions that honor exceptional writing. For more information, please visit sarabandebooks.org.